PENGUIN  CLASSICS

THE MABINOGION

ADVISORY EDITOR: BETTY RADICE

THE MABINOGION has come to be accepted as a composite title for eleven medieval Welsh prose tales, the result of centuries of oral storytelling. Although influenced by the growth and development of the Arthurian legend on the Continent, these tales are essentially native in origin, and despite circumstances unfavourable to transmission, they preserve much of the colour and energy of the early Celtic world.

JEFFREY GANTZ received a doctoral degree in Celtic Languages and Literatures from Harvard University in 1972. He is engaged on several other translations and lives near New Hope in Pennsylvania.

THE MABINOGION

Translated with an introduction by
JEFFREY GANTZ

PENGUIN BOOKS

PENGUIN BOOKS

Published by the Penguin Group
Penguin Books Ltd, 27 Wrights Lane, London W8 5TZ, England
Viking Penguin, a division of Penguin Books USA Inc.
375 Hudson Street, New York, New York 10014, USA
Penguin Books Australia Ltd, Ringwood, Victoria, Australia
Penguin Books Canada Ltd, 2801 John Street, Markham, Ontario, Canada L3R 1B4
Penguin Books (NZ) Ltd, 182–190 Wairau Road, Auckland 10, New Zealand

Penguin Books Ltd, Registered Offices: Harmondsworth, Middlesex, England

This edition first published 1976
13 15 17 19 20 18 16 14 12
Printed in England by Clays Ltd, St Ives plc
Set in Linotype Baskerville

To my family

CONTENTS

INTRODUCTION

1. THE MABINOGION

On the bank of the river he saw a tall tree:
from roots to crown one half was aflame and
the other green with leaves.

'Peredur' (p. 243)

OF all the strange and supernatural images in *The Mabinogion*, none captures the essence of these medieval Welsh tales so concisely as does this vertically halved tree: the green leaves symbolizing the rich and concrete beauty of the mortal world, the flames symbolizing the flickering shadowy uncertainty of the otherworld, and the whole emblematic of the tension and mystery which characterize all forms of Celtic art.[1]

The Mabinogion itself is something of a mystery, both as to origin and as to content. Some clarification is, however, feasible:

1. The title 'Mabinogion', while familiar and convenient, actually grew up round a nineteenth-century misconception (see Section 7, p. 31). 'Tales from the White Book of Rhydderch' (one of the manuscripts in which the stories appear) would better describe these eleven distinct and largely unrelated narratives.

2. The tales of *The Mabinogion* are not the product of a single hand, even individually. On the contrary, they

---

1. The initial *C* of Celtic may be pronounced either soft (*s*) or hard (*k*). Inasmuch as the Greeks, whose sources were oral rather than written, spelt their word for the Celts *Keltoi* and inasmuch as *c* in Modern Irish and Welsh is without exception hard, we can assume that the Celts themselves pronounced this initial consonant as a *k*.

evolved over a span of centuries: passed on from story-teller to storyteller, they were by turns expanded and distorted, improved and misunderstood. It follows that the versions we possess are not the most original, and not necessarily the most coherent.

3. While we in fact possess only one version of each tale, it is quite possible that other, substantially different, versions also existed at one time.

4. Our manuscripts by no means commemorate the first occasion on which these stories were committed to paper. While the White Book of Rhydderch (our earliest more-or-less complete manuscript) dates to *c.* 1325, the tales of *The Mabinogion* appear to have existed in written form for a considerable period before that. In all likelihood, the copyists, through ignorance and carelessness, introduced additional errors, a consideration which reinforces the observation made above that these tales altered appreciably in passing from one hand to the next.

5. As to content, *The Mabinogion* draws upon the myths, folklore, history and pseudo-history of Celtic Britain: four well-springs that are often well-nigh indistinguishable. Set largely within the British Isles, the tales nonetheless create a dreamlike atmosphere by tele-scoping Saxon- and Norman-dominated present into the misty Celtic past of has been and never was.

Sad to say, while a relatively large number of inter-related and well-ordered medieval Irish tales have survived, this is the only Welsh collection of the kind which we possess. As a repository of myth and history, *The Mabinogion* is highly corrupt, while the circumstances of its transmission all but precluded the development of those qualities commonly associated with literary excellence. Even so, these tales preserve, albeit in garbled form, much of the primitive, fantastic, fascinating world of Celtic myth, and they exemplify the heroic, romantic, idealistic world of Celtic literature. If the beginnings of

The Mabinogion remain a mystery, its continued appeal does not.

The tales themselves comprise an ensemble of rather heterogeneous parts. The text identifies the first four – 'Pwyll', 'Branwen', 'Manawydan' and 'Math' – as the Four Branches of the Mabinogi: composed largely of mythological fragments, and unified by a network of thematic parallels and a consistent point of view, these stories possess a structural and stylistic identity which must suggest the hand of a single redactor. 'How Culhwch Won Olwen' incorporates a treasure trove of traditional lore (including King Arthur's first appearance in Celtic prose) within its embracing central theme of the hero's quest for the giant's daughter, a folktale seemingly built on a regeneration myth. 'The Dream of Maxen' and 'Lludd and Llevelys' relate pseudo-historical accounts of British courage and intelligence in Roman and pre-Roman days, while 'The Dream of Rhonabwy' contrasts the splendour of the legendary Arthur (and of Celtic legends in general) with the more prosaic realities of twelfth-century Wales. Finally, 'Owein', 'Peredur' and 'Gereint' – that part of *The Mabinogion* closest in feeling to the tales of Crestiens de Troyes and Thomas Malory – use Arthur's court as backdrop and ancient themes as material for the heroic and romantic exploits of three of his champions.

2. THE CELTS

The people responsible for *The Mabinogion* – that is, the Welsh – are descendants of the Celts, a distinct Indo-European linguistic and cultural group who seem to have surfaced in Bohemia during the early centuries of the last millennium before Christ.[2] By the time of Herodotus they

2. A majority view; however, in *Celtic Realms* (pp. 1–2, 214) Myles Dillon and Nora Chadwick advance the view that the Celts constituted a distinct cultural group as early as 2000 B.C.

had established themselves north of the Alps; in 390 B.C. they sacked Rome, and in 279 Delphi. A vigorous and energetic people, the Celts were quick to expand their area of control, but having no tolerance for centralized authority, even among themselves, they were unable to consolidate their gains; after Caesar's defeat of Vercingetorïx at Alesia in 52 B.C. Gaul was doomed to give way to the Romans, and by A.D. 400 Gaulish culture was virtually extinct. Even so, the extent of Gaulish influence can be seen today in the Celtic names which survive for major cities like Paris, Milan and Vienna (London?, Berlin?) and major rivers like the Thames, the Seine, the Rhine and the Danube.

In Britain, pressure from first the Romans and later the English drove the Celts back into Scotland, Wales, Cornwall and Brittany; Ireland, while not subjected to these indignities, was raided and colonized by Viking marauders, and of course Christianity made substantial inroads on Celtic culture everywhere. Even by the time of the first *Mabinogion* manuscripts this culture was irrevocably on the wane.

By Mediterranean standards the Celts were tall and powerfully built, with fair skin, blue eyes and blond hair. The men wore moustaches. In temperament they were reckless, impulsive, vainglorious, generous to guests, fond of feasting and drinking and entertainment and jewellery and bright colours. Celtic art, as evidenced by, for example, the coins of the Osimii, the warrior's head from Mšecké Žehrovice and the Book of Kells, tends to stylization and abstraction, while the literature of the Irish and the Welsh – we have none from Gaul – is characterized by a partiality to ambiguity and paradox, and a sharply defined aversion to the dour realities of time, place and everyday life.

3. STORYTELLING AND THE ORAL TRADITION

Foremost among the entertainments of which the Celts were so fond was storytelling; thus, in 'Math', Gwydyon assures his enthusiastic welcome at Rhuddlan Teivi simply by disguising himself as a bard. Like other storytellers, the Celtic bards possessed a large repertoire, and like other storytellers they accomplished this feat by memorizing not every word of a tale – a prodigiously difficult task – but only the outline, for they could fill in the details extemporaneously. This process of oral composition, a technique by which *The Iliad* and *The Odyssey* were also told, helps to explain the fluid state in which these tales were passed along. Inasmuch as the Celts were a conservative people, many ancient and primitive themes find a haven in *The Mabinogion*. But the very freedom which characterizes oral transmission ineluctably led to oversights and misunderstandings which contributed to the deterioration of the plot and the obfuscation of the original themes and structures; neither could the tales ever hope to attain the coherence and internal consistency of stories conceived and fashioned in one piece.

4. THE STORYTELLERS' SOURCES

The Celtic storytellers' sources fall into two broad categories: myth and folklore on the one hand, history and pseudo-history on the other. Inasmuch as the Celts, true to their escapist nature, tended to view history as what ought to have happened rather than as what actually did, fact and fiction in *The Mabinogion* are not easy to distinguish. Moreover, such myths as are preserved in these tales are so obscure and fragmentary that restoration is difficult if not impossible. A number of factors have contributed to this confusing situation.

1. The Celts were decentralized culturally as well as politically. While Gaulish reliefs and inscriptions testify to the worship of numerous different gods, these were local in nature and formed no national pantheon or hierarchy. Neighbouring tribes might easily worship the same gods under different names, if not different gods altogether, a situation which did little to promote the development of a national mythology. The tendency of many deities to relate to a specific natural feature such as a mound or a stream simply reinforced their local character.

2. Such myths as may have existed must have been coloured (in Gaul and Britain) by Roman thought, and influenced everywhere by Christianity. Many of the statues and reliefs from Gaul and Britain exhibit decidedly Roman traits, and often the name of a Roman deity accompanies (where it does not actually replace) the Celtic one. The contemporary accounts of Celtic religion given by Caesar and others reflect Roman prejudice and predisposition and are not totally reliable; similarly, the early Irish tales, which contain obvious references to Christianity, may also be coloured by Christian thought in subtler and less evident ways.

3. Such accounts of Gaulish mythology as may have been committed to paper have not survived, nor have the Irish and Welsh tales been preserved in early (pre-A.D. 1000) manuscripts. Our earliest written fragments of *The Mabinogion* date only to the thirteenth century, by which time it is clear that the material has been greatly altered. To give just one example, both Irish and Welsh traditions have been almost entirely euhemerized: characters like Rhiannon and Math (in the Four Branches), while exhibiting divine aspects and powers, are treated as human, even historical figures.

There remains, however, what Proinsias Mac Cana has called 'an imbroglio of anecdotes, allusions, motifs and

characters which under close scrutiny reveal the out-
lines of a number of familiar mythological paradigms
within a British setting'.[3] One such paradigm, a regeneration motif, recurs throughout *The Mabinogion*;
in its most prevalent and important reflex two men con-
test one woman:

'Pwyll': Arawn, Arawn's wife, Pwyll; Pwyll, Rhiannon,
  Gwawl.
'Branwen': Brân, Branwen, Mallolwch.
'Manawydan': Manawydan, Rhiannon, Llwyd.
'Math': Math, Goewin, Gilvaethwy; Lleu, Blodeuedd,
  Goronwy.
'Culhwch': Culhwch, Olwen, Ysbaddaden; Gwynn, Crei-
  ddylad, Gwythyr.
'Owein': Owein, Countess of the Fountain, Knight in
  Black.
'Gereint': Gereint, Enid, Knight of the Kestrel or the
  Brown Earl.

Of course this plot is a common one; however, its very
frequency here suggests a unifying theme, and many of
the particulars suggest regeneration. R. S. Loomis has
pointed out that, in the first episode of 'Pwyll', Arawn is
dressed in a grey-brown hunting outfit, and that the name
of Arawn's enemy, Havgan, means 'summer-white';[4] grey-
brown does not necessarily signify winter, nor is the in-
terpretation of the name Havgan beyond question, but
the two points in conjunction strengthen the case for a
seasonal reading of the Arawn–Havgan dispute. Throughout the First Branch of the Mabinogi events occur at
year-intervals – Pwyll sojourns in Annwvyn one year be-

3. *Celtic Mythology*, p. 18.
4. *Wales and the Arthurian Legend*, p. 81; see also *Celtic Heritage*,
pp. 285–6. In the Irish tale 'Bricriu's Feast', the drably outfitted Cú
Roí tests Cú Chulaind, just as Arawn (in effect) tests Pwyll. Both
Arawn and Cú Roí anticipate the Green Knight who tests Gawain.

fore encountering Havgan; he loses Rhiannon to Gwawl
one year after first meeting her, and wins her back one year
after losing her – while in 'Culhwch' Gwynn and Gwythyr
are ordered to fight over Creiddylad every May Day, the
first day of summer in the Celtic calendar.[5] Also suggestive
of a seasonal pattern is the movement of the women in
the Four Branches: Arawn's wife passes from Arawn to
Pwyll and back to Arawn; Rhiannon from Pwyll to Gwawl
and back; Branwen from Brân to Mallolwch and back;
Rhiannon from Manawydan to Llwyd and back; Goewin
from Math to Gilvaethwy and back; Blodeuedd from Lleu
to Goronwy and back (after a fashion).[6]

Variants of this motif present segments of the seasonal
cycle, focusing on the advent or absence of regenerative
force. Summer is often personified by a young hero who
defeats an older, feebler opponent: Culhwch taking Olwen from her father Ysbaddaden (the giant's insistence
that he will die when his daughter marries renders Culhwch a rival and not just a prospective son-in-law); Gilvaethwy's rape of his uncle's foot-holder[7] – just as Ysbaddaden cannot live without Olwen, so Math must have
Goewin with him; perhaps, too, Owein, who after dis-
patching the Knight in Black and succeeding him as husband to the Countess of the Fountain must subsequently
defend both fountain and lady against Arthur's best
knights.

Summer may also be brought back from the other-

5. The theme of a May Day abduction forms the basis of Crestiens' *li chevaliers a la charette*; in that tale Guinevere is abducted
and Lancelot rescues her.

6. This shuttle pattern survives also in the Conchobar–Derdriu–
Noísi and Find–Gráinne–Díarmuid triangles of Irish saga, and in
the Arthur–Guinevere–Lancelot and Tristan–Iseult–Mark triangles
of Arthurian Romance. One can even see traces of it in such a relatively contemporary work as *The Return of the Native*.

7. As descent in the northern Branches appears to be matrilinear,
Gilvaethwy would be Math's successor.

world, much as Hermes brings Persephone back from Hades. In an early Welsh poem, 'The Booty of Annwvyn', the men of Britain attempt to carry off a cauldron of rebirth; in 'Branwen' a similar raid is made upon Ireland with the object of rescuing Branwen – and, in an earlier version, perhaps, the cauldron as well. In 'Manawydan', Rhiannon and Pryderi attempt to remove a golden bowl from Llwyd's *caer* (fortified place), but their feet stick to a marble slab, just as Theseus and Peiríthoos stick to their chairs in Hades when they try to carry off Persephone. Similarly, Owein's removal of the bowl from the fountain precipitates first a destructive hailstorm and then the arrival of the fountain's defender. The process by which Manawydan outbargains Llwyd and rescues Rhiannon and Pryderi from the otherworld (again in 'Manawydan') may suggest a kind of verbal raid; while Arthur's journey to Ireland for the cauldron of Diwrnach (in 'Culhwch') represents yet another version of the Welsh poem mentioned above. In each of these episodes a journey to the otherworld or a foreign land is undertaken in quest of a bowl or cauldron, or else a woman, but in any case a symbol of woman's regenerative power.

Winter, on the other hand, may be seen in the abduction or incapacitation of the masculine regenerative principle. The abductions of Gwri/Pryderi in 'Pwyll' and Mabon[8] in 'Culhwch' parallel Hades' rape of Persephone as a seasonal myth, while the ill-health of the hero is often linked to the barrenness of the land. Near the end of 'Branwen' Brân is wounded in the foot with a poisoned spear; both Ireland and Britain fall waste, and in the next tale, 'Manawydan', Dyved is completely devastated. In 'Peredur' the lameness of the hero's Fisher King uncle is made the cause of strife and battle in the land. In subsequent Grail stories Bran or Bron is the name of a Fisher

---

8. Mabon: from the Celtic *Maponos*, 'Great Son'. His mother's name, Modron, descends from *Màtrona*, 'Great Mother'.

King who has been wounded through both thighs; moreover the less reticent Wolfram von Eschenbach makes it clear in his *Parzival* that the Fisher King has been sexually incapacitated by a poisoned-spear thrust, while Crestiens' first continuator establishes a connection between ailing king and wasteland. This idea of a sympathetic relationship between the potency of the king and the fertility of the land is supported by Irish texts which hint that a king might be ritually married to the tutelary earth goddess of the tribe. In any case, it seems clear that the descriptions in *The Mabinogion* are euphemistic, that both Brân and Peredur's uncle were rendered sterile, and that, according to the underlying patterns, their lands were afflicted as a result.

Even in the absence of an underlying paradigm, *The Mabinogion*'s debt to myth and to the supernatural is evident. Euhemerized gods abound. Like the Irish hero Cú Chulaind, Pryderi (in 'Pwyll') and Lleu (in 'Math') grow at twice the normal rate, and the birth of Pryderi, like that of Cú Chulaind, is associated with that of colts – perhaps a totem animal. Pryderi's mother Rhiannon is herself a euhemerized horse goddess – no other explanation will do[9] – with a counterpart in the Irish goddess Macha.[10] Arawn, Havgan and Llwyd are all otherworld rulers, while Casswallawn, Math and Gwydyon, more thoroughly rationalized, nonetheless retain their special powers: Casswallawn possesses a cloak of invisibility, Math enjoys acute hearing, and he and Gwydyon can both do magic at will. The Corannyeid of 'Lludd and Llevelys' can also hear everything, while the talents of the figures in 'Culhwch' are literally too numerous to mention. And this list is only a small sample.

9. See *Rh*, pp. 64, 67, Chapter V. Rhiannon is from *Rigantona*, 'Great Queen'.

10. The story of Macha, who can outrun any horse, is told in 'The Incapacitation of the Ulstermen'. Like Rhiannon, she marries a rash mortal.

At the opposite extreme, the storytellers' sources encompass history and pseudo-history, predominantly the latter, for in *The Mabinogion* the harsh realities of history are softened by a generous application of wishful thinking; thus, as a record of the Celtic past, a story like 'The Dream of Maxen' is quite untrustworthy. Maxen himself is a composite of two historical figures: he bears the name of a certain Maxentius, but his story (fortified by some imaginative reconstruction) is that of the Maximus who led his troops from Britain to Rome in an abortive attempt to become emperor. Even Maxen's wife Elen is a composite of two Helenas. The Welsh retelling differs most noticeably at the conclusion, for Maxen really does regain his throne, though it is stressed that he, a Roman (in this version), could not have succeeded without the aid of his British brothers-in-law. Similarly, 'Lludd and Llevelys' owes more to traditions of the kind embodied in Geoffrey of Monmouth's *History of the Kings of Britain* than it does to genuine fact.

Frequently a historical name (or derivative) is applied to an entirely fictitious character. Casswallawn the magician and usurper of 'Branwen' and 'Manawydan' is not the Cassivellaunos who fought against Caesar, though he bears the same name; Caradawg son of Brân is no longer the Caratācus whom Cartismandua handed over to the Romans. Peredur, Gwrgi, Owein, Uryen, Selyv, Kynan and Maelgwn of Gwynedd are names from Britain of the sixth and seventh centuries, but in the context of *The Mabinogion* they are just names. It is not clear whether Osla Bigknife is to be identified as Offa or Octha; whether March son of Meirchyawn belongs to history or to legend (Mark in *Tristan*) – or to both. Madawg son of Maredudd of Powys is a historical reality of the twelfth century, but in 'The Dream of Rhonabwy' that reality is merely a frame for the heart of the story: the dream.

Best known of these historical and pseudo-historical

figures is Arthur, who appears in five of the tales. Invariably he rules over the noblest and most glorious court in Britain, but whereas in the Romances this court is set in south Wales, both 'Culhwch' and 'Rhonabwy' place it at Kelli Wig in Cornwall – an earlier tradition? Arthur himself does not play a central role in any of the tales: he is a king rather than a hero, and the heroism which made him king is largely in the past. He has already married his wife Gwenhwyvar (Guinevere), and with one exception – Iddawg's reference to Medrawd (Mordred) and the Battle of Camlann in 'Rhonabwy' – there is no mention of the very different material drawn on by Geoffrey of Monmouth. Unfortunately, then, *The Mabinogion* does not reveal very much about the development of Arthur in Celtic literature, except that by the time of 'Culhwch' – seemingly an early tale – he was already an established figure.

A last amusing example of 'history' in *The Mabinogion* is provided by the onomastic episodes in 'Branwen', 'Math', 'Maxen', 'Lludd' and 'Culhwch': over-ingenious and inherently improbable explanations which seem to have arisen out of desperation rather than from genuine knowledge. Thus the storytellers of 'Math' explain the numerous occurrences of Mochdrev (Pig Town) in Wales by routing Gwydyon's retreat north – with the pigs – through as many of these as possible. Some names appear to have been misunderstood: in 'Branwen', the place name Tal y Bolyon (End of the Ridges) is explained by the episode of the colts which were made over to Mallolwch – the storyteller evidently understood (or chose to understand) the name as Tal Ebolyon (Payment of Colts). A few personal names – Culhwch (Pig Run) and Olwen (White Track) – are also victimized by the storytellers' imagination, but the results, no matter how unlikely, are invariably amusing.

5. THE FORMATION OF THE TALES

Given the oral traditions which underlie *The Mabinogion* it is difficult to say how, and at what time, the individual stories took shape. Peniarth 6, the earliest manuscript to preserve even fragments of the Four Branches, dates only to *c.* 1225, and so offers nothing to scholars who feel that the Mabinogi achieved written form by 1100 or earlier. Presumably, these tales approached their present form between 1000 and 1250 – what they were like before that is simply beyond conjecture. Within this period Welsh scholars tend to favour the earlier terminus – they naturally want to maximize the extent of their ancestors' contribution to *The Mabinogion* – while French scholars, with the same idea in mind, argue for 1200 or 1250. Ifor Williams, in proposing 1060 as a likely date for the codification of the Four Branches, advances a number of arguments: the occurrence of outdated word-forms in the text, the paucity of French loan-words, references to extinct or outdated customs, and the suitability of the peaceful period 1055–63 as a time for bards from north and south to visit and exchange tales. On the French side, Morgan Watkin argues that the Four Branches do in fact reflect French influence in matters of vocabulary, styles of dress, customs and ideas.

Neither scholar marshals especially compelling evidence. Williams bases his case primarily on a very limited number of word-forms, and ignores the possibility of conscious or unconscious archaism on the redactor's part. The outdated customs may well have been outdated when the tales were put together; the question of the French loan-words is disputed by Watkin; and the rest of the case, while attractive, is still speculation. Watkin, on the other hand, attributes to the French many items and ideas – grey horses, splendid dwellings, single combats, the precocious growth of the hero – which also appear in early Irish sagas, in contexts where they are indisputably of native, Celtic origin. There are, in fact, at least two good reasons why the problem cannot admit of an easy solution: the virtually total absence of any reference to contemporary events in *The Mabinogion*, and the lack of any radical change in the Welsh language (such as would facilitate dating) during the period in question.

What really matters, though, with regard to these stories, is not the date of formation, but rather the degree to which they reflect Celtic or French culture – if *The Mabinogion* incorporates genuine Celtic themes and patterns, then a late date is of no consequence; conversely, if it is permeated with French ideas, no claims of an early date can make it more Celtic. Early Irish sagas, which are relatively uncontaminated, provide a good basis for comparison:

1. *Location.* The action of most Irish tales is restricted to Ireland and the otherworld; *The Mabinogion* is less conservative in this respect, but only marginally. Part of 'Maxen' – a late tale – is set in Rome, and in 'Lludd' – another late story – France is visited. Otherwise the action is confined to the British Isles.

2. *Setting.* Dwellings in *The Mabinogion* are described in such vague terms that it is difficult to demonstrate influence from any quarter. But the elaborate Irish houses described in 'Bricriu's Feast' and 'The Destruction of Dá Derga's Hostel', to name just two tales, provide sufficient analogues for the courts and dwellings in these Welsh tales.

3. *Nomenclature.* With the exception of Maxen and perhaps Gwiffred Petit (the Little King in 'Gereint'), the people of *The Mabinogion* all bear indigenous Celtic names; the people of Crestiens' Romances, by contrast, can hardly claim to bear indigenous French names. But the uncharacteristically vague sense of geography exhibited by

the Welsh Romances is suspicious and suggests dependence on a French predecessor.

4. *Costume.* By contrast with the Irish sagas, *The
Mabinogion* seems little concerned with the specifics of
dress. It stresses texture rather than colour, and where the
material is worth mentioning, it is invariably silk. This
point too is suspicious, in that the Welsh word for silk,
pali, appears to have been borrowed from French *paille*.
'Pwyll', 'Rhonabwy' and the Romances are the most
attentive to details of costume.

5. *Manners.* Dialogue in Irish tales is often terse, abrupt,
even cryptic: these tales applaud courage and valour
rather than courtesy and good manners. *The Mabinogion*
is more concerned with hospitality – the greeting of guests,
and their seating at table and their being graciously and
generously served. 'Pwyll', 'Manawydan' and the Romances seem the least Irish in this respect.

6. *Modes of combat.* The Celts of Caesar's time fought
from chariots, or else drove to battle and fought on foot;
these chariots survive in the tales of Cú Chulaind, but not
in *The Mabinogion*. In the Four Branches all fighting is
done on foot, excepting the mounted encounter at the ford
between Pwyll and Havgan. (In this connection it may be
worth noting that much of Morgan Watkin's evidence is
drawn from 'Pwyll', and that Saunders Lewis has suggested the presence of considerably later elements in the
First Branch of the Mabinogi.)[11] In 'Culhwch', Arthur
and his men fight on foot, but in 'Rhonabwy' they ride, and
in the Romances they wear armour, fight with lances and are
called knights. It is difficult to trace the first appearance
of armour in *The Mabinogion*, or the rise of the concept
of knighthood, because the Welsh language did not de-
velop new words for them: *arveu*, originally 'weapons',
came to mean 'armour' as well, while *marchawg*, 'horseman', came to mean 'knight', and it is not always clear

11. *Llên Cymru*, IV, pp. 230–33.

which is meant. The heroes of the Romances, however, are definitely knights, and do wear armour.

These considerations offer some clue as to the development of the Welsh story, out of an ambience similar to that of the Cú Chulaind tales to one more nearly approximating the Romances of Crestiens. While there has been considerable accretion of foreign material, the basic themes, as set forth in Section 4, are distinctively Celtic. The qualities which characterize the Celts, moreover, are present in abundance: pleasure in feasting and entertainment, juxtaposed with a yearning for the timeless joy of the otherworld, and with a sense of tension and ambivalence between the two. To these and other qualities has been added a sense of tenderness in human relationships which, irrespective of its source, constitutes a definite improvement. Finally, comparison of any passage in the Welsh Romances – not the earliest tales in *The Mabinogion* by any means – with its counterpart in Crestiens will reveal how very much more effusive and subjective and moralistic the latter is, and how much more closely the style of *The Mabinogion* resembles that of the Irish sagas.

As to relative dating, the earliest stratum of Celtic material appears to lie in 'Culhwch' and in the two Branches of the Mabinogi set in northern Wales, 'Branwen' and 'Math'; the two Branches from the south of Wales, 'Pwyll' and 'Manawydan', naturally betray more evidence of French influence, for that part of the country was more accessible to outsiders. The dream sequence in 'Rhonabwy' preserves much of the primitive Irish atmosphere; however, the kaleidoscopic descriptive passages bespeak a later period, and in any case the setting of the dream in twelfth-century Powys shows that the tale cannot have assumed its present shape before 1150.

The dating of the remaining five tales involves a special problem: their relationship to the works of Geoffrey of Monmouth and Crestiens de Troyes. Both 'Maxen' and

'Lludd' bear a marked resemblance to material found in the *History of the Kings of Britain* or in its Welsh translation, and inasmuch as their setting and tone set them apart from the rest of *The Mabinogion*, it seems likely that their present form has been influenced either by Geoffrey's work, or by its sources. ('Culhwch', by contrast, appears entirely free of such influence, though, awkwardly enough, neither does it seem to have influenced Geoffrey.)

The relationship between the Welsh Romances and those of Crestiens is difficult to assess because of its inconsistency. On the whole, 'Owein', 'Peredur' and 'Gereint' draw on native Celtic material – even Crestiens admits, for example, that Perceval (Peredur) is a Welshman – so that, thematically, they do not seem very different from the earlier tales of *The Mabinogion*. But their presentation is another matter: more genteel and romantic than those earlier tales, overlaid with continental notions of chivalry and good manners. The lack of specific geography is strange, and moreover certain episodes clearly related by Crestiens are distorted and confused in the Welsh, as if through faulty recollection. R. L. Thomson has suggested that the original versions (he was speaking of 'Owein' and Crestiens' *Yvain* only, but the same logic can be applied to the other Romances) crossed to France, were reworked, and eventually passed to Crestiens, who rewrote them further; and that the Welsh versions which we possess today have come to us by way of France (though not necessarily by way of Crestiens).[12] In other words, that both the Romances of Crestiens and those of *The Mabinogion* derive from French reworkings of Celtic originals. This explanation may seem a trifle artificial, but it does account for the veneer of French manners in the Welsh Romances.

12. *Owein*, pp. xcv–xvcii.

6. THE STORYTELLERS' ARTISTRY

It has often been stated that *The Mabinogion* is a literary
masterpiece. Its virtues are, in fact, so abundant that its
flaws can be cheerfully and confidently owned – in any
case, most of the shortcomings were, given the circumstances of its composition, quite unavoidable. In the first
place, the demands of oral composition are such that some
degree of inconsistency is inevitable – even Homer's work
is not perfect in this respect. And secondly, the manuscripts which we possess were not approved by the storytellers themselves; they rather resemble the bad quartos of
a Shakespearian play, subjected to innumerable mishear-
ings and misreadings. The Welsh storytellers' audiences
must have enjoyed a much higher level of artistry than is
evident in the surviving manuscripts.

Some inconsistencies arise from simple oversight. When
Manawydan and Pryderi return from their eighty-seven
year sojourn in the otherworld, they find Casswallawn
(who had usurped the throne prior to their departure)
still ruling, though by rights he should be long since dead.
In 'Culhwch', Arthur's servant Cacamwri drowns during
the hunting of Twrch Trwyth; a few lines later, however,
we are told that he is being sent in to wrestle with the
Black Witch. The hag who upbraids Peredur refers to the
mysteries at the castle of the first uncle (the Lame King),
when Peredur actually saw them at the castle of the second.
(A natural mistake – why there should be two uncles at
all is a mystery in itself.) Other inconsistencies stem from
the storytellers' attempt to preserve conflicting traditions.
When Gwydion asks for the swine of Annwvyn, Pryderi
first states that they may not leave Dyved until they have
bred twice their number, but later says that he may neither
sell the pigs nor give them away. Clearly the storyteller
knew of two versions and wished to preserve both – a ten-

able position – but at some point in the process of transmission his explanation of how Pryderi fulfils the first condition – that the pigs should breed twice their number – has been lost.

The Mabinogion suffers from two kinds of structural problem. The later tales, like the Irish sagas, are episodic and tend to ramble. 'Peredur' is the worst offender: like its hero, it wanders about aimlessly, heaping incident upon unrelated incident and ignoring every question relevant to the plot; moreover, its 'explanation' of the events at the castle of the second uncle is sketchy, contrived and altogether unsatisfactory. 'Maxen', 'Owein' and 'Gereint' all vitiate their climaxes with unintegrated afterthoughts, episodes which belong to the tradition but which found no place in the main body of the tale. 'Culhwch', while as episodic as any, is undermined by its own tremendous size: having enumerated some thirty-nine tasks, the text manages to describe the fulfilment of barely half, including three not on the list. Even in this truncated form, 'Culhwch' is as long as any tale in *The Mabinogion*.

The other kind of structural weakness stems from the apparent composite nature of two of the Four Branches, 'Pwyll' and 'Math'. Each of these appears to incorporate three distinct and originally independent parts: Pwyll and Arawn; Pwyll and Rhiannon; Teirnon and Gwri in 'Pwyll'; Goewin and Gilvaethwy; Aranrhod and Lleu; Lleu and Blodeuedd in 'Math'. Thematically these episodes have been remarkably well integrated, but at the plot level there are omissions and inconsistencies. In the third section of 'Pwyll' numerous loose ends remain: Who abducted Gwri? Why? Why leave him on Teirnon's doorstep? What of Teirnon's missing colts? And in 'Math', why, when Goewin was raped, does Aranrhod bear the child? Why does Gwydyon rear that child as a father? What purpose does Dylan serve?

But *The Mabinogion* also offers up a heady portion of

artistic pleasures and delights – more than enough to out-
weigh its shortcomings. 'Manawydan' and 'Rhonabwy'
are coherent and well-integrated tales, devoid of structural flaws, while 'Branwen', with its neatly balanced
halves and its parallel and crossing thematic motifs, is a
jewel of organization. Distinctive personalities abound:
Pwyll and Pryderi are prone to act first and think later;
Rhiannon has a sharp tongue; Mallolwch is greedy but
timorous, Manawydan prudent and peace-loving, Gwydyon clever but unscrupulous. Owein is bold, enterprising,
gracious but forgetful of his wife; Peredur is naïvely con-
fident and something of a lady's man; Gereint is sensible
and courageous, but also uxorious and stubborn and
sulky. Evnissyen, the controlling force in 'Branwen', is a
story by himself: progressively insecure and envious, cruel
and sadistic, clever and resourceful, repentant and self-
sacrificing.

Yet the real artistic strengths of *The Mabinogion* lie
elsewhere: in the vibrant and imaginative nature of the
Celtic tradition; in the deft and sensitive handling
through which this tradition is rationalized and presented;
and in the degree to which characteristic (courage, generosity, hospitality) and uncharacteristic (patience,
moderation, a sense of fair play) Celtic virtues inform the
action. The colour and energy of *The Mabinogion*, and
its wealth of bizarre and fantastic episodes, scarcely require
comment; yet imagination is never completely divorced
from reality. There is throughout a tension between rigid
and plastic, concrete and abstract, real world and otherworld, necessity and desire – a tension which contributes
richly to the detached, almost dreamlike quality of these
tales: tangible and yet not quite real.

The storytellers, for their part, have woven this material,
permeated as it is with grotesque and baroque episodes,
into a series of dramatic and compelling narratives. The
Four Branches comprise a tightly structured matrix of

thematic parallels, of action and ineluctable reaction. In
the very opening pages of the First Branch, for example,
Pwyll's one unjust action precipitates a chain of events
which determine the course of the entire story. Note, too,
how delicately Pwyll and Arawn fence with each other at
their first meeting, and how the storyteller creates suspense
by completely masking the protagonist's intentions with
regard to Arawn's wife. One can also admire the control
with which Gwydyon is rehabilitated in 'Math', and the
manner in which his punishment is thematically integrated (lust for lust); and the meticulous blending of
ancient and contemporary in all Four Branches. Elsewhere, one can revel in the flamboyance and sheer panache
of 'Culhwch', the descriptive virtuosity and genial satire of
'Rhonabwy', the ingenuous wit of 'Peredur', the exuber-
ance and romanticism of 'Owein' and 'Gereint' and the
direct and unpretentious approach which characterizes the
entire work.

7. THE HISTORY OF THE MABINOGION

Just how extensively these stories found their way into
writing is not certain. Our earliest copy of the complete
Mabinogion appears in the Red Book of Hergest (*c.* 1400);
an earlier manuscript, the White Book of Rhydderch (*c.*
1325), is now incomplete – only fragments of 'Lludd', 'Culhwch' and 'Owein' remain, and 'Rhonabwy' is missing
altogether – but probably contained all eleven tales when
whole. Fragments of these tales appear in a few other
manuscripts, the earliest of which, Parts i and ii of
Peniarth 6 (*c.* 1225), contain a few lines of 'Branwen' and
'Manawydan' respectively. Whether the Red Book is a
copy of the White or whether both derive from a common
(lost) original is not certain, but the differences between
the two manuscripts, while of interest to the linguist, are
of no literary importance. Neither is any significance ap-

parent in the arrangement of the tales. In the White Book the Four Branches come first, followed by other material, then 'Peredur', 'Maxen', 'Lludd', (probably) 'Rhonabwy', 'Owein', more intervening material, 'Gereint' and 'Culhwch'; in the Red Book 'Rhonabwy' is followed by other matter, then 'Owein', 'Peredur', 'Maxen', 'Lludd', the Four Branches, 'Gereint' and 'Culhwch'. Three groupings emerge: the Four Branches; 'Peredur', 'Maxen', 'Lludd'; 'Gereint', 'Culhwch'; and perhaps a fourth in 'Rhonabwy', 'Owein'. Note that while the Four Branches of the Mabinogi always appear in order and as a unit, the Three Romances do not. Curiously, 'Culhwch', which may have been the earliest tale to take shape, brings up the rear in both compilations.

Surprisingly, too, the influence of these tales – at least, the direct influence – upon Arthurian legend appears to have been minimal. A few names find their way into Crestiens and Malory: Bedwyr becomes Bedivere, Kei Kay, Owein Uwayne, Gwenhwyvar Guinevere. Brân turns up as Bran or Bron the Fisher King. But many pairs are just tantalizingly similar: Peredur and Perceval, Gwalchmei and Gauvain. Perhaps, as G. W. Goetinck suggests, this is due to faulty transmission: 'One can picture a French storyteller reflecting, "Now what was that name? Gwal something or other." '[13] Unfortunately it is just as easy, and logical, to envision a Welsh storyteller botching an unfamiliar French name (though for other reasons this is not likely to have been the case). Moreover, most of the important names in the Four Branches – Pwyll (Pelles?), Rhiannon (Niniane?), Gwawl, Teirnon, Mallolwch, Branwen, Evnissyen, Manawydan, Llwyd, Math, Gwydyon, Aranrhod, Lleu (Lancelot?), Blodeuedd, Goronwy – seem to be absent from Arthurian literature altogether. A few motifs and patterns do recur: the hunter Arawn's testing of Pwyll by offering his wife must have contributed to

13. *Llên Cymru*, VIII, p. 235.

Sir Gawain and the Green Knight, while Gorsedd Arberth may well anticipate the Siege Perilous. And of course the Holy Grail undoubtedly owes much to the numerous vessels and platters in *The Mabinogion*: the cauldron in 'Branwen', the bowl in 'Manawydan', the cauldron in 'Culhwch', the bowl in 'Owein' and the salver in 'Peredur'.

The Mabinogion's lack of influence during this period may be attributed to the fact that it does not seem to have been very well known, not even to Welsh literature. It lay so dormant that it was not translated into English until 1849, when Lady Charlotte Guest's version appeared. Lady Charlotte also supplied the title *Mabinogion* – previously the tales were simply identified as being part of this or that manuscript – and for this title some explanation is due. Each of the Four Branches ends with some form of the phrase, 'So ends this Branch of the Mabinogi.' Inasmuch as the Welsh word *mab* means 'boy', Lady Charlotte concluded that *mabinogi* was a noun meaning 'a story for children' and that *mabinogion* was the plural of the word. In fact, the word *mabinogion* does not exist in Welsh, though it appears once by mistake in 'Pwyll'. *Mabinogi* is a genuine Welsh word, but in these texts it applies only to the Four Branches in which it appears. Strictly speaking, this collection ought to be called 'The Mabinogi and Other Early Welsh Tales', but that is cumbersome, while 'The Mabinogion' is established and convenient.

Unfortunately, the *meaning* of the word *mabinogi* in the present context is still a problem. Professor Ifor Williams was able to show that *mabinogi* generally designates the story of someone's early years, and he suggested that the Four Branches originally told the story of Pryderi.[14] If this was indeed the case, then Pryderi's part in these tales has been considerably reduced, not just in the northern stories, but in 'Pwyll' and 'Manawydan' as well. One must

14. *Pedeir Keinc y Mabinogi*, pp. xlii–liii.

ask why there is scarcely any trace of the missing Pryderi material in Welsh tradition; why a coherent Pryderi-cycle should have been broken up into four distinct and unrelated narratives; and why the no-longer-applicable title was not dropped from the end of each Branch. Also, if perhaps Pryderi's fleeting appearance in 'Branwen' isn't rather an attempt to provide the Four Branches with a unifying figure. Alternatively, Rachel Bromwich has suggested that *mabinogi* came to signify 'a tale of descendants', and that the Four Branches actually deal with the children of the early Celtic deities: the families of Llŷr and Dôn, and Pryderi son of Pwyll.[15] While stretching the meaning of *mabinogi* somewhat, this theory does rebut the objections raised above. Still, one cannot completely discount the possibility that Pryderi was once the focal point of the Four Branches.

8. TEXTS, TRANSLATIONS AND SCHOLARSHIP

The diplomatic edition of the White Book of Rhydderch was done by J. Gwenogvryn Evans in 1907; it has since been reprinted by the University of Wales Press (1973) with a new introduction (in Welsh) by R. M. Jones. For the Red Book of Hergest version there is the 1887 diplomatic edition by J. Gwenogvryn Evans and John Rhys. Most of the tales have appeared in individual editions as well: Ifor Williams has done the Four Branches, 'Maxen' and 'Lludd', while Melville Richards has produced an edition of 'Rhonabwy'. The notes to 'Maxen' and 'Lludd' are in English; otherwise, introductions and notes to these volumes are in Welsh. The Dublin Institute has published editions of three tales, with introductions, notes and vocabularies all in English: 'Pwyll' and 'Owein' by R. L. Thomson and 'Branwen' by Derick Thomson. For

15. *Studies in Early British History*, Cambridge, 1954, p. 103.

'Culhwch', 'Peredur' and 'Gereint' there are only the diplomatic editions.

Of the three English translations, Lady Charlotte Guest's includes a twelfth tale, 'The Story of Talyessin', not found in the early manuscripts, but it also excises passages which she considered indelicate. In 1927, T. P. Ellis and John Lloyd produced a second translation from the Red Book, this one unabridged, while in 1948 there finally appeared a translation from the White Book, the work of Thomas Jones and Gwyn Jones. This last is the most scrupulously accurate, though its literalness sometimes makes for unidiomatic English. There is also the 1913 French translation by Joseph Loth.

Full-length studies of *The Mabinogion* are not exactly abundant. The theories which W. J. Gruffydd advances in his studies of 'Math' and 'Pwyll/Manawydan' are highly speculative but often compelling; Proinsias Mac Cana's more objective *Branwen Daughter of Llŷr* eschews reconstruction in favour of outlining the tale's numerous sources. Morgan Watkin's *La Civilisation française dans les Mabinogion* explores the extent of French influence upon the earlier tales, while in his *International Popular Tale* Kenneth Jackson points out parallels between the Mabinogi and popular folktales. For those who read Welsh, there are the introductions to the editions mentioned above, as well as some useful articles by G. W. Goetinck and R. M. Jones in current Welsh periodicals. Among contemporary retellings, Evangeline Walton has devoted a fantasy to each Branch of the Mabinogi, while in his novel *The Owl Service* Alan Garner reinterprets the Lleu–Blodeuedd–Goronwy section of 'Math'.

9. THIS TRANSLATION

The aim of the present volume is two-fold: to present an accurate, readable rendering into modern English, and to provide an assortment of helpful background materials. With regard to the translation I have not attempted to be absolutely literal. The surviving texts of *The Mabinogion* are often tedious, repetitive and unclear, and I have therefore varied sentence structure, eliminated a few duplications and occasionally replaced personal pronouns with proper names (or vice versa); the result, I hope, will sound as natural to the modern reader as the original did to its medieval audiences. The order of the tales is that of the Jones translation, not for the sake of tradition, but because the Four Branches belong at one end and the Arthurian stories at the other – 'Culhwch' may have been the first tale to take shape, and 'Rhonabwy' the last, but they have a number of characters in common and are not so very unlike each other in tone and setting.

The pronunciation guide is only an approximation, but it should render the Welsh names in the text less formidable. Similarly, the locations on the map are often the result of guesswork, but they are roughly accurate; I have drawn freely on Welsh scholarship in order to include as many place names as possible, and the great majority of them are represented. The bibliography covers all texts and major critical works, as well as selected background material; for the sake of brevity articles have generally been excluded, but those who read Welsh may be referred to the periodical *Llên Cymru*.

I would like to thank W. G. Cooke and J. H. Gough for their help in xeroxing the text; my brother Timothy for his numerous valuable suggestions; my editor Mrs Betty Radice for her patient perusal of my typescript; and those scholars without whose work this translation would not be what it is.

BIBLIOGRAPHY

NOTE: (W) after a text indicates that the introduction and notes are written in Welsh; (W/E) indicates that the introduction is in Welsh and the notes in English.

Although *Math vab Mathonwy* and *Trioedd Ynys Prydein* have Welsh titles, they are written in English.

DIPLOMATIC EDITIONS

The White Book Mabinogion, edited by J. Gwenogvryn Evans, Pwllheli, 1907; reprinted as *Llyfr Gwyn Rhydderch* (The White Book of Rhydderch) with introduction (W) by R. M. Jones, Cardiff, 1973.

The Text of the Mabinogion and other Welsh Tales from the Red Book of Hergest, edited by John Rhys and J. Gwenogvryn Evans, Oxford, 1887.

TEXTS

Pedeir Keinc y Mabinogi (The Four Branches of the Mabinogi), edited (W) by Ifor Williams, Cardiff, 1930.

Pwyll Pendeuic Dyuet (Pwyll Lord of Dyved), edited by R. L. Thomson, Dublin, 1957.

Branwen uerch Lŷr (Branwen Daughter of Llŷr), edited by Derick Thomson, Dublin, 1961.

Breuddwyd Maxen (The Dream of Maxen), edited (W/E) by Ifor Williams, third edition, Bangor, 1928.

Cyfranc Lludd a Llevelys (The Adventure of Lludd and Llevelys), edited (W/E) by Ifor Williams, second edition, Bangor, 1932.

Breudwyt Ronabwy (The Dream of Rhonabwy), edited (W) by G. Melville Richards, Cardiff, 1948.

Owein, or *Chwedyl Iarlles y Ffynnawn* (Owein, or the Tale of the Countess of the Fountain), edited by R. L. Thomson, Dublin, 1968.

TRANSLATIONS

The Mabinogion from the Llyfr Coch o Hergest, and other ancient Welsh manuscripts, translated by Lady Charlotte Guest, London, 1838–49.

Les Mabinogion, translated (into French) by Joseph Loth, second edition, Paris, 1913.

The Mabinogion, translated by T. P. Ellis and John Lloyd, Oxford, 1929.

The Mabinogion, translated by Gwyn Jones and Thomas Jones, London, 1948.

CRITICAL STUDIES

Gruffydd, W. J., *Rhiannon*, Cardiff, 1953; *Math vab Mathonwy*, Cardiff, 1928.

Mac Cana, Proinsias, *Branwen Daughter of Llŷr*, Cardiff, 1958.

Newstead, Hélaine, *Brân the Blessed*, New York, 1939.

Watkin, Morgan, *La Civilisation française dans les Mabinogion*, Paris, 1963.

Jackson, Kenneth, *The International Popular Tale and Early Welsh Tradition*, Cardiff, 1961.

Foster, Idris Llewelyn, '*Culhwch and Olwen* and *Rhonabwy's Dream*' and '*Gereint, Owein* and *Peredur*', both in *Arthurian Literature in the Middle Ages*, edited by R. S. Loomis, London, 1959.

Loomis, R. S., *Arthurian Tradition and Chrétien de Troyes*, New York, 1949; *Wales and the Arthurian Legend*, Cardiff, 1956.

Williams, M. Rh., *Essai sur la composition du roman gallois de Peredur*, Paris, 1909.

RELATED WORKS

Geoffrey of Monmouth, *Historia Regum Britanniae*, edited by Acton Grissom, London, 1929; translated by Lewis Thorpe, Harmondsworth, 1966.

Crestiens de Troyes, *li contes del graal*, or *Perceval*, edited (as *Le roman de Perceval*) by William Roach, Paris, 1959;

translated (as *The Story of the Grail*) by Robert White Linker, Chapel Hill, 1952; *li chevaliers au lyon*, or *Ivain*, edited by T. B. W. Reid, Manchester, 1942; translated (as *Yvain: The Knight of the Lion*) by Robert W. Ackerman and Frederick W. Locke, New York, 1957; *Erec et Enide*, edited by Mario Rocques, Paris, 1952; translated by W. W. Comfort in *Arthurian Romances by Chrétien de Troyes*, London, n.d.

Ancient Irish Tales, edited by T. P. Cross and C. H. Slover, London, 1937; reprinted, New York, 1969.

The Earliest Welsh Poetry, translated by Joseph Clancy, Cardiff, 1970.

Trioedd Ynys Prydein (The Triads of the Island of Britain), edited and translated by Rachel Bromwich, Cardiff, 1961.

GENERAL INTEREST

Powell, T. G. E., *The Celts*, London, 1958.

Dillon, Myles, and Chadwick, Nora, *The Celtic Realms*, New York, 1967.

Filip, Jan, *Celtic Civilisation and its Heritage*, Prague, 1960.

Vries, Jan de, *Keltische Religion*, Stuttgart, 1961.

Rees, Alwyn and Brinley, *Celtic Heritage*, London, 1961.

Mac Cana, Proinsias, *Celtic Mythology*, Feltham, 1970.

CONTEMPORARY RETELLINGS

Walton, Evangeline, *Prince of Annwn*, New York, 1974; *The Children of Llyr*, New York, 1971; *The Song of Rhiannon*, New York, 1972; *The Island of the Mighty*, New York, 1970 (originally published as *The Virgin and the Swine*, 1936).

Garner, Alan, *The Owl Service*, London, 1967.

ABBREVIATIONS
USED IN THE NOTES

See the Bibliography for full details of the works referred to.

ALMA	*Arthurian Literature in the Middle Ages*
BDL	*Branwen Daughter of Llŷr*
BR	*Breudwyt Ronabwy*
BuL	*Branwen uerch Lŷr*
PKM	*Pedeir Keinc y Mabinogi*
PPD	*Pwyll Pendeuic Dyuet*
Rh	*Rhiannon*
TYP	*Trioedd Ynys Prydein*

NOTE ON THE PRONUNCIATION
OF WELSH NAMES

While they may look odd to the English speaker, the names of
the people and places in *The Mabinogion* are not difficult to
pronounce, and the following will serve as a rough guide:

Consonants. As in English, with a few exceptions:

c : *c*ane, never *c*inder
ch : Scottish lo*ch* or German Ba*ch*, never *ch*urch
dd : *th*en, never *th*istle
ff : *f*urze
g : *g*irl, never *g*em
ll : as if *hl*, with a hissing *h*
rh : as if *hr*, with a hissing *h*
s : *s*in, never ro*s*e.
th : *th*istle, never *th*en

Vowels. Roughly as in continental languages:

a : f*a*ther
e : m*e*t
i : p*i*n
o : n*o*t
u : p*i*n, or French t*u*
w : n*oo*k – but consonantal before vowels (except *y*) and in
    G*w*res, G*w*lwlwyd, G*w*lyddyn, G*w*enwledyr.
y : p*i*n – but consonantal before vowels (except *w*).

The addition of a circumflex lengthens a vowel.

Diphthongs. Usually as a combination of the two vowels:

ae, ei, eu, ey : t*i*ger
aw : *ou*t
oe : *oi*l
wy : d*ewy*. Following *g* or at the beginning of a syllable:
    *wi*n. However, *gŵy* : *gooey*.

Stress. On the next to last syllable. Note however Ánnwvyn,
    Brónllavyn, Dývynarth, Dývynwal.

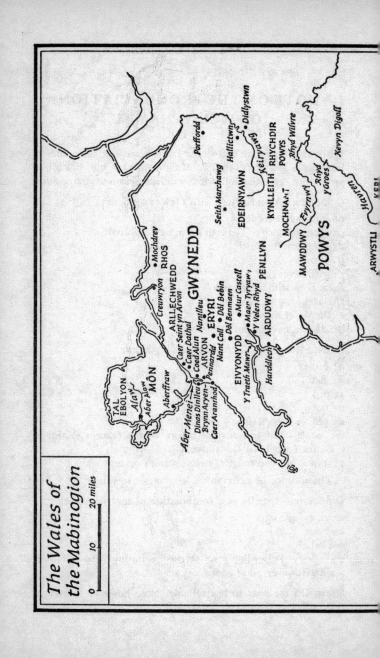

The Wales of
the Mabinogion

0   10   20 miles

Porffordd

Didlystwn

Hallictwn

Seith Marchawg

Mochdrev

RHOS

ARLLECHWEDD

GWYNEDD

EDEIRNYAWN

Keiryawg

Rhyd Wilvre

RHYCHDIR

KYNLLEITH

POWYS

Kevyn Digoll

Creuwryon

Caer Seint yn Arvon

Caer Dathal

Nantlleu

ERYRI

Dôl Bebin

MOCHNANT

Rhyd
y Groes

Evyrnwl

Havren

Coed Alun

Mur Castell

Eyrnwl

Dinas Dinlleu

Aber

Aber Alaw

MÔN

TAL
EBOLYON

Alaw

Aberffraw

Brynn Aryen

Pennardd

ARVON

Nant Call

EIVYONYDD

Y Traeth Mawr

Dôl Benmaen

Maen Tyryaw

Y Velen Rhyd

Mur Castell

PENLLYN

MAWDDWY

POWYS

ARWYSTLI

KEDI

Havren

Caer Arianrhod

Aber Menei

Hardlech

ARDUDWY

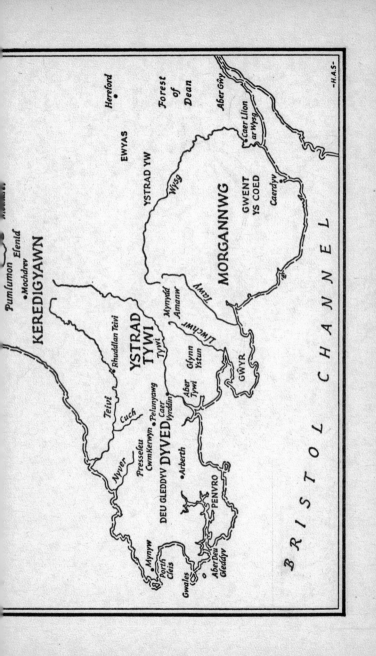

KEREDIGYAWN

Pumlumon
Elenid
• Mochdrev

Teivi
Cuch

Nyver
Presseleu
Cwmkerwyn DYVED
Pe? unyawg
Caer
Vyrddin

Mynyw
Porth
Cleis

Gwales
Aber Deu
Gleddyv

Arberth

PENVRO

DEU GLEDDYV

Rhuddlan Teivi

YSTRAD
TYWI

Tywi

Aber
Tywi

Gfynn
Ystun

Mynydd
Amanw

Llwchwr

GWYR

Tawy

Hereford •

Forest
of
Dean

EWYAS

YSTRAD YW

Wysg

Aber Gŵy

Caer Llion
ar Wysg

MORGANNWG

GWENT
YS COED

Caerdyv

B R I S T O L   C H A N N E L

—H.A.S—

THE MABINOGION

PWYLL LORD OF DYVED

PWYLL, while confined entirely to the south of Wales, comprises three distinct parts. The plot of the first parallels that of an Irish tale, 'The Wasting Sickness of Cú Chulaind': a mortal hero is asked to fight for an otherworld king, and is offered an otherworld woman as reward – though Pwyll's self-denial, suggesting as it does the extent to which continental chivalry has informed the tale, represents a major innovation. The second part recalls Odysseus' reclaiming of Penelope, while the third may reflect similar Irish traditions about the birth of Cú Chulaind, which was also accompanied by the birth of colts.

Structurally, the first two parts run parallel: in each section Pwyll is required to repair the consequences of an initial blunder. His victory over Havgan atones for the appropriation of Arawn's stag, while his forbearance in the matter of Arawn's wife is fittingly rewarded by the appearance of Rhiannon in the second part. Pwyll's second mistake differs from the first in showing a want of good judgement rather than of goodwill, but the result is the same: he must prove himself again. Part Two also differs in being appreciably less well constructed: the storyteller effectively vitiates any feeling of suspense by revealing every step of Rhiannon's plan in advance. Part Three is simpler in theme but very confused as to plot – possibly at an earlier stage Rhiannon was accused of giving birth to a foal, hence her bizarre punishment and the confusion over Teirnon's colts. The primary concerns in this section, however, are those of kindness and courtesy.

Pryderi's original role in 'Pwyll' is difficult to assess. The manner of his birth, his fosterage, his two names and his precocity all liken him to the Irish hero Cú Chulaind; on the other hand, his early life is simply passed over here, and there is little mention of him elsewhere in Welsh tradition.

Pwyll Lord of Dyved

Pwyll [1] Lord of Dyved ruled over the seven cantrevs [2] of that land. One day, when he was in his chief court at Arberth, his thoughts and desires turned to hunting. Glynn Cuch [3] was the part of his realm he wanted to hunt, so he set out that evening from Arberth and went as far as Penn Llwyn on Bwya, [4] where he spent the night. At dawn the next day he rose and made for Glynn Cuch, in order to turn his hounds loose in the forest; he blew his horn and began to muster the hunt, but in riding after the hounds he became separated from his companions. As he listened to the baying of his pack he perceived the cry of another pack, a different cry which was advancing towards him. He spied a clearing in the forest, a level field, and as his pack reached the edge of this field he saw the other pack with a stag running before it, and near the centre of the clearing this other pack overtook the stag and brought it down. Pwyll at once remarked the pack's colour, without bothering to look at the stag, for no hound he had ever seen was the colour of these: a dazzling shining white with red ears, and as the whiteness of the dogs shone so did the redness

1. Pwyll: sense, judgement.
2. cantrev: (literally one hundred homesteads) an administrative unit.
3. Glynn: glen.　　　4. Penn: peak, headland.

of their ears. Even so he approached and drove off the strange hounds and baited his own upon the stag.

As Pwyll was about this he saw beyond the other pack a rider approaching on a great dapple-grey horse, wearing a hunting horn round his neck and a hunting dress of greyish-brown material. This horseman rode up to him and said, 'Chieftain, I know who you are, but I will not greet you.' 'Well,' replied Pwyll, 'perhaps your rank prevents your doing so.' 'God knows, it is not the degree of my rank which prevents me.' 'What else, chieftain?' asked Pwyll. 'Between me and God,' said the stranger, 'your own rudeness and discourtesy.' 'Chieftain, what discourtesy have you seen in me?' 'In no man have I seen greater discourtesy than driving away the pack which has killed a stag and baiting one's own pack upon it. That was your discourtesy, and though I will take no vengeance, between me and God, I will dishonour you to the value of a hundred stags.' 'Chieftain,' said Pwyll, 'if I have done wrong, I will earn your friendship.' 'How?' asked the other. 'As befits your rank – only I do not know who you are.' 'I am a crowned king in my own land.' 'Lord, good day to you,' said Pwyll. 'What land do you come from?' 'Annwvyn,'[5] said the other. 'I am Arawn King of Annwvyn.' 'Lord, how can I earn your friendship?' 'This is how,' said Arawn. 'There is a man – Havgan King of Annwvyn – whose realm borders on mine, and he is constantly waging war against me. By ridding me of his oppression, which you can do easily, you will earn my friendship.' 'I will do that gladly,' said Pwyll, 'only tell me how I can.'

'That I will,' said Arawn. 'We will make a strong bond of friendship. I will send you into Annwvyn in my place, and give you the loveliest woman you have ever seen to sleep with every night; moreover I will endow you with my shape and appearance so that no chamberlain, no officer,

5. Annwvyn: not-world? *v. PPD* pp. 25–6.

no follower of mine will know that you are not I. All this
for a year and a day, and then we will meet again here.'
'Fair enough,' said Pwyll. 'But even if I stay in your land
for a year, how am I to find the man of whom you speak?'
'A year from tonight,' said Arawn, 'he and I are to meet at
the ford. You will be there in my place; strike him one
blow, which he will not survive, and if he asks you to
finish him off hold your hand, no matter how much he
begs you. For however often I struck him, the next day
he would be fighting as well as before.' 'Very well,' said
Pwyll, 'but what will I do with my own kingdom?' 'I will
see that neither man nor woman knows that I am not you,
for I will go in your place.' 'Then I will be glad to go.'
'Your journey will be free of trouble; nothing will im-
pede your progress to my kingdom, for I myself will guide
you.'[6]

Arawn then led Pwyll to where they could see the court
and the other dwellings. 'This court and kingdom are now
yours. Make straight for the court; no one there will fail
to recognize you, and as you observe people's behaviour
you will learn our customs.' Pwyll rode towards the court,
and once inside he saw dwellings and halls and chambers
and the finest assembly of buildings anyone had seen. He
entered the hall to change; youths and servants appeared
and pulled off his boots, and each one greeted Pwyll as he
went by. Two horsemen came to remove his hunting garb
and clothe him in a garment of gold brocade. Then the
hall was made ready; he could see troops and companies
entering, the finest looking and best equipped troops anyone had seen, and with them the queen, dressed in shining
gold brocade, the most beautiful woman anyone had seen.
Everyone washed and went to sit down; the queen sat on

6. From this point until Pwyll regains his own shape, he is not
called by name, rather he is identified as 'he' or 'the man who was
in Arawn's place' Perhaps in an earlier version the protagonist's
name was not Pwyll. *v. Rh*, pp. 36–7.

one side of Pwyll, and the earl (so he surmised) on the
other. Pwyll began to talk to his queen, and of all the
women he had ever talked with, she was the least affected,
and most gracious in disposition and conversation. They
passed the time eating and drinking and singing and
carousing, and of all the courts he had ever seen, this was
the best supplied with golden plate and royal jewels.

When it was time to sleep Pwyll and his queen went to
bed, and as soon as they were in the bed he turned his face
to the edge and his back to her, nor did he speak another
word before morning. The next day tenderness and affec-
tionate conversation were resumed, but however affec-
tionate they were by day, not one night during the
following year was different from the first one.

Pwyll spent that year hunting and singing and carousing, in fellowship and in pleasant talk with his companions, up to the night of the meeting, which the men
in the most distant parts of the kingdom remembered as
well as he did himself. He was accompanied by the nobles
of the realm, and as they reached the ford a horseman rose
and said, 'Nobles, listen well. This encounter lies between
the two kings, in single combat, for each one claims the
land and the domain of the other; therefore let everyone
else stand back.' With that the two kings drew near and
met in the middle of the ford. On the first rush the man
who was in Arawn's place struck Havgan's shield in the
centre of the boss so that it split into two halves; Havgan's
armour shattered, and he himself was thrown an arm
and a spear's length over his horse's hindquarters to the
ground, where he lay mortally wounded. 'Chieftain,' he
said, 'what right did you have to kill me? I made no claim
against you, nor do I know of any reason why you should
kill me.[7] But since you have begun so, finish me off now.'
'Chieftain, I may yet regret doing to you what I have done.

7. Havgan apparently knows that his opponent is Pwyll and not
Arawn.

He who wishes to may strike you again, but I will not.'
'Loyal followers,' said Havgan, 'carry me away, for my end
is now certain, and I can no longer maintain you.' 'Sirs,'
said the man who was in Arawn's place, 'talk among yourselves and decide who ought to be my men,' and they
answered, 'Lord, all men ought to be, for there is over
Annwvyn no king but yourself.' 'Good. Let those who
offer their submission be received, and those who are un-
willing be compelled by the sword.' Thus he received the
homage of the men and began to rule the land, and by
noon of the following day both realms were in his power.

Pwyll then set out for the meeting-place. He made for
Glynn Cuch, and when he arrived Arawn was there waiting for him, and each was glad to see the other. 'God reward your friendship,' said Arawn. 'Well,' said Pwyll,
'when you arrive in your own land, you will see what I
have done for you.' 'For what you have done, God reward
you.' Then Arawn restored Pwyll's shape and appearance,
and took back his own, so that each man was himself
again.

Arawn set out for his court in Annwvyn, and he was
happy to see the companies and troops which he had
missed for so long; they however knew nothing of his absence, and his arrival was no greater novelty than it had
ever been. He spent the day in pleasure and merrymaking,
in sitting and talking with his wife and his nobles, and
when it was time to sleep rather than to carouse they went
to bed. Arawn got into the bed and his wife came to him,
and at once he began to talk to her, to hold her and
caress her lovingly. She had not been so treated for the
past year, and she thought, 'My God, how different he is
tonight from what he has been.' She thought a long time;
he woke, and spoke to her, a second time, and even a
third, but she gave no answer. 'Why do you not answer
me?' he asked, whereupon she said, 'I tell you that for a
year now I have not spoken at all in this place.' 'How can

that be? We have always talked in bed.' 'Shame on me,'
she said, 'if since a year from yesternight this bed has seen
conversation or pleasure between us, or even your turning
your face to me, let alone anything more.' That set Arawn
to thinking. 'Lord God,' he said, 'what a faithful comrade
I took for a friend!' Then he said to his wife, 'Lady, do
not blame me, for I have neither lain down nor slept with
you this past year.' He told her what had happened, and
she said, 'I confess to God, you made a strong pact for your
friend to have fought off the temptations of the flesh and
kept faith with you.' 'Lady, that was my thought when I
was silent.' 'No wonder,' she said.

Meanwhile Pwyll Lord of Dyved arrived in his own
realm and country, and began to question his nobles as
to how he had ruled the past year compared with previous
ones. They answered, 'Lord, never have you been so per-
ceptive, nor so kind; never have you distributed your
goods more freely, never was your discernment so marked.'
'Between me and God,' said Pwyll, 'you ought rather to
thank the man who was with you,' and he told them what
had happened. 'Well, lord, thank God you made such a
friend. As for the rule we have known this past year,
surely you will not take it from us?' 'Between me and
God,' said Pwyll, 'I will not.'

From that time on the friendship between Pwyll and
Arawn increased. Each sent the other horses and hounds
and hawks and whatever treasure he thought his friend
might like. Moreover, because of Pwyll's year-long sojourn
in Annwvyn, because of his having reigned there so prosperously and his having united the two realms through
valour and prowess, the name Pwyll Lord of Dyved fell
into disuse, and he was called Pwyll Head of Annwvyn
ever after.

One day Pwyll was in his chief court at Arberth, where
a feast had been prepared and a great number of men
assembled. After the first sitting he rose to take a walk,

setting out for Gorsedd Arberth,[8] the hill which rose above
the court. One of his men said, 'Lord, it is the property of
this hill that whenever a man of royal blood sits on it, one
of two things happens: he receives blows and wounds, or
else he sees a wonder.' 'I do not expect to receive blows
or wounds in the company of such a host,' said Pwyll, 'and
I would be glad to see a wonder. I will go and sit on the
hill.'

This Pwyll did. As they were sitting they saw a woman
dressed in shining gold brocade and riding a great pale
horse approaching on the highway which ran past the
hill, and anyone who saw the horse would have said it
was moving at a slow steady pace as it drew level with the
hill. 'Men,' said Pwyll, 'does anyone know that horsewoman?' 'No, lord,' they answered. 'Then let someone go
find out who she is.' A man rose, but by the time he reached
the highway she had already gone past. He followed on
foot as best he could, but the greater his speed the farther
ahead she drew, and when he saw that his pursuit was in
vain he returned and told Pwyll, 'Lord, it is pointless for
anyone to follow her on foot.' 'All right,' said Pwyll, 'go to
the court and take the fastest horse you know and go after
her.' The man fetched the horse and set out; he reached
open country and showed his mount the spurs, but the
more he pricked it on the farther ahead she drew, all the
while going at the same pace as before. His horse tired,
and when it slowed to a walk he brought it back to where
Pwyll was waiting, and said, 'Lord, it is useless for anyone to follow that lady. I know of no horse in the entire
kingdom faster than this one, and I could not overtake
her.' 'All right,' said Pwyll, 'but there is some hidden
meaning here. Let us return to the court.'

They did that and spent the day there, and the next

8. Gorsedd: mound. A noun followed by a proper name always
indicates possession – Gorsedd Arberth: the Mound of Arberth.

one as well, until dinner time. After the first sitting Pwyll
said, 'Well, let those who went out yesterday accompany
me to the hill now. And you,' he said to one of the lads,
'bring along the fastest horse you know of in the field,' and
the lad did that. They went out to the hill and the horse
with them, and as they were sitting there they saw the
woman in the brocade garment riding the same horse
along the highway. 'There is the horsewoman of yesterday,' said Pwyll. 'Lad, be ready to find out who she is.'
'Gladly, Lord,' said the lad. The horsewoman drew opposite; the lad mounted his horse, but before he could settle
into the saddle she had gone past and put a clear distance
between them, all the while travelling at the same pace as
the day before. He put his horse to a walk, thinking that
as slow as he went he would still overtake her, but he did
not. He gave the horse its head, but even then he was no
nearer to her, and the more he urged his horse the farther
ahead she drew. When he perceived that pursuit was useless he turned back to where Pwyll was waiting. 'Lord, the
horse cannot do better than you have seen.' 'I have seen
it is useless for anyone to pursue her,' said Pwyll, 'but
between me and God she had an errand for someone on
this plain, had her obstinacy not prevented her declaring
it. Let us return to the court.'

They did that and spent the night singing and carousing, and the next day as well until dinner time; and when
all had sat down to dinner Pwyll said, 'Where are the men
who went to the top of the hill yesterday and the day before?' 'Here we are, lord.' 'Then let us go to the hill and
sit there. And you,' he said to a stableboy, 'saddle my horse
well and bring it to the highway, and bring my spurs along
too.' The lad did this. They reached the hill and sat down,
and almost immediately they saw the horsewoman coming
along the highway, in the same dress and travelling at the
same pace. 'Lad,' said Pwyll, 'I see our horsewoman coming; give me my horse.' Pwyll climbed into the saddle,

but no sooner had he done so than the lady rode past him. Giving his spirited prancing mount its head he turned to follow, supposing he would overtake her at the second or third bound; yet he drew no closer than before. He pushed his horse to its utmost speed, until he saw that pursuit was fruitless.

Pwyll then called out, 'Lady, for the sake of the man you love best, stop for me!' 'I will, gladly,' said she, 'and it would have been better for your horse had you asked me that earlier.' The lady then reined in and halted, and drew up the part of her veil which covered her face; she fixed her gaze on him and they began to talk. 'Lady,' said Pwyll, 'where do you come from, and where are you going?' 'I am doing my errands,' she said, 'and I am glad to see you.' 'I welcome you,' said Pwyll, for it seemed to him that the beauty of every girl and woman he had ever seen was nothing compared to the face of this lady. 'Lady, will you tell me anything of your errands?' 'Between me and God I will. My most important errand was to try to see you.' 'That seems to me the best errand you could have come on. Will you tell me your name?' 'Lord, I will. I am Rhiannon daughter of Heveydd the Old. I am being given to a man against my will; I have not wanted any husband, and that because of my love for you. Even now I will not have him unless you reject me, and it is to hear your answer to me that I have come.' 'Between me and God, here is my answer. Had I my choice of every girl and woman in the world, I would choose you.' 'Well, if that is how you feel, then set a time for us to meet, before I am given to another man.' 'The best time for me would be the soonest, in whatever place you like. Set the date.' 'That I will, lord: a year from tonight in Heveydd's court. I will see that a feast is prepared for your arrival.' 'I will certainly keep that appointment,' said Pwyll. 'Lord, farewell, and remember to keep your promise. I will leave you now.' So they parted and he returned to his troops and his company, and whenever they inquired about the lady he would turn to other topics.

That year passed, and when the time came Pwyll and ninety-nine companions equipped themselves and rode to the court of Heveydd the Old.[9] There was great joy at their arrival: a huge assembly rejoicing to see them and a great feast set out and all the resources of the court placed at Pwyll's disposal. The hall was made ready and they entered and sat down: Heveydd sat on one side of Pwyll and Rhiannon on the other, and everyone else according to rank. They ate and caroused and conversed, and as they began to carouse after the first course they saw a tall, auburn-haired, noble-looking youth in a silk garment enter the hall, approach the upper end, and greet Pwyll and his companions. 'God's greeting to you, friend,' said Pwyll, 'sit down.' 'I will not, for I am a suppliant and I have an errand.' 'Go on,' said Pwyll. 'Lord, it is with you my errand lies, for I have come to ask you a favour.' 'Whatever you ask, so far as it lies within my power you shall have it.' 'Alas, why did you answer him so?' said Rhiannon; but the youth said, 'Lady, he has given his answer in the presence of these nobles.' 'Friend,' asked Pwyll, 'what is your request?' 'The woman I love best you are to sleep with tonight. It is to ask for her, and for the preparations and the feast, that I have come.'

Pwyll fell silent, for there was no answer he could give. 'You had better not say any more,' said Rhiannon, 'for I have never seen such a feeble-witted performance.' 'Lady, I did not know who he was.' 'This is the man to whom I was to be given against my will: Gwawl son of Clud,[10] a powerful lord with many followers. As you have given your word, you had better give me to him before you dis-

9. Inasmuch as Arawn and Rhiannon are otherworld beings, the story is understandably unclear as to the location of their courts.

10. Gwawl: wall; Clud=Clyde. Probably a humorous reference to the Celts of northern Britain, *v. PPD*, p. 34.

honour yourself.' 'Lady, I do not know what sort of answer that is. I could never bring myself to do as you say.' 'Give me to him, and I will arrange it so that he will never have me.' 'How can that be?' asked Pwyll. 'I will give you a little bag, which you must keep with you. He will ask for the preparations and the feast, but those do not lie within your power, for I will give the feast to your host and your company, and this will be your answer to him concerning that.

'As for me, I will set a date, a year from tonight, for him to sleep with me, and at that time you, with your bag and your ninety-nine horsemen, must station yourselves in the orchard above the court. When Gwawl is in the midst of feasting and carousing you must enter, dressed in shabby clothes and with the bag in your hand, and you must ask for nothing more than the filling of the bag with food, for I will see that even if all the food and drink in these seven cantrevs is put into the bag it will be no fuller than before. After a great deal has been put in Gwawl will ask you if your bag will ever be full, and you must answer that it will not unless a very powerful noble rises and presses down the food with both feet and says, "Enough has been put inside." I will persuade Gwawl to rise and tread down the food in the bag, and when he does, turn the bag so that he is upside down inside and tie the strings of the bag into a knot. Wear a hunting horn round your neck, and when Gwawl is securely in the bag sound the horn, and let that be the signal between you and your horsemen: when they hear your horn, they are to descend upon the court.'

'Lord,' said Gwawl, 'it is high time I had an answer to my request.' Pwyll answered, 'You shall have as much of your request as is in my power.' 'Friend,' said Rhiannon, 'as for the preparations and the feast which are here, I have already given them to the troops and companies of Dyved, and I cannot allow them to be given to anyone else. But a year from tonight in this court a feast will be prepared for you, my friend, and you shall sleep with me.'

Gwawl set out for his kingdom, Pwyll returned to Dyved, and each spent the following year waiting for the feast in the court of Heveydd the Old. Gwawl son of Clud set out for the feast which had been prepared for him, and when he arrived at the court he was greeted joyfully; Pwyll Head of Annwvyn went to the orchard with his ninety-nine horsemen and his bag, just as Rhiannon had commanded, and wearing a shabby ragged outfit with big rag boots on his feet. Perceiving that the carousing after the first course had begun Pwyll made for the hall, and when he reached the upper end he greeted Gwawl son of Clud and the latter's companions, both men and women. 'God be good to you,' said Gwawl, 'and His welcome to you.' 'Lord, God reward you,' said Pwyll. 'I am a suppliant.' 'Your request is welcome, and if it is reasonable I will gladly grant it.' 'It is reasonable, lord, for I ask only to ward off hunger. This is my request: the filling of the little bag you see here with food.' 'A modest request that, and I will gladly grant it. Bring him food.' A great number of servants rose and began to fill the bag, but however much they put in, it was no fuller than before. 'Friend, will your bag ever be full?' asked Gwawl. 'Between me and God, it will not, unless a nobleman of land and possessions rises and presses the food down into the bag with both feet and says, "Enough has been put inside." ' 'Champion, rise at once,' said Rhiannon to Gwawl. 'Gladly,' said Gwawl, and he rose and put both feet in the bag, which Pwyll turned so that he was head over heels inside. Pwyll then closed it quickly and knotted the strings and blew on his horn, and at this his company fell upon the court and took prisoner the host that had come with Gwawl, while Pwyll threw off his rags and tatters and his rag boots. Upon entering, each of Pwyll's number struck the bag and asked, 'What is this?' 'A badger,' the rest of the men replied.

This is how they played the game: each man would strike
the bag with his foot or his staff, and as he did so he would
ask, 'What game are you playing?' 'The game of Badger
in the Bag,' they would all answer. This was the first playing of Badger in the Bag.

'Lord,' said the man in the bag, 'if you would listen to
me, death in a bag is no proper end for me.' 'What he says
is true, lord,' said Heveydd the Old. 'You ought to listen to
him, that is no proper death.' 'Then I will follow your
advice in this matter,' said Pwyll, whereupon Rhiannon
said, 'This is what you should do. You are in a position
where it is customary to satisfy the requests of suppliants
and minstrels. Require Gwawl there to give the presents
on your behalf, and have him swear that he will make no
claim and seek no revenge. That is punishment enough.'
'He will get that gladly,' said the man in the bag. 'I will
gladly accept the advice of Heveydd and Rhiannon,' said
Pwyll. 'Well, that is our advice.' 'Then I will take it.'
Heveydd said, 'Obtain sureties for yourself; we will answer
for his conduct until his men are free to do so,' and with
that Gwawl was released from the bag and his men were
freed. Then Heveydd said, 'Now ask for your sureties –
we know what ought to be asked for,' and he drew up a
list of sureties. 'Arrange your own conditions,' said Gwawl,
but Pwyll answered, 'I am satisfied with what Rhiannon
has drawn up,' and the sureties were arranged on those
terms. Then Gwawl said, 'Lord, I am injured and have
sustained many wounds; I have need of a healing bath
and so, with your permission, I will go now. But I will
leave men behind on my behalf to answer anyone who
might have a request.' 'Gladly,' said Pwyll, so Gwawl departed for his own kingdom.

Then the hall was made ready for Pwyll and his company and the company of Heveydd's court; they entered
and sat down, and as they had sat the year before so they
sat now. They feasted and caroused, and when bed-time

came Pwyll and Rhiannon retired to their chamber and
spent the night in pleasure and delight. The next morning Rhiannon said, 'Lord, rise now and begin to content
the minstrels, and do not refuse anyone who desires a
gift.' 'Gladly,' said Pwyll, 'today and every day, as long as
the feast lasts.' He rose and called for silence, asking all
suppliants and minstrels to present themselves and announcing that every whim and fancy would be satisfied.
This was done; the feast went on and on, and while it
lasted no one was turned away. When it ended Pwyll said
to Heveydd, 'With your permission, lord, I will depart for
Dyved tomorrow.' 'Godspeed, then,' said Heveydd, 'and
will you set a time for Rhiannon to follow you?' 'Between
me and God, we will leave together.' 'Is that your will,
lord?' 'Between me and God, it is.' The next day they left
for Dyved, making for the court at Arberth where a feast
was being prepared. An assembly of the noblest men and
women in the land and the kingdom came, and not one of
them, man or woman, left Rhiannon without being given
a memorable gift, a brooch or a ring or a precious
stone.

Pwyll and Rhiannon ruled Dyved prosperously the first
year and the second. The third year, however, the men of
Dyved began to fret at seeing that this man whom they
loved as their lord and foster-brother was still childless;
consequently they summoned Pwyll to a meeting in
Presseleu.[11] 'Lord, we realize you are not as old as some
men in the land, but we fear your wife will never bear you
a child. Take another woman so that you may have an
heir. You will not last forever, and though you may wish
matters to remain as they are, we will not permit it.' 'Well,
even now we have not been together long, and much may
yet happen,' answered Pwyll. 'Give me another year; at the
end of that time we will meet again and I will accept your
advice.'

11. Presseleu = Prescelly.

They set a date, and before the year was up Rhiannon bore Pwyll a son in Arberth. On the night of his birth women were brought in to look after mother and child, but these women and Rhiannon all fell asleep. Six women had been brought into the chamber, and they did watch for part of the night, but they were asleep before midnight and woke only at dawn; upon waking they searched round where they had left the boy, but there wasn't a trace of him. 'Alas! The boy is lost!' said one woman. 'Yes,' said another, 'and they would consider it getting off lightly if we were only burned or executed.' 'Is there any hope for us?' 'There is – I have a good plan.' 'What is it?' they all asked. 'There is a deerhound here with pups. We can kill some of the pups, smear Rhiannon's hands and face with the blood, throw the bones before her and insist that she destroyed her own child – it will be her word against that of us six.'

They settled on this plan. Towards daybreak Rhiannon woke and asked, 'Women, where is the child?' 'Lady, do not ask us for the lad; we are nothing but blows and bruises from struggling with you, and we are certain that we have never seen such fight in any woman, so that all our struggling was in vain.' 'Poor souls,' said Rhiannon, 'by the Lord God who knows all things, do not accuse me falsely. God who knows all things knows your words are false. If you are afraid, by my confession to God, I will protect you.' 'God knows that we will not bring harm on ourselves for anyone's sake.' 'Poor souls, you will come to no harm for telling the truth.' But whether her words were kind or pleading, Rhiannon got only the one answer from the women.

At this Pwyll Head of Annwvyn rose, with his company and his retinue, and the incident could not be kept from them. The story went round the land and all the nobles heard it, and they assembled and sent to Pwyll to ask him to separate from his wife because of the terrible outrage

she had committed. Pwyll answered, 'You have no reason
to ask me to put away my wife, except for her being childless, and since I know that she has borne a child I will not
part from her. If she has done wrong, let her be punished.'
Rhiannon summoned teachers and wise men, and as she
preferred being punished to arguing with the women, she
accepted her punishment. She had to remain for seven
years at the court of Arberth, where she was to sit every
day by the mounting-block near the gate and tell her story
to anyone who might not already know it; she was also to
offer to carry guests and strangers to the court on her back,
though it was seldom that anyone let himself be so trans-
ported. Rhiannon spent part of a year thus.

At that time the lord of Gwent Ys Coed [12] was Teirnon
Twrvliant,[13] the best man in the world. Teirnon had a
mare in his house, and there was not a handsomer horse
in the realm. Every May Eve [14] she foaled, but no one ever
knew anything of the colt, so that Teirnon, in talking one
night with his wife, said, 'Wife, we are fools to lose the
foal of our mare every year without getting even one of
them.' 'What can you do about it?' 'It is May Eve tonight,'
said he. 'God's revenge on me if I do not find out what fate
the foals have met with.' So he had the mare brought inside, while he armed himself and began to watch.

As night fell the mare foaled, a big colt without a flaw
and standing already. Teirnon rose to remark the sturdi-
ness of the colt, and as he did so he heard a great noise,
whereupon a great claw came through the window and
seized the colt by the mane. Teirnon drew his sword and
hacked the arm off at the elbow, so that the colt and part

12. Gwent Ys Coed: Gwent Below the Woods.
13. Twrvliant: thunder of waters? *v. PKM*, pp. 146–7, *PPD*, p.
39.
14. May Eve: (Walpurgisnacht) the beginning of summer in the
Celtic calendar. On this night visits from the otherworld were common.

of the arm were inside with him; hearing a loud crash and, simultaneously, a scream, he opened the door and rushed out after the noise, but the night was so dark he could see nothing. He was about to rush off and follow when he remembered that he had left the door open, and when he returned, he found by the door a small boy in swaddling clothes and wrapped in a silk mantle.

Teirnon picked up the lad and observed that he was strong for his age; then he closed the door and made for his wife's chamber. 'Lady, are you asleep?' 'No, lord; I was, but I woke as you came in.' 'Here is a boy for you, if you want him, for that is the one thing you have never had.' 'Lord, what story is this?' she asked, so he told her what had happened. 'See, lord, what kind of cloth is this the boy is wrapped in?' 'A brocade mantle.' 'Then he is the son of noble folk. Lord, if you approve, this could be a joy and a comfort to me. I will take some women into my confidence, and we will let out that I have been pregnant.' 'I will gladly agree to that,' said Teirnon.

This was done. The boy was baptized in the manner usual for that time, and was given the name Gwri Golden Hair, because what hair was on his head was as yellow as gold. He was brought up at the court, and before he was a year old he could walk and was sturdier than a well-grown three-year-old. At the end of the second year he was as strong as a six-year-old, and by the time he was four he was bargaining with the stableboys to let him water the horses. 'Lord,' said Teirnon's wife, 'where is the colt you rescued on the night you found the boy?' 'I gave it into the care of the stableboys,' answered Teirnon, 'and ordered it to be looked after.' 'Would it not be a good idea to have it broken in and given to the boy? After all, you found the lad on the same night that the colt was born and rescued.' 'I will not argue against that – I will let you give it to him.' 'God reward you, lord, I will do that.' So the horse was given to the lad, and Teirnon's wife went to the stableboys and grooms to command them to look after the colt and break it in for when the boy would go riding and there would be a story about him.

Meanwhile they heard the news of Rhiannon and her punishment, and because of the find he had made, Teirnon listened to all the tales and made constant inquiries, so that he heard from those who came from Arberth numerous laments over Rhiannon's misfortune and disgrace. He thought over these accounts and looked closely at the boy, and it was clear to him that as regards appearance he had never seen father and son who resembled each other so much as did Pwyll Head of Annwvyn and this lad. Pwyll's appearance was well known to Teirnon, who had once been his man; thus as Teirnon looked now he was seized by anxiety, for he realized how wrong it was to keep a boy whom he knew to be another's son. As soon as he was alone with his wife, Teirnon told her it was not right for them to keep the lad and allow so noble a lady as Rhiannon to be punished when the boy was actually Pwyll's son. His wife agreed to send Gwri back to Pwyll, 'for we will gain in three ways, lord: thanks and gratitude for releasing Rhiannon from her punishment, Pwyll's thanks for rearing the boy and returning him, and finally, if the boy grows into a good man, he will be our foster-son and will always do the best he can for us.'

So they decided to give the boy back. No later than the next day Teirnon and three companions equipped themselves and set out, with the boy as a fourth on the horse Teirnon had given him, and made for Arberth, and it wasn't long before they arrived. When they reached the court they saw Rhiannon sitting by the mounting-block, and as they drew near she said, 'Chieftain, come no nearer. I will carry each one of you to the court, since that is my punishment for killing my son and destroying him with my own hands.' 'Lady,' answered Teirnon, 'I do not suppose any of us will allow you to carry him.' 'Let him be

carried who will,' said the boy, 'but I will not.' 'God
knows, friend, none of us will,' said Teirnon.

When they entered the court there was great rejoicing
at their arrival. A feast was about to begin; Pwyll himself
had just returned from a circuit of Dyved, so they all went
in to wash, and Pwyll was glad to see Teirnon. They sat
down thus: Teirnon between Pwyll and Rhiannon, and
his two companions above Pwyll with the boy between
them. After the first course everyone began to talk and
carouse, and Teirnon told the tale of the mare and the
boy, how the latter had been in the care of himself and his
wife and how they had brought him up, and he said to
Rhiannon, 'Lady, look upon your son, for whoever lied
about you did wrong. When I heard of your grief I was
sorrowful and griefstricken myself. I do not suppose that
anyone in this company will deny that the lad is Pwyll's
son.' 'No, we have no doubt that he is,' they all said.
'Between me and God,' said Rhiannon, 'what a relief from
my anxiety if all this is true!' 'Lady, you have named your
son well,' said the Chieftain of Dyved,[15] 'for Pryderi son
of Pwyll Head of Annwvyn is the name which suits him
best.' Rhiannon answered, 'Ask if his own name does not
suit him better.' 'What was his name?' asked the Chieftain
of Dyved. 'We called him Gwri Golden Hair.' 'Then
Pryderi should be his name,' said the Chieftain of Dyved,
and Pwyll said, 'It is right to name the boy after what his
mother said when she received good news of him.' So they
named him Pryderi.[16]

Then Pwyll said, 'Teirnon, God reward you for bringing up the boy all this time. If he grows into a good man
he too ought to reward you.' 'Lord, my wife reared the

15. Chieftain of Dyved: in the text, Pendaran Dyved. Pendaran
may instead be a proper name. *v. TYP*, p. 488.

16. An attempt to explain the name Pryderi, not a very good one,
either, since pryderi actually means anxiety, and not, as the text
suggests, relief. *v. PPD*, p. 41.

boy, and no one in the world could grieve more over losing him than she does. He ought to remember, for my sake and hers, what we have done for him.' 'Between me and God,' said Pwyll, 'I will maintain both you and your land, so long as I am alive and able to maintain myself, and if he lives, it would be more fitting that he support you. If you and these nobles agree, since you have reared him until now, we will send him to be fostered by the Chieftain of Dyved henceforth, and you shall all be companions and foster-fathers to him.' Everyone agreed that this was a good idea, so the boy was given to the Chieftain of Dyved and the nobles all allied themselves with him. Teirnon and his companions then set out for their own land and dominions, amid gladness and rejoicing; Teirnon did not leave without being offered the finest jewels and the best horses and dogs, but he would accept nothing.

They remained in their own realms after that, and Pryderi son of Pwyll was brought up carefully, as was proper, until he was the most perfect lad and the handsomest and most accomplished at every feat in the kingdom. Thus they passed the years until Pwyll's life came to an end and he died. Pryderi ruled the seven cantrevs of Dyved prosperously, beloved by his country and by all around him; moreover he conquered the three cantrevs of Ystrad Tywi [17] and the four cantrevs of Keredigyawn, [18] and these are now called the seven cantrevs of Seissyllwch. [19] He campaigned until it was time for him to take a wife, and he took Kigva [20] daughter of Gwynn the Splendid son of Gloyw Wide Hair [21] son of the ruler Casnar, one of the nobles of this island. With that this Branch of the Mabinogi ends.

17. Ystrad: vale. 18. Keredigyawn = Cardigan.

19. Seissyll united the cantrevs of Ystrad Tywi and Keredigyawn in 730.

20. Kigva = Ciocba, wife of a son of Partholón in the Irish *Book of Invasions*.

21. Gwynn: white; Gloyw: shining.

BRANWEN DAUGHTER OF LLŶR

SET in northern Wales and Ireland, 'Branwen' encompasses a broader geography than does 'Pwyll', for it states that Brân is ruler over all of Britain – in this respect it adheres more closely to Geoffrey of Monmouth than to the First Branch. The plot represents a variant of the early Welsh poem 'The Booty of Annwvyn' in which Arthur and the men of Britain raid the otherworld and attempt to carry off a magic cauldron; the poem does not say if the prize is obtained, but it does tell us that only seven men return. The parallels with 'Branwen' – the expedition to the otherworld (here Ireland), the magic cauldron and the seven survivors – are too salient to be coincidental, and it may be that in an earlier version the cauldron and not Branwen was the primary object of the raid. The presence of Brân (the sexually incapacitated Fisher King of later Arthurian tales) and the cauldron, and the destruction of both Ireland and Britain, may also suggest that this is an early and primitive version of the Grail legend.

Structurally 'Branwen' forms two overlapping and counterbalancing sections. In Part One the British (through Evnissyen's maiming of the horses) insult the Irish, who first accept compensation and then (by mistreating Branwen) reject it; in Part Two the British (outraged by Branwen's sufferings) initially accept compensation and then (through Evnissyen again) reject it. A troublemaker in the tradition of the Norse Lóki and the Irish Bricriu, Evnissyen is the motivating factor throughout this tale, but his remorse and self-sacrifice come too late to save more than seven of his companions. The coda describes the timeless joys of the otherworld, and, touchingly, in the guise of an insatiable curiosity, man's yearning for the mortal world in which he belongs.

Branwen Daughter of Llŷr

Brân [1] the Blessed son of Llŷr [2] was the crowned king of this island, having been raised to the throne of London. One afternoon he was at a court of his at Harddlech [3] in Ardudwy; he was sitting on the rock of Harddlech overlooking the sea, accompanied by his brother Manawydan son of Llŷr, and his two brothers on his mother's side, Nissyen and Evnissyen, and such noblemen as ought to surround a king. The two brothers on his mother's side were the sons of Eurosswydd and Brân's mother Penarddun, [4] daughter of Beli son of Mynogan: one of these youths was a good lad, for he would make peace between the most hostile of forces, and his name was Nissyen; Evnissyen, however, would bring about fighting between the most loving of brothers.

As these nobles were sitting thus they saw thirteen ships coming from the south of Ireland and making for the coast, moving easily and swiftly, running before the wind and approaching rapidly. 'I see ships out there making boldly for our land,' said Brân. 'Tell the men of the court to equip themselves and go learn what our visitors want.' The men made ready and descended to the ships below, and seeing them close up they were certain they had never

1. Brân: raven.
2. Llŷr (= Lir in Irish): sea.
3. Harddlech = Harlech.
4. 'Triad 52' names Llŷr as the prisoner of Eurosswydd, *v. TYP*, p. 141.

seen ships better turned out than these, with their fine,
graceful, handsome ensigns of brocade. They could see
one of the ships drawing ahead of the others, and on that
ship a shield was raised above the deck with the point
uppermost as a sign of peace. The strangers made for land
in order to talk: they put out boats and sailed in to shore
and greeted the king, who could hear everything from his
seat on the rock above. 'God be good to you,' said Brân,
'and may you be welcome. Whose host of ships is this, and
who is your leader?' 'Lord, Mallolwch [5] King of Ireland is
here, and these are his ships.' 'What is it he wishes? Will
he come ashore?' 'No, lord,' they said. 'He has a request
for you, and unless you grant it he will not come.' 'What
is this request?' asked Brân. 'Lord, he wishes to make an
alliance with you. He has come to ask for Branwen [6]
daughter of Llŷr, and if you wish he will ally the Island
of the Mighty [7] with Ireland so that both will be stronger.'
'Then let him come ashore while we discuss the matter,'
answered Brân. That answer went back to Mallolwch,
who replied, 'I will gladly come.' He came ashore and
was welcomed, and between his host and Brân's there
was a great multitude in the court that night.

First thing the next day the men of the Island of the
Mighty held a council, and their decision was to give
Mallolwch Branwen; she was one of the three great queens [8]
of the island, and the most beautiful girl in the world. A
time was set for the couple to sleep together and everyone set out, Mallolwch and his host in their ships, Brân
and his party by land, until they all reached Aberffraw. [9]
There the feast began, and this is how they sat: the King

5. Mallolwch: also spelt Matholwch, it may be a borrowing of
the Irish name Máel Sechlainn. *v. BDL*, p. 30n., *TYP*, pp. 450–51.

6. Branwen: Bronwen (white breast), which appears once in the
text, may be the original form, *v. TYP*, p. 287.

7. Island of the Mighty: Britain.

8. queens: or perhaps ancestors, though Branwen has no descendants.   9. Aber: estuary.

of the Island of the Mighty with Manawydan son of Llŷr on one side of him and Mallolwch on the other, and Branwen next to Mallolwch. They feasted not in a house but in tents, for Brân had never been able to fit inside any house; they began to carouse, and to talk, and when they perceived it was better to sleep than to continue carousing they went to bed, and that night Mallolwch slept with Branwen.

The next day the entire complement of the court rose and the household officers began to discuss the quartering of Mallolwch's horses and grooms, and these were then quartered in every region, as far as the sea. One day Evnissyen, the quarrelsome man we mentioned above, happened upon the quarters of Mallolwch's horses and asked whose animals they were. 'These are the horses of Mallolwch King of Ireland,' replied the grooms. 'What are they doing here?' 'The King of Ireland himself is here; he has slept with your sister Branwen, and these are his horses.' 'Have they given away so excellent a girl as my sister without my consent?' said Evnissyen. 'They could not have hit upon a greater insult.' Straightway he struck at the horses: he cut their lips through to the teeth and their ears down to their heads and their tails through to their backs, and where he could get hold of their eyelids he cut them through to the bone; thus the horses were so badly disfigured that they were of no use to anyone.

News of this deed reached Mallolwch: he was told how his horses had been maimed and disfigured so that there was no profit to be had from them. 'Well, lord,' said one Irishman, 'they have insulted you, and the insult was intended.' 'God knows,' said Mallolwch. 'I marvel though that when they contemplated this insult they first gave me a girl as excellent and noble and beloved of her people as Branwen is.' 'Lord, you see it made plain,' said another man. 'There is nothing for you to do but make for the ships.' So they sought the ships.

News reached Brân that Mallolwch was leaving the court, though he had neither asked permission nor received it, and so messengers left to ask the King of Ireland why. Iddig son of Anarawd [10] and Heveydd the Tall were the messengers who went; they overtook Mallolwch and inquired about his intentions and why he was leaving. 'God knows,' he answered, 'had I only known I should not have come here. Still, a strange thing has happened to me.' 'What is that?' 'First I was given as wife Branwen daughter of Llŷr, one of the three great queens of this island and the daughter [11] of the King of the Island of the Mighty, and then I was insulted. I find it strange that the intended insult was not done before so excellent a girl as she was given to me.' 'God knows, lord, no one at court, no counsellor desired that you be insulted, and though you consider it an insult this affront and trick has offended Brân even more than it has you.' 'Well, I suppose that is true,' said Mallolwch. 'Nevertheless, he cannot retract the insult.'

The messengers took that answer to Brân and told him what Mallolwch had said. 'Well,' said the king, 'we are undone if he goes away angry; therefore we will not let him go.' 'Then send more messengers after him, lord.' 'That I will. Manawydan son of Llŷr, Heveydd the Tall, Unig Strong Shoulder, rise and go after Mallolwch; tell him that he shall have a sound horse for every one that was injured, and moreover as an honour-price a silver staff as thick as his little finger and as tall as himself, and a golden plate as broad as his face. Tell him what sort of man did this, and how it was done against my will; tell him that my half-brother did it, and that it would not be easy for me to have him killed or destroyed. Or let Mallolwch come to see me, and I will make peace on whatever terms he likes.'

10. Anarawd = Honorātus.

11. At the beginning of the tale it is stated that Brân is king; here his father Llŷr is made ruler over the island of Britain.

The messengers went after Mallolwch and repeated these words in a friendly way, and he listened to them. 'Men,' he said then, 'let us hold council.' They did that, and the conclusion they came to was that if they rejected the offer they were more likely to suffer greater shame than obtain a greater reparation. So Mallolwch decided to accept the offer, and the Irish returned to the court in peace; the tents and pavilions were arranged as if in a hall, and they went to eat, and as they had sat at the beginning of the feast so they sat now.

Mallolwch and Brân began to talk, but Brân found his companion's conversation listless and uninspired, whereas the man had been full of constant good cheer prior to the insult. He supposed that the Irish chieftain considered the compensation too meagre, so he said, 'Sir, you are not as good a talker tonight as you were earlier. If it is because you feel your compensation is too small, then I will increase it as much as you wish, and the horses will be made over to you tomorrow.' 'God reward you, lord,' said Mallolwch. 'I will add even more to your compensation,' said Brân, 'for I will give you a cauldron, the property of which is this: take a man who has been slain today and throw him into it, and tomorrow he will fight as well as ever, only he will not be able to speak.' Mallolwch thanked Brân and felt exceedingly pleased with the gift. The next day the horses were made over to him as long as there were tamed horses to be had, and then they journeyed to another commot [12] where he was given colts until the payment was complete. That commot was known as Tal Ebolyon [13] ever after.

As the host sat together on the second night Mallolwch asked, 'Lord, where did you find the cauldron which you have given me?' and Brân answered, 'I got it from a man

12. commot: subdivision of a cantrev.
13. Tal Ebolyon: actually 'End of the Ridges', *v.* Introduction, p. 20.

who was in your country, and for all I know it was there he found it.' 'Who was that?' 'Llassar Llaes Gyngwyd. He came here with his wife Kymidei Kymeinvoll after their escape from an iron house in Ireland – the house was made white-hot round them but they escaped from it. I am surprised that you know nothing of this.' 'I do know, lord,' said Mallolwch, 'and as much as I know I will tell you. I was hunting in Ireland one day, at the top of a mound which overlooks a lake called the Lake of the Cauldron, and I saw a huge man with yellow-red hair emerging from the lake with the cauldron on his back; he was a great monstrous man with an evil thieving look about him. His wife followed, and if he was huge she was twice as big. They drew near and greeted me, and I asked, "How goes it with you?" "This is how it goes with us, lord," the man said. "In a month and a fortnight this woman will conceive, and the boy that she bears at that time will be a fully-armed warrior." I took them with me and maintained them, and they stayed with me for a year. For that first year I kept them willingly, but thereafter they became a burden to me. By the end of the fourth month of the second year they had caused themselves to be hated and detested throughout the land; they committed outrages, and harassed and importuned gentlemen and ladies. My subjects gathered round to ask that I part with these people, and bade me choose between my realm and the strangers; I referred the matter to the council of the country to see what should be done, for the strangers would not go of their own will, and because of their fighting ability there was no need for them to go against their will.

'In these difficult circumstances it was decided to make a chamber entirely of iron;[14] when this was ready all the smiths of Ireland were summoned to bring their hammers and tongs, and charcoal was piled up to the top of

14. A similar iron house appears in two Irish tales: 'The Intoxication of the Ulstermen' and 'The Destruction of Dind Rig'.

the chamber. Inside the man and his wife and their children were served with great quantities of food and drink until it was clear that they were all drunk, whereupon those outside began to fire the charcoal round the chamber and work the bellows round the house. There was one man to each bellows, and these men blew until the house was white-hot round its occupants. The strangers inside held a council in the middle of the chamber; they waited until the wall was white-hot, and then the man, by reason of his great strength, was able to rush it and break it down with his shoulder, so that he and his wife alone escaped. After that I suppose the couple came over to you, lord.' 'Indeed he did come here,' said Brân, 'and he gave the cauldron to me.' 'How did you receive them, lord?' 'I quartered them in every part of the realm, and they are numerous and prosper everywhere; wherever they are they fortify the place with the best men and arms anyone has seen.'

That night they continued to talk and sing and carouse as long as they liked, and when they saw that it was better to sleep than to continue sitting up they went to bed. Thus they spent an enjoyable feast, and when it ended Mallolwch and Branwen set out; thirteen ships left Aber Menei and sailed for Ireland, where they were greeted with great rejoicing. No gentleman or lady of Ireland who came to visit Branwen left without being given a brooch or ring or treasured royal jewel, and it was a marvellous sight to watch these being carried off: little wonder, then, that Branwen acquired a great reputation in the course of the year, or that she flourished in honour and with many friends. Meanwhile it happened that she became pregnant, and when the proper time came she gave birth to a son; they named him Gwern [15] son of Mallolwch and sent him to be fostered in the best place for men in Ireland.

15. Gwern: alder.

At the end of the second year, however, people began to grumble about the insult that Mallolwch had sustained in Wales, about the disgrace he had suffered due to the maimed horses. His foster-brothers and closest friends taunted him and made no effort to conceal their feelings; ultimately there was such an uproar in the land that there was no peace for him until he avenged the outrage. This is the revenge they took: Branwen was driven from her husband's chamber and made to cook for the court, and the butcher came every day, after he had finished cutting up the meat, to box her ear, and that was her punishment.[16] 'Now, lord,' said the Irish, 'forbid all ships and coracles from going to Wales, and impound those boats which arrive from Wales, so that news of Branwen might not spread,' and that was done.

Not less than three years passed thus, during which time Branwen reared a starling on the edge of her kneading trough. She taught it words and told it what sort of man her brother was, and then she brought a letter telling of the punishment and disgrace she was suffering; she fastened this to the base of the starling's wing and sent the bird to Wales. When it arrived at this island it found Brân at an assembly of his at Caer Seint yn Arvon;[17] it alighted on his shoulder and ruffled its wing until the letter was noticed and they perceived that the bird had been reared in a house. The letter was taken and looked at, and when it was read Brân was saddened to hear of Branwen's disgrace, and immediately he began to muster the island. He had the full complement of one hundred and fifty-four districts assemble, and he himself complained of the punishment his sister was being made to undergo. They held a council and decided to set out for Ireland, leaving seven men behind as leaders, with

16. In 'Triad 52', Mallolwch himself strikes Branwen just once.
17. Caer Seint yn Arvon = Caernarvon. The Roman Segontium.

Caradawg [18] son of Brân as chief, and seven horsemen as
well. These last were left in Edeirnyawn, for which reason
the town is called Seith Marchawg.[19] The seven leaders
were Caradawg son of Brân, Heveydd the Tall, Unig
Strong Shoulder, Iddig son of Anarawd Curly Hair, Ffodor
son of Ervyll, Wlch Bone Lip and Llassar son of Llassar
Llaes Gyngwyd, and the Chieftain of Dyved (who was a
young lad) with them.[20] These seven stayed behind as
stewards in charge of the island, and Caradawg son of
Brân was their chief steward.

Brân and the host we spoke of set sail for Ireland, and
since the sea was not deep he waded through. At that
time there were only two rivers, Lli and Archan, but
thereafter the sea widened and overflowed the kingdoms.
Brân took all the string musicians on his back and made
for Ireland.

One day Mallolwch's swineherds were by the sea, watching over their pigs, and the sight they saw caused them to
run to their king. 'Greetings, lord,' they said. 'God be good
to you,' said Mallolwch. 'What news have you?' 'Lord,
we have wondrous news: we have seen a forest upon the
sea where we never before saw so much as one tree.' 'A
strange thing that. Did you see anything else?' 'Lord, we
did. We saw a huge mountain close to the forest, and it
was moving. There was a high ridge on the mountain
and a lake on each side of the ridge and the forest and
the mountain and everything were all moving.' 'Well,'
said Mallolwch, 'no one here would know anything of
that, except possibly Branwen – go ask her.' The messengers went to Branwen and said, 'Lady, what do you make
of this?' 'Though I am no lady, I know what it is: the
men of the Island of the Mighty have heard of my dis-

18. Caradawg = Caratācus.

19. Seith Marchawg: seven horsemen.

20. In 'Pwyll' the Chieftain of Dyved is Pryderi's foster-father; in
'Branwen' he is a lad and Pryderi is a man.

grace and are coming.' 'What is the forest that was seen on the sea?' 'The masts and yardarms of the ships.' 'Alas! What is the mountain that was seen alongside the ships?' 'That was my brother Brân wading to shore – there was no ship into which he could fit.' 'What was the high ridge and the lake on either side of the ridge?' 'He was looking at this island, for he is angry. The two lakes on either side of the ridge are his two eyes on either side of his nose.'

This caused the fighting men of Ireland and the coastal areas to assemble hastily and hold a council. 'Lord,' said his men, 'you have no choice but to retreat across the Liffey (a river in Ireland)[21] and put the river between you and Brân and then destroy the bridge; there are loadstones at the bottom of the river, so that no ship or other vessel can cross it.' The Irish retreated across the river and destroyed the bridge, and when Brân and his ships reached land and crossed to the river bank his men said to him, 'Lord, you know the property of this river: no one can cross it, nor is there any bridge. What do you propose for a bridge?' 'Simply this,' said Brân, 'let him who is a chief be a bridge.' (This is the first time these words were spoken, and the proverb is still current.) Brân then lay down across the river and hurdles were placed upon him, and so the host crossed over on top of him.

As soon as he rose, there were Mallolwch's messengers approaching, greeting him and saluting him as Mallolwch's kinsman and assuring him that through their king's good will nothing but good would befall him. 'Mallolwch is giving the kingship to your nephew Gwern, the son of your sister, and will invest him in your presence to

21. Liffey: in the text, Llinon, which must represent either the Liffey or the Shannon. As the Liffey flows into the Irish Sea, it is not a suitable line of defence; moreover Llinon might be an approximation of Irish Sinann (Shannon). On the other hand, the placing of hurdles upon Brân clearly refers to Baile Átha Clíath (Dublin in Irish): 'Town of the Hurdle Ford'.

make up for the wrong and the injury done to Branwen. So either here or in the Island of the Mighty, whichever you wish, make some provision for Mallolwch.' 'Well, if I cannot obtain the kingship for myself,' said Brân, 'perhaps I will call a council to discuss your offer. You shall have no answer from me until you bring a different proposal.' 'We will bring you the best answer we can get, if you will wait for it.' 'I will wait, as long as you return quickly,' answered Brân. The messengers returned to Mallolwch and said, 'Lord, prepare a better answer for Brân, for he would have none of the one we took him.' 'What is your advice, men?' 'Lord, there is only one choice. Brân has never fitted inside a house. Build one in his honour so that it will contain the men of the Island of the Mighty in one half and your men in the other; then place the kingship at his disposal and become his men. The honour of having a house into which he can fit – for he has never yet had one – will induce him to make peace with you.' The messengers took that proposal to Brân; he held a council, with the result that he accepted. This was due to the pleading of Branwen, who feared that otherwise the land would be laid waste.

The peace was made and the house was built large and sturdy. But the Irish set a trap: they fixed a peg on every one of the hundred pillars in the house, and hung a leather bag on each peg and put an armed man in every bag. When Evnissyen entered the house ahead of the men of the Island of the Mighty he examined it with a ferocious, merciless stare, and he noticed the leather bags along the posts. 'What is in this bag?' he asked an Irishman, and the man answered, 'Flour, friend,' whereupon Evnissyen fumbled with the bag until he found the warrior's head, and then he squeezed it until he perceived his fingers sinking through the bone and into the brain. He moved on and put his hand on another bag and asked, 'What is in here?' and the Irishman answered, 'Flour.' Evnissyen played the same trick on every warrior until of the two hundred men there was only one left alive. When he came to the last bag he asked, 'What is this?' and the Irishman answered, 'Flour, friend.' Evnissyen fumbled about until he found the head, and as he had squeezed the others so he squeezed this one, and he perceived that it wore armour. He did not leave the man until he had killed him, and then he sang this englyn: [22]

> There is in these bags a kind of flour:
> Champions, fighters, attackers in battle,
> Warriors ready for the foe.

Then the hosts entered the house: the men of Ireland went into one half and the men of the Island of the Mighty into the other. As soon as they had sat down they made peace, and the boy was invested with the kingship. When the peace had been concluded Brân called the boy over to him; from Brân Gwern went to Manawydan, and everyone who saw the boy loved him. Nissyen son of Eurosswydd called the boy to come from Manawydan to him, and Gwern went willingly. At that Evnissyen said, 'Why does my nephew, the son of my sister, not come to me?' 'Let him go, gladly,' said Brân, and Gwern went gladly. 'By my confession to God,' thought Evnissyen, 'this outrage I am about to commit is one the household would never expect.' He rose and took Gwern by the feet, and at once, before a man in the house could lay a hand on him, he thrust the boy headfirst into the flames. When Branwen saw her son burning in the fire, she made as if to leap after him from where she was sitting between her two brothers, but Brân seized her with one hand and his shield with the other. Everyone in the house sprang up, and there arose the greatest commotion ever caused by a host in one house as everyone reached for his arms. This was when Pierced

22. englyn: a kind of verse. For possible puns, v. BuL, p. 35, BDL, pp. 70–71, PKM, pp. 203–4.

Thighs[23] said, 'Dogs of Gwern, beware of Pierced Thighs!'
As each man went after his weapons Brân protected Branwen between his shield and his shoulder.

The Irish, however, began to kindle a fire under the cauldron of rebirth; corpses were thrown in until it was full, and next morning the warriors sprang forth as fierce as ever, except that they could not speak. When Evnissyen saw these corpses and no room anywhere in the cauldron for the men of the Island of the Mighty, he thought, 'Alas, God, wretched am I who brought this about on the men of the Island of the Mighty, and shame on me if I do not seek to deliver them.' He crept in among the Irish dead, and two bare-bottomed Irishmen found him and threw him in with the rest; Evnissyen stretched out inside the cauldron until he broke it into four pieces, and then his heart broke also. Consequently such victory as there was went to the men of the Island of the Mighty, though there was no victory save for the escape of seven men, and at that Brân had been wounded in the foot with a poisoned spear. The seven who escaped were Pryderi,[24] Manawydan, Glinyeu son of Taran, Talyessin, Ynawg, Gruddyeu son of Muryel and Heilyn son of Gwynn the Old.

Brân commanded them to cut off his head. 'Take my head,' he said, 'and carry it to the White Hill[25] in London, and bury it there with the face turned towards France. You will be a long time on the road; you will spend seven years feasting at Harddlech, with the Birds of Rhiannon singing to you, and the head will be as good

23. Pierced Thighs: possibly a reference to Brân, anticipating his wound (v. Introduction, pp. 17-18); or perhaps Mighty Thigh, or even, as a personal name, Morddwyd Tyllyon. v. *BDL*, pp. 162-5.

24. Pryderi's only appearance in 'Branwen'. Did he play a more important part in an earlier version, or is this reference an afterthought?

25. White Hill: Tower Hill, or perhaps where St Paul's now stands.

a companion as it ever was. After that you will spend eighty years at Gwales in Penvro,[26] and as long as you do not open the door to the Bristol Channel on the side facing Cornwall you may stay there and the head will not decay. Once you have opened that door, however, you must not delay, but set out at once to bury the head in London. Now, however, you must cross the sea.' So they cut off the head and made to cross the sea with it, the seven of them and Branwen. They landed at Aber Alaw in Tal Ebolyon and sat down and rested, but Branwen looked at Ireland and the Island of the Mighty, at what she could see of them, and said, 'Alas, son of God, woe that I was ever born, for two good islands have been destroyed on my account.' And with that her heart broke. They made a four-sided grave and buried her on the bank of the Alaw.

Then the seven took the head and set out for Harddlech, and as they journeyed along a company of men and women approached. 'What news?' asked Manawydan. 'None,' they answered, 'except that Casswallawn son of Beli has conquered the Island of the Mighty and is a crowned king in London.' 'What has happened to Caradawg son of Brân and the men who were left with him?' 'Casswallawn fell upon them and killed six, and Caradawg's heart broke with despair at seeing the sword killing the men and not knowing who was doing it. Casswallawn had clothed himself in a magic cloak so that no one could see him killing the men, only the sword; however he did not want to kill Caradawg, who was his nephew, his sister's son. (Caradawg was thus one of the Three who Broke their Hearts with Grief.) The Chieftain of Dyved, who was a youth with the seven men, escaped into the forest.'

The seven then continued on to Harddlech, where they sat down and began to enjoy food and drink; as they did so three birds appeared and began to sing, and all the

26. Gwales=Grassholm? Penvro=Pembroke.

singing they had ever heard was nothing compared to this. They looked far out over the ocean to see the birds, yet they saw as clearly as if the creatures were close at hand. Seven years passed thus, and at the end of that time they set out for Gwales in Penvro, where they found a great handsome royal hall overlooking the sea; they entered and found two doors open and the third closed, the one on the Cornwall side. 'There is the door we must not open,' said Manawydan. They spent that night in joyous feasting, and remembered nothing of all the grief they had seen and suffered, and nothing of any other sorrow in the world. Eighty years they spent at Gwales and they could not remember having spent a happier or more joyful time; never was it more tedious than when they first arrived, nor could any tell by looking at his companions that it had been so long, nor was having the head there more disagreeable than when Brân had been alive and with them. By reason of the eighty years this was called the Assembly of the Wondrous Head, while the one which went to Ireland was called the Assembly of Branwen and Mallolwch.

One day Heilyn son of Gwynn said, 'Shame on my beard if I do not open this door to see if what is said about it is true.' He opened the door and looked out at the Bristol Channel and Cornwall, and as he did so they all became as conscious of every loss they had suffered, of every friend and relative they had lost, of every ill that had befallen them, as if it had all just happened; above all they felt for their lord. From that moment they could not rest; they took the head and set out at once for London. However long they were on the road they came at last to London and buried the head in the White Hill, and that burial was one of the Three Happy Concealments, and one of the Three Unhappy Disclosures when it was disclosed. For while the head was concealed no plague came across the sea to this island.

According to the story this is the tale of 'The men who

went to Ireland'. In Ireland, meanwhile, there was not a man left alive, only five pregnant women in a cave in the wilderness, and these women all bore sons at the same moment. The boys were reared until they grew into big lads; their thoughts turned to women and they desired to take wives, so each one in turn slept with his companions' mothers. They lived in the land and ruled it and divided it among the five of them, and because of that division the five parts of Ireland are still called fifths. They scoured the land wherever there had been battles; they found gold and silver and became wealthy.

So ends this Branch of the Mabinogi, about the blow struck at Branwen (one of the Three Unhappy Blows of this island), about the Assembly of Brân, wherein the hosts of one hundred and fifty-four districts went to Ireland to avenge that blow, about the seven years' feasting in Harddlech, about the singing of the Birds of Rhiannon and about the Assembly of the Head which lasted eighty years.

MANAWYDAN SON OF LLŶR

ALONE among the tales of *The Mabinogion*, 'Manawydan', with its peculiar opening sentence ('After the seven men we mentioned above ...'), shows an awareness of and a dependence on outside material – in this case the first two Branches. The story is set in the southern Wales of 'Pwyll', but it also incorporates episodes set in England, and in recognizing Casswallawn as ruler of all Britain displays the expanded geographic consciousness of 'Branwen'. Obviously the redactor was familiar with 'Pwyll' and 'Branwen', and one must wonder how much of this tale is old, and how much it owes to traditions later established by the first two Branches.

Although Manawydan himself is the Welsh counterpart of the Irish god Manandán son of Lir (whether one name derived from the other is not certain), no Irish adventures parallel those of the Third Branch. The sources include motifs similar to those found in 'Branwen': two attempts upon the otherworld (the occupation of Gorsedd Arberth and the removal of the golden bowl in Llwyd's fortress) and two consequent disasters (the disappearance of the court at Arberth and the disappearance of Llwyd's fortress). In 'Manawydan', however, these are more thoroughly rationalized, being subsumed into a form of the folktale (the Eustace legend) in which the hero patiently endures every sort of misfortune. Even more than in 'Pwyll', the storytellers stress the importance of gentle and gracious behaviour:

Pryderi's kindness and generosity towards Manawydan, Manawydan's chivalrous behaviour towards Kigva, the happiness of the two couples during their circuit of Dyved, and the good faith which Manawydan and Llwyd show in their bargaining.

The second title mentioned at the end remains a mystery. Is it an irrelevant afterthought, or does it point to material buried hopelessly below the surface of the present narrative?

Manawydan Son of Llŷr

After the seven men we mentioned above had buried Brân's head in the White Hill in London, with the face towards France, Manawydan looked at the town and at his friends, gave a great sigh and felt an immense sadness and longing. 'Alas, almighty God, woe is me!' he said. 'Among all those here I alone have no place for the night.' 'Lord, be not so heavy-hearted,' said Pryderi. 'Your cousin[1] is king over the Island of the Mighty, and if he has wronged you,[2] still, you have never claimed land or property – you are one of the Three Ungrasping Chieftains.' 'Even though the king is my cousin,' answered Manawydan, 'it saddens me to see anyone in my brother Brân's place, and I could not be happy in the same house as Casswallawn.' 'Then will you listen to some more advice?' 'I need advice. What is yours?' 'The seven cantrevs of Dyved were left to me,' said Pryderi, 'and my mother Rhiannon is there. I will give her to you, along with authority over the seven cantrevs, and if you have no ter-

1. According to 'Branwen', Casswallawn is Manawydan's uncle, not his cousin. Perhaps Beli and Penarddun should be brother and sister rather than father and daughter.
2. As Brân's brother, Manawydan is the rightful heir.

ritory but these cantrevs, there are nonetheless no seven better than they. Kigva daughter of Gwynn the Splendid is my wife.[3] Though the title to the land is mine, let it be you and Rhiannon who enjoy it, and should you ever desire territory perhaps you will have that too.' 'I do not desire that, chieftain,' said Manawydan, 'but God reward your friendship.' 'The truest friendship in my power shall be yours, if you want it.' 'I do want it, friend, and God reward you. I will go with you now to see Rhiannon and the territory.' 'That is the right thing to do,' said Pryderi. 'I do not imagine you have ever heard a lady talk better than she does; moreover when she was in her prime there was no lovelier woman, and even now her appearance will not disappoint you.'

They set out, and though their journey was long they finally reached Dyved, where Rhiannon and Kigva had prepared and set out a feast for them. Manawydan and Rhiannon sat together and began to talk; gradually his thoughts and desires grew tender towards her, and it pleased him that he had never seen a lovelier or more beautiful woman. 'Pryderi, I will accept your offer,' he said, whereupon Rhiannon asked, 'What offer was that?' Pryderi answered. 'Lady, I have given you as wife to Manawydan son of Llŷr.' 'I accept that gladly,' she said. 'So do I,' said Manawydan, 'and God reward the man who gives me such true friendship.' Before the feast ended, then, the couple slept together.

'Continue with what remains of the feast,' said Pryderi, 'while I go to England to offer my submission to Casswallawn son of Beli.' 'Lord, Casswallawn is now in Kent,' said Rhiannon. 'You can continue with the feast and wait until he is nearer.' 'Then we will wait,' said Pryderi. They continued the feast, and then they began a circuit of Dyved; they hunted and enjoyed themselves, and for

3. This sentence interrupts the train of thought and seems misplaced.

roaming the countryside they had never seen a more
delightful land, nor a better hunting-ground nor one better stocked with honey and fish. Such friendship arose
among the four that none of them wished to be without
the others day or night. It was during this time that
Pryderi went to see Casswallawn at Oxford, where he was
received joyfully and thanked for offering his submission.

When Pryderi returned he and Manawydan feasted and
took their ease. They began the feast at Arberth, since
that was the chief court where every celebration began,
and after the evening's first sitting, while the servants were
eating, the four companions rose and went out to Gorsedd
Arberth, taking a company with them. As they were sitting on the mound they heard thunder, and with the loud-
ness of the thunder a mist fell, so that no one could see
his companions. When the mist lifted it was bright everywhere, and when they looked out at where they had once
seen their flocks and herds and dwellings they now saw
nothing, no animal, no smoke, no fire, no man, no
dwelling – only the houses of the court empty, deserted,
uninhabited, without man or beast in them; their own
company was lost too, and they understood only that the
four of them alone remained.

'Alas, lord God,' said Manawydan, 'what has happened
to our company and the rest of our people? Let us go
and look.' They returned to the hall, but no one was
there; they searched the chambers and the sleeping quarters but found nothing, while the kitchen and the mead-
cellar were equally desolate. The four began another feast;
they hunted and enjoyed themselves, and they all roamed
the land trying to spot a house or dwelling, but only wild
beasts did they see. When they had finished with their
feasting and their food they began to live off the animals
they hunted, and off fish and wild honey; they passed one
happy year thus, and then a second. At length they grew
weary. 'God knows, we cannot go on like this,' said

Manawydan. 'Let us go to England and there seek a trade by which we can support ourselves.'

So they set out for England, and when they had settled in Hereford they took up saddlemaking. Manawydan shaped and coloured the pommels as he had seen Llassar Llaes Gyngwyd do with blue enamel; he made this enamel exactly as Llassar had done, and for this reason it is still called *calch llassar* [4] – because Llassar Llaes Gyngwyd made it. As for the work, so long as a saddle or pommel could be got from Manawydan it would not be bought from any other saddler in Hereford. When these other saddlers realized that they were selling only what Mana-wydan could not supply they formed a conspiracy and decided to kill their rival and his companion; the strangers received a warning, however, and they in turn held a council to decide whether they should leave town. 'Be-tween me and God, I do not think we ought to leave – better to kill these churls,' said Pryderi, but Manawydan answered, 'No, for if we fought with them we should earn a bad reputation, and be thrown into prison. Better for us to seek another town and earn our living there.'

The four made for another city. 'What trade shall we take up here?' asked Pryderi. 'We will make shields,' said Manawydan. 'Do we know anything about shieldmaking?' 'We will try it,' Manawydan answered. They began to make shields, shaping them to resemble the good ones they had seen and colouring them as they had coloured the saddles. Their work prospered so that no shield was bought elsewhere in the town unless it could not be had from them. They worked swiftly and made countless shields, and this went on until their competitors became angry and conspired to kill them; however, they were told of these plans. 'Pryderi, these men want to kill us,' said Manawydan. 'We ought not to take that from the rascals. Let us go and kill them,' said Pryderi, but Manawydan

4. calch llassar: azure chalk or enamel.

answered, 'No, for Casswallawn and his men would hear of it, and then we should come to grief. Let us go to another town.'

They did that, and Manawydan said, 'What craft shall we take up here?' 'Whichever one you prefer of the two we know,' said Pryderi, but Manawydan answered, 'No, we should take to shoemaking, for shoemakers are not bold enough to kill us or forbid our working.' 'I know nothing of that trade,' said Pryderi. 'Well, I do,' said Manawydan, 'and I will show you how to stitch. We will not bother to tan the leather; instead we will buy it already dressed and work from that.' They bought the best cordovan that was to be had in the town, for everything except the soles. Manawydan visited the best goldsmith in town; he had the latter make gilded buckles for the shoes, and moreover he watched until he knew how to do the gilding himself – for that reason he was called one of the Three Golden Shoemakers. So long as a shoe or boot could be had from him it would not be bought from any other shoemaker in town, and his competitors perceived that they were losing business, for Pryderi stitched the shoes as expertly as Manawydan cut them out. These shoemakers held a council in which they decided to do away with their competitors. 'Pryderi, the shoemakers are planning to kill us,' said Manawydan. 'Why should we take that from the thieving churls and not kill them?' asked Pryderi, but Manawydan answered, 'No, we will not fight them, nor will we remain here. Let us return to Dyved.'

Though their journey was long they came at last to Dyved and made for Arberth, where they kindled a fire and began to support themselves by hunting; they spent a month thus, assembling their dogs and going to hunt, and so a year passed. One morning Pryderi and Manawydan rose to hunt. They made their dogs ready and set out from the court; some of the dogs ran ahead towards a small copse which was near by, but having entered it they re-

treated at once, trembling violently with fear, and returned to the men. 'Let us ride over to that copse and see
what is inside,' said Pryderi. As he and Manawydan
approached the copse, a shining white boar burst forth
and the dogs, at the men's urging, raced after it. The
boar left the copse and retreated a little way from the men,
and until they drew near it would stand at bay against
the dogs; whenever the men closed in, though, it would
retreat and break away. They pursued the boar until they
saw a great tall fortress, a new building where they had
never before seen any kind of stone or work, and when the
boar and the dogs had gone inside they marvelled to see
this fortress where they had never seen any before. From
the top of the mound they listened for the dogs' barking,
but as long as they stayed they heard not a sound from
any of the dogs.

'Lord,' said Pryderi, 'I will enter the fortress and seek
news of the dogs.' 'God knows, that is not a good idea,'
said Manawydan. 'I have never seen this fortress before,
and if you take my advice you will not enter it, for whoever placed the enchantment on the land must have caused
this building to appear.' 'God knows, I will not give up
my dogs,' said Pryderi. Manawydan's advice notwith-
standing he entered the fortress but once inside he could
see neither man nor beast nor boar nor dogs nor house nor
dwelling; what he did see, as if in the middle of the fortress, was a fountain with marble stone round it, and a
golden bowl fastened to four chains, the bowl set over a
marble slab and the chains extending upwards so that he
could see no end to them. Ecstatic over the beauty of the
gold and the fine craftsmanship of the bowl he walked over
to the vessel and grasped it, but as soon as he did so his
hands stuck to the bowl and his feet to the slab he was
standing on, and his speech was taken so that he could not
say a single word. There he stood.

Manawydan waited until evening, and late in the after-

noon, being certain he would get news neither of Pryderi
nor of the dogs, he made for the court. As he entered
Rhiannon looked at him and asked, 'Where is your companion, and where are the dogs?' 'This is the story,' he
said, and he told her everything. 'God knows,' she said,
'you have been a bad companion and lost a good one,' and
with those words she left, making for where he had told
her the man and the fortress would be. She found the gate
open and nothing concealed, and when she entered she
discovered Pryderi holding the bowl and walked over to
him. 'Alas, my lord, what are you doing here?' Then she
too grasped the bowl, and at once her hands stuck to it
and her feet to the slab, nor could she utter a word. When
night came thunder rolled and a mist fell; the fortress
vanished, and they with it.

When Kigva, Pryderi's wife and the daughter of Gwynn
the Splendid, saw that she and Manawydan were alone in
the court, she lamented that being alive was no better
than being dead. Noticing this, Manawydan said, 'God
knows, you are mistaken if you weep for fear of me. I give
you God as surety that you have not seen a truer friend
than you will find me, so long as God will have it so.
Between me and God, were I in the prime of youth I
would still be loyal to Pryderi, and for your sake too I
would be true, so do not be afraid. Between me and God,
you shall have such friendship from me as you would wish,
while it is in my power, however long God wills this misery
and distress upon us.' 'God reward you – that is what I
expected,' said Kigva, and she cheered up and took courage. 'Well, friend,' said Manawydan, 'this is no place for
us to stay, for we have lost our dogs and cannot support
ourselves. Let us make for England – it will be easier
there.' 'Gladly,' she answered.

They returned to England, and Kigva said, 'Lord, what
craft will you take up? Choose a clean one.' 'I will choose
nothing but shoemaking, as I did before.' 'Lord, its clean-

liness scarcely suits a man of your rank and talents.'
'Well, that is what I will take up.' Manawydan began to
practise his trade, fashioning the shoes from the best cordovan there was to be had in the town. As in the other
city he fastened the shoes with gold buckles, so that the
work of all the other shoemakers in the town seemed a
paltry wasted effort beside his own, and so long as a shoe
or boot could be had from him it would not be bought
from anyone else. A year passed thus, until the other shoemakers grew jealous and envious, and soon Manawydan
was warned that they were planning to kill him. 'Lord,
why do we tolerate this from these churls?' Kigva asked,
but Manawydan answered, 'We do not. We will return to
Dyved.'

They did that, and when they set out Manawydan took
a load of wheat with him, and when they reached Arberth
they settled there. Nothing was pleasanter to Manawydan
than seeing Arberth and the land he had once hunted, he
and Pryderi, and Rhiannon with them. He began to catch
fish, and wild animals in their lairs, and he began to till
the soil: he sowed one croft, then a second and a third.
The wheat that grew was the best in the world; moreover
all three crofts flourished alike, so that no man had seen
better wheat. Manawydan waited out the seasons of the
year until harvest time, when he went to look at one of
his crofts and saw that it was ripe, and he said to himself,
'I will reap this tomorrow.'

That night he returned to Arberth, and the following
morning, when he came in the grey dawn intending to
reap the croft, he found only the naked stalks; each one
had been broken off where the ear grows out of the
stalk, and the ears had all been carried away and the stalks
left bare. He marvelled greatly at that, and then went to
another croft and saw that it was now ripe. 'God knows,
I mean to reap that one tomorrow,' he said to himself, but
when he came the next day he found nothing but bare

stalks. 'Alas, lord God, who is completing my downfall? This I know: the one who started it is now finishing it, and he has ruined the country along with me.' He went to look at the third croft and saw that it was ripe, and thought, 'Shame on me if I do not guard this tonight. Whoever carried off the other wheat will come after this croft, and then I will find out who it is.' He took up his weapons and began to watch over the croft, and he told Kigva what had happened. 'Well, what are you planning?' she asked. 'To watch the croft all night.'

Manawydan watched. Towards midnight he heard the greatest uproar in the world, and when he looked there was the largest host of mice ever – neither number nor measure could be set upon it. Before he could move the mice had fallen upon the croft: each creature climbed up a stalk and, pulling it down, broke off the ear and carried it away, leaving the stalk behind, and as far as he could tell there was not a single stalk without a mouse to it. They were all running off, carrying the ears with them, and with the anger and dismay he felt Manawydan rushed in among the mice, but he could no more focus on one than if they had been gnats or birds. One mouse, however, was very heavy, and observing that it could not move quickly he chased and caught it; he put it in his glove and tied the opening shut with string, and took the glove with him when he returned to the court.

When he reached the chamber where Kigva was he put more wood on the fire and hung the glove by its string on a peg. 'What is that, lord?' asked Kigva. 'A thief that I caught stealing from me.' 'What sort of thief could fit inside your glove?' 'This is what happened,' and Manawydan told her how his crofts had been ruined and destroyed, and how the mice had come to the last croft before his very eyes. 'One of them was very heavy and I caught it; it is now inside my glove, and I will hang it tomorrow. By my confession to God, had I caught them all

I would hang them.' 'Lord, that would not be strange,' said Kigva. 'But it is hardly proper for a man of your rank and dignity to hang that sort of creature. If you would do what is right, do not bother with it, rather let it go.' 'Shame on me if I did not hang every one I caught – but I will hang the one I did catch.' 'Well, lord, there is no reason for me to plead for this creature except to prevent your being dishonoured; therefore do as you will.' 'Lady, if I knew of any reason in the world why you should plead for this creature I would take your advice, but as I know of none I intend to destroy it.' 'Then do as you wish,' said Kigva.

Manawydan set out for Gorsedd Arberth, taking the mouse with him, and once there he placed two forks on the highest point of the mound. As he did so he could see a scholar coming towards him, dressed in poor, old, worn clothes. It was seven years since Manawydan had seen man or beast, save for the four who were together until two of them vanished. 'Lord, good day to you,' said the scholar. 'God be good to you, and welcome. Where are you going, scholar?' asked Manawydan. 'Lord, I come from singing in England – why do you ask?' 'These past seven years I have not seen one man here, save for four of us who were set apart, until you yourself this minute.' 'Well, lord, I am just passing through on my way to my own country. But what sort of work are you about?' 'Hanging a thief I caught stealing from me,' Manawydan answered. 'Lord, what sort of thief? The creature I see in your hand is like a mouse, and it is scarcely fitting for a man of your rank to handle an animal such as that. Let it go.' 'Between me and God, I will not,' said Manawydan. 'I caught it stealing, and I will execute upon it the punishment for stealing, which is hanging.' 'Lord, I will give you a pound I received as alms to let the creature go.' 'Between me and God, I will not let it go, nor will I sell it.' 'Do as you like lord – if it did not seem to me degrading for a man of your rank to handle such a creature I would not trouble myself.' With that the scholar went on.

As Manawydan was fixing the crossbeam upon the forks he saw a priest coming towards him on a richly equipped horse. 'Lord, good day to you,' said the priest. 'God be good to you,' said Manawydan, 'and I ask your blessing.' 'The blessing of God be upon you. What sort of work are you about?' 'Hanging a thief I caught stealing from me.' 'What sort of thief, lord?' 'A creature in the form of a mouse,' said Manawydan; 'it has stolen from me, and so I intend to punish it as a thief.' 'Lord, rather than see you handle that creature I will buy it from you. Let it go.' 'By my confession to God, I will not sell it and I will not let it go.' 'True, lord, for no price has been set. Rather than see you defile yourself with that animal I will give you three pounds to let it go.' 'Between me and God,' said Manawydan, 'I will not take any price in lieu of what it deserves, which is to be hanged.' 'Very well, lord, do as you wish.'

The priest rode off and Manawydan drew the string round the mouse's neck, and as he drew the creature up there appeared a bishop's retinue; Manawydan could see the baggage and the company and the bishop himself coming forward, so he halted his work. 'Lord bishop, I ask your blessing.' 'God bless you,' said the bishop. 'What sort of work are you about?' 'Hanging a thief I caught stealing from me.' 'Isn't that a mouse I see in your hand?' asked the bishop. 'Yes, that is the thief.' 'Well, since I have come upon the destruction of the creature, I will buy it from you. Lest such a noble man be seen destroying such a worthless animal I will give you seven pounds for it; let it go, and you shall have the money.' 'Between me and God, I will not let it go.' 'If you will not let it go for that I will give you twenty-four pounds in ready money, only let it go.' 'By my confession to God, I would not let it go for twice as much money.' 'If you will not let it go for

that, I will give you all the horses you see on this plain,
and the seven loads of baggage you see on these seven
horses.' 'Between me and God, I will not accept that.'

'As you will not take that,' said the bishop, 'I ask you to
name your price.' Manawydan answered, 'I want the release of Pryderi and Rhiannon.' 'You shall have that.'
'Between me and God, that is not all.' 'What else?' 'The
removal of the spell and enchantment from the seven
cantrevs of Dyved.' 'You shall have that too, only free
the mouse.' 'Between me and God, I will not. I wish to
know who the mouse is.' 'She is my wife – otherwise I
would not ransom her.' 'How did she come to me?'
'Plundering. I am Llywd son of Kil Coed,[5] and it was I who
enchanted the seven cantrevs of Dyved. I did this for revenge, out of friendship for Gwawl son of Clud; Pwyll
Head of Annwvyn ill-advisedly played Badger in the Bag
with Gwawl at the court of Heveydd the Old, and therefore I took revenge on Pryderi. After hearing that you were
dwelling in the land my company came to me and asked
to be turned into mice, in order that they might destroy
your corn: they went the first night, and the second as
well, and they destroyed the first two crofts. The third
night the ladies of the court came and asked to be trans-
formed, and I did that. My wife was pregnant; had she not
been you would not have caught her, but since she was,
and you did, I will give you Pryderi and Rhiannon, and
lift the spell and enchantment from Dyved. I have told
you who the mouse is – now release her.'

'Between me and God, I will not,' said Manawydan.
'What else do you wish?' 'Your promise that there will
never be any spell on the seven cantrevs of Dyved, and
that none ever be cast.' 'You shall have that, only release
my wife.' 'Between me and God, I will not.' 'What else

5. Llwyd son of Kil Coed: perhaps related to the Irish name Líath
son of Celtchar; both Llwyd and Líath mean grey. Kil Coed is in the
parish of Eglwys Lwyd (Ludchurch) in Pembroke. Coed: wood.

do you wish?' 'Your promise that no revenge ever be taken
on Pryderi or Rhiannon, or on me, because of this.' 'You
shall have all that. God knows, that was a good thought.
Had you not struck on that all the harm would have
landed on your own head.' 'Yes,' replied Manawydan,
'that is why I protected myself.' 'Now release my wife,'
said Llwyd. 'Between me and God, I will not do so until
I see Pryderi and Rhiannon coming towards me.' 'They
are coming now.'

Pryderi and Rhiannon appeared; Manawydan rose to
meet them and greeted them and they all sat down. Llwyd
said, 'Now, sir, free my wife, for you have everything you
asked for.' 'Gladly,' said Manawydan; he released the
mouse, and Llwyd struck it with a magic wand and turned
it back into the loveliest young woman anyone had seen.
Then Llwyd said, 'Look round at the land and you will
see every house and dwelling as it was at its best.' Manawydan rose and looked, and he saw all the land inhabited
and complete with its herds and dwellings.

'What sort of servitude have Pryderi and Rhiannon
performed?' asked Manawydan then, and Llwyd answered,
'Round his neck Pryderi would wear the gate-hammers
of the court; round hers Rhiannon would wear the collars
of the asses after they had been carrying hay – that has
been their imprisonment.' By reason of that imprisonment this story was called the Mabinogi of the Hay-Collars
and the Gate-Hammers.[6] So ends this Branch of the
Mabinogi.

6. The introduction of a punishment for Rhiannon and Pryderi
reflects the storyteller's understanding of the difficult title Mabinogi
Mynweir a Mynordd. Gruffydd proposes that the original title was
'The Mabinogi of Gweir and Modron', and that the original Third
Branch was a Mabon–Modron story, with Gweir (another famous
prisoner from 'Triad 52') mistakenly substituted for Mabon, v. *Rh*,
pp. 96–7. Ellis and Lloyd (vol. I, p. 97) suggest that the present title
reflects the names of two villages: Mynwear (at the end of Milford
Haven) and Manordean (in Cilgerran).

MATH SON OF MATHONWY

LIKE 'Pwyll', 'Math' is geographically restricted (to north Wales), and comprises three distinct parts. The first of these is by far the most complex: themes of the otherworld raid and the wasted, forbidden lover (Amnon and Phaedra, but also Ailill in the Irish 'Wooing of Étaín') are skilfully integrated into a regeneration context (old king, young hero, woman), but one whose outcome is governed by humanistic ideas, so that the nephews' treachery is only partially mitigated by the extent of Gilvaethwy's anguish – rather than sully Étaín's honour Ailill suffers in silence – and so that Math rather than Gwydyon emerges as the hero. The nephews' punishment is as appropriate as it is bizarre.

Part Two opens on a confusing note: although Goewin was raped, it is Aranrhod who bears two apparently fatherless children. Either the two women were originally one – in which case Aranrhod's animosity towards Gwydyon is explained – or else reference to the divine father of Dylan and Lleu has been omitted in the process of euhemerization. The appearance of Dylan here seems to be an unintegrated tradition. Fittingly, Gwydyon, who made a woman out of Goewin, can give Lleu no mortal wife, but only a flower girl.

The Samson and Delilah theme of Part Three is found also in the Irish 'Death of Cú Roí'. The love of Blodeuedd (from *blodeu*, 'flowers') blooms and fades and has not the constancy of mortal feeling; this artificial quality in her character, along with her forced marriage to Lleu (recalling the plight of Rhiannon) and her genuine devotion to Goronwy must be set against the couple's treachery and shabby rationalizing. The tensed, finely balanced result lies in the shadow of the curse which Gwydyon's actions in Part One have placed upon his nephew.

Pryderi's appearance and surprising major role in Part One seem to be an integral part of the narrative; inasmuch as this point suggests that the young Lord of Dyved was well-known in the north, too, it advances the case for his having once been a central figure in Welsh tradition. His actions here are entirely in character with those of 'Manawydan', and with those of his father in the First Branch: both Pwyll and Pryderi are bold and enterprising, but rash to the point of foolishness. In 'Math', Pryderi thoughtlessly and greedily parts with the presents of Arawn, so that his downfall, while pathetic, is not entirely undeserved.

Math Son of Mathonwy

Math son of Mathonwy was Lord of Gwynedd, while Pryderi son of Pwyll was lord of the twenty-one cantrevs of the south – that is, the seven cantrevs of Dyved, the seven of Morgannwg,[1] the four of Keredigyawn, and the three of Ystrad Tywi. At that time Math son of Mathonwy could not live unless his feet were in the folds of a virgin's lap,[2] except when the tumult of war prevented this.

1. Morgannwg = Glamorgan.
2. This odd custom would ensure that the foot-holder remained a virgin – cf. Ysbaddaden (in 'Culhwch'), who also can only live while his daughter remains a virgin.

The virgin who was with him was Goewin daughter of Pebin, from Dôl Bebin[3] in Arvon, for she was the most beautiful girl known in those parts. Math used to rest at Caer Dathal;[4] he could make no circuit of the land, so his nephews Gilvaethwy son of Dôn[5] and Gwydyon son of Dôn – that is, his sister's sons – would go for him, accompanied by his retinue.

Now Goewin was always with Math, and Gilvaethwy son of Dôn set his heart on her and loved her so that he did not know what to do; his colour and looks and shape were all wasting away, and it was not easy to recognize him. One day his brother Gwydyon looked at him closely and said, 'Lad, what is wrong?' 'Why, what is wrong with me?' replied Gilvaethwy. 'I can see that you are losing your looks and your colour – what is the matter?' 'Lord, brother, it is impossible for me to tell anyone what has happened.' 'Why, friend?' asked Gwydyon, and Gilvaethwy answered, 'You know of Math's gift: once the wind has caught a man's softest whisper, he is certain to hear it.' 'Then be silent. I know your mind: you love Goewin.' When Gilvaethwy realized that his brother had read his mind, he gave the heaviest sigh in the world. 'Leave off your sighing, friend – you will not win her that way,' said Gwydyon. 'As there is nothing else to be done, I will see that Gwynedd and Powys and Deheubarth[6] are mustered, so that the girl can be got at. Cheer up, I will arrange it for you.'

They went to see Math son of Mathonwy, and Gwydyon said, 'Lord, I hear there have arrived in the south creatures such as never before came to this island.' 'What are they called?' asked Math. 'Pigs, lord.' 'What kind of animals

3. Dôl Bebin : dale of Pebin.

4. Caer : fortress, stronghold, encampment.

5. Dôn = Dana, an Irish goddess. Túatha Dé Dannan : people of the goddess Dana. Perhaps related to the name Danube.

6. Deheubarth : the southern part of Wales.

are they?' 'Small animals whose flesh is better than that of
oxen,' answered Gwydyon. (But they are small and have
changed their name: now they are called swine.) 'Who
owns them?' Math asked. 'Pryderi son of Pwyll. They were
sent to him by Arawn King of Annwvyn.' (Thus there survive the phrases *hanner hob* and *hanner hwch*.)[7] 'How
will you obtain the swine from Pryderi?' 'I will go as one
of twelve men in the guise of bards, lord, to ask for the
animals.' 'He may refuse your request.' 'My plan is not
bad, lord, nor will I return without the swine.' 'Go, then,
gladly,' said Math.

Gwydyon and Gilvaethwy and ten others rode to
Keredigyawn, to what is now called Rhuddlan Teivi,
where Pryderi was holding court. The twelve men dressed
as bards entered and were welcomed joyfully. Gwydyon
was seated to one side of Pryderi, who said, 'Well, we
would enjoy hearing a story from one of these young
men.' 'Lord,' answered Gwydyon, 'it is our custom that,
on the first night in the house of a great man, it is the
chief bard who begins. I will gladly tell a story.' Gwydyon was the best storyteller ever, and that night he enter-
tained the court with pleasant tales and stories until
everyone there praised him, and Pryderi was happy to
converse with him. At length Gwydyon said, 'Lord, can
anyone word my request to you better than I myself?'
'No,' replied Pryderi, 'for you have a good tongue in your
head.' 'Then here is my errand, lord: to ask you for the
animals that were sent you from Annwvyn.' 'That would
be the easiest thing in the world, except that it was agreed
between me and my people that the swine would remain
here until they had bred twice their number.' 'Lord, I can
free you from those words,' answered Gwydyon. 'Do not
give me the swine tonight, and do not refuse me either —
tomorrow I will show you an exchange for them.'

7. hanner bob, hanner hwch: half a pig. Hob and hwch were
presumably out-of-date words for pig; Gwydyon uses moch.

That night Gwydyon and his companions went to their lodging and held a council. 'Men,' said Gwydyon, 'the swine are not to be had for the asking.' 'Well then, what plan do you have for getting them?' 'I will see that they are got,' and Gwydyon drew upon his arts and began to display his magic: he conjured up twelve stallions, and twelve greyhounds, all black with white breasts, and twelve collars and leashes. Anyone who looked at the collars and leashes would think they were gold; moreover there was a saddle for each horse, and all the places that ought to have been iron were solid gold, and the bridles were of the same workmanship. Gwydyon brought the horses and the dogs to Pryderi, saying, 'Good day to you, lord.' 'God be good to you, and welcome.' 'Lord,' continued Gwydyon, 'here is the way out of what you said last night about the swine, that you could neither sell them nor give them away: you may exchange them for something better. I will give you these twelve horses, equipped as they are with saddles and bridles, and the twelve greyhounds that you see, with their collars and leashes, and the twelve shields that are here.' (These last he had conjured up out of toadstools.) 'Well, we will hold a council,' said Pryderi, and in the council they decided to give the swine to Gwydyon and to take his horses and greyhounds and shields.

Gwydyon and his men said farewell and set out with the swine. 'Lads, we will have to hurry,' said Gwydyon, 'the magic will not last more than a single day.' They reached the hills of Keredigyawn, and the place where they halted is still called Mochdrev.[8] Next morning they pushed on, crossing Elenid and stopping that night between Keri and Arwystli, in a town which is now also called Mochdrev; from there they went on to a commot in Powys which is now called Mochnant,[9] where they spent the night. The next day they made for the cantrev of Rhos, spending the

8. Mochdrev: pig town.   9. Mochnant: pig brook.

night in a town now called Mochdrev, and the next day
Gwydyon said, 'Men, we will make for the stronghold of
Gwynedd with these animals, for there is a host after us.'
They headed for the Upper Town [10] of Arllechwedd and
there made a sty for the swine, and so the town is now
called Creuwryon.[11]

When this sty was finished they went to Caer Dathal to
see Math son of Mathonwy, and as they arrived the people
were being mustered. 'What is going on here?' asked
Gwydyon, and the answer came, 'Pryderi is mustering
twenty-one cantrevs in your pursuit. Strange how slowly
you have travelled!' 'Where are the animals you went
after?' Math asked. 'A sty has been made for them and
they are in another cantrev,' said Gwydyon. They heard
trumpets and the mustering of the people, so they
equipped themselves and set out for Pennardd in Arvon.
That night, however, Gwydyon and his brother Gilvaethwy returned to Caer Dathal, and Gilvaethwy and
Goewin were put to sleep together in Math's own bed;
the other girls were forced out of the chamber, and Goewin
was taken against her will.

When they saw the next day dawn the brothers made
for the place where Math and his host were; as they arrived, the men were preparing to discuss where they ought
to await Pryderi and the men of the south, so Gwydyon
and Gilvaethwy took part in the council, and it was decided to wait in the stronghold of Gwynedd in Arvon.
They waited in the middle of two towns, Pennardd and
Coed Alun; Pryderi attacked and joined battle, and there
was great slaughter made on both sides until the men of
the south were forced to retreat to what is now known
as Nant Call. The pursuit led to another great battle, and

10. Upper Town: the cantrev of Arllechwedd is divided into upper
and lower commots.

11. Creu: sty. If wryon could be read wydyon, the name would
mean Gwydyon's sty.

the southerners fled to what is now Dôl Benmaen; there they rallied and sought a truce, and to secure this truce Pryderi gave as hostages Gwrgi Gwastra and the sons of twenty-three nobles.

The forces then travelled under the white flag as far as Y Traeth Mawr, but when they reached Y Velen Rhyd [12] the foot soldiers could no longer be restrained from shooting at each other; Pryderi therefore sent messengers to have the opposing forces separated, and to ask that the issue be left to him and Gwydyon, since Gwydyon was the cause of the war. Upon hearing the message Math said, 'Between me and God, if Gwydyon is agreeable I will gladly leave off. I will not force anyone to fight without our doing all we can.' 'God knows,' said the messenger, 'Pryderi feels that the man who did him this injury ought to face him in single combat and allow the two hosts to stand back.' 'I swear by my confession to God,' said Gwydyon, 'I will not ask the men of Gwynedd to fight on my account when I can meet Pryderi. I will gladly meet him in single combat.' That answer was sent to Pryderi, who said, 'Well, I will not ask anyone to seek compensation for me.'

The two men were set apart. They armed themselves and fought, and by reason of strength and skill and magic and enchantment Gwydyon was the victor and Pryderi was killed; he was buried at Maen Tyryawg above Y Velen Rhyd, and there his grave is. The men of the south then set out for their own land, weeping bitterly, and that was not strange: they had lost their lord and many of their nobles, and their horses and the greater part of their weapons. The men of Gwynedd returned elated and rejoicing, and Gwydyon said to Math, 'Lord, ought we not to release to the men of the south their nobleman, the one they gave us as hostage against the truce? We should

12. Y Traeth Mawr: the big strand. Y Velen Rhyd: the yellow ford.

not keep him imprisoned.' 'Release him,' said Math, and so Gwrgi and the other hostages were allowed to follow after the men of the south.

Math then made for Caer Dathal, but Gilvaethwy and his retinue made a circuit of Gwynedd as was their custom, rather than returning to the court. Math went to his chamber and had them prepare him a place to rest, so that he might place his feet in the virgin's lap, but Goewin said, 'Lord, look for another virgin to hold your feet – I am a woman.' 'How is that?' 'I was assaulted openly, nor was I silent – everyone in the court knew of it. Your nephews Gwydyon and Gilvaethwy, your sister's sons, raped me and dishonoured you by sleeping with me in your chamber and your very bed.' 'Well, I will do what I can,' said Math. 'First I will seek compensation for you, and then for myself. I will take you for my wife and give you authority over this realm.'

Meanwhile the nephews did not return to the court but continued their circuit of the land until Math forbade anyone to give them food or drink. At first they would not return, but finally they came. 'Lord, good day to you,' they said. 'Well, have you come to make it up to me?' asked Math. 'Lord, we are subject to your will.' 'Had I my will, I would not have lost what I have of men and weapons. You cannot make good my shame, nor the death of Pryderi, but since you have come to do my will, I will begin to punish you.' Math took his magic wand and struck Gilvaethwy so that the latter became a large hind; then he quickly seized Gwydyon (who wanted to escape but could not) and struck him so that he became a stag. 'Since you are in league with each other I will make you go off together; you shall mate, and shall have the nature of wild deer, and when those animals bear their young you shall bear yours. Return here a year from today.'

At the end of the year Math heard a great din outside his chamber, and the dogs of the court barking in reply.

'Go and see what is outside,' he said, and a man replied, 'Lord, I have looked: there are a stag and a hind, and a fawn with them.' Math rose and went outside and saw the three wild beasts: a stag and a hind and a sturdy fawn. He lifted his magic wand and said, 'The one of you that has been a hind this past year shall be a wild boar, and the one that has been a stag shall now be a wild sow.' He struck them with the magic wand. 'The boy however I will take, and arrange for him to be baptized and fostered.' He gave the boy the name Hyddwn. 'Go now: one of you shall be a wild boar and the other a wild sow, and you shall have the nature of wild swine. Be here outside this wall a year from today, and bring your offspring with you.'

At the end of the second year they heard the barking of the dogs outside the chamber wall and the uproar of the court in reply, so Math went out and saw three beasts: a wild boar and a wild sow and a sturdy young one with them, strong for its age. 'Well, I will take this one and see that it is baptized,' and he struck the young pig with his magic wand so that it became a handsome lad with thick auburn hair, and this lad he named Hychdwn. 'As for you, the one that has been a wild boar this past year shall be a she-wolf now, and the one that has been a wild sow shall be a wolf.' He struck them with his wand so that they became wolf and she-wolf. 'You shall have the nature of wolves, and you are to be here outside this wall a year from today.'

That day a year later Math heard a clamour and a barking outside his chamber wall; he rose and went out and found a wolf and a she-wolf and a sturdy wolf-cub with them. 'I will take the cub and arrange for his baptism, for the name Bleiddwn [13] is ready for him. These three boys are yours, namely:

13. Hydd: deer; Hwch: pig; Bleidd: wolf.

Three sons of false Gilvaethwy,
Three true champions:
Bleiddwn, Hyddwn, Hychdwn the Tall.'

Then Math struck the two with his wand so that they recovered their own forms. 'Men, if you wronged me you have been punished enough – it is a great disgrace that each of you has had children by the other. Now draw a bath for these two and wash their heads and dress them.'

After the two nephews had been cleaned up they went to see Math, who said, 'Men, you have earned peace, and you shall have friendship. Now advise me which virgin to choose.[14] Gwydyon replied, 'Lord, that is an easy choice: Aranrhod [15] daughter of Dôn, your niece and your sister's daughter.' The girl was sent for, and when she arrived Math said, 'Girl, are you a virgin?' 'I do not know but that I am.' Math took his wand and bent it, saying, 'Step over that, and if you are a virgin I will know.' Aranrhod stepped over the wand, and with that step she dropped a sturdy boy with thick yellow hair; the boy gave a loud cry, and with that cry she made for the door, dropping a second small something on the way, but before anyone could get a look at it Gwydyon snatched it up and wrapped it in a silk sheet and hid it in a little chest at the foot of his bed. 'Well,' said Math, 'I will arrange for the baptism of this one,' referring to the yellow-haired boy, 'and I will call· him Dylan.' The boy was baptized, whereupon he immediately made for the sea, and when he came to the sea he took on its nature and swam as well as the best fish. He was called Dylan son of Ton,[16] for no wave ever broke beneath him. The blow which killed him was struck by his uncle Govannon,[17] and that was one of the Three Unfortunate Blows.

14. Math has survived without a foot-holder for three years.

15. Aranrhod: silver wheel? *v. TYP*, pp. 277–8.

16. Dylan: sea; Ton: wave.

17. Govannon = Goibniu, the blacksmith of the Irish gods. Govan: smith.

One day, when Gwydyon was just waking up, he heard a cry from the foot of the bed. Though this cry was not loud it was loud enough for him to hear, so he rose quickly and opened the chest and saw a small boy thrusting his arms out from the folds of the sheet and pushing it away. Gwydyon took the boy and made for the town, where he knew of a woman who was nursing, and bargained with her to suckle the child. The boy was reared for a year; and at the end of it his size would have been large had he been twice as old, and by the end of the second year he was a big boy who could go to the court by himself. Gwydyon himself took notice of the lad on his visits there, and the boy grew to know Gwydyon and loved him more than any other man. He was brought up in the court until he was four, and it would have been remarkable for an eight-year-old to be as big.

One day he followed Gwydyon out walking. The latter made for Caer Aranrhod and the boy with him, and when they reached her court Aranrhod rose to welcome and greet them. 'God be good to you,' said Gwydyon. 'What boy is that who is following you?' asked Aranrhod. 'Your son.' 'Alas, what has prompted you to disgrace me and prolong my shame and maintain it so?' 'If you suffer no disgrace worse than my rearing so fine a boy, you will have little to be ashamed of.' 'What is the boy's name?' 'God knows, he has none as yet.' 'Well, then,' said Aranrhod, 'I will swear this fate upon him, that he shall have no name until he obtains one from me.' 'I swear by my confession to God, you are a wicked woman,' said Gwydyon, 'but the lad shall have a name, though you be the worse for it. Being a woman now, you are angry because you are no longer called a virgin – never again will you be called a virgin!'

Gwydyon went away angry and made for Caer Dathal and spent the night there. The next day he rose and took the boy and went for a walk along the shore between

Caer Dathal and Aber Menei, and when he found red sea-weed and kelp he conjured up a ship; out of the kelp and the seaweed he created a great amount of cordovan, and he coloured it so that no one had seen more beautiful leather. Then he equipped the ship with a sail, and he and the boy sailed to the harbour entrance of Caer Aranrhod, where they began to cut out shoes and stitch them. They were observed from the fortress, and perceiving this Gwydyon changed their appearance so they would not be recognized. 'What people are in the ship?' Aranrhod asked. 'Shoemakers,' she was told. 'Go and see what kind of leather they have and what sort of work they do.' People went, and when they reached the ship Gwydyon was colouring the cordovan with gold, so they returned and told Aranrhod. 'All right,' she said, 'measure my foot and ask the cobbler to make me a pair of shoes.' Gwydyon made the shoes, not the right size but too big, and had them sent to her, and they were too large. 'These are too big,' said Aranrhod. 'He shall be paid for them, only let him also make some that are smaller.' Gwydyon made others that were much smaller than her feet and sent them to her. 'Tell him that neither pair fits,' said she, and Gwydyon was told that. 'Then I will not make shoes for her until I see her feet,' he said, and when she heard that she said, 'Very well, I will go to him.'

Aranrhod went to the ship, and when she arrived Gwydyon was cutting out shoes and the boy was stitching them. 'Lady, good day to you,' said Gwydyon. 'God be good to you,' she answered. 'I am surprised that you could not make shoes to measure.' 'I could not before, but I can now.' At that moment a wren alighted on the ship; the boy aimed at it and hit it between the sinew and the bone of the leg. She laughed, 'God knows, the light-haired one hit it with a skilful hand.' 'That he did,' said Gwydyon, 'and God's curse upon you. The lad has got a name, and a good enough one: Lleu [18] Skilful Hand he shall be from now on.' Everything turned back into kelp and seaweed and Gwydyon did no more work, but for this he was known as one of the Three Golden Shoemakers.[19] 'God knows,' said Aranrhod, 'you shall fare no better for hurting me.' 'I have not hurt you yet,' said Gwydyon, and he released himself and Lleu from the spell so that they had their own appearance. 'Very well,' said Aranrhod, 'I swear this fate on the boy, that he shall have no weapons until I arm him myself.' 'Between me and God,' said Gwydyon, 'this springs from your wickedness. But Lleu shall have arms.'

The two returned to Dinas Dinlleu,[20] where Lleu Skilful Hand was brought up until he could ride every horse, and until he had matured in appearance and reached his full size and growth. Gwydyon noticed that he was growing idle for want of horses and weapons, so he called to him, 'Lad, we will go, you and I, on an errand tomorrow, so be more cheerful than you have been.' 'That I will,' answered the boy. At dawn the next day they rose and rode along the seashore up to Brynn Aryen,[21] and at the top of Kevyn Clun Tyno [22] they prepared their horses to ride out to Caer Aranrhod. They changed their appearance and made for the gate disguised as two young men, save that Gwydyon's expression was more sober than the boy's. 'Gatekeeper,' said Gwydyon, 'go inside and say that bards from Morgannwg are here.' The gatekeeper went in, and Aranrhod said, 'Greetings to them, let them enter.' Everyone rejoiced at their arrival; the hall was prepared and they all went to eat. The meal being finished Aranrhod began to talk with Gwydyon about stories and storytelling, for Gwydyon was a good storyteller; when the

18. Lleu (= Lug in Irish): bright, shining.
19. Actually 'Triad 67' names Lleu, not Gwydyon, as one of the Three Golden Shoemakers.
20. Dinas: fort.　　21. Brynn: hill.　　22. Kevyn: ridge.

time for carousing had ended, however, a chamber was prepared for the guests and they went to bed.

The next day Gwydyon rose early and called on his magic and his power, and by dawn there was a great running about and trumpeting and crying out all through the land. When day broke they heard a knock on the chamber door and Aranrhod asking them to open it; Lleu rose and opened the door and she and a girl came in. 'Good sirs, we are in a bad state,' she said. 'Yes,' said Gwydyon, 'we hear shouting and trumpets – what do you make of it all?' 'God knows we cannot see the colour of the ocean for all the ships assembled on it, and they are making for land as fast as they can. What are we to do?' 'Lady, there is nothing we can do except close up the fortress and make the best possible defence.' 'Well, God reward you,' said Aranrhod. 'Prepare our defence, you will find weapons enough here,' whereupon she went after arms and returned with two girls and arms for two men. 'Lady, arm this youth,' said Gwydyon, 'and with the girls' help I will arm myself.' 'Gladly,' said Aranrhod, and of her own will she armed Lleu completely. 'Is the youth's arming completed?' asked Gwydyon. 'It is,' she said. 'So is mine. We will put off our arms now, there is no need for them. 'Alas, why? Look at the ships surrounding the house,' said Aranrhod. 'Woman, no fleet is outside.' 'Alas, what sort of host was this?' 'A host to avert the fate you swore for your son by obtaining arms for him. He has them now, no thanks to you.' 'Between me and God,' said Aranrhod, 'you are an evil man – many a lad might have lost his life in the muster you brought about in this cantrev today. I will swear a fate on the boy: he shall have no wife of the race that is on this earth at this time.' 'You were always an evil woman,' said Gwydyon, 'and no one ought to serve you. Lleu shall have a wife all the same.'

Then Gwydyon and Lleu went to Math and made the most persistent complaints ever against Aranrhod, telling

him how Gwydyon had obtained arms for Lleu, and Math
said, 'Let us use our magic and enchantments to conjure
up a woman out of flowers.' By then Lleu had the stature
of a man and was the handsomest lad anyone had seen.
Math and Gwydyon took the flowers of oak and broom
and meadowsweet and from these conjured up the loveliest and most beautiful girl anyone had seen; they baptized her with the form of baptism that was used then,
and named her Blodeuedd.[23]

After the couple had slept together at the wedding-feast
Gwydyon said, 'It is not easy for a man with no land to
support himself.' 'Very well,' said Math, 'I will give him
the best cantrev there is for a young man to have.' 'Which
cantrev is that?' 'The cantrev of Dinoding,' said Math.
(It is now called Eivyonydd and Ardudwy.) Lleu set up
his court in the place called Mur Castell,[24] in the hills of
Ardudwy; he settled there and governed the land, and all
were content with his rule.

One day he left for Caer Dathal to visit Math. The day
of his departure his wife was stirring about the court when
she heard a horn blown and saw an exhausted stag going
by with dogs and hunters in pursuit, followed by a company of men on foot. 'Send a lad to find out who these
people are,' she said, so the lad went out and asked what
lord they served; 'Goronwy the Staunch, Lord of Penllyn,' was the answer, and the lad reported that to
Blodeuedd. Goronwy pursued the stag until he overtook it
at Avon Gynvael,[25] and there he killed it, and what with
killing the stag and feeding his dogs he was there until
night closed in. As day ended and night drew near he
came to the gate of the court.

'God knows, we will be disgraced for letting this chieftain go elsewhere at this hour and not asking him in,' said
Blodeuedd. 'God knows, lady, we should ask him in,'

23. Blodeu: flowers.   24. Mur Castell: castle wall.
25. Avon: river.

said her attendants. Messengers were sent, and Goronwy was glad to accept the invitation; he entered the court and she came to welcome and greet him. 'Lady, God reward you for this welcome,' he said, and then they changed and went to sit down. Blodeuedd looked at Goronwy, and as she looked there was no part of her that was not filled with love for him; he returned her gaze, and the feeling that had overcome her overcame him also. He could not conceal his love for her and so he told her; this made her very happy, and their talk that night was of the love and affection they felt for each other. Nor did they hesitate to embrace – that night they slept together.

The next day Goronwy made to leave, but Blodeuedd said, 'God knows, you must not go from me tonight,' so they spent that night together also, planning how they might stay together. 'There is only one way,' said Goronwy, 'you must try to learn from your husband how his death might be brought about – you can do so by feigning concern for his well-being.' The next day Goronwy made to leave, but Blodeuedd said, 'God knows, I do not advise you to leave me today.' 'God knows, since you feel that way, I will not go. Though I am considering the danger that the chief whose court this is will return.' 'All right, I will let you go tomorrow.' The next day he prepared to leave and she did not hinder him. 'Now remember what I told you,' he said, 'speak privately with him, feign affection, and learn how he can be killed.'

That night Lleu returned home. He and his wife spent the day singing and carousing and talking, and at night they went to sleep together, and he spoke to her, and then a second time, but not one word did he get in reply. 'What has happened to you – are you all right?' he asked. 'I am thinking of something you would not expect from me,' she answered, 'that is, I am worried about your death, about your going before I do.' 'Well, God reward you for your concern,' said he. 'But unless God strikes me down, it will not be easy for anyone to kill me.' 'Then for God's sake and mine, tell me how you can be killed, for my memory is a better safeguard than yours.' 'Gladly. It will not be easy for anyone to strike me, since he would have to spend a year working on the spear, and no work may be done except when people are at Mass on Sundays.' 'Are you certain of that?' 'I am. I cannot be killed indoors or out of doors, on horse or on foot.'[26] 'Then how can you be killed?' 'I will tell you. Make a bath for me on a river bank, with a good snugly thatched roof over the tub; then bring a buck goat and put it alongside the tub. If I put one foot on the goat's back and the other on the edge of the tub, whoever struck me then would bring about my death.' 'Well, I thank God for that,' she said, 'for this can easily be avoided.'

No sooner had Blodeuedd obtained the information than she sent it to Goronwy the Staunch. Goronwy worked over the spear until, at the end of the year, it was ready, and he told Blodeuedd that very day. 'Lord,' she said to her husband, 'I am thinking of how what you told me earlier might come about. If I prepare the bath, will you show me how you would stand on the goat and the edge of the tub?' 'I will,' said Lleu, whereupon she sent for Goronwy and told him to wait in the shadow of the hill now called Brynn Kyvergyr, on the bank of Avon Gynvael; then she had men gather all the goats they could find in the cantrev and bring them to the far side of the river, the side facing Brynn Kyvergyr. The next day she said, 'Lord, I have had the roof and the bath prepared, and everything is ready.' 'Then let us go and look,' said Lleu. The next day they came to look at the bath. 'Will you step into the bath, lord?' she asked. 'Gladly,' he said. 'Lord, here are those animals you said were called buck goats.' 'Then have them catch one and bring it here.' The goat

26. When he is killed, Lleu is also standing neither on dry land (the goat's back) nor in water (the edge of the tub).

was brought; Lleu rose from the bath and put on his
trousers, then put one foot on the edge of the tub and the
other on the goat's back. At once from the hill called
Brynn Kyvergyr Goronwy rose to one knee and cast the
poisoned spear at Lleu and struck him in the side so that
the shaft stuck out but the head stayed in. Lleu flew up
in the form of an eagle and gave a horrible scream, and
he was not seen again.

As soon as he had disappeared Goronwy and Blodeuedd
set off for the court, and that night they slept together.
The next day Goronwy rose and subdued Ardudwy and
ruled over it, so that both Ardudwy and Penllyn were in
his power. Upon hearing of this Math was grieved and
heavy-hearted, and Gwydyon was sadder still. 'Lord, I
cannot rest until I get news of my nephew,' said he, and
Math replied, 'Go then, and God be your strength.'
Gwydyon set out on his journey; he searched Gwynedd
and every part of Powys, and after looking everywhere he
came to Arvon and stopped at a peasant's house in the
stronghold of Pennardd, where he dismounted and spent
the night. When the man of the house and his household entered, the swineherd came last, and the master said
to his swineherd, 'Lad, has your sow come in this evening?' 'She has just come in to the swine.' 'What sort of
journey does this sow make?' asked Gwydyon. 'Every day
when the sty is opened she goes out; no one can hold her,
nor do we know where she goes any more than if she went
into the earth.' 'Will you do something for me?' asked
Gwydyon. 'Do not open the sty until I am standing by.'
'I will do that,' said the swineherd.

They went to sleep that night, and when the swineherd
saw the light of day he woke Gwydyon, who rose and
dressed and went out and stood by the sty. The swineherd opened the sty, and at once the sow bolted out and
raced away, with Gwydyon in pursuit. She headed upstream and made for the valley which is now called Nant-

lleu, and there she halted and began to feed. Gwydyon
walked under the tree to see what she was feeding on,
and he found her eating rotten flesh and maggots. Then
he looked up into the top of the tree and there was an
eagle; when the eagle shook, worms and rotten flesh fell
away and the sow would eat. Gwydyon thought that the
eagle was Lleu, so he sang this englyn:

> An oak [27] grows between two lakes,
> Dark sky and glen.
> If I speak truly
> This comes from Lleu's feathers.

At that the eagle dropped into the middle of the tree.
Gwydyon then sang another englyn:

> An oak grows on a high plain;
> Rain soaks it no more than does putrefaction. [28]
> It has supported twenty crafts; [29]
> In its branches is Lleu Skilful Hand.

At that the eagle dropped down into the lowest branch
of the tree, and Gwydyon sang still another englyn:

> An oak grows on a slope,
> The refuge of a handsome prince.
> If I speak truly
> Lleu will come to my lap.

At that the eagle dropped down onto Gwydyon's knee,
and Gwydyon struck him with his magic wand so that he
regained human form. No one had ever seen such a pitiful
sight of a man – he was nothing but skin and bone.
Gwydyon took him to Caer Dathal; all the good doctors
in Gwynedd were brought, and well before the end of the
year he was cured.

Lleu then said to Math, 'Lord, it is time to demand

27. oak: one of the flowers from which Blodeuedd was made.

28. Lleu's rotting flesh falls like rain.

29. Lug is master of many crafts – perhaps that is the significance
of the twenty crafts mentioned here.

compensation from the man who did me this injury.' 'God
knows, he cannot continue to keep it from you,' said Math.
'Well, the sooner I receive compensation the better I
will feel.' So they mustered the forces of Gwynedd and
made for Ardudwy, and Gwydyon rode ahead to Mur
Castell. When Blodeuedd heard that they were coming
she took her women with her and made across Avon Gynvael to a court which was on the mountain; these women,
however, were so afraid that they would only advance with
their faces turned backwards, and so they knew nothing
until they had fallen into the lake and drowned, all but
Blodeuedd. Gwydyon overtook her and said, 'I will not
kill you, but I will do what is worse: I will let you go in
the form of a bird. Because of the shame you have brought
on Lleu Skilful Hand, you are never to show your face to
the light of day, rather you shall fear other birds; they
will be hostile to you, and it will be their nature to maul
and molest you wherever they find you. You will not lose
your name but will always be called Blodeuwedd.[30]
(Blodeuwedd means owl in the language of our day, and
therefore birds are hostile to the owl.)

Goronwy the Staunch set out for Penllyn, from where
he sent messengers to ask Lleu Skilful Hand if he would
accept land or territory or gold or silver for the injury.
'I swear by my confession to God, I will not,' said Lleu.
'He must come to where I was when he cast the spear at
me, while I am standing where he was, and must let me
throw a spear at him. That is the least I will accept.' This
was told to Goronwy, who replied, 'Well, I must do that.
Nobles, troops, foster-brothers, will any of you take the
blow in my stead?' 'God knows, we will not,' they all said,
and because of their refusal to stand and take the blow
for their lord they were known as one of the Three Disloyal Companies.

'Then I must take the blow,' said Goronwy. The two

30. Blodeuwedd: flower face.

men went to the bank of Avon Gynvael; Goronwy stood where Lleu had been when the spear was thrown, and Lleu where Goronwy had been. But Goronwy went to Lleu and said, 'Lord, since it was through a woman's bad influence that I struck you, I beg this of you in God's name. I see a stone by the river bank – let me put that between myself and the blow.' 'God knows I will not refuse you that,' said Lleu. 'God reward you,' said Goronwy, and he took up the stone and put it between himself and the blow. Then Lleu threw the spear and pierced both the stone and Goronwy; Goronwy's back was broken and he was killed. The stone still stands on the bank of Avon Gynvael in Ardudwy, with the spear through it, and so it is called Llech Oronwy.[31] But Lleu Skilful Hand subdued the land a second time and ruled over it prosperously, and according to the storytellers he was Lord of Gwynedd thereafter. So ends this Branch of the Mabinogi.

31. Llech Oronwy: stone of Goronwy.

THE DREAM OF MAXEN

'MAXEN' is a mixture of history and pseudo-history and reflects traditions found also in Geoffrey's *Historia*. Maxen himself is a composite figure. He draws his name from Maxentius, Roman emperor from A.D. 306 to 312, but the source of the tale is the career of the Spaniard Magnus Maximus (in Geoffrey identified with the Roman senator Maximianus, another confusion). Maximus served with the Roman army in Britain from A.D. 368 until 383, when the disenchanted troops proclaimed him emperor. He crossed the Channel, defeated Gratian and became master of Gaul and Spain, and even of northern Italy; subsequently Theodosius defeated him twice, however, and in 388 Maximus was captured and beheaded. In Geoffrey's version the Roman senator Maximianus is invited to Britain to marry the daughter of Octavius (Eudav in 'Maxen') and to rule the island. This daughter is not named, but only a few pages earlier in the *Historia* Coel's daughter Helena (Elen in 'Maxen') is married to the wise and courageous Roman senator Constantius, and it seems that through further confusion Elen became the name of Maxen's wife. Geoffrey's Conanus, the nephew of Octavius, appears in 'Maxen' as Eudav's son Kynan, but the part he plays is very different.

The debt of 'Maxen' to Geoffrey is difficult to determine. It is clear that Geoffrey's history is the more accurate, and that 'Maxen' has departed from the tradition of the *Historia* by making the ruler a wise and courageous hero, by making his expedition to Rome (to *recapture* the throne) a success, and most of all by claiming that Maxen could not have retaken Rome without the help of his wife's relatives. As told, 'Maxen' extols the beauty of Elen, and the courage and intelligence of Kynan and Avaon.

The Dream of Maxen

The ruler Maxen was Emperor of Rome, and he was handsomer and wiser and better suited to be emperor than any of his predecessors. One day, at an assembly of kings, he said to his friends, 'I wish to go hunting tomorrow.' So the next morning he set out with his host; they rode to the valley of the river which flows through Rome and hunted until noon. There were with Maxen thirty-two crowned kings, all his men, and it was not so much for the pleasure of hunting that the emperor rode out as because he had been made a man of such rank that he was lord over all these kings. The sun was high overhead and with the great heat Maxen grew sleepy, so his chamberlains made a castle round him by setting their shields on their spear shafts to protect him from the sun, and they placed a gold-chased shield under his head. Thus the emperor slept.

In his sleep Maxen had a dream. He saw himself travelling to the end of the valley and reaching the highest mountain in the world – it seemed as high as the sky – and having crossed this mountain he saw himself journeying through the flattest and loveliest land that anyone had seen. Great broad rivers flowed from the mountain to the sea, and he made along these rivers to their outlets, and though his journey was long he finally reached the mouth of the greatest river anyone had seen. There he saw a great city, and a great fortress within with many tall towers

of different colours. At the mouth of the river he saw a
fleet, the greatest he had seen, and one of the ships was
much bigger and more beautiful than any of the others;
insofar as the ship was visible above the water he could see
one plank of gold and another of silver. A bridge of ivory
led from ship to shore, and along that bridge Maxen saw
himself going aboard, whereupon the sail was hoisted and
the ship set out across the sea until it came to the loveliest
island in the world. When he had crossed this island from
one sea to the other, to the very farthest reaches, he saw
steep slopes and high crags and a harsh rough land whose
like he had never seen, and beyond it an island in the sea.
Between him and this island he saw a land where the plain
was as broad as the sea and the forest as broad as the
mountain; from this mountain a river ran through the
land and down to the sea, and at the mouth of the river
stood a great fortress, the handsomest ever. The gate was
open and he entered.

Inside Maxen saw a fine hall: its roof seemed all of
gold, its sides of luminous stones all equally precious, its
doors all of gold. There were golden couches and silver
tables, and on the couch facing him two auburn-haired
lads playing gwyddbwyll [1] with a silver board and golden
men. These lads were dressed in pure black brocade, with
headbands of red gold restraining their hair, and precious
luminous stones therein, rubies and gems and imperial
stones in alternation, and shoes of new cordovan on their
feet, strapped on with bands of red gold. By the base of a
pillar Maxen saw a white-haired man sitting in a chair of
elephant ivory, on which was an image of two eagles in
red gold; he wore gold armlets, and rings on his fingers
and a gold torque round his neck, with a gold hairband,
and he had an impressive quality about him. A gold board

1. gwyddbwyll (=fidchell in Irish): wood sense. A board game in
which one side's king attempts to escape to the edge of the board,
and the other side attempts to capture him.

for gwyddbwyll lay before him; in his hands he held a bar
of gold and a file, and he was carving men for the game.

Sitting before him Maxen also saw a girl in a chair of
red gold, and looking at the sun at its brightest would be
no harder than looking at her beauty: she wore shifts of
white silk with red gold fastenings across the breast, and a
gold brocade surcoat and mantle, the latter fastened by a
brooch of red gold, a hairband with rubies and gems and
pearls and imperial stones in alternation, and a belt of
red gold. She was the loveliest sight man had ever seen.
From her golden chair she rose to Maxen, and he threw
his arms round her neck, and they sat down in the chair,
which was as comfortable for two as it had been for her
alone. His arms were round her neck, and they were sitting cheek to cheek, but what with the hounds straining
at their leashes, and the edges of the shields banging together and the spear shafts rubbing together and the
stamping and whinnying of the horses the emperor woke
up.

When Maxen woke, there was no life or being or existence in him because of the girl he had seen in his dream –
not a knuckle-bone, not the tip of a fingernail, let alone
anything more, was not full of love for her. His retainers
said, 'Lord, it is past your mealtime,' so the emperor, the
saddest man ever seen, mounted his palfrey and rode back
to Rome, and thus he remained for a week. When his retinue went to drink wine and mead from golden cups he
stayed behind; when they went to listen to songs and entertainments he stayed behind. He did nothing but sleep,
for then he would dream of the woman he loved best, and
when he was awake he cared for nothing about him because he did not know where she was.

One day a chamberlain spoke to the emperor (though
he was a chamberlain he was also King of the Romani),
'Lord, your men all slander you.' 'Why?' 'Because you
give them neither the speech nor the errands that men

expect from their lord,' and the emperor answered, 'Summon the wise men of Rome, and I will tell you why I am sad.' The wise men of Rome were summoned, and Maxen told them, 'I have had a dream, and in that dream I have seen a girl, and because of her there is not life nor being nor existence in me.' 'Lord,' said the wise men, 'as you have asked us, we will advise you. For the next three years send messengers to the three parts of the earth in search of your dream. Since you will never know at what time of day or night good news might arrive, that much hope will sustain you.' The messengers were sent to roam the world seeking news of the emperor's dream, but when they returned at the end of a year they knew not a word more than they had when they set out, and the emperor was saddened to think that he would never get news of the woman he loved most.

The King of the Romani then said to him, 'Lord, set out to hunt where you saw yourself, whether east or west.' The emperor did this; he found the river bank and said, 'This is where I was in my dream, and I was moving westward upstream.' Thirteen men set out as the emperor's messengers, until they saw before them a mountain which seemed to reach to the sky. These messengers journeyed thus: each one wore a sleeve of his cape in front as a sign that he was a messenger, so that whatever warring land they might pass through they would come to no harm. Having crossed the mountain they saw great level expanses with broad rivers flowing through them and they said, 'Look, here is the land our lord saw.' They travelled along the estuaries of the rivers until they reached a major river which flowed into the sea; they found a great city at the mouth of the river, and within a great fortress with many tall towers of various colours, and at the mouth of the river the largest fleet in the world, and one ship larger than any of the others. 'Here again is the dream our lord

saw,' they said. They boarded the great ship and sailed to
the island of Britain, and then they journeyed through
that island until they reached Eryri.[2] 'And here is the
rough land our lord saw,' they said. They went on until
they could see Môn[3] opposite, and Arvon as well, and
again they said, 'There is the land our lord saw in his
dream.' They saw Aber Seint[4] and a fortress at the mouth
of the river; finding the gate open they entered and saw
a hall. 'Look, the hall our lord saw in his dream.'

The messengers then entered the hall and saw the two
lads playing gwyddbwyll on the golden couch and the
white-haired man seated in the ivory chair at the base of
the column carving gwyddbwyll men; they saw the girl
seated in the chair of red gold, and they knelt down before
her and hailed her as Empress of Rome. 'Sirs, you have
the look of noblemen, as well as the badge of messengers,'
she said. 'Why then do you mock me?' 'Lady, we do not.
The Emperor of Rome has seen you in a dream, and now
life and being and existence have all left him. We give
you a choice: you may come with us and be made empress
in Rome, or else the emperor will come here to make you
his wife.' 'Men,' she answered, 'I do not doubt what you
say, but I do not believe it overmuch either. If it is I whom
the emperor loves, let him come for me.'

The messengers rode day and night getting back; when
their horses failed they left them and bought new ones,
and when they reached Rome they went to greet the
emperor and ask for their reward, which they got even as
they were asking. 'Lord, we will guide you by land and
sea to the woman you love best; we know her name and
her relatives and her birth,' they said. At once the emperor
and his host set out, taking the messengers along as guides.
They crossed ocean and sea to the island of Britain, which

2. Eryri=Snowdon.   3. Môn=Anglesey.
4. Aber Seint: estuary where stood the Roman fort Segontium.

Maxen took by driving Beli son of Mynogan and his sons
into the sea, and pushed on to Arvon, and he recognized
the land as soon as he saw it. Upon seeing Aber Seint he
said, 'There is the fortress where I saw the woman I love
best.'

Maxen entered the fortress, and inside the hall he saw
Kynan son of Eudav and Avaon son of Eudav playing
gwyddbwyll, and Eudav son of Caradawg sitting in the
ivory chair carving gwyddbwyll pieces, and the girl from
his dream sitting in the red gold chair. 'Hail to the Empress
of Rome,' he said, and he embraced her, and that night he
slept with her. The next morning she asked for her gift,
as he had found her a virgin, and he told her to name her
own gift. She asked for the island of Britain for her father,
from the English Channel to the Irish Sea, and the three
offshore islands[5] for the Empress of Rome, and three
strongholds to be made for her in the island of Britain,
in the places she chose. She asked that the chief fortress
be built in Arvon, and soil from Rome was brought so
that it would be healthier for the emperor to sit and
sleep and move about. The other fortresses were none
other than Caer Llion[6] and Caer Vyrddin.[7]

One day Maxen went to hunt at Caer Vyrddin; he went
to the top of Y Vrenni Vawr[8] and pitched his tent there,
and the tent ground has been known as Cadeir Vaxen[9]
ever since. Caer Vyrddin, on the other hand, was so called
because it was built by a multitude of men. Afterwards,
Elen thought to have highways built from one fortress to

5. The three offshore islands are the isles of Wight, Man, and either
Anglesey or the Orkneys.

6. Caer Llion (=Caerleon on Usk): Roman Castra Legionum,
'Encampment of the Legions'.

7. Caer Vyrddin=Carmarthen. Explained here as if it were derived from myrdd, 'myriad'; elsewhere explained as the fortress of
Myrddin (Merlin). The Roman name is Maridunum.

8. Y Vrenni Vawr: the big prow.

9. Cadeir Vaxen: encampment of Maxen.

another across the island; these were built, and are now called the highways of Elen of the Hosts, because of her British origin – that is, because the men of the island would not have assembled for anyone but her.

The emperor spent seven years in this island, and at that time it was a custom of the Romans that whenever an emperor stayed conquering in another land for seven years, he must stay abroad and not be allowed to return to Rome. A new emperor was elected, and he sent Maxen a threatening letter, no more than this: *If you come, and if you ever come to Rome.* This letter with its contents reached Maxen at Caer Llion, and he in turn sent a letter to the man who claimed to be Emperor of Rome, no more than this: *If I go to Rome, and if I go.* Then Maxen and his host set out for Rome. On the way he conquered France and Burgundy, and then he laid siege to Rome, but after a year before the fortress he was no closer to taking it than he had been the first day.

There had followed Maxen from the island of Britain a small band led by the brothers of Elen of the Hosts, and there were better fighters in that small band than among twice as many Romans. The emperor was told how this band had been seen dismounting and pitching their tents near his own, and how no one had ever seen a finer band nor one better equipped, nor with handsomer standards for their size. Elen of the Hosts went to look, and she recognized the standards of her brothers; thus Kynan and Avaon came to see Maxen, and he threw his arms about them and welcomed them. They all went to look at the Roman assault on the stronghold, and Kynan said to his brother, 'We should look for a cleverer way to take this stronghold.' At night they measured the height of the wall, and then they sent their carpenters into the forest and had a ladder made for every four men, and soon the ladders were ready. Every day at noon the two emperors would stop fighting and eat their meal. The British, how-

ever, took their food and drink in the morning, until
they were in high spirits, and so when the two emperors
were eating the British approached the wall and set their
ladders against it, and at once they scaled the wall and
dropped over inside. The new emperor had no oppor-
tunity to arm himself before they were upon him; they
killed him and many others, and three days and nights
they spent overcoming the host in the fortress and in
conquering the castle, while another part of them were
on watch lest any of Maxen's host should enter before
they had finished.

Maxen said to Elen of the Hosts, 'Lady, I marvel greatly
that it is not for me that your brothers have conquered
this fortress,' and she answered, 'Lord, my brothers are
the wisest men in the world. Go and ask for the stronghold, and if they control it they will gladly give it to you.'
So Maxen and Elen went to ask for the fortress, and Maxen
was told that its capture and surrender to him was the
doing of none save the men of the island of Britain. The
gate to the fortress of Rome was then opened, and the
emperor sat in his chair and the Romans did him homage.

Maxen then said to Kynan and Avaon, 'Sirs, I have regained control over my empire, and now I will give you
this host, that you might conquer any territory you like.'
The brothers went out and conquered lands and castles
and cities; they killed all the men but left all the women
alive, and this continued until the young lads who had
come with them were white-haired with the time they had
been conquering. Kynan said to his brother Avaon, 'Do
you want to stay in this land or return to your own
country?' Avaon and many of his men decided to go
home, but Kynan and another group stayed, and they
determined to cut out the tongues of the women, lest
their own British language be contaminated. Because the
women were silent and the men could speak, the men of
Brittany were called Bryttanyeid, and there have often

come and still do come men of that language from Brittany.[10]

This tale is called the Dream of the Ruler Maxen, and this is its end.

10. The Welsh name for Brittany, Llydaw, is here interpreted as Lled-taw, 'half silent'.

LLUDD AND LLEVELYS

LIKE 'The Dream of Maxen', 'Lludd and Llevelys'
reflects traditions of the sort found in the *Historia*: although the tale of Llevelys and the three
plagues does not appear in Geoffrey's Latin
original, it turns up almost verbatim in the subsequent Welsh translations. Geoffrey does state
that Heli had three sons – Lud, Cassibelaunus
and Nennius – and that the eldest, Lud, rebuilt the
walls of Trinovantum, the city thereafter being
called Kaerlud and Kaerlundein – that is, he had
access to the same episode with which 'Lludd'
opens. Lludd, Casswallawn and Nynnyaw are the
usual Welsh forms of Geoffrey's Latin names,
while the discrepancy between Geoffrey's Heli
and the Beli of 'Lludd' must be attributed to
scribal error. Mynogan is the result of another
error, one that tradition took over from the his-
torian Nennius. The explanation of how London
acquired its name is a bit strained – why should
Lud turn into Lundein? – and moreover quite
untrue, as the city bore the name Londinium in
Roman times.

Like 'Maxen', 'Lludd' extols the virtues of the
British Celts: Llevelys' shrewdness, Lludd's
prowess in battle. The elements of the three
plagues are drawn from disparate strands of tradition. The Corannyeid, who, like Math, can hear
the faintest whisper, appear to survive in the Kor-
riganed (faery folk) of the Bretons. The story of
the dragons is told by Nennius, although its
original significance – the warring dragons were

preventing the completion of Vortigern's citadel
– is no longer apparent. As for the third plague,
the man with the basket has analogues in Beowulf's Grendel and Teirnon's horse thief, both of
whom attack in the night; like Beowulf, Teirnon
and Manawydan, Lludd must sit up and watch.

Lludd and Llevelys

Beli the Great, son of Mynogan, had three sons: Lludd
and Casswallawn and Nynnyaw, and according to this
story there was a fourth son, Llevelys. After Beli's death
the kingdom of Britain passed into the hands of the eldest
son Lludd, and Lludd ruled it prosperously. He rebuilt
the walls of London and surrounded the city with innumerable towers, and then he ordered its inhabitants to
build houses such as no other kingdom possessed. Moreover, he was a good fighter, and generous and open-
handed in giving food and drink to all who sought them.
Though he had many strongholds and fortresses he loved
London best; he spent most of the year there, and so it
was called Caer Lludd, later Caer Llundein, though after
the foreigners came it was called Lundein or Lwndrwys.[1]

Of his brothers Lludd loved Llevelys best, for the latter
was both handsome and wise. When Llevelys heard that
the King of France had died and left a daughter as his
only heir, putting the kingdom in her hands, he went to
ask advice and help of his brother Lludd, not so much for
his own advantage as to seek to augment the honour and
dignity and worth of their family by going to France and
asking the girl to be his wife. Lludd was of the same
opinion, so that Llevelys was glad to take his advice; at
once ships were fitted out and nobles brought aboard and
they set out for France. Upon their arrival messengers were

1. Lwndrwys = Londres, the French name for London.

sent to inform the French nobles of their errand, whereupon the nobles and princes held a council and decided
to give Llevelys both the girl and the crown of the realm.
Thereafter Llevelys ruled with honesty and dignity, as
long as he lived.

After some time had passed, however, there fell upon
the island of Britain three plagues the like of which no
one had ever seen. The first of these was the arrival of a
people called the Corannyeid, the extent of whose knowledge was such that there was no conversation anywhere
in the island, however hushed, that they did not hear,
provided the wind caught it; consequently no harm could
be done to them. The second plague was a scream that was
heard every May Eve over every hearth in the island; it
pierced the hearts of the people and terrified them so that
men lost their colour and strength, women suffered mis-
carriages, children lost their senses, and animals and trees
and soil and water all became barren. The third plague
was this: however much provision had been prepared in
the king's courts, though it might be a year's supply of
food and drink, none of it ever remained after the first
night. The first plague was evident to all, but no one knew
the meaning of the other two, and therefore they had more
hope of being delivered from the first than from the second
or third.

King Lludd was greatly perplexed by and concerned
over these plagues, nor did he know how to rid the island
of them. He summoned his nobles and sought their advice as to how he should proceed, and it was the unani-
mous opinion of his men that he should ask counsel of his
brother Llevelys, the King of France, for Llevelys was a
wise man and a good counsellor. A fleet was fitted out,
silently and in secret, so that no one but the king and his
advisers should know the reason for the voyage, and when
this was ready Lludd and those he had chosen went aboard
and began to cleave the seas towards France. Upon hearing

of this Llevelys, who did not know why his brother was coming, took a large fleet and sailed out to meet him; and seeing Llevelys' fleet Lludd left his ships out at sea, all except for the one in which he went to meet his brother, who himself came forth in a single ship. When these ships met Lludd and Llevelys embraced and greeted each other with brotherly love.

When Lludd told his brother the purpose of his errand Llevelys said that he knew already why Lludd had come. Then they sought some different way to discuss the problem, so that the wind could not carry it off and the Corannyeid learn of their conversation. Llevelys ordered a long horn of bronze to be made, and they spoke through that, but whatever one said to the other came out as hateful and contrary. When Llevelys perceived there was a devil frustrating them and causing trouble he ordered wine to be poured through the horn to wash it out, and the power of the wine drove the devil out.

Thereafter they conversed unhindered. Llevelys told his brother that he would give him some insects, and that Lludd should keep some alive for breeding, in case the plague returned, but that he should take the remaining insects and mash them with water, for Llevelys assured his brother that this mixture would be effective in destroying the Corannyeid. When Lludd arrived home he was to summon all the people of his realm, both his own race and that of the Corannyeid, under pretence of making peace between them, and when all were assembled he was to take this purifying water and throw it over everyone, for Llevelys assured him that the water would poison the Corannyeid without killing or injuring his own people.

'The second plague in your realm,' said Llevelys, 'is a dragon. A dragon of another race, a foreign one, is fighting with it and struggling to overcome it, and therefore your dragon screams horribly. This is how you can see for yourself: when you arrive home measure the length and breadth of the island, and where you find the exact centre have a pit dug; in the pit place a vat full of the best mead that can be made, with a silk sheet over the vat, and guard all this yourself. You will see the dragons fighting in the shape of monstrous animals until they finally rise into the air as dragons, and when they have wearied of their horrid and frightening combat they will sink onto the sheet in the form of two little pigs; they will drag the sheet to the bottom of the vat, and there they will drink the mead and fall asleep. When that happens you must wrap the sheet round them and lock them in a stone chest, and bury them in the earth within the strongest place you know of in the island. As long as they are within that strong place no plague will come to Britain.

'As for the third plague, a mighty magician is carrying off your food and drink from the banquet table. His spells and enchantments cause everyone to fall asleep, so you will have to stand watch yourself – lest sleep overcome you too, have a vat of cold water close by, and when you feel sleepy step into the vat.'

Then Lludd returned to his own country, and at once he summoned both his own people and the Corannyeid. He mashed the insects with water as Llevelys had instructed, and threw this mixture over the entire assembly, and at once destroyed all of the Corannyeid without harming any of the British. A little later Lludd had the length and breadth of the island measured and found its centre to be in Oxford. There he had a pit dug, and in the pit he set a vat of the best mead that could be made, with a silk sheet over the vat, and he himself watched that night and saw the dragons fighting. When they were tired and worn out they sank onto the sheet and dragged it down to the bottom of the vat, where they drank up the mead and fell asleep. Lludd wrapped the sheet round them and locked them in a stone chest in the most secure place he could find in Eryri, and thereafter the place was called

Dinas Emreis,[2] though before it had been Dinas Ffaraon Dandde.[3] (Ffaraon Dandde was one of the Three Noble Youths who broke his heart with dismay.) Thus ended the tempestuous screaming in the kingdom.

Then Lludd ordered a great feast to be set out, and a vat of cold water to be prepared and set nearby, and he himself stood guard, armed with his weapons. About the third watch of the night he heard many songs and much excellent entertainment, until the drowsiness of sleep stole over him; lest this sleep overcome him and frustrate his intent he immersed himself in the water repeatedly. Finally a huge man clad in strong heavy armour entered with a basket, and as was his custom he put all the food and drink that had been prepared and set out into the basket and made off. Lludd thought nothing so strange as that the basket could hold so much. He set off after the giant, crying, 'Stop! Stop! Though you have done many wrongs and inflicted many losses you shall do so no more, unless your skill at arms proves you to be stronger and more able than I.' The giant dropped his basket and waited; a violent encounter ensued, during which sparks flew from their weapons, but at length Lludd took hold of his opponent, and destiny saw that the victory fell to him as he threw the oppressor to the ground. Having been conquered by force and might the giant begged for mercy. 'How can I grant mercy in view of the number of losses and wrongs you have inflicted upon me?' said Lludd. 'I will make good every loss,' said the giant, 'and I will commit no further outrages, but will be your faithful follower hereafter.' Lludd accepted this.

Thus Lludd rid the island of the three plagues, ruling it peacefully and prosperously as long as he lived. This tale is called the Adventure of Lludd and Llevelys, and here it ends.

2. Emreis = Ambrosius.
3. Ffaraon Dandde: flaming pharaoh? a reference to Vortigern?

HOW CULHWCH WON OLWEN

As in *Jason and the Golden Fleece*, the hero of
'Culhwch' has to undertake a number of seemingly
impossible tasks, all of which he is to perform in
the process of winning the daughter of his opponent. But the Welsh version differs in a number
of respects. Ysbaddaden's insistence that he must
die when his daughter weds underlines the primitive nature of the young hero–old king–woman
plot. Moreover, whereas Jason leads the other
Argonauts in the quest for the Golden Fleece,
Culhwch is all but invisible among his more
talented companions.

The major disparity, however, lies in the number of tasks assigned the hero, a staggering thirty-
nine in the Welsh tale. Fortunately for both
audience and reader, only half of these are mentioned as being fulfilled, and only two – the rescue of Mabon and the hunting of Twrch Trwyth
– are described in any detail. On the other hand,
the even more staggering catalogue of heroes
whose aid Culhwch invokes is a veritable kitchen
sink, with genuine Arthurian figures like Kei and
Bedwyr quickly giving way to confusion (Corvil
Bervach for Conall Cernach), desperation
(Someone son of Caw) and outright self-parody
(Sufficiency son of Surfeit). As a whole, though,
'Culhwch' is remarkably coherent.

Arthur, in what is probably his earliest appearance in Welsh prose, has a disappointingly minor
role; already established as the great king of the
British, he displays little personality. While the

exploits which made him king lie in the Celtic past, the distinguishing characteristics which made him famous seem to lie in the continental future.

How Culhwch Won Olwen

Kilydd son of the ruler Kelyddon wanted a wife as well-born as himself, and the woman he chose was Goleu-ddydd [1] daughter of the ruler Amlawdd. After he had slept with her the country went to pray for the couple to have children, and because of these prayers a son was born. Once she had become pregnant Goleuddydd went mad and would enter no house, but when her time came her senses returned; she was near a swineherd and his herd of pigs, and out of fear of the pigs she delivered. The swineherd kept the boy until he came to court, where the lad was baptized and given the name Culhwch, because he had been found in a pig-run; [2] nevertheless he was a well-born lad, Arthur's first cousin, and he was sent out to be nursed.

After that his mother Goleuddydd fell ill, and she called her husband to her; 'I shall die of this illness, and you will want to take another wife. Although wives are gift-givers, still you should not disinherit your son. I ask you not to look for another woman until you see a two-headed thorn on my grave.' He promised her that. Then she summoned her confessor and ordered him to trim the grave every year lest anything grow there. The queen died, and every morning thereafter the king sent a lad to see whether anything was growing on the grave. After seven years the confessor neglected his promise to the queen. The king, who was out hunting, visited the graveyard to see her

1. Goleuddydd: bright day.
2. Culhwch: interpreted as pig run.

grave, and finding the thorn he promptly sought advice
as to where he could find a wife. One of his advisers said,
'I know a good woman who would suit you: the wife of
King Doged.' They decided to go and seek her; they
killed Doged and brought back the woman, with her only
daughter, and seized her husband's land.

One day the good woman was out walking when she
came to the house of an old hag without a tooth in her
head. 'Woman, for God's sake,' she said, 'tell me what I
ask you: Where are the children of this man who has
carried us off by force?' 'He has no children.' 'Woe that I
have come to a childless man!' Then the hag said, 'No
need for that – it is foretold that he will have a child,
and as he has not had it by any other woman he must
have it by you. Do not be sad, either, for he does have
one son.'

Then the queen went home happy and asked her husband, 'Why are you hiding your son from me?' The king
answered, 'I am not hiding him.' So the lad was sent for
and came to court, and his stepmother said to him, 'You
would do well to take a wife, and I have a daughter fit
for any noble in the world.' 'I am not old enough for a
wife,' said Culhwch. 'Then I swear this destiny upon you:
your side shall never touch that of woman until you win
Olwen daughter of Chief Giant Ysbaddaden.' The lad
blushed, and though he had never seen the girl love for
her entered into every limb. His father said, 'Lad, why
do you blush so? What has happened to you?' 'My stepmother has sworn that I shall have no wife until I win
Olwen daughter of Chief Giant Ysbaddaden.' 'That will
not be difficult,' said his father. 'Arthur is your first
cousin; go to him and have your hair trimmed, and ask
for Olwen as your reward.'

Culhwch set off on a steed with a glossy grey head, four
years old; it was firmly crotch-jointed, hollow-hoofed and
had a tubular gold bridle bit in its mouth. The lad sat

in a precious gold saddle, holding two sharpened silver
spears and a battle axe half a yard across from ridge to
edge, an axe which would draw blood from the wind, and
which was swifter from stalk to ground than the swiftest
dewdrop in the month of June, when the dew is heaviest.
He had also a sword with a gold hilt and blade, a gold-
chased buckler the colour of lightning, with an ivory
boss, and two brindled white-breasted greyhounds wearing
red-gold collars from shoulder to ear. The greyhound on
the right side would run to the left and the one on the
left side would run to the right, and so they sported about
him like two terns, while his steed's hooves dug up four
clods as if they were four swallows in the air overhead,
now before him, now behind. Culhwch wore a four-
cornered purple mantle with a red-gold apple in each
corner; each apple was worth a hundred cows, while his
footgear and stirrups, from the top of his thigh to the tip
of his toe, were worth three hundred cows in precious
gold. So smooth was his steed's gait that not a hair on
his head stirred as he journeyed to Arthur's court.

When he reached the gate Culhwch asked, 'Is there a
gatekeeper?' 'There is, and may your head not be yours
for asking such a question. I am gatekeeper to Arthur
every first of January, while for the rest of the year my
lieutenants are Huandaw and Gogigwr and Llaesgymyn
and Penpingyon, who travels on his head to save his feet,
neither skyward nor earthward but like a rolling stone on
the floor of the court.' 'Open the gate.' 'I will not.' 'Why
will you not?' 'Knife has gone into meat, and drink into
horn, and there is a throng in Arthur's hall. Excepting the
king of a lawful dominion or a craftsman who brings his
craft no one may enter. You shall have mash for your dogs
and corn for your horse, and for yourself hot peppered
chops and an abundance of wine and entertaining songs;
food for fifty men shall come to you in the guesthouse
where eat strangers and lads from foreign lands who bring

no craft, and you shall have a woman to sleep with and
entertaining songs to listen to. Tomorrow morning, when
the gate is opened for the multitude that came here today, you shall be first in, and you may sit wherever you
choose in Arthur's hall, from the upper end to the lower.'

Culhwch replied, 'I will have none of that. If you open
the gate, well and good; if not, I will bring dishonour to
your lord, and give you yourself a bad name. I will give
three shouts at the entrance to this gate such as will be no
less audible on Penryn Penwaedd [3] in Cornwall, and in
the depths of Dinsol in the north, and in Ysgeir Oervel [4]
in Ireland. Any pregnant woman in this court will mis-
carry, and the wombs of those who are not pregnant will
be oppressed and will overturn, so that the women will
never again bear children.' Glewlwyd Strong Grip replied, 'However much you rail against the customs of
Arthur's court, you shall not enter until I have gone inside and spoken with Arthur.'

Glewlwyd entered the hall, and Arthur said, 'Have you
news from the gate?' 'Two-thirds of my life have gone by,
and two-thirds of yours as well. I have been in Caer Se
and Asse, in Sach and Salach, in Lotor and Fotor, in
Greater India and Lesser India, and in the battle between
the two Ynyrs [5] when the twelve hostages were brought
from Norway. I have been in Europe and Africa, in the
islands of Corsica, in Caer Brythwch and Brythach, and in
Nerthach. I was there when you overcame the troops of
Gleis son of Merin, [6] when you killed Mil the Black son of
Dugum; I was there in the eastern part of the world when
you conquered Greece, in Caer Oeth and Anoeth, and in
Caer Nevenhyr Nineteeth. We have seen handsome noble-

3. Penryn Penwaedd = Penwith Point between Land's End and
Mousehole in Cornwall, *v. TYP*, p. 234.
4. Ysgeir Oervel = Sescenn Úairbeóil in Leinster, as found in the
Irish tale 'Bricriu's Feast'.
5. Ynyr = Honorius.   6. Gleis: stream; Merin: sea.

looking men, but I have never seen a man like the one who now stands at the entrance to the gate.' Arthur replied, 'If you came in walking go out running – an injunction upon the one who opens his eye and looks at the light and shuts his eye. Let some serve the lad with gold drinking horns, and others with hot peppered chops, until he has had his fill of meat and drink, for it is a wretched thing to leave out in the wind and rain such a man as you describe.' 'By my companion's hand,' said Kei, 'if you took my advice, you would not abandon the custom of the court for this lad's sake.' 'Not so, good Kei. We are noble men so long as others come to us, and the more gifts we distribute, the greater will be our reputation and fame and glory.'

So Glewlwyd returned to the gate and opened it for the lad, but whereas everyone else dismounted outside at the mounting-block, Culhwch rode in on his steed. 'Hail to the chief lord of this island!' he said. 'May the lower couches of this house be no worse than the upper, and may my greeting apply equally to your nobles and your company and your troops, without omitting anyone. As I greeted you properly, so may your trust and grace and glory be proper throughout this island.' 'In God's truth, so be it, chieftain. Hail to you also! Sit between two warriors and you shall have entertaining songs, and the status of a prince, an heir to the kingdom, for the length of your stay; moreover when I distribute presents to guests and foreigners I will begin with you.'

Culhwch replied, however, 'I did not come here to beg for food and drink. If my request is granted I will repay it and I will praise you; otherwise I will bear your shame to the farthest extent of your reputation in the four corners of the world.' 'Chieftain,' said Arthur, 'even though you do not stay, you shall have the request that head and tongue name, as far as the wind dries, as far as the rain wets, as far as the sun rises, as far as the sea stretches, as far as the earth extends, excepting only my ship, my mantle, my sword Caledvwlch,[7] my spear Rhongomynyad,[8] my shield Wynebgwrthucher,[9] my knife Carnwennan and my wife Gwenhwyvar.[10] 'In God's truth?' 'Name what you want, and you shall have it gladly.' 'I want my hair trimmed.' 'You shall have that,' and Arthur took a gold comb and silver-handled scissors and combed the lad's hair and asked who he was, saying, 'My heart grows tender towards you, and I know that you must come from my lineage. Tell me who you are.' 'I am Culhwch son of Kilydd son of the ruler Kelyddon, and Goleuddydd daughter of the ruler Amlawdd is my mother.' Arthur said, 'That is true. You are my first cousin – therefore state your desire and you shall have it, whatever mouth and tongue may name.' 'In God's truth, and the truth of your kingdom?' 'You shall have it gladly.' 'Then I ask for Olwen daughter of Chief Giant Ysbaddaden, and I invoke her in the name of your warriors.'

Culhwch invoked Olwen in the name of Kei, Bedwyr, Greidyawl Enemy Subduer, Gwythyr son of Greidyawl, Greid son of Eri, Kynddilig the guide, Tathal Honest Deceitful, Maelwys son of Baeddan,[11] Cnychwr son of Nes, Cubert son of Daere, Fercos son of Poch, Luber Beuthach, Corvil Bervach,[12] Gwynn son of Esni, Gwynn son of Nwyvre, Gwynn son of Nudd,[13] Edern son of Nudd, Cadwy son of Gereint, the ruler Fflewdwr Fflam, Rhuvawn[14] the

---

7. Caledvwlch=Excalibur.   8. Rhongomynyad: cutting spear.

9. Wynebgwrthucher: face of evening.

10. Gwenhwyvar: white phantom? The Irish Findabair of *The Cattle Raid of Cooley*?

11. Maelwys: noble pig; Baeddan: boar.

12. These names are borrowed from Irish tales. Cnychwr son of Nes=Conchobar son of Ness; Cubert son of Daere=Cú Roí son of Dáire; Fercos son of Poch=Fergus son of Róech; Luber Beuthach=Lóegaire Búadach; Corvil Bervach=Conall Cernach.

13. Nudd=Nodons, a British deity.

14. Rhuvawn=Rōmānus.

Radiant son of Deorthach, Bradwen son of Moren the
Noble, Moren the Noble himself, Dalldav son of Cunyn
Cov, the son of Alun of Dyved, the son of Seidi, the son of
Gwryon, Uchdryd Battle Protector, Kynwas Cwryvagyl,
Gwrhyr Fat Cattle, Ysberyr Cat Claw, Gallgoid the Killer,
Duach and Brathach and Nerthach the sons of Gwawr-
ddur Hunchback (these men were sprung from the high-
lands of Hell), Kilydd Hundred Holds, Canhastyr [15]
Hundred Hands, Cors Hundred Claws, Ysgeir Gulhwch
Govyncawn, [16] Drwst Iron Fist, Glewlwyd Strong Grip,
Llwch [17] Windy Hand, Anwas the Swift, Sinnoch son of
Seithved, Wadu son of Seithved, Naw [18] son of Seith-
ved, Gwenwynwyn son of Naw son of Seithved, Bedyw
son of Seithved, Gobrwy son of Echel Pierced Thigh, [19]
Echel Pierced Thigh himself, Mael son of Roycol,
Dadweir Blind Head, Garwyli son of Gŵyddawg
Gŵyr, [20] Gŵyddawg Gŵyr himself, Gormant [21] son of
Rica, Menw son of Teirwaedd, [22] Digon son of Alar, [23]
Selyv son of Sinoid, Gusg son of Achen, Nerth son of
Cadarn, [24] Drudwas son of Tryffin, Twrch [25] son of
Peryv, Twrch son of Anwas, Iona King of France, Sêl son
of Selgi, [26] Teregud son of Iaen, Sulyen son of Iaen, Brad-
wen son of Iaen, Moren son of Iaen, Siawn son of Iaen,
Caradawg son of Iaen, all men from Caer Dathal, and

15. Canhastyr: hundred holds.

16. Ysgeir Gulhwch Govyncawn: ridge of Culhwch the Reed-
cutter?

17. Llwch: borrowed from Irish Lug? The pronunciation is similar.

18. Seithved: seventh; Naw: nine.

19. Echell=Achilles. Pierced Thigh: v. p. 79 n. 23. Brân, like
Achilles, is shot in the foot.

20. gŵyr: bent, crooked, or Gŵyr=Gower.

21. Gormant: excess.

22. Teirwaedd: three cries.

23. Digon: sufficiency; Alar: surfeit.

24. Nerth: might; Cadarn: strong.

25. Twrch: boar; Peryv: lord.

26. Sêl: watch; Selgi: watchdog.

related to Arthur on his father's side, Dirmyg [27] son of
Caw, Iustig son of Caw, Edmyg [28] son of Caw, Angawdd
son of Caw, Govan son of Caw, Kelyn [29] son of Caw,
Conyn [30] son of Caw, Mabsant [31] son of Caw, Gwyngad
son of Caw, Llwybyr [32] son of Caw, Coch [33] son of Caw,
Meilyg son of Caw, Kynwal son of Caw, Ardwyad [34] son of
Caw, Ergyryad [35] son of Caw, Neb [36] son of Caw, Gildas
son of Caw, Calcas son of Caw, Hueil son of Caw, who
never submitted to a lord's hand, Samson Dry Lip, Chief
Bard Talyessin, Manawydan son of Llŷr, Llara [37] son of
the ruler Casnar, Ysberin son of King Fflergant [38] of Brit-
tany, Garanhon son of Glythvyr, Llawr [39] son of Erw,
Anynnawg son of Menw son of Teirwaedd, Gwynn son of
Nwyvre, Fflam [40] son of Nwyvre, Gereint son of Erbin,
Ermid son of Erbin, Dywel son of Erbin, Gwynn son of
Ermid, Kyndrwyn son of Ermid, Heveydd One Cloak,
Eiddon the Magnanimous, Rheidwn the Rough, Gormant son of Rica [41] (Arthur's brother on his mother's
side; his father was chief elder of Cornwall), Llawvrodedd
the Bearded, Nodawl Trimmed Beard, Berth son of
Cadwy, Rhun son of Beli, Ysgonan the Generous, Ysga-
wyn son of Panon, Morvran son of Tegid [42] (no man struck
him at Camlann [43] – because of his ugliness everyone

27. Dirmyg: contempt.
28. Edmyg: honour.
29. Kelyn: holly.
30. Conyn: stalk.
31. Mabsant: patron saint.
32. Llwybyr: path.
33. Coch: red.
34. Ardwyad: protector.
35. Ergyryad: attack.
36. Neb: someone.
37. Llara: meek.
38. Fflergant = Alan Fyrgan, Duke of Burgundy 1084–1112. An in-
terpolation?
39. Llawr: earth; Erw: acre.
40. Fflam: flame; Nwyvre: firmament.
41. Gormant son of Rica: some people are named twice.
42. Morvran: great raven; Tegid = Tacitus.
43. Camlann: perhaps the Roman fort of Camboglanna on
Hadrian's Wall, v. *TYP*, pp. 160–62. Geoffrey places it in Cornwall.

thought he was a devil helping, for there was hair on his face like the hair of a stag), Sanddev Angel Face (no man struck him at Camlann — because of his beauty everyone thought he was an angel helping), Saint Kynwyl (who was one of the three men to escape from Camlann; he was the last to leave Arthur, on his horse Hen Groen),[44] Uchdryd son of Erim, Eus son of Erim, Hen Was the Swift son of Erim, Hen Beddestyr son of Erim,[45] Sgilti Light Foot [46] son of Erim (three properties had these three men: Hen Beddestyr never found a man who could keep up with him, either on horseback or on foot; no four-footed creature could stay with Hen Was the Swift for even an acre, let alone anything more; when the desire to undertake an errand for his lord came upon Sgilti Light Foot, he never took the road so long as he knew his way, but if there was a forest he travelled along the tree tops, and if there was a mountain he travelled on the tips of the reeds, and never did a reed bend, much less break, so light of foot was he), Teithi the Old son of Gwynnan (whose kingdom the sea overran, and who came to Arthur after barely escaping; no hilt would remain attached to the blade of his knife, and for that reason he grew sick and feeble while he lived, and then he died), Carnedyr son of Govynyon the Old, Gwenwyn-wyn son of Naw, Arthur's premier fighter, Llygadrudd Emys [47] and Gwrvoddw the Old, both uncles of Arthur, his mother's brothers, Culvanawyd [48] son of Gwryon, Llenlleawg the Irishman from the headland of Gamon,

---

44. Hen Groen: old skin.
45. Hen Was: old servant; Hen Beddestyr: old walker.
46. Sgilti Light Foot = Caîlte of the Irish Find tales.
47. Llygadrudd: red eye; Emys: stallion.
48. Culvanawyd: slender awl.

Dyvynwal [49] the Bald, Dyvynarth King of the North, Teirnon Twrvliant, Tegvan the Lame, Tegyr the Cup Bearer,
Gwrddywal son of Evrei, Morgant the Wealthy, Gwystyl [50]
son of Nwython, Rhun son of Nwython, Llwydeu son of
Nwython, Gwydre son of Llwydeu by Gwenabwy daughter
of Caw (his uncle Hueil stabbed him, and the wound was
the source of a feud between Hueil and Arthur),[51] Drem
son of Dremidydd [52] (who from Kelli Wig [53] in Cornwall
could see a gnat rise with the sun at Penn Blathaon [54] in
Scotland), Eiddoel son of Ner, Gwlyddyn, the carpenter
who built Arthur's hall Ehangwen,[55] Kynyr Elegant Beard
(who was said to be Kei's father; he said to his wife,
'Woman, if there is anything of me in your son, his heart
will always be cold, nor will there be any warmth in his
hands; if he is my son, he will be stubborn; whenever he
carries a burden, whether great or small, it will be visible
neither from the front nor the rear; no one will brave fire
and water as well as he, nor will there be any official or
servant like him'), Hen Was and Hen Wyneb and Hen
Gedymddeith,[56] another Gallgoig (whenever he came to a
town, if he needed anything he would let no man sleep,
though there might be three hundred homes in the town),
Berwyn son of Kerenhyr,[57] Paris King of France (which is
why the city is called Paris), Osla Big Knife [58] (who carried

49. Dyvynwal=Dubnoualos.

50. Gwystyl: hostage.

51. On the quarrel between Hueil and Arthur, *v. TYP*, pp.
408–10.

52. Drem: sight; Dremidydd: sighter.

53. Kelli: wood. The exact location of Kelli Wig is uncertain,
v. TYP, pp. 3–4.

54. Blathaon: probably John o'Groats or Dunnet Head in Caith-
ness, *v. TYP*, pp. 233–4.

55. Ehangwen: wide and spacious.

56. Hen Wyneb: old face; Hen Gedymddeith: old companion.

57. Kerenhyr=Carantorix, 'king of kinsmen'.

58. Osla=Octha son of Hengist? *v. ALMA*, p. 42. Or Offa King
of Mercia 757–96? *v. BR*, p. 46.

Bronllavyn Short Broad; when Arthur and his troops came to a cresting flood, they would find a narrow spot; the knife in its sheath would be laid across the flood and that would be bridge enough for the three armies of the island of Britain and the three offshore islands, with all their plunder), Gŵyddawg son of Menestyr, who killed Kei and whom Arthur killed in revenge, Garanwyn [59] son of Kei, Amren son of Bedwyr, Eli, Myr, Rheu Easy Difficult, Rhun Red Alder, Eli and Trachmyr, Arthur's chief huntsmen, Llwyd son of Kil Coed, Huabwy son of Gwryon, Gwyn Godyvron, Gweir Servant of Birds and Gweir son of Cadellin Silver Brow and Gweir Brave Wicked and Gweir White Spear Shaft, all uncles of Arthur, his mother's brothers, the sons of Llwch Windy Hand from beyond the fierce sea, the Irishman Llenlleawg, who was the exalted one of Britain, Cas son of Seidi, Gwrvan Shaggy Hair, Gwilenhin King of France, Gwitart son of Aedd [60] King of Ireland, Garselid the Irishman, Panawr Battle Leader, Fflewdwr son of Naw, Gwynn Hyvar Steward of Devon and Cornwall, one of the nine who planned the Battle of Camlann, Kelli, Cuel, Gilla Stag Shank, who could leap three hundred acres in a single bound, and who was the chief leaper of Ireland, Sol and Gwadyn Osol and Gwadyn Oddeith [61] (Sol could stand all day on one foot; if Gwadyn Osol stood on the highest mountain in the world, it would become a level plain under his feet; like a warm mace drawn from the forge were the bright sparks from Gwadyn Oddeith's soles when he struck something hard, and he cleared the way for Arthur in battle), Erwm the Tall and Atrwm the Tall (the day they came to a feast they would seize three cantrevs for their wants and they would eat until noon and drink until night; when they went to sleep they would devour the heads of insects out of hunger, as if they had

59. Garanwyn: white shank.
60. Aedd=Áed in Irish.
61. Gwadyn: sole; Oddeith: bonfire.

never eaten; when they went to a feast they left neither fat nor lean, hot nor cold, pure nor fresh, green nor salted), Huarwar son of Avlawn [62] (who requested his fill of Arthur. He was one of the three great plagues of Devon and Cornwall until he had eaten his fill, and never was there seen on him a trace of a smile unless he was sated), Gwarae Golden Hair, the two pups of the bitch Rhymhi, Gwyddrud, Gwydden the Difficult, Sugyn son of Sugynedydd [63] (who could suck up a sea on which there were three hundred ships until it was nothing but a dry strand; he had a red heart hidden within him), Cacamwri, Arthur's servant (show him a barn, and though there be a track for thirty ploughs within, he would strike the barn with an iron flail until the planks and cross-beams were no better off than the small oats at the bottom), Llwng, Dygyvlwng, Anoeth the Bold, Eiddyl the Tall and Amren the Tall (two of Arthur's servants), Gwevyl son of Gwastad [64] (when he was sad he would let one lip droop to his navel and raise the other until it was a hood over his head), Uchdryd Cross Beard, who could throw his fixed red beard over fifty rafters in Arthur's hall, Elidyr the Guide, Ysgyrdav and Ysgudydd (two servants of Gwenhwyvar; on an errand their feet were as swift as their thoughts), Brys [65] son of Brysethach from the valley of black fernery in Scotland, Gwydolwyn the Dwarf, Bwlch, Kyvwlch and Syvwlch sons of Cleddyv Kyvwlch [66] grandsons of Cleddyv Divwlch (three bright shinings their three shields, three piercing stabs their three spears, three sharp blades their three swords, Glas, Glessig and Gleisyad their three dogs, Call, Cuall and Cavall [67] their three horses,

62. Avlawn: not full.

63. Sugyn: suction; Sugynedydd: pump.

64. Gwevyl: lip; Gwastad: level.   65. Brys: haste.

66. Bwlch: gap; Kyvwlch: complete; Cleddyv: sword; Divwlch: continuous.

67. Call: wise; Cuall: foolish; Cavall: horse.

Hwyrddyddwg, Drwgddyddwg and Llwyrddyddwg[68] their
three wives, Och, Garym and Diasbad[69] their three grandchildren, Lluched, Neued and Eissywed[70] their three
daughters, Drwg, Gwaeth and Gwaethav Oll[71] their three
maids), Eheubryd daughter of Kyvwlch, Gorasgwrn[72]
daughter of Nerth, Gwaeddan daughter of Kynvelyn,[73]
Keudawg Half Wit, Dwnn[74] the Vigorous Chief, Eiladar
son of Penn Llarcan, Kynedyr the Wild son of Hetwn
Silver Brow, Sawyl High Head, Gwalchmei son of Gwyar,
Gwalhaved[75] son of Gwyar, Gwrhyr Interpreter of
Languages, who knew all tongues, Kethtrwm the Priest,
Clust son of Clustveinydd[76] (were he buried seven fathoms
in the earth he would hear an ant stirring from its bed
in the morning fifty miles away), Medyr son of Medyredydd[77] (who from Kelli Wig could hit a wren in Ysgeir
Oervel in Ireland through both legs), Gwiawn Cat Eye
(who could cut a corner from a gnat's eye without harming
the eye), Ôl son of Olwydd[78] (whose father's pigs were
carried off seven months before he was born; when he
grew up he tracked down the pigs and brought them home
in seven herds), the bishop Bidwini, who blessed food and

68. Hwyrddyddwg: late bringer; Drwgddyddwg: evil bringer;
Llwyrddyddwg: complete bringer.

69. Och: groan; Garym: shout; Diasbad: outcry.

70. Lluched: plague; Neued: want; Eissywed: need.

71. Drwg: bad; Gwaeth: worse; Gwaethav Oll: worst of all.
As Cavall is elsewhere the name of Arthur's dog (the name notwith-
standing), and as Hwyrddyddwg, Drwgddyddwg and Llwyrddyddwg
seem more appropriate for horses than for wives, it is possible that
Glas, Glessig and Gleisyad refer to the swords, Call, Cuall and Cavall
to the dogs, etc.

72. Gorasgwrn: big bone; Nerth: might.

73. Kynvelyn=Cunobelinos, Cymbeline.

74. Dwnn: brown.

75. Gwalhaved: probably no connection with Galahad.

76. Clust: ear; Clustveinydd: hearer.

77. Medyr: aim; Medyredydd: aimer.

78. Ôl: track; Olwydd: tracker.

drink, and finally the gentle gold-torqued women of this
island: the first lady of the island Gwenhwyvar, her sister
Gwenhwyach, Rathtyen the only daughter of Clememyl,
Kelemon daughter of Kei, Tangwen daughter of Gweir
Servant of Birds, Gwenn Alarch [79] daughter of Kynwal
Hundred Hogs, Eurneid daughter of Clydno of Edin-
burgh,[80] Eneuawg daughter of Bedwyr, Enrydreg daughter
of Tuduathar, Gwenwledyr daughter of Gwawrddur the
Hunchback, Erdudvyl daughter of Tryffin, Eurolwyn
daughter of Gwydolwyn the Dwarf, Teleri daughter of
Peul, Indeg daughter of Garwy the Tall, Morvudd daughter of Uryen of Rheged,[81] Gwenn Lliant,[82] a fair and
generous girl, Creiddylad daughter of Lludd Silver
Hand [83] (the most majestic girl ever in Britain or the three
offshore islands; for her Gwythyr son of Greidyawl and
Gwynn son of Nudd fight every May Day until the Judgement), Ellylw daughter of Neol Hang Cock, who lived
three generations, Essyllt White Neck and Essyllt Slender
Neck [84] – in the name of all these Culhwch invoked his
request.

Arthur then said, 'Chieftain, I have heard nothing of
this girl, nor of her parents, but I will gladly send messengers to learn of her.' That night messengers set out,
and when at the end of a year they had found nothing
Culhwch said, 'Everyone else has obtained his request but
I am still waiting. I will leave, and bear your shame with
me.' 'Chieftain, you are not fair to Arthur,' said Kei.

79. Gwenn Alarch: white swan.

80. Clydno: famous, renowned. Edinburgh: the area surrounding
the present city of Edinburgh. Clydno appears to have been a leader
of northern Britain in the late sixth century.

81. Uryen of Rheged: according to Nennius, Uryen and Morgant
and Gwallawg fought against the Northumbrians Hussa and Theodric
in the late sixth century. Uryen=Ōrbogenos, 'well born'.

82. Gwenn Lliant: white flood.

83. Lludd Silver Hand: probably a mistake for Nudd, cf. the
Irish name Núadu Silver Hand.   84. Essyllt=Isolt, Isolde.

'Come with us – until you say that the girl does not exist or until we find her we will not leave you.' Kei rose then. He had this talent: nine days and nine nights his breath would last under water, and nine days and nine nights he could go without sleep. No doctor could cure the wound from Kei's sword. He could be as tall as the tallest tree in the forest when he pleased, while when the rain was heaviest a hand's span about what was in his hand would be dry by reason of the heat he generated, and when his companions were coldest that would be kindling for the lighting of a fire.

Arthur also summoned Bedwyr, who never avoided any errand on which Kei went. No one in the island was as handsome as Bedwyr, save only Arthur and Drych [85] son of Kibddar, and though he was one-handed no three warriors on the same field could draw blood faster than he; moreover he would make one thrust with his spear and nine counter-thrusts. Arthur called upon Kynddilig the Guide, saying, 'Accompany the chieftain on this errand,' for Kynddilig was no worse guide in a country he had never seen than in his own; he summoned Gwrhyr Interpreter of Languages, who knew every tongue, and Gwalchmei son of Gwyar, since the latter never returned without fulfilling his errand, and was moreover the best walker and rider, and was Arthur's nephew, his sister's son and his first cousin as well. Finally Arthur summoned Menw son of Teirwaedd, for if they came to a pagan land Menw could cast a spell through which they could see everyone and no one could see them.

This party rode out until they reached a great level plain and saw a fortress, the strongest one ever. They journeyed throughout the day, and when they expected to reach the fortress they were no nearer than at first; yet as they travelled along the plain they could see a great flock of sheep with neither end nor limit to it, and a shepherd

85. Drych: look, appearance.

watching from the top of a mound, a cloak of skins on him, and a shaggy mastiff at his side, larger than a nine-year-old stallion. He had never lost a lamb, much less a sheep, nor did there pass him any company which he did not harm or wound mortally, for his breath had burned every dead tree and bush on the plain to the ground.

Kei said to Gwrhyr Interpreter of Languages, 'Go and talk to that man over there.' 'Kei, I never promised to go any farther than you did, so let us go together,' said Gwrhyr, and Menw son of Teirwaedd said, 'Do not worry – I will put a spell on the dog so that it harms no one.' They approached the shepherd and said, 'You are well off, shepherd.' 'May you never be better off than I,' was the reply. 'By God, because you are the head man.' 'Apart from my wife, no wound annoys me.' 'Whose sheep are you tending, and whose is the fortress?' 'Everyone knows that this is the fortress of Chief Giant Ysbaddaden.' 'And who are you?' 'Custenhin [86] son of Mynwyedig, and because of my wife Chief Giant Ysbaddaden has ruined me. And who are you?' 'Messengers of Arthur who have come for Olwen.' 'God protect you, men – for all the world, do not say that, for no one who made that request has ever left here alive.'

Then the shepherd rose, and Culhwch gave him a gold ring; he tried to put it on but it did not fit, so he put it in the finger of his glove and went home and gave it to his wife. She took the ring out and asked, 'Where did this ring come from? It is not often you find treasure.' 'I went to the sea to find sea-food, and what did I see but a body washing in on the tide. I never saw so beautiful a body, and on its finger I found this ring.' 'The sea strips dead men of their jewels – show me the body.' 'Wife, you will see the owner of that body here soon.' 'Who is he?' she asked. 'Culhwch son of Kilydd son of the ruler Kelyddon, by Goleuddydd daughter of the ruler Amlawdd – he has

86. Custenhin=Constantine.

come for Olwen.' The woman had divided feelings: she was happy that her nephew, her sister's son, was coming, but she was sad because she had never seen anyone who came with that request depart with his life.

The visitors came on to the gate of the shepherd Custenhin's court, and when his wife heard the clamour of their arrival she ran out to give them a joyful welcome. Kei drew a log from the woodpile as she approached and sought to embrace them, and when he thrust the log between her two hands she squeezed it into a twisted coil. 'Woman, had it been I whom you squeezed so, no one else would ever need to love me,' said Kei. 'A bad sort of love yours!' They entered the house and their needs were seen to, and after a while, when everyone was busy, the woman opened a chest near the hearth and out jumped a lad with curly yellow hair. Gwrhyr said, 'A shame to hide such a lad as this. I know it is not his own fault that he is so treated,' and the woman replied, 'He is the last one; Chief Giant Ysbaddaden has killed twenty-three of my sons, and there is no more hope for this one than there was for the others.' Kei said, 'Let him come along as my companion; he shall not be slain unless I am.'

Then they ate, and the woman asked, 'On what errand have you come?' 'We have come to ask for Olwen.' 'As no one from the fortress has yet seen you, for God's sake, turn back!' 'God knows, we will not turn back until we have seen the girl – will she come to some place where she can be seen?' 'She comes here every Saturday to wash her hair; she leaves her rings in the washing bowl, and neither she nor her messenger ever comes after them.' 'Will she come if she is sent for?' 'God knows, I will not sell myself by betraying the one who trusts me, but if you swear to do her no harm I will send for her.' 'We swear.' Messengers were sent and Olwen came, dressed in a flame-red silk robe, with a torque of red gold round her neck, studded with precious pearls and rubies. Her hair was yellower

than broom, her skin whiter than sea-foam, her palms and
fingers were whiter than shoots of marsh trefoil against
the sand of a welling spring. Neither the eye of a mewed
hawk nor the eye of a thrice-mewed falcon was fairer than
hers; her breasts were whiter than the breast of a white
swan, her cheeks were redder than the reddest foxgloves,
and anyone who saw her would fall deeply in love.
Wherever she went four white trefoils appeared behind
her, and for that reason she was called Olwen.[87]

She entered the house and sat between Culhwch and
the best chair, and he recognized her as soon as he saw her.
'Lady, it is you I love – will you come with me?' 'I may
not, for fear of bringing sin upon us both. My father has
made me promise that I will not go without his consent,
for he can live only until I take a husband. I will give
you advice, however, if you will take it: go to my father
and ask for me, and whatever he asks you for promise to
get it, and then you shall have me; if he doubts you,
however, you will not get me, and you will be fortunate to
escape with your life.' 'I promise to do that, and I will
obtain everything,' said Culhwch.

Olwen went to her room then; they rose and followed
her to the fortress, where they killed nine gatekeepers at
nine different gates, without a man making a sound, and
nine mastiffs without so much as a growl being raised.
They entered the hall and said, 'Hail, Chief Giant
Ysbaddaden, in the name of God and man!' 'Where are
you all going?' 'We are seeking your daughter for
Culhwch son of Kilydd.' 'Where are those good-for-
nothing servants of mine? Prop up the forks under my
eyelids so I can see what my son-in-law is like,' said the
Chief Giant, and this was done. Then he said, 'Come
back tomorrow and I will have some sort of answer for
you.' They rose to go, but Ysbaddaden seized one of the
three poisoned stone spears that were near at hand and

87. Olwen: interpreted as white track.

threw it at them; Bedwyr caught it and threw it back and struck Ysbaddaden right in the kneecap. 'You cursed barbarian of a son-in-law! Now it will be harder to walk uphill. The poisoned iron has hurt like the sting of a gadfly; cursed be the smith who made it and the anvil on which it was made – that's how painful it is.'

They slept that night in Custenhin's house, and next day they put fine combs in their hair and made a majestic entrance into the hall and said, 'Chief Giant Ysbaddaden, give us your daughter in exchange for her marriage fee and the virgin's gift to you and her two kinswomen; otherwise you shall meet your death on her account.' 'She and her four great-grandfathers and her four great-grandmothers are still alive, and I must confer with them.' 'Then do so – we will go to eat.' As they rose Ysbaddaden took a second stone spear which he had nearby and threw it after them, but Menw son of Teirwaedd caught it and threw it back so that it pierced him in the chest and came out in the small of his back. 'You cursed barbarian of a son-in-law! That hard iron hurt me like the bite of a hole-headed leech. Cursed be the forge on which it was heated, for now when I go uphill I will suffer from chest pains and stomach aches and frequent loss of appetite.'

They went to eat then, and when they returned the third day they said, 'Chief Giant Ysbaddaden, shoot at us no more, do not be the cause of your being injured and wounded and killed.' 'Where are my servants? Raise up the forks under my eyelids – they have drooped over my eyeballs – so that I may see what my son-in-law is like.' Then they rose, whereupon Ysbaddaden took a third poisoned stone spear and threw it after them, but Culhwch caught it and threw it back, aiming at the Chief Giant's eyeball so that the spear came out through the base of his neck. 'You cursed barbarian of a son-in-law! The sight of my eyes will be that much worse as long as I live, and when the wind blows in my face they will water, and I will suffer headaches and dizzy spells every new moon. The poisoned spear has pierced me like the bite of a mad dog – cursed be the forge on which it was heated.'

The company went to eat, and the next day they returned to the court and said, 'Do not shoot at us any more; do not seek harm and injury and martyrdom for yourself, or even worse if you insist. Give us your daughter.' 'Where is he who was told to ask for my daughter?' 'I am he,' said Culhwch son of Kilydd. 'Come here so I can see you.' A chair was brought and the two sat face to face, and Chief Giant Ysbaddaden said, 'Are you the one who seeks my daughter?' 'I am.' 'I want you to promise that you will not be less than fair to me.' 'I promise.' 'When I get what I ask for then you shall have my daughter.' 'Then name what you want.'

'That I will,' said Ysbaddaden. 'Do you see that great thicket out there?' 'I do,' said Culhwch. 'I want it uprooted and burned on the ground, down to cinders and ashes for manure; I want it ploughed and sown so that by the time the dew has dried in the morning it is ready for harvest, so that it can be made into food and drink for the wedding guests of my daughter and yourself. And I want all this done in one day.' 'It will be easy for me to get that, though you think otherwise.'

'Though you get that, there are things you will not get. I want a ploughman to till the land; no one but Amathaon son of Dôn will do, and he will not come of his own free will, nor can you compel him.' 'It will be easy for me to get that, though you think otherwise.'

'Though you get that, there are things you will not get. Govannon son of Dôn is to come to the headland to deliver the irons; he will not do the work of his own will, except for a rightful king, nor can you compel him.' 'It will be easy for me to get that, though you think otherwise.'

'Though you get that, there are things you will not get.

The two oxen of Gwlwlwyd Chestnut Hair [88] to be yoked together and to plough this rocky ground; he will not give them up of his own will, nor can you compel him.' 'It will be easy for me to get that, though you think otherwise.'

'Though you get that, there are things you will not get. I want the Yellow Pale-White and the Spotted Ox [89] yoked together.' 'It will be easy for me to get that, though you think otherwise.'

'Though you get that, there are things you will not get. There are two horned oxen, one on the far side of Mynydd Bannawg [90] and one on the near side; I want them yoked under one harness. They are Nynnyaw and Peibyaw, and God turned them into oxen because of their sins.' 'It will be easy for me to get that, though you think otherwise.'

'Though you get that, there are things you will not get. Do you see that ploughed field?' 'I see it.' 'When I first met the mother of my daughter nine hestors of linseed were sown there, and neither black nor white has appeared. I have the measure still, and I want the linseed sown in that newly ploughed soil to make a linen veil for my daughter on her wedding day.' 'It will be easy for me to get that, though you think otherwise.'

'Though you get that, there are things you will not get. Honey nine times sweeter than that of a first swarm, but without drones or bees; I want to make bragget for the wedding feast.' 'It will be easy for me to get that, though you think otherwise.'

'Though you get that, there are things you will not get. The cup of Llwyr [91] son of Llwyryon, which holds the best

88. 'Triad 45' refers to the chestnut ox of Gwlwlwyd, rather than the ox of chestnut-haired Gwlwlwyd.

89. Yellow Pale-White, Spotted Ox: also mentioned in 'Triad 45'.

90. Mynydd Bannawg: horned mountain.

91. Llwyr: complete.

drink, for it is the only cup in the world which can hold such strong drink. He will not yield it of his own will, nor can you compel him.' 'It will be easy for me to get that, though you think otherwise.'

'Though you get that, there are things you will not get. The hamper of Gwyddno Long Shank, for were the entire world to gather round it, twenty-seven men at a time, everyone would find the food he liked best. I want to eat from it on the night my daughter sleeps with you – Gwyddno will not give it to you of his own will, nor can you compel him.' 'It will be easy for me to get that, though you think otherwise.'

'Though you get that, there are things you will not get. We want to pour that night from the horn of Gwlgawd of Gododdin;[92] he will not give it to you of his own will, nor can you compel him.' 'It will be easy for me to get that, though you think otherwise.'

'Though you get that, there are things you will not get. I want the harp of Teirtu to entertain me that night. When a man pleases it will play by itself, or it will be silent if silence is wanted. Teirtu will not give it to you of his own will, nor can you compel him.' 'It will be easy for me to get that, though you think otherwise.'

'Though you get that, there are things you will not get. The Birds of Rhiannon, who wake the dead and lull the living – I want them to entertain me that night.' 'It will be easy for me to get that, though you think otherwise.'

'Though you get that, there are things you will not get. I want the cauldron of Diwrnach the Irishman, steward to Odgar son of Aedd King of Ireland, to boil meat for the wedding feast.' 'It will be easy for me to get that, though you think otherwise.'

'Though you get that, there are things you will not get. I must wash my hair and shave my beard, and I want the

92. Gododdin: the territory of the Votadini in northern Britain.

tusk of Chief Boar Ysgithyrwyn [93] in order to shave, nor will I be any better for it unless it is taken while the boar is still alive.' 'It will be easy for me to get that, though you think otherwise.'

'Though you get that, there are things you will not get. The tusk can be drawn only by Odgar son of Aedd King of Ireland.' 'It will be easy for me to get that, though you think otherwise.'

'Though you get that, there are things you will not get. I will not entrust this tusk to anyone but Caw of Scotland, who possesses the sixty cantrevs of Scotland; he will not leave his kingdom of his own will, nor can you compel him.' 'It will be easy for me to get that, though you think otherwise.'

'Though you get that, there are things you will not get. I must untangle my beard before I can shave it, and it will never straighten out until you get the blood of the Black Hag, daughter of the White Hag, from the headland of the Valley of Distress in the highlands of Hell.' 'It will be easy for me to get that, though you think otherwise.'

'Though you get that, there are things you will not get. The blood will not be effective unless you get it while it is still warm, and no vessel anywhere will keep liquid warm save the bottles of Gwydolwyn the Dwarf: these retain the heat of what is poured in the east until one reaches the west. He will not give them to you of his own will, nor can you compel him.' 'It will be easy for me to get that, though you think otherwise.'

'Though you get that, there are things you will not get. Some will want milk, but there will be no getting milk for everyone unless you first get the bottles of Rhynnon Stiff Beard, for no liquid in those bottles ever sours. He will not give them of his own will, nor can you compel him.' 'It will be easy for me to get that, though you think otherwise.'

93. Ysgithyrwyn: white tusk.

'Though you get that, there are things you will not get. In all the world there are no comb and shears that can straighten out my tangled hair, except for the comb and shears that lie between the ears of Twrch Trwyth [94] son of the ruler Taredd. He will not give them of his own will, nor can you compel him.' 'It will be easy for me to get that, though you think otherwise.'

'Though you get that, there are things you will not get. Twrch Trwyth cannot be hunted until you first get Drudwyn, the pup of Greid son of Eri.' 'It will be easy for me to get that, though you think otherwise.'

'Though you get that, there are things you will not get. There is in all the world no leash that will hold Drudwyn save for the leash of Cors Hundred Claws.' 'It will be easy for me to get that, though you think otherwise.'

'Though you get that, there are things you will not get. There is no collar in the world that will hold the leash save for the collar of Canhastyr Hundred Hands.' 'It will be easy for me to get that, though you think otherwise.'

'Though you get that, there are things you will not get. The chain of Kilydd Hundred Holds must attach the collar to the leash.' 'It will be easy for me to get that, though you think otherwise.'

'Though you get that, there are things you will not get. No houndsman in the world can manage that hound, except for Mabon son of Modron,[95] who was abducted from his mother when he was three nights old. No one knows where he is, or whether he is alive or dead.' 'It will be easy for me to get that, though you think otherwise.'

'Though you get that, there are things you will not get. Gwynn Dun Mane, the horse of Gweddw (swift as a wave) for Mabon to ride when hunting – Gweddw will not yield the horse of his own will, nor can you compel him.' 'It will be easy for me to get that, though you think otherwise.'

94. Twrch: boar; Trwyth: cf. Irish *tríath*, boar?
95. Mabon son of Modron: *v.* Introduction, pp. 17–18.

'Though you get that, there are things you will not get. Since you do not know where Mabon is, you will never find him unless you first seek out Eiddoel son of Ner; he is Mabon's first cousin and will be ardent in the search for his kinsman.' 'It will be easy for me to get that, though you think otherwise.'

'Though you get that, there are things you will not get. Garselid the Irishman is the chief houndsman of Ireland, and Twrch Trwyth cannot be hunted without him.' 'It will be easy for me to get that, though you think otherwise.'

'Though you get that, there are things you will not get. A leash from the beard of Dillus the Bearded, since nothing else will hold the two pups – but it will be of no use unless it is drawn from his face while he is still alive and plucked out with wooden tweezers. He will not allow that while he lives, and if he is dead the beard will be of no use, for it will be brittle.' 'It will be easy for me to get that, though you think otherwise.'

'Though you get that, there are things you will not get. No houndsman in the world can hold the two pups except for Kynedyr the Wild son of Hetwn the Leper; he is nine times wilder than the wildest beast on the mountain, and you will never get him, nor my daughter either.' 'It will be easy for me to get that, though you think otherwise.'

'Though you get that, there are things you will not get. You cannot hunt Twrch Trwyth until you first get Gwynn son of Nudd, in whom God has set the energy of the demons of Annwvyn, in order to prevent the destruction of this world, and Gwynn cannot be let loose.' 'It will be easy for me to get that, though you think otherwise.'

'Though you get that, there are things you will not get. No horse in the world will avail Gwynn in hunting Twrch

Trwyth save Du[96] the horse of Moro Battle Leader.' 'It
will be easy for me to get that, though you think otherwise.'

'Though you get that, there are things you will not get.
Twrch Trwyth cannot be hunted unless Gwilenhin King
of France comes; it would be wrong for him to leave his
country and he will never come.' 'It will be easy for me
to get that, though you think otherwise.'

'Though you get that, there are things you will not get.
Twrch Trwyth can never be hunted unless you get the
son of Alun of Dyved to come; he is a good unleasher.'
'It will be easy for me to get that, though you think otherwise.'

'Though you get that, there are things you will not get.
Twrch Trwyth can never be hunted unless you get Aned
and Aethlem; they are swift as a gust of wind, and never
were they loosed on an animal they did not kill.' 'It will
be easy for me to get that, though you think otherwise.'

'Though you get that, there are things you will not get.
Arthur and his companions must come and hunt Twrch
Trwyth, for he is a powerful man; yet he will not come,
for he is under my thumb.' 'It will be easy for me to get
that, though you think otherwise.'

'Though you get that, there are things you will not get.
Twrch Trwyth can never be hunted until you get Bwlch
and Kyvwlch and Syvwlch, the sons of Kilydd Kyvwlch
and grandsons of Cleddyv Divwlch. Three bright shinings
their three shields, three piercing stabs their three spears,
three sharp blades their three swords, Glas, Glessig and
Gleisyad their three dogs, Call, Cuall and Cavall their
three horses, Hwyrddyddwg, Drwgddyddwg and Llwyrddyddwg their three wives, Och, Garym and Diasbad their
three grandchildren, Lluched, Neued and Eissywed their
three daughters, Drwg, Gwaeth and Gwaethav Oll their

96. Du: black. Du Moro is mentioned in 'Triad 44', *v. TYP*, pp.
113–14.

three maids. When these men sound their horns everyone will come and cry out, until the sky could fall and no one would care.' 'It will be easy for me to get that, though you think otherwise.'

'Though you get that, there are things you will not get. The sword of Wrnach the Giant, who cannot be killed save with this sword. He will give it to no one, not for price nor blessing, nor can you compel him.' 'It will be easy for me to get that, though you think otherwise.'

'Though you get that, there are things you will not get. In seeking these things you will lie awake at night, but you will not get them, nor will you get my daughter.' 'I have horses and horsemen, and my lord and cousin Arthur will get everything for me; I will win your daughter and you shall lose your life.' 'Then go – you shall not be responsible for feeding and clothing my daughter. Seek these things, and when you find them you shall have my daughter.'

They rode all day until evening, when they saw a fortress built of finished stone, the largest fortress in the world, and a black man, greater than three men of this world, coming from it. 'Where are you coming from?' they asked. 'From the fortress you see,' the man answered. 'Whose fortress is it?' 'How slow-witted you are! There is no one in the whole world who does not know that this is the fortress of Wrnach the Giant.' 'How are guests and foreigners received here?' 'God save you from asking, chieftain. No guest who ever came here has left alive, nor is anyone allowed in unless he brings a craft.'

Then they made for the gate, where Gwrhyr the Interpreter asked, 'Is there a gatekeeper here?' 'There is, and for asking that may your head not be yours.' 'Open the gate.' 'I will not.' 'Why not?' 'Knife has gone into meat, drink into horn, and there is a great throng in Wrnach's hall. Except for a craftsman who brings his craft the gate will not be opened.' 'Gatekeeper, I have a craft,'

said Kei. 'What is that?' 'I am the best burnisher of swords
in the world.' 'I will go and tell Wrnach the Giant, and
will return with an answer.'

The gatekeeper entered the hall and Wrnach said,
'Have you news from the gate?' 'I have. There is a company at the entrance to the gate, and they wish to enter.'
'Ask whether they have any skills.' 'I did that, and one of
them said he could burnish swords.' 'I need such a man,
for I have spent some time looking for someone to burnish
my sword without finding anyone. Since he has brought a
craft, let that man enter.' The gatekeeper went and opened
the gate, and Kei entered by himself and greeted Wrnach.
A chair was brought for him, and then Wrnach said, 'Is
it true what is said about your being able to burnish
swords?' 'I do that,' said Kei. The sword was brought in,
and he took a marked whetstone from under his arm and
asked, 'Do you prefer it dark-hilted or light-hilted?' 'Do
what you like, just as if it were your own sword.' Kei
cleaned half of one side of the blade and put it in the
giant's hand, asking, 'Are you content with that?' 'I
would rather the whole of it looked as well than everything in my kingdom. A pity a man like you has no companions.' 'Well, sir, I do have a companion, though he does
not practise the same craft.' 'Who is he?' 'Let the gatekeeper go out and I will tell you about his talents. The
head of his spear will leave its shaft and draw blood and
then return to the shaft.' So the gate was opened and
Bedwyr entered, and Kei said, 'Bedwyr has a wonderful
gift, though he does not practise this craft.'

Outside there was among the men a great argument.
Kei and Bedwyr entered, and a young lad, the only
son of the shepherd Custenhin, went in at the same
time; he and those companions who stayed with him went
over the three walls as if they thought it nothing, until
they reached the fortress, whereupon his companions said,
'Custenhin's son is the best of men,' and thereafter he

was called Goreu [97] son of Custenhin. These men made for
the separate lodgings in order to kill the lodgekeepers
without the giant's knowing.

The burnishing of the sword being finished Kei gave
the weapon to Wrnach, as if to let him see whether he
was satisfied. The giant said, 'This is good work and I am
content with it.' Then Kei said, 'It is your scabbard which
has damaged your sword; give it to me, and I will take
out the wooden sidepieces and make new ones.' He took
the scabbard in one hand and the sword in the other,
and held them over the giant's head as if he meant to
sheathe the sword, but instead he thrust it into the giant
and took his head off with one blow. Then they plundered
the fortress and took such treasure as they wanted, and
after exactly one year they returned to Arthur's court,
bringing the sword with them. They told how they had
fared, and Arthur said, 'Which of these wonders should
we seek first?' 'It would be best to go after Mabon son of
Modron,' they said, 'and there is no getting him until his
kinsman Eiddoel son of Ner is found.'

So Arthur and the warriors of Britain rose and went
forth to seek Eiddoel, and they came to the outer wall of
Glini's fortress, where Eiddoel was held prisoner. Glini
stood on top of the wall and said, 'Arthur, since you will
not leave me in peace on this rock, what do you want of
me?·I have no good and no pleasure here, neither wheat
nor oats, and now you come to do me harm.' 'I have not
come to do you harm,' Arthur replied, 'only to ask for the
prisoner you hold.' 'I did not intend to give him to anyone, but I will give him to you, and you shall have my
support and strength as well.' Then the men said to
Arthur, 'Lord, go back, for you ought not to accompany
the host on this sort of petty errand.' 'Gwrhyr Interpreter

97. Goreu: best. Possibly an error for Gorneu – Custenhin Gorneu:
Custenhin the Cornishman. In 'Gereint', Custenhin is the father of
the Cornish ruler Erbin, *v. TYP*, pp. 346–7.

of Languages,' said Arthur, 'it will be proper for you to go on this errand, for you know all tongues and can speak with some of the birds and animals. Eiddoel, it is right for you to accompany my men in seeking your cousin. Kei and Bedwyr, I hope that you will obtain whatever you seek – go on this errand on my behalf.'

These men went on until they found the Ousel of Kilgwri, and Gwrhyr asked, 'For God's sake, do you know anything of Mabon son of Modron, who when three nights old was stolen away from between his mother and the wall?' 'When I first came here,' answered the ousel, 'there was a smith's anvil. I was a young bird then, and since that time no work has been done on the anvil except by my beak every night. Today there is not so much as a nut that has not been worn away, and yet God's revenge on me if in all that time I have heard anything of the man you seek. Nevertheless I will do what is right by Arthur's messengers. There is a kind of creature which God made even before me, and I will guide you to it.'

They then went to the Stag of Rhedenvre, and said, 'Stag of Rhedenvre, we are Arthur's messengers, and we have come to you because we know of no animal which is older. Tell us if you know anything of Mabon son of Modron, who was stolen from his mother when three nights old.' 'When I first came here,' said the stag, 'there was only a single antler on either side of my head, and no tree here but a single hazel oak which then grew into an oak of one hundred branches; thereafter the tree fell and today there is nothing left but a red stump. I have been here since that day and have heard nothing of the man you seek, but since you are Arthur's messengers, I will guide you to an animal which God made before me.'

They came to the Owl of Cwm Cawlwyd [98] and said, 'Owl of Cwm Cawlwyd, these are messengers from Arthur. Do you know anything of Mabon son of Modron, who was

98. Cwm: valley, glen.

stolen from his mother when three nights old?' 'If I knew I would tell you. When I first came here the great valley which you see before you was a wooded glen; the race of man came and destroyed it, whereupon a second forest grew up, and this forest is the third. As for me, my wings are now nothing but stumps. To this day I have heard nothing of the man you seek, but I will guide Arthur's messengers to the oldest animal in the world and the one which has travelled the most, the Eagle of Gwernabwy.'

Gwrhyr then said, 'Eagle of Gwernabwy, we are messengers from Arthur who have come to ask if you know anything of Mabon son of Modron, who was stolen from his mother when three nights old.' 'I came here long ago,' answered the eagle, 'and when I first came I had a stone from the top of which I pecked at the stars every evening, and now that stone is not a hand's-breadth in height. I have been here from that day to this, and I have heard nothing of the man you seek except when I made a trip to look for food at Llyn Llyw.[99] There I sank my claws into a salmon, expecting that it would feed me for a long time, but it drew me down into the water, so that I barely escaped. I returned with all my relatives to destroy the fish, but it sent messengers to make peace, and came itself to have fifty tridents pulled out of its back. Unless this salmon knows something of the one you seek I know of none who might know anything. I will guide you to it.'

They came to that place, and the eagle said, 'Salmon of Llyn Llyw, I have come with Arthur's messengers to ask if you know anything of Mabon son of Modron, who was stolen from his mother when three nights old.' 'I will tell you as much as I know. I swim upstream on every tide until I reach Gloucester, where I found such evil as I had never found before. That you may believe me let one of you ride on my shoulders.'

99. Llyn: lake.

So Kei and Gwrhyr rode on the salmon's shoulders
until they came to the prisoner's enclosure, and they heard
moaning and wailing from the other side of the wall, and
Gwrhyr said, 'Who is crying in this stone house?' 'Alas,
there is reason for this man to lament: Mabon son of
Modron is here, and no one was ever so harshly imprisoned, not Lludd Silver Hand, not Greid son of Eri.'[100]
'Is there any hope of securing your release through gold
or silver or worldly wealth, or through battle and fighting?' 'Such release as is got for me will be got by fighting.' So they returned to Arthur and told him where
Mabon's prison was; Arthur summoned the warriors of
this island and went to Gloucester where Mabon was
prisoner, but Kei and Bedwyr rode on the salmon's shoulders. While Arthur's men were fighting at the fortress Kei
broke through the wall of the enclosure and rescued the
prisoner on his back, besides fighting with the men; then
Arthur returned home, and with him Mabon, a free man.

'Which of these wonders should we go after now?' asked
Arthur. 'We ought to seek the two pups of the bitch
Rhymhi.'[101] 'Is her whereabouts known?' 'She is at Aber
Deu Gleddyv.'[102] Arthur went to the house of Tringad in
Aber Cleddyv and asked, 'Have you news of Rhymhi
round here?' 'What shape is she in?' 'In the shape of a she-
wolf, and she has two pups.' 'She kills my stock frequently;
just now she is down in a cave in Aber Cleddyv.' So
Arthur sailed out to sea in his ship Prydwen,[103] while
others went to hunt the bitch on land, and thus they surrounded her and her two pups; God changed the wolves
back into their own shapes, and Arthur's host dispersed
by ones and twos.

100. 'Triad 52' names the Three Famous Prisoners at Mabon,
Llŷr and Gweir.

101. Ysbaddaden requests neither the pups of Rhymhi, nor the
pups of Glythvyr Ledewig, nor Gwrgi Severi.

102. Aber Deu Gleddyv (= Milford Haven): estuary of two swords.

103. Prydwen: fair face.

One day as Gwythyr son of Greidyawl was crossing a mountain he heard crying and fierce sobbing, a terrible noise to hear. He sprang forth and drew his sword and struck the anthill to the ground so that the ants were saved from the fire. They said, 'Take God's blessing and ours, and what no person on earth can find we will deliver.' Thereafter they brought the nine hestors of linseed which Chief Giant Ysbaddaden had asked of Culhwch, the entire measure save for a single seed, and a lame ant brought that in before nightfall.

As Kei and Bedwyr were sitting on Pumlumon,[104] on Carn Gwylathyr,[105] in the greatest wind in the world, they looked round and saw a great smoke blowing towards the south far away, and not being blown by the wind, and Kei said, 'By my companion's hand, that is the fire of a warrior.' They made for the smoke and approached and saw from a distance Dillus the Bearded singeing a wild boar. He was the greatest warrior who ever avoided Arthur. Bedwyr asked Kei, 'Do you recognize him?' 'I do – that is Dillus the Bearded. No leash in the world will hold Drudwyn the pup of Greid son of Eri save one from the beard of the man you see before you, nor will that avail us unless it is plucked with wooden tweezers while he is still alive, for if he is dead it will be brittle.' 'What is your plan?' asked Bedwyr. 'We will let him eat his fill of meat, and after that he will fall asleep,' said Kei, and while Dillus was stuffing himself they were making wooden tweezers. When Kei was certain that Dillus was asleep he made the biggest pit in the world under his feet and then struck him an infinitely powerful blow; they pressed him down into the pit until his beard had been entirely plucked out with the wooden tweezers, and then they killed him outright. From there the two made for Kelli Wig in Cornwall, taking with them the leash from the beard of Dillus

104. Pumlumon (= Plynlimon): five peaks.
105. Carn: cairn.

the Bearded and giving it to Arthur, and Arthur sang
this song:

> Kei made a leash
> From the beard of Dillus son of Eurei;
> If Dillus were alive he would kill you.

Kei became angry, so that the warriors of this island could
barely make peace between him and Arthur; nevertheless
Kei would have nothing to do with Arthur from then on,
not when the latter was wanting in strength or when his
men were being killed.

Arthur said, 'Which wonder should we seek now?' 'We
should seek Drudwyn, the pup of Greid son of Eri.' A
short time before Creiddylad daughter of Lludd Silver
Hand had gone to Gwythyr son of Greidyawl, but before he could sleep with her Gwynn son of Nudd came and
carried her off by force. Gwythyr collected an army and
went to fight Gwynn, but Gwynn conquered, taking
prisoner Greid son of Eri, Glinyeu son of Taran, Gwrgwst
Half Naked and his son Dyvynarth, Penn son of Nethawg,
Nwython and his son Kyledyr the Wild. Gwynn killed
Nwython and cut out his heart, and forced Kyledyr to
eat his father's heart, and that is how Kyledyr went mad.
When Arthur heard of this he went into the north and
called on Gwynn and freed the nobles from prison, and
peace was made between Gwynn and Gwythyr:
Creiddylad was left in the house of her father undisturbed
by either side, and every May Day the two men would
fight, and the one who conquered on the Judgement Day
would keep the girl. When the two lords had been re-
conciled Arthur obtained Dun Mane the horse of Gweddw,
and the leash of Cors Hundred Claws, and then he went
to Brittany with Mabon son of Mellt and Gwarae Golden
Hair after the two dogs of Glythvyr Ledewig: having
taken them he went with Odgar son of Aedd King of Ireland to the west of Ireland in search of Gwrgi Severi, and

from there to the north where he caught the madman Kyledyr.

After that they went after Chief Boar Ysgithyrwyn, with Mabon son of Mellt and the two pups of Glythvyr Ledewig at hand, and Drudwyn, the pup of Greid son of Eri, and Arthur himself went, with his dog Cavall. Caw of Scotland mounted Arthur's mare Llamrei and rushed the boar; he snatched up a hatchet and bravely and vigorously made for the boar and split its head in two and then took the tusk.[106] It was not the dogs that Ysbaddaden named to Culhwch which killed the boar, but Arthur's own dog Cavall.

After Chief Boar Ysgithyrwyn had been killed Arthur and his men returned to Kelli Wig in Cornwall, and from there Menw son of Teirwaedd was sent to see if the treasures were between the ears of Twrch Trwyth, lest Arthur be shamed by going there to fight and not finding the treasures. Twrch was there, however, and he had destroyed a third of Ireland. Menw went after the treasures and found them in Ysgeir Oervel; he changed himself into a bird and alighted on the lair and tried to seize one of them, but he got only a bristle. Moreover Twrch rose boldly and stirred so that some of the poison overtook Menw, who thereafter was never completely without injury.

Then Arthur sent a messenger to Odgar son of Aedd King of Ireland to seek the cauldron of his steward Diwrnach. Odgar asked Diwrnach to give it up, but Diwrnach said, 'God knows, even were Arthur the better for just one glimpse of the cauldron, he would not get it.' Arthur's messenger returned with a refusal, so Arthur and a small force set out in his ship Prydwen, and when they reached Ireland they made for the house of Diwrnach, where the troops remarked their strength. When his men

106. Ysbaddaden required that the tusk be taken while the boar is alive, but this is overlooked.

had eaten and drunk their fill Arthur asked for the cauldron, but Diwrnach answered, 'Were I to give it to anyone I would have given it at the request of Odgar King of Ireland.' At this refusal Bedwyr rose and seized the cauldron and set it on the back of Hygwydd, who was the half-brother (by the same mother) of Cacamwri, another of Arthur's servants; his task was to carry Arthur's cauldron and keep a fire lit under it. Llenlleawg the Irishman seized Caledvwlch, swung it round in a circle and killed Diwrnach the Irishman and his entire retinue; the troops of Ireland came and fought, and when these troops were put to flight Arthur and his force boarded the ship in their presence, with the cauldron filled with the treasures of Ireland,[107] and they disembarked at the house of Llwyd son of Kil Coed at Porth Kerddin[108] in Dyved, and that is now Messur y Peir.[109]

Then Arthur collected all the warriors that were in Britain and the three offshore islands, in France, Brittany, Normandy and the Summer Country,[110] along with selected dogs and renowned horses, and that entire army went to Ireland; at their coming there was fear and trembling in that island. When Arthur landed the saints of Ireland came to him seeking protection, and when he granted them that they gave him their blessing. The men of Ireland also came, bringing a gift of food. After that Arthur went to Ysgeir Oervel, where Twrch Trwyth and his seven young pigs were; from all sides dogs were unleashed at Twrch, and the Irish fought with him all day until evening, and at that he destroyed a fifth part of Ireland. The next day Arthur's troops fought with him, but

107. This entire episode is suggestive, cf. the invasion of Ireland and the cauldron of 'Branwen', the Irish tale of the 'Children of Tuirenn' and the story of Balin in Malory.

108. Porth: harbour.

109. Messur y Peir: measure of the cauldron.

110. Summer Country=the Mediterranean area? Somerset?

except for the harm they suffered they got nothing; the
third day Arthur himself fought with Twrch, nine days
and nine nights, and killed nothing more than one piglet.
His men asked him about the meaning of the pig and
Arthur said, 'He was a king, but because of his sins God
turned him into a pig.'

After that Arthur sent Gwrhyr Interpreter of Languages
to try to talk with Twrch. In the form of a bird Gwrhyr
alighted on the lair of Twrch and the seven young pigs
and said, 'For the sake of Him who put this shape upon
you, if you can speak, I ask one of you to come and talk
with Arthur.' Grugyn Silver Bristle (like silver wings were
all his bristles, and the path he took through forest or
plain could be told by the way the bristles glittered)
answered, 'For the sake of Him who put this form upon
us, we will neither say nor do anything for Arthur. God
did us injury enough, making pigs out of us, without your
coming to fight us.' 'I can tell you that Arthur will fight
you for the comb and razor and shears [111] that lie between
the ears of Twrch Trwyth.' 'Until you take his life, you
will not get the treasures. Tomorrow we will start out for
Arthur's country, and once there we will do the greatest
possible damage.'

Then the pigs made for the sea and swam towards
Wales; Arthur and his troops and horses and dogs boarded
Prydwen and at once saw the swine and Twrch Trwyth
landing at Porth Cleis in Dyved. Arthur reached Mynyw [112]
that evening, and the next day he was told that Twrch
had already passed through; they overtook him killing
the cattle of Kynwas Cwryvagyl, after he had killed the
men and beasts in Deu Gleddyv prior to Arthur's arrival.

111. Ysbaddaden does not mention the razor. *v.* Nennius (39)
where Germanus refers to razor, scissors and comb in connection
with Vortigern's son; subsequently the boy goes to his father and asks
to have his hair trimmed.

112. Mynyw=St David's.

Twrch Trwyth then set out for Presseleu, and Arthur
went after him with all the forces in the world, and sent
his men into the hunt: Eli and Trachmyr, and Drudwyn
the pup of Greid son of Eri with them, Gwarthegydd
son of Caw with the two dogs of Glythvyr Ledewig at
hand, and Bedwyr with Arthur's dog Cavall at his side,
and Arthur deployed all his men along the banks of the
Nyver.[113] The three sons of Cleddyv Divwlch came also,
men who had won great renown at the slaying of Chief
Boar Ysgithyrwyn. But Twrch made from Glynn Nyver
and went as far as Cwm Kerwyn, where he stood at bay
and killed four of Arthur's champions: Gwarthegydd son
of Caw, Tarawg of Dumbarton, Rhun son of Beli Adver
and Ysgonan the Generous, and having killed these men
Twrch stood at bay a second time in the same place and
killed Gwydre son of Arthur, Garselid the Irishman, Glew
son of Ysgawd and Ysgawyn son of Panon, and he himself
was wounded.

The next morning at daybreak some of Arthur's men
overtook Twrch, and the boar killed Huandaw, Gogigwr
and Penpingyon the three servants of Glewlwyd Strong
Grip, so that God knows Glewlwyd had no servant to hunt
with him except Llaesgymyn, who was of no use to anyone.
Twrch killed many other men of the country as well, including Gwlyddyn the Carpenter, Arthur's master builder,
before Arthur overtook him at Pelunyawg, where Twrch
killed Madawg son of Teithyon, Gwynn son of Tringad
son of Neued and Eiryawn Penlloran. From there he went
to Aber Tywi, where he stood at bay and killed Kynlas
son of Kynan and Gwilenhin King of France, and then
he went to Glynn Ystun and both men and dogs lost his
trail.

Arthur summoned Gwynn son of Nudd and asked if he
knew anything of Twrch Trwyth but Gwynn did not, so
all the houndsmen went out to hunt the pigs, as far as

113. Nyver=Nevern.

Dyffryn Llwchwr,[114] where Grugyn Silver Bristle and Llwydawg the Killer attacked so that only one man escaped with his life. Then Arthur and his troops came to where Grugyn and Llwydawg were and all the dogs brought for that purpose were unleashed. With the shouting and barking that followed Twrch Trwyth (who had not seen them all since they crossed the Irish Sea) came up to help, and men and dogs attacked him; he made his way to Mynydd Amanw,[115] and there one of the piglets was killed. They went at each other life and death, first the piglet Twrch Llawin was killed, and then Gwŷs; Twrch then went to Dyffryn Amanw and there lost two more piglets, Banw and Benwig,[116] so that there escaped alive with him only Grugyn Silver Bristle and Llwydawg the Killer. Twrch went to Llwch Ewin [117] and Arthur overtook him, but he killed Echel Pierced Thigh and Garwyli son of Gŵyddawg Gŵyr and many others as well. From there they went to Llwch Tawy, but Grugyn Silver Bristle separated from them and made for Din Tywi, and after that for Keredigyawn; he was followed by Trachmyr and Eli and many others, and when he reached Garth Grugyn [118] he was killed, but not before killing Rhuddvyw Rhys and many other men. Llwydawg the Killer went on to Ystrad Yw, where the men of Brittany met him; he killed Peissawg the Tall King of Brittany and Arthur's uncles Llygadrudd Emys and Gwrvoddw, the brothers of his mother, and then Llwydawg himself was killed.

Then Twrch Trwyth passed between Tawy and Ewyas, whereupon Arthur summoned Devon and Cornwall to meet him at the mouth of the Havren,[119] and there he

114. Dyffryn: valley.
115. Amanw: is the storyteller forming a connection with banw, 'pig'?
116. Gwŷs: pig; Banw: pig; Benwig: sow.
117. Llwch: lake.   118. Garth: hill, ridge.
119. Havren=Severn.

said to the warriors of this island, 'Twrch Trwyth has killed a number of my men. By the courage of man, he shall not go into Cornwall while I am alive, nor will I pursue him further, rather I will pit my life against his. You men may do as you wish.' On Arthur's advice a troop of horsemen were sent out, along with the dogs of this island; they went as far as Ewyas and turned Twrch back towards the Havren, and there the battle-tested warriors of this island met him and drove him into the river by force. Mabon son of Modron, mounted on Gwynn Dun Mane, the horse of Gweddw, went into the river with him, and so did Goreu son of Custenhin and Menw son of Teirwaedd, between Llyn Lliwan and Aber Gwy.[120] Then Arthur and the champions of Britain joined the fight; Osla Big Knife drew near, and Manawydan son of Llŷr and Arthur's servant Cacamwri and Gwyngelli; they closed in and grasped Twrch's feet and dunked him in the river until the currents rolled over him. On one side Mabon son of Modron spurred on his steed and seized the razor; from the other Kyledyr the Wild advanced on his steed and seized the shears. Before they could get the comb, however, Twrch found his feet, and when he reached land neither dog nor man nor horse could stay with him as he made for Cornwall. For all the harm they came to in seeking the treasures, they came to worse trying to save two men from drowning, for as Cacamwri was being pulled out he was dragged to the bottom by two millstones, while Osla Big Knife lost his knife from its sheath in running after the boar; the sheath filled with water, and as he was being pulled out it dragged him down to the bottom.

After that Arthur and his men overtook Twrch in Cornwall. The harm they had come to already was nothing compared to what they suffered in seeking the comb, but though they went from one disaster to another the comb was finally obtained. Twrch was hunted out of

120. Gwy=Wye.

Cornwall and driven into the sea, and from then on it is not known where he went, or Aned and Aethlem either. Arthur himself went to Kelli Wig in Cornwall to bathe and rest, and there he asked, 'Is there any wonder that has not been obtained?' 'There is: the blood of the Black Hag, daughter of the White Hag, from the headland of the Valley of Distress in the highlands of Hell.'

So Arthur set out for the north and the hag's cave. On the advice of Gwynn son of Nudd and Gwythyr son of Greidyawl, Cacamwri and his brother Hygwydd were sent to fight with the hag, but as they entered the cave she sprang at them, catching Hygwydd by the hair and throwing him to the floor. Cacamwri grabbed her by the hair and pulled her away from his brother, whereupon she turned on him, and having stripped them both of their armour and weapons drove them out yelling and screaming. Arthur was angry to see his servants half-dead, and wanted to go at the hag himself, but Gwynn and Gwythyr said, 'We cannot enjoy seeing you wrestle with her – send Amren the Tall and Eiddyl the Tall into the cave.' They went, but if the first pair emerged in a bad state, these two came out even worse, so that God knows not one of the four could have left the place in any way other than being all loaded on Arthur's mare Llamrei. Then Arthur sprang to the cave entrance and threw his knife Carnwennan at the hag, so that it struck her down the centre and made two vats of her, and Caw of Scotland took the blood and kept it with him.

After that Culhwch set out with Goreu son of Custenhin and all those who were ill-disposed towards Chief Giant Ysbaddaden, and they took the wonders to the giant's court. Caw of Scotland came to shave the giant's beard, flesh and skin right to the bone and both ears completely. 'Have you been shaved?' asked Culhwch. 'I have,' said Ysbaddaden. 'Is your daughter mine now?' 'She is. And you need not thank me, rather Arthur, who won her for you; of my own will you would have never got her. Now it is time for you to kill me.' Goreu son of Custenhin seized Ysbaddaden by the hair and dragged him along to the dunghill, where he cut off his head and set it on a stake on the wall. They seized the fortress and the land, and that night Culhwch slept with Olwen, and as long as he lived she was his only wife. Then Arthur's men dispersed to their own lands.

This is how Culhwch won Olwen, the daughter of Chief Giant Ysbaddaden.

THE DREAM OF RHONABWY

THE most literary of the tales in *The Mabinogion*, 'Rhonabwy' may also be the last to have taken shape. Madawg son of Maredudd – a genuine historical figure – died in 1159, and his brother Iorwerth a few years later; thus the framework of the story cannot be much older than 1200. On the other hand, the stark simplicity of the gwyddbwyll match, and its counterpointing in the battle between Owein's ravens and Arthur's squires, recalls the dreamlike atmosphere of the opening pages of 'Pwyll'. In many ways, 'Rhonabwy' is closer in feeling to 'Culhwch' than to the Romances. As in 'Culhwch', Arthur's court appears to be in Cornwall and not in Wales. Owein is nearly Arthur's equal here; moreover armour, jousting and the concept of knighthood are all absent – strongly indicating that 'Rhonabwy', however late its composition, largely preserves the ambience of the earlier tales.

On one level, this story satirizes the twelfth-century Welshmen. The miserable reception accorded Rhonabwy and his companions at the house of Heilyn the Red provides the greatest possible contrast both to the generosity characteristic of Celtic tales, and to the glory and splendour of Arthur's legendary court. And yet this legendary glory is itself under attack: Arthur and his bishop look foolish as they are soaked by a passing horse; and later we are told that his bards' song is so obscure that no one can understand it. The contrast between fictive past and the all-too-real present is accented by the panoply of colours and metals and elaborate crests which Arthur's men bear, an assortment which renders 'Rhonabwy' a storyteller's *tour de force*, the visual counterpart to the list of names in 'Culhwch'.

The Dream of Rhonabwy

Madawg son of Maredudd ruled Powys from one end to the other, that is, from Porffordd as far as Gwavan in the highlands of Arwystli. He had a brother, a man of lesser rank, and this brother, Iorwerth son of Maredudd, was extremely agitated and distressed at seeing the honour and power that Madawg enjoyed, while he himself had nothing. He sought out his comrades and foster-brothers for advice, and they decided that some of them should go to Madawg and ask for maintenance for Iorwerth. Madawg offered to make his brother head of his troops, with equal rank, honour, arms and horses, but Iorwerth rejected that and went off to raid England, where he slaughtered many and burned houses and took prisoners. Madawg conferred with the men of Powys, and they decided to put one hundred men in every three commots to look for Iorwerth. They considered Rhychdir Powys,[1] from Aber Keiryawg to Hallictwn as far as Rhyd Wilvre[2] on Evyrnwy, as the equal of the best three commots in Powys, for the man and troops who did not thrive in Rhychdir Powys would not thrive anywhere else.

These men were quartered in Didlystwn, a townlet in Rhychdir, and one of their number was named Rhonabwy. Rhonabwy and Kynwrig Red Freckles, a man from Mawddwy, and Cadwgawn the Stout, from Moelvre in Kynlleith, came to seek shelter at the house of Heilyn the Red son of Cadwgawn son of Iddon; when they reached

1. Rhychdir: arable land.   2. Rhyd: ford.

his house they saw an old pitch-black hall with a straight front and smoke enough coming from it. Inside they saw a bumpy pitted floor: where there were bumps a man could scarcely stand, so slimy was this floor with cow dung and urine, and where there were holes a man might sink to his instep in the mixture of water and urine, and it was all strewn with holly stems whose tips the cattle had been eating. When they reached the fore-court they found a dusty threadbare floor and an old hag before the fire at one end, and when she was cold she would throw a lapful of chaff onto the fire, so that it was not easy for any man to put up with the smoke that entered his nostrils. At the other end they saw a yellow ox-skin, and lucky the man who was privileged to sleep on that.

When they had sat down they asked the hag where the people of the house were, but she answered gruffly. At that the people came: a red man, absolutely bald and very withered, with a bundle of sticks on his back, and a skinny little grey woman with another armful. The guests received a cool welcome; the woman kindled a fire with the sticks and went to cook, and then food was brought, barley-bread and cheese and watery milk. After that a wind and rainstorm arose, so that it was not easy for anyone to go outside and relieve himself, and then with the restlessness of their journey they grew drowsy. But when they looked at their bed it was nothing but dusty flea-ridden bits of straw with large branches strewn everywhere after the oxen had eaten all the straw above their heads and below their feet; a threadbare greyish-red blanket was spread over the straw, then a torn, tattered sheet with a half-empty pillow and an absolutely filthy pillowcase. They went to bed, and Rhonabwy's two companions fell asleep only after being tormented by the fleas and the discomfort; Rhonabwy, however, could neither sleep nor rest, and it seemed to him that he might be less uncomfortable sleeping on the yellow ox-skin on the platform.

There he did fall asleep, and at once a vision came: he and his companions were crossing the plain of Argyngrog, and his thoughts and feelings seemed directed towards Rhyd y Groes [3] on the Havren. As he journeyed he heard a commotion the like of which he had never heard before, and looking back he saw a young man with curly hair and a newly trimmed beard riding a yellow horse. This man was green from the tops of his legs and his kneecaps down, and wore a tunic of yellow brocade sewn with green thread; on his thigh was a gold-hilted sword, with a scabbard of new cordovan and a gold buckle. Over the tunic he wore a mantle of yellow brocade sewn with green silk, and the green of the rider's outfit and his horse's was the colour of fir needles, while the yellow was the colour of broom. His bearing was so awesome that they became frightened and fled, but he gave chase; when his horse breathed out they drew ahead, but when it breathed in they were as near as its chest.

At length they were overtaken and asked for mercy. 'You shall have that gladly, do not be afraid,' said the rider. 'Since you have granted us mercy, chieftain, tell us who you are,' said Rhonabwy. 'I will not conceal my identity – I am Iddawg son of Mynyo, yet I am better known by my nickname.' 'Will you tell us what that nickname is?' 'I will. I am called Iddawg the Churn of Britain.' 'Chieftain, why are you called that?' asked Rhonabwy. 'I will tell you. I was one of the messengers at the Battle of Camlann between Arthur and his nephew Medrawd. I was a high-spirited young man, so eager for battle that I stirred up bad feeling between them: when the Emperor Arthur sent me to remind Medrawd that Arthur was his uncle and foster-father, and to ask for peace lest the sons and nobles of the island of Britain be killed, though Arthur spoke as kindly as he could I repeated his words to Medrawd in the rudest possible way.

3. Rhyd y Groes: ford of the cross.

Thus I am called Iddawg the Churn of Britain, and that is
how the Battle of Camlann was woven. Nevertheless, three
nights before the end of the battle I left and went to Y
Llech Las [4] in Scotland to do penance, and I remained
there seven years before I earned forgiveness.'

At that they heard a commotion far louder than the
earlier one, and when they looked in its direction they
saw a young man with yellow-red hair, but neither beard
nor moustache, cutting a noble figure on a great horse.
From the point of its withers and from its kneecaps down
the horse was yellow, while its rider was dressed in red
brocade sewn with yellow silk, and yellow fringes on the
mantle; the yellow of his clothing and his horse was the
colour of broom, while the red was the colour of the
reddest blood in the world. This rider overtook them and
asked Iddawg for a share of the little fellows he had with
him, but Iddawg said, 'I will grant you what is fair: to be
their companion, just as I am.' The rider accepted that and
then went away. 'Iddawg, who is that rider?' asked Rhonabwy. 'Rhuvawn the Radiant son of the ruler Deorthach.'

They crossed the great plain of Argyngrog to Rhyd y
Groes on the Havren, and a mile from the ford, on every
side of the road, there were tents and pavilions and the
gathering of a great host. Upon reaching the bank they
saw Arthur seated on a flat islet below the ford, with the
Bishop Bidwini on one side of him and Gwarthegydd son
of Caw on the other, and standing before them a big
auburn-haired lad with his sheathed sword in his hand.
This lad wore a tunic and cap of jet black brocade; his
face was as white as elephant ivory and his eyebrows as
black as jet, and what one might see of his wrist between
glove and sleeve was whiter than a lily and thicker than
the small of a warrior's leg.

Iddawg and his companions went before Arthur and
greeted him. 'God be good to you, Iddawg,' said Arthur.

4. Y Llech Las: the grey stone.

'Where did you find these little men?' 'Lord, I found them up the road.' Then Arthur smiled grimly, and Iddawg asked, 'Lord, what are you laughing at?' 'I am laughing out of the sadness I feel at this island's being in the care of such puny men as these, after the sort that held it before.' Then Iddawg said, 'Rhonabwy, do you see the ring with the stone on the emperor's hand?' 'I do.' 'It is a property of that stone that you will remember all that you have seen here tonight; had you not seen the stone you would have remembered nothing.'

After that Rhonabwy saw a troop coming towards the ford. 'Iddawg, what troop is that?' he asked. 'The companions of Rhuvawn the Radiant son of the ruler Deorthach; mead and bragget are set out in their honour, and they are privileged to court the royal daughters of the island of Britain without stint, for that is their right. In every danger they ride both before and behind the emperor.' Rhonabwy could see on the horses and men of that troop no colour that was not as red as blood; if one of the riders were to separate from the troop, he would appear as a column of fire rising into the sky. They pitched their tents above the ford.

After that another troop was seen approaching the ford: from the pommels of their saddles upwards they were as white as the lily, and from that point downwards as black as jet. A rider forged ahead and spurred his horse into the ford so that the water splashed over the head of Arthur and the bishop and their advisers until they were as wet as if they had been dragged out of the river. As this rider turned his horse's head, the lad who was standing before Arthur struck the animal with the sword in its scabbard, so that it would have been a marvel if even iron had been unscathed, let alone flesh or bone. The rider drew his sword half out of its scabbard and said, 'Why did you strike my horse – as an insult, or out of desire to advise me?' 'You need advice. What foolishness

caused you to ride so recklessly as to splash the water of
the ford over the heads of Arthur and the holy bishop
and their advisers, until they were as wet as if they had
been dragged from the river?' 'I will accept that as advice,'
said the rider, and he turned his horse and returned to
his troop. 'Iddawg, who was that rider?' asked Rhonabwy.
'A young man considered the wisest and most accomplished in the kingdom: Avaon son of Talyessin.' 'And
who is the man who struck his horse?' 'A perverse and
overanxious lad, Elphin son of Gwyddno.'

Then a proud handsome man of bold and eloquent
speech said that it was a wonder how a large force could
be contained in such a confined area, the more so as they
had promised to be at the Battle of Baddon [5] by noon in
order to fight against Osla Big Knife. 'You may choose to
go or not to go, but I will go,' he said, and Arthur
answered, 'What you say is true. We will set out together.'
'Iddawg, who is the man who spoke so boldly to Arthur?'
asked Rhonabwy. 'A man who has the right to speak as
bluntly as he wishes: Caradawg Strong Arm, son of Llŷr
of the Sea, Arthur's chief adviser and his first cousin.'

After that Iddawg took Rhonabwy up behind him, and
with each troop in place that great host set out towards
Kevyn Digoll; when they reached the middle of the ford
Iddawg turned the horse's head round and Rhonabwy
looked at the Havren valley: two quieter troops were approaching the ford, and then a shining white troop, everyone wearing cloaks of white brocade with jet black fringes.
The kneecaps and legs of the horses were pure black, but
everywhere else they were pure white, and the troop's
standards were pure white with a pure black tip.
'Iddawg, what is that pure white troop?' 'The men of
Norway, led by March son of Meirchyawn,[6] Arthur's first
cousin.' Then Rhonabwy saw a troop dressed all in pure

5. Baddon=Bath?
6. March=Marcus; Meirchyawn=Marciānus.

black, with pure white fringes on their mantles. The knee-caps and legs of the horse were pure white, but everywhere else they were pure black, and the troop's standards were pure black with a pure white tip. 'Iddawg, what is that pure black troop?' 'The men of Denmark, led by Edern son of Nudd.'

By the time these troops overtook the host, Arthur and his force had descended below Caer Vaddon;[7] Rhonabwy could see that he and Iddawg were going the same way as Arthur, and when they too had descended he heard a great commotion among the host: the men at the edge of the host were running to the centre, and the men at the centre were making for the edge. A rider arrived, armed in mail: its rings were as white as the whitest lily, its rivets as red as the reddest blood, and the rider was careering through the host. 'Iddawg, is the host fleeing before me?' 'The Emperor Arthur has never fled, and had that remark been overheard you would now be a dead man. No, the rider you see is Kei, the handsomest man in Arthur's kingdom. The men at the edge of the host are rushing to the centre to see Kei riding, while the men at the centre are fleeing to the edge to avoid being trampled by Kei's horse – that is the meaning of the commotion among the host.'

Then they heard Cadwr Earl of Cornwall being summoned, and saw him rise with Arthur's sword in his hand, with a design of two serpents on the golden hilt; when the sword was unsheathed what was seen from the mouths of the serpents was like two flames of fire, so dreadful that it was not easy for anyone to look. At that the host settled down and the commotion subsided, and the earl returned to his tent. 'Iddawg, who is the man who brought Arthur's sword?' 'Cadwr Earl of Cornwall, the man whose task it is to arm the king on the day of battle and conflict.'

Then they heard summoned Eiryn the Splendid son of

7. Caer Vaddon: fortress of Baddon.

Peibyn, Arthur's servant, a rough, ugly, red-haired man
with a red moustache and combed hair; he approached on
a big red horse with its mane parted on both sides of its
neck, and carried a fine pack. This large red-haired man
dismounted before Arthur, drew a gold chair and a ribbed
brocade mantle from the pack, spread the mantle – there
was a red-gold apple in each corner – and set the chair
on it, a chair so large that three armed warriors could sit
in it. Gwenn [8] was the name of the mantle, and one of
its properties was this: a man wrapped in it could see
everyone, but no one could see him, nor would it allow
any colour on it but its own. Arthur sat on the mantle,
with Owein [9] son of Uryen standing before him, and said,
'Owein, will you play gwyddbwyll?' 'I will, lord,' said
Owein. So the red-haired man brought them the gwyddbwyll set, whose men were gold and whose board was
silver.

Owein and Arthur began to play, and they were deep
into the game when from a white red-topped pavilion
with the image of a pure-black serpent – bright-red
poisonous eyes in its head and a flame-red tongue – came
a young man with curly yellow hair and blue eyes and the
beginnings of a beard. He wore a surcoat of yellow brocade, stockings of thin, yellow-green cloth on his legs, and
on his feet buskins of mottled cordovan with gold buckles
fastening them across his insteps; he carried a heavy gold-
hilted triple-grooved sword, and a black cordovan scabbard tipped with pure red gold. He came to where the
emperor and Owein were playing gwyddbwyll and greeted
Owein. The latter wondered that the lad had greeted him
and not Arthur, but Arthur read his thoughts and said,
'Do not wonder that the lad greeted you just now, for he
greeted me earlier, and besides, his message is for you.'
The lad said to Owein, 'Lord, is it with your permission
that the emperor's young lads and servants are harassing

8. Gwenn: white.   9. Owein=Eugenius.

and molesting your ravens? If not, then have the emperor forbid it.' 'Lord, do you hear what the page is saying?' said Owein. 'If you please, call your men off my ravens.' 'Your move,' said Arthur, whereupon the page returned to his pavilion.

They finished their game and started another, and towards the middle of that game they saw a ruddy young man with curly auburn hair, sharp-eyed and tall with a trimmed beard, coming out of a pavilion of pure yellow with the image of a pure red lion on top. This man wore a tunic of yellow brocade reaching down to the small of his leg and sewn with red silk thread, stockings of thin white buckram, buskins of black cordovan with gold buckles; in his hand he carried a great heavy three-grooved sword, and a red deerskin scabbard with a gold tip. He approached the gwyddbwyll players and greeted Owein, who was not happy about being greeted, though Arthur was no more disturbed than before. 'Lord, is it with your permission that the emperor's pages are stabbing your ravens, killing some and wounding others?' asked the page. 'If it is not, ask him to call them off.' Owein said, 'Lord, if you please, call off your men,' but Arthur answered only, 'Your move,' and the page returned to his pavilion.

They finished their game and began another, and as they were making the first move they saw far off a spotted yellow pavilion, the largest anyone had seen, and the image of a gold eagle with a precious stone in its head. They saw a page with bright yellow hair, handsome and well-shaped; he wore a mantle of green brocade with a gold brooch at the right shoulder as thick as a warrior's middle finger, stockings of fine cloth and shoes of mottled cordovan with gold buckles. This youth had a noble countenance, a white face with red cheeks and large hawk-keen eyes, and in his hand a stout speckled yellow spear with a freshly sharpened head and a prominent standard.

Violently angry, he galloped towards the gwyddbwyll players and they perceived his anger; he greeted Owein and told him how the noblest ravens had been killed, and those that were not dead had been molested and wounded so badly there was not one that could lift its wings an inch off the ground. 'Lord, call off your men,' said Owein. 'If you please, play on,' said Arthur. Then Owein told the page, 'Go, and where you see the fiercest fighting raise the standard, and let God's will be done'.

The page went off to where the fighting was going badly for the ravens; he raised the standard, and at that the ravens rose, full of anger and violence and joy as well, to let the wind into their wings and to cast off fatigue. Having recovered strength and the will to fight they swooped down in anger and joy on the men who had earlier inflicted wounds and injuries and losses upon them. Some carried off heads, some eyes, some ears, some arms, and as they rose into the air their fluttering and gleeful cawing set up a great din, while another such commotion was raised by the men who were being pecked and stabbed and even killed.

While playing gwyddbwyll Arthur and Owein were amazed to hear such a noise, and as they looked round they saw a rider on a dapple-grey horse. This horse was a remarkable colour: dapple-grey, with a pure red right leg, and from the top of its legs to its hooves pure yellow; and both horse and rider were clothed in strange heavy armour. The horse was covered from the pommel up in pure red linen, and from the pommel down in pure yellow linen. The youth wore a great gold-hilted one-edged sword on his thigh, with a new pure green scabbard and a tip of Spanish brass, while the sword belt was of blackish-green cordovan with gilt crossbeams and a clasp of elephant ivory with a pure black tongue. On his head he wore a gold helmet, set with precious stones of great value, and on the crest a yellow-red leopard with two blood-red stones in its head, so that it was dreadful for any warrior, however stout-hearted, to look at the leopard's face, let alone the rider's; in his hand he carried a long heavy green-shafted spear, blood-red from the grip up and the blade covered with ravens' blood and feathers. This rider approached the gwyddbwyll players and they saw that he was tired and angry; he greeted Arthur and said that the ravens were killing the squires and pages, whereupon Arthur looked at Owein and said, 'Call off your ravens.' Owein replied, 'Your move, lord.' They played on; the page returned to the battle and the ravens were no more called off than before.

When they had played a while they heard a great uproar and the screams of men and the cawing of strong ravens carrying the men up into the air and pulling them apart and letting the pieces fall to the ground. From this commotion came a rider on a pale white horse with a pure black left leg, right down to the hoof. Both horse and rider were clothed in great heavy green armour: he wore a cloak of ribbed yellow brocade with green fringes, while his horse was covered in pure black with pure yellow fringes. The lad wore a great heavy three-grooved sword on his thigh, with a scabbard of embossed red leather and a belt of new red deerskin with many gilt crosspieces, and an ivory clasp with a pure black tongue; on his head he wore a gold helmet with a powerful sapphire and on the crest the image of a yellow-red lion with a foot-long flame-red tongue and poisonous blood-red eyes in its head, while in his hand he carried a thick ash spear with a new blood-stained blade and silver rivets. This page greeted the emperor and said, 'Lord, your pages and squires have been killed, and the sons of the nobles of Britain too, so that from now on it will not be easy to defend this island.' 'Owein, call off your ravens,' said Arthur. 'Your move, lord,' said Owein.

They finished their game and began another, and as

they were finishing that game they heard a great uproar and the screaming of men, and then the cawing of ravens and the flapping of their wings and their dropping undented armour and pieces of men and horses to the ground. After that came a rider on a handsome black high-headed horse: from the top of its left leg it was pure red, and from the top of its right leg down to the hoof pure white, and both horse and rider were clothed in spotted yellow armour speckled with Spanish linen; his cloak and that of the horse were in halves, white and pure black with purple-gold fringes. He carried a gleaming gold-hilted three-grooved sword, with a belt of yellow gold-cloth and a clasp from the eyelid of a pure black whale with a tongue of yellow gold; on his head he wore a helmet of yellow linen with gleaming crystals, and on the crest the image of a griffin with a powerful stone in its head, while in his hand he carried a ridge-shafted ash spear coloured with blue lime, the blade covered with fresh blood and riveted with pure silver. This rider approached Arthur angrily and said that the ravens had killed his retinue and the sons of the nobles of this island, and asked him to have Owein call the ravens off. Arthur asked Owein to do so, and he squeezed the gold men on the board until they were nothing but dust; then Owein ordered Gwres son of Rheged to lower the banner, and when this was done there was peace on both sides.

Rhonabwy asked Iddawg about the first three men who had come to tell Owein that his ravens were being killed, and Iddawg answered, 'Men who took Owein's loss badly, fellow chieftains and companions: Selyv son of Kynan White Shank from Powys, Gwgawn Red Sword [10] and Gwres son of Rheged, the man who carries Owein's banner on the day of battle and conflict.' 'Who were the last three who came to tell Arthur that the ravens were killing his

10. Welsh tradition makes Selyv and Gwgawn present at the Battle of Chester in 616.

men?' 'The best and bravest men and those who took any loss of Arthur's the hardest: Blathaon son of Mwrheth,[11] Rhuvawn the Radiant and Heveydd One Cloak.'

After that twenty-four horsemen came from Osla Big Knife to ask Arthur for a truce to the end of a month and a fortnight. Arthur rose and went to seek advice; he walked towards a big man with curly auburn hair who stood a little way off, and his advisers were brought: Bishop Bidwini, Gwarthegydd son of Caw, March son of Meirch-yawn, Caradawg Strong Arm, Gwalchmei son of Gwyar, Edern son of Nudd, Rhuvawn the Radiant son of the ruler Deorthach, Rhioganedd son of the King of Ireland, Gwen-wynwyn son of Naw, Howel son of Emhyr[12] of Brittany, Gwilym[13] son of the ruler of France, Daned son of Oth, Goreu son of Custenhin, Mabon son of Modron, Peredur Long Spear, Heveydd One Cloak, Twrch son of Peryv, Nerth son of Cadarn, Gobrwy son of Echel Pierced Thigh, Gweir son of Gwestyl, Drystan[14] son of Tallwch, Moren the Noble, Granwen son of Llŷr, Llacheu son of Arthur, Llawvrodedd the Bearded, Cadwr Earl of Cornwall, Morvran son of Tegid, Rhyawdd son of Morgant, Dyvyr son of Alun of Dyved, Gwrhyr Interpreter of Languages, Avaon son of Talyessin, Llara son of the ruler Casnar, Fflewdwr Fflam, Greidyawl Enemy Subduer, Gilbert son of Cadgyffro,[15] Menw son of Teirwaedd, the ruler Gwerth-mwl, Cawrdav son of Caradawg Strong Arm, Gildas son of Caw, Cadyryeith[16] son of Seidi and many men from Norway and Denmark and Greece besides – it was a large enough host that came to the council.

'Iddawg, who is that auburn-haired man to whom they have come?' asked Rhonabwy. 'Rhun son of Maelgwn[17]

11. Mwrheth=Murchada (Murphy) in Irish.
12. Emhyr: emperor. Perhaps not originally a proper name.
13. Gwilym=William.   14. Drystan=Tristan.
15. Cadgyffro: battle tumult.   16. Cadyryeith: fair speech.
17. Maelgwn (=Maglocunos): hound prince. According to Nennius, a sixth-century ruler of Anglesey.

of Gwynedd, a man whose status is such that everyone comes to him for advice.' 'And why was a lad as young as Cadyryeith son of Seidi brought into the council of such high-ranking men?' 'Because no one in Britain gives better advice.' At that Arthur's bards began to chant a song, which no man there except Cadyryeith himself understood, except that it was in praise of Arthur. Then twenty-four donkeys came with baskets of gold and silver, and with each donkey a tired exhausted man bringing Arthur tribute from the islands of Greece. Cadyryeith son of Seidi asked that Osla Big Knife be granted a truce to the end of a month and a fortnight, and that the donkeys which brought the tribute be given to the bards, along with the baskets, as a reward for their patience, and that during the truce they be rewarded for their songs, and all this was agreed upon. 'Rhonabwy,' said Iddawg, 'would it not be wrong to prevent a young man who gives such abundant advice from attending his lord's council?' Then Kei rose and said, 'Whoever wishes to follow Arthur, let him be in Cornwall tonight, and let everyone else come to meet Arthur at the end of the truce.' With the great turmoil that followed Rhonabwy woke; he was on the yellow ox-skin, having slept three days and three nights.

This story is called the Dream of Rhonabwy, and the reason is that no one, neither bard nor storyteller, knows the Dream without a book, because of the many colours of the horses and the variety of strange colours of armour and equipment and precious mantles and powerful stones.

OWEIN, or
THE COUNTESS OF THE FOUNTAIN

ALTHOUGH 'Owein', 'Peredur' and 'Gereint' –
traditionally known as the three Welsh Romances
– very closely resemble the *Yvain*, *Perceval* and
Erec of Crestiens de Troyes, it is not likely that a
single hand is primarily responsible for all three.
These tales do not appear together in any of the
manuscripts; moreover 'Gereint' is appreciably
more refined than the other two, just as 'Peredur'
is appreciably less well-constructed.

'Owein' and 'Gereint' are actually mirror versions of the same theme: the hero's knightly obli-
gations balanced against his devotion to his lady.
Thus, while Owein leaves his wife for Arthur's
banquet hall, Gereint addresses himself totally to
Enid and neglects his court. The present tale is,
however, more obviously dependent on the regeneration motif which informs the entire
Mabinogion: the journey to the otherworld; the
fountain and the bowl (as at Llwyd's *caer* in
'Manawydan'; the challenge of the otherworld
ruler. In this version, the victorious challenger re-
places his opponent both as husband to the
countess and as defender of the fountain.

Even in 'Owein', however, this motif has been
considerably rationalized – see how delicately the
hero's suit must be advanced in the face of the
widow's natural grief and resentment. The importance of kindness and courtesy is also stressed.
Owein's generosity in saving the lion (the influence of Androcles is obvious) earns him the aid

of a powerful friend, and his defeat of the besieging earl puts to shame the second countess's reservations about the high cost of hospitality. Luned's faith and charity are amply repaid by Owein's defeat of the squires. By contrast, Kei's rude boasting serves only to bring about his own discomfiture.

Owein, or *the Countess of the Fountain*

The Emperor Arthur was at Caer Llion ar Wysg,[1] and one day he was sitting in his chamber with Owein son of Uryen and Kynon[2] son of Clydno and Kei son of Kynyr, while Gwenhwyvar and her handmaidens were sewing by a window. Now though it is said that there was a gatekeeper at Arthur's court there was not; however, Glewlwyd Strong Grip was there acting as gatekeeper, greeting guests and foreigners, beginning to honour them, telling them the customs and habits of the court, and informing those who had the right to go to the hall or the chamber, or who merited lodging. The Emperor Arthur was sitting in the middle of the chamber on a pile of green rushes with a cloth of yellow-red brocade under him and a red-brocade-covered cushion under his elbow, and he spoke and said, 'Men, if you would not be offended, I would like to sleep until it is time to eat. You can tell stories to each other, and Kei will fetch you a pitcher of mead and some chops.'

Thus Arthur slept, while Kynon son of Clydno asked Kei for what Arthur had promised. 'I want the good story that was promised me,' said Kei, and Kynon answered, 'Well, it would be fairer to fulfil Arthur's promise first,

1. Caer Llion ar Wysg = Caerleon on Usk.
2. Kynon (=Cunonos): great hound. The Welsh poem 'Gododdin' states that Kynon was present at the Battle of Catraeth, *c.* 600.

and then we will tell you the best tale we know.' So Kei went to the kitchen and the mead cellar and returned with a pitcher of mead and a gold cup, and his hands full of skewers with chops on them; they took the chops and began to drink the mead, and then Kei said, 'Now let me have my story.' 'Kynon, tell Kei his story,' said Owein. 'God knows, you are a better storyteller than I,' said Kynon, 'for you have seen more strange things. You tell Kei his tale.' 'Well, begin with the strangest thing that you know,' said Owein.

'Very well,' said Kynon. 'I was the only son of my mother and father. I was very high-spirited and very arrogant, and I did not suppose that anyone in the world could surpass me at any feat. After I had learned every feat known to my country I equipped myself and travelled to the outer reaches and deserts of the world, until I happened upon the loveliest valley possible: the trees were all the same height and a river ran through the valley and a path alongside the river. I followed this path until noon and then crossed and rode on until evening, when I reached a great plain, at the end of which stood a great shining fortress with an ocean close by. I approached that fortress, and there I saw two lads with curly yellow hair and gold headbands. Each wore a tunic of yellow brocade, buskins of new cordovan on his feet with gold buckles fastening them across the instep; each carried a bow of elephant ivory with strings of deer sinew, and arrows with shafts of walrus ivory and points of gold and peacock feathers, and knives with gold blades and bosses of walrus ivory, and they were shooting at their knives. A little way off there stood a man in his prime, with curly yellow hair and his beard newly trimmed; he wore a tunic and mantle of yellow brocade with a ribbon of gold thread in the mantle, and buskins of mottled cordovan with gold buttons.

'When I saw this man I approached and greeted him, but he was so courteous as to greet me before I could greet

him, and he accompanied me to the fortress. There were
no inhabitants save for the people in the hall, but twenty-
four girls were embroidering by a window, and I tell you,
Kei, that the least beautiful of them was in my opinion
lovelier than the most beautiful girl in the island of
Britain [3] – the least beautiful of them was lovelier than
Arthur's wife Gwenhwyvar at her loveliest, Christmas
or Easter at Mass. These women rose to meet me. Six of
them took my horse and drew off my boots, while six others
took my armour and had it polished in a burnisher until
it was as white as the whitest thing; another six laid a
cloth on the table and set out food, while the last six
drew off my travel clothes and dressed me in other garments: a shirt and trousers of fine linen, and a tunic and
mantle of yellow brocade with a wide border; and they
drew under me and around me many cushions covered in
red linen. I sat down, while the six who had taken my
horse stabled it as well as the best grooms in Britain could
have done. Silver bowls with water for washing appeared,
and towels, some of white linen and some of green, so we
washed, and the man I spoke of went to sit at the table
I sat next to him, and below me sat the women who were
not serving. The table was silver and the napkins linen,
and not a single vessel was not of gold or silver or wild
ox-horn. Then our food arrived, and I am certain, Kei,
that I have neither seen nor tasted food or drink that I
did not see there, and the service was better there than
anywhere else.

'We ate until the meal was half over, and neither the
man nor the girls spoke a word to me, but when the man
perceived that I would sooner talk than eat he asked me
what errand I was on and what sort of man I was; I
answered that it was high time I had someone to talk with,
and that at court there was nothing worse than a poor

3. Is Kynon no longer in Britain? Geography in this tale is non-
existent.

talker. "Lord," said the man, "we would have spoken earlier had it not interfered with your meal, but we will talk now." Then I told the man who I was and what my errand was, and said I was looking for someone to overcome me, or whom I might overcome; the man looked at me and smiled and said, "Did I not believe that too much harm would follow, I would guide you to your goal." At that I felt grief and disappointment, and perceiving this the man then said, "Since you wish me to tell you of evil rather than good I will do so. Spend the night here, and tomorrow rise and take the road that brought you to this valley until you reach the wood which you passed through, and a short distance into that wood you will find a fork: take the right hand path and continue until you come to a great cleared field with a mound in the centre, and on that mound you will see a great black man, no smaller than two men of this world. He has one foot, and one eye in the middle of his forehead,[4] and he carries an iron spear which you can be certain would be a burden for any two men. Though ugly, he is not an unpleasant man. He is keeper of the forest, and you will see a thousand wild animals grazing about him. Ask him where to go from the clearing; he will be cross with you, but nevertheless he will show you how to find what you seek."

"That night seemed endless. In the morning I rose and dressed and mounted my horse and set out for the valley and the forest, and I found the fork in the road and the clearing that the man had described. When I arrived the wild animals I saw there were three times as pleasing as the man had said. The black man was sitting on the mound; my host had told me he would be big, but he was far bigger than I expected, and as for the iron spear which was to be a burden for two men – Kei, I am certain it would be a burden for four warriors, and yet this black man held it in his hand. I greeted him but he replied

4. Lug and Ódin also appear in one-eyed and one-legged forms.

uncivilly, so I asked him what power he held over the animals. "Little man, I will show you," he said, and he took his cudgel and struck a stag a great blow so that it roared; with that wild animals came until they were like stars in the sky, so that there was scarcely room for me to stand among the serpents and vipers and lions and animals of all sorts. He looked at them and ordered them to graze, and they bowed their heads and worshipped him as obedient men do their lord. Then he said, "Well, little man, you see the power I hold over these animals."

'Then I asked him the way. He was short with me, but he did ask me where I wished to go, and I told him what sort of man I was and what I sought. "Take the path at the head of the clearing," he said, "and climb the slope until you reach the summit; there you will see a vale like a great valley, and in the middle a great tree with branches greener than the greenest fir. Beneath that tree is a fountain, and beside the fountain a great stone, and on the stone a silver bowl, and a silver chain so that bowl and stone cannot be separated. Take the bowl and fill it and throw the water on the stone, and you will hear a tremendous thundering, such that you will expect heaven and earth to shake with the noise, and after that a cold shower which you will barely survive. Hailstones will fall, and when the weather clears, the tree will not have one leaf that the shower has not carried away. A shower of birds will come and sit in the tree, and in your own country you have never heard such singing as theirs, but when their song is most pleasant to you a great moaning and groaning will come towards you through the valley, and you will see a rider on a pure black horse dressed in pure black brocade, with a standard of pure black linen on his spear. He will attack you at once; if you flee he will overtake you, and if you stand mounted he will leave you on foot, and if you do not find trouble in this you will never find it as long as you live."

'I took the path and climbed the slope and saw everything the black man had described; I came to the tree
and saw the fountain underneath and the marble stone
alongside and the silver bowl and chain. I took up the
bowl and threw the water on the stone, and at once there
was thunder, much louder than the black man had said,
and then a shower. Kei, I was certain that neither man nor
beast whom this shower overtook would escape with his
life, for not one hailstone stopped until it had gone
through skin and flesh to the bone. Turning my horse's
hindquarters into the shower I put the point of my shield
over its head and mane and pulled down my visor, and
so we survived. My life was on the point of leaving my
body when the shower stopped, and when I looked at the
tree there was not a leaf on it. The weather cleared, and
birds alighted on the tree and began to sing, and I am
certain, Kei, that I had never heard before – nor have I
since – singing the like of that, but when it was pleasantest
for me to be listening to their music I heard the groaning
of which I had been told coming through the valley and
towards me. "Horseman, what do you want of me? What
evil did I ever inflict on you that you should do to me
and my realm what you have done today – do you not
know that today's shower has left alive in my kingdom
neither man nor beast that it found out of doors?"

'At that there appeared a rider on a pure black horse,
dressed in pure black brocade with an emblem of fine pure
black linen on his spear. I made an attack, and though it
was a fierce one I was quickly thrown to the ground. My
opponent passed his spear shaft through the bridle rein of
my horse and took the animal away and left me there,
as he did not think it worth his while to take me
prisoner or strip off my armour. I returned by the road I
had taken before; when I reached the clearing the black
man was there, and I tell you, Kei, it is a wonder I did

not melt into a pool with the shame that man heaped upon me.

'That night I made my way back to the fortress. I was greeted more joyfully than I had been the night before, and better fed, and I was able to talk with men and women as much as I wished; however no one spoke of my journey to the fountain, nor did I mention it myself. I spent the night there, and when I rose the next morning I found saddled and ready a bay-black palfrey with a pure red mane the colour of the reddest lichen. After putting on my armour and leaving my blessing I returned to my own court; the horse remains in the stable yonder, and Kei, between me and God, I would not exchange it for the best palfrey in the island of Britain. God knows, Kei, no man ever spoke against himself a more embarrassing tale than this, and I have told it out of surprise at never hearing of anyone – neither before nor since – who might know more of this adventure, for the matter lies somewhere in the realm of the Emperor Arthur without being discovered.'

'Men,' said Owein, 'would it not be a good idea to set out and try to find this place?' 'By the hand of my companion,' said Kei, 'such things are more often spoken by you than they are performed.' 'God knows, you should be hanged before you speak such disgraceful words to such a man as Owein,' said Gwenhwyvar, and Kei replied, 'By the hand of my companion, lady, you have never praised Owein any more than I do now.' At that Arthur woke and asked if he had been asleep. 'You slept for a while,' said Owein. 'Is it time for us to eat?' 'It is, lord,' said Owein. A horn was sounded for time to wash, and so the emperor and his company went to eat.

When the meal was ended Owein slipped away to his lodging and made ready horse and armour and at dawn the next day he armed himself, mounted his horse, and set out for the far reaches and the desolate mountains of the world. Finally he reached the valley Kynon had told him of and he was certain it was the right one. He travelled through the valley alongside the river, and having crossed to the opposite bank came to a vale and journeyed through that until he saw the fortress. As he approached the young men were shooting at their knives where Kynon had seen them, and the yellow-haired man was standing near by, and as Owein was about to greet the man the latter greeted him. Owein went forward to the fortress and saw a chamber and entered; he saw the girls sitting in gold chairs and embroidering silk, and they seemed far more beautiful and delightful than Kynon had said. They rose to serve Owein as they had served Kynon, and the meal was even more wonderful than Kynon had said. When this meal was half-finished the yellow-haired man asked Owein what errand he was on, and Owein told him everything, concluding, 'I wish to seek out the knight who guards the fountain.' The yellow-haired man smiled, and it was hard for him to tell Owein of the adventure, just as it had been hard to tell Kynon, but he did tell everything.

They went to sleep, and the next morning the girls saddled his horse and Owein rode along until he reached the clearing with the black man, who was more impressive than Kynon had said. He asked for directions and the man gave him them and he rode along the path Kynon had taken until he came to the green tree and the fountain and the bowl. Owein took the bowl and threw the water on the stone, and there followed the thunder and the shower, much more severe than Kynon had said, and after that the sky brightened, though when Owein looked at the tree there was not a leaf on it. Birds alighted on the tree and began to sing, and when their song was most pleasing to Owein he saw the horseman coming through the valley.

At that Owein attacked, and a fierce encounter ensued:

having broken their spears they hewed at each other with their swords. At length Owein struck his opponent a blow that pierced helmet, mail cap and hood, passing through skin and flesh and bone until it entered the brain. When the man in black perceived that he had been mortally wounded he turned his horse's head and took flight; Owein pursued, and though he was not far behind the knight was beyond his sword's reach. Ahead a great city glittered; they raised the fortress gate for the knight in black and then let it down on Owein, and striking him just behind the saddle it went through the rowels of his spurs and cut his horse in half. The gate dropped to the ground – the rowels of his spurs and the back part of the horse were outside and Owein and the rest of the horse inside between two gates, for the inner gate had been dropped lest he escape, and thus he was in need of a plan.

In this state Owein saw through the join of the gate a road, and a row of houses on each side of the road, and a girl with curly yellow hair and a gold headband, dressed in yellow brocade and wearing buskins of mottled cordovan. This girl approached the gate and asked for it to be opened. 'God knows, lady,' said Owein, 'the gate will not be opened from out here, any more than you can rescue me from in there.' 'God knows, it is a shame that you cannot be rescued,' answered the girl. 'It would be right for a woman to help you, for God knows, I have never seen a better man for a woman than you. If you had a woman-friend she would be the best of woman-friends, and if you had a lover she would be the best of lovers; therefore I will do what I can to help you. Take this ring and put it on your finger, and keep the stone in your hand and close your fist over it, for as long as you conceal it it will conceal you. Those in the castle will come to put you to death because of the man you killed, but when they do not see you they will be annoyed. I will wait for you by the mounting-block, and though I will not see you, you will see me; put your hand on my shoulder to tell me you have come, and then follow me.'

She left Owein, and he did what she had told him. Men came from the court to put him to death, but they saw only half a horse, and that annoyed them; meanwhile Owein slipped away and found the girl and put his hand on her shoulder, and she led him to the door of a large handsome upper chamber. She opened the door and they entered, and then she closed it behind them, and as Owein looked round he saw not a single nail uncoloured with a precious colour, and not a single plank without a different gold image. The girl kindled a fire with charcoal, then took a silver bowl with water in it and a towel of fine white linen on her shoulder and gave the water to Owein to wash. After that she set before him a gilded silver table with a cloth of yellow linen and brought him dinner; Owein was certain he had never seen any food which was not there in large quantity, and moreover the service was better than anywhere else. He had never seen so many excellent gifts of food and drink, nor was he served from cups other than of silver and gold.

Owein ate and drank until evening, when he heard a crying out in the fortress, and he asked the girl, 'What outcry is this?' 'They are anointing the nobleman who owns this fortress,' she answered. Then he went to sleep, and the bed she made up for him of scarlet and fur and brocade and fine linens was worthy of Arthur himself. Towards midnight they heard a frightful crying, and Owein asked, 'What crying is this now?' 'The nobleman who owns this fortress has just died.' A short while after dawn they heard another cry and immeasurably loud shouting, and Owein asked, 'What is the meaning of this shouting?' 'They are taking the body of the nobleman who owns this fortress to church.'

Then Owein rose and dressed himself, and when he opened the chamber window and looked out at the fort-

ress he saw neither end nor limit to the crowds which were
filling the streets, and they were all armed; many women,
both mounted and on foot, were there, and all the clergy-
men of the fortress were chanting, and he felt the air
reverberate with the shouting and trumpeting and clergy-
men chanting. In the midst of this host was a bier covered
with a cloth of white linen, round which many wax
candles burned, while in the procession there was no man
of lesser rank than baron. Owein was certain he had never
seen a handsomer looking host in such brocade and silk
and linen. There followed a woman whose yellow hair
flowed over her shoulders and whose head was covered
with many bloody wounds; she wore a torn outfit of yellow
brocade and buskins of mottled cordovan, and it was a
wonder that her fingertips did not break the way she
wrung her hands together. Owein was certain that had she
been herself he would never have seen such a beautiful
woman. She cried more loudly than any man or horn of
the host, and as he looked upon her he was kindled with
a love that filled every part of him.

Owein asked the girl who this lady was. 'God knows, a
woman who can be said to be the most beautiful of
women, the most loyal, the most generous and the wisest
and noblest – she is my lady, the Countess of the Fountain
she is called, the wife of the man you killed yesterday.'
'God knows, she is the woman I love best,' said he. 'God
knows, she does not love you at all, not even a little bit,'
said the girl. Then she rose and kindled a fire of charcoal
and filled a cauldron with water and set it to heat; she
took a white linen towel and put it round his neck, and
then she brought out a cup of elephant ivory and a silver
bowl, which she filled with warm water, and she washed
his head. She opened a wooden chest and took out a razor
with a handle of elephant ivory and two golden grooves
in the blade, and she shaved his beard and dried his head
and neck with the towel; then she set up a table for him

and brought him dinner, and he was certain he had never eaten a better meal, nor one more perfectly served. After dinner she made up the bed and said, 'Go to sleep now, and I will go courting on your behalf.' So Owein slept.

The girl closed the chamber door and went out to the fortress; there she found nothing but sorrow and distress, and the countess herself was in her chamber, unable to see anyone for grief. Luned[5] went and greeted her, but receiving no answer she became angry and said, 'What is wrong with you that you do not answer?' 'Luned,' said the countess, 'what a nerve you have, not coming to console me. It is I who made you wealthy, and it was wrong of you not to come and offer condolence.' 'God knows, I thought you would show better sense,' said Luned. 'You should be thinking of making good the loss of your husband, rather than wishing for what you cannot have.' 'Between me and God, I could not make good the loss of my lord with any other man in the world.' 'You could by taking a husband who would be as good, if not better,' said Luned. 'Between me and God,' said the countess, 'were it not hateful to me to kill a creature that I reared myself, I would have you put to death for such a disloyal suggestion. I will have you banished.' Luned answered, 'I am glad that you have no reason save that I gave you good advice when you could not find the way. Shame on the one of us who first sends for the other, whether it is I who invite you or you who invite me.'

As Luned went out, the countess rose and went to her chamber door and coughed aloud; Luned looked back, the countess nodded and Luned came back. 'Between me and God, you have a wicked mind,' said the countess, 'but since you spoke for my own good, tell me how it might come about.' 'That I will. You know that your realm cannot be held except by strength of arms – therefore you must at once find someone to defend it.' 'How am I to do

5. Luned: is this name drawn from the Lunette of Crestiens?

that?' 'If you cannot defend the fountain you cannot defend the realm, and the fountain can only be defended by one of Arthur's men. I will go to Arthur's court, and shame on me if I do not bring back a warrior who will defend the fountain as well as or better than the man who preceded him.' 'That will not be easy,' said the countess, 'but you have my permission to try.'

Luned set out as if to go to Arthur's court, but returned to her chamber instead, and she and Owein remained there until it was time for her to return from Arthur's court. Then she dressed and went to see the countess, who was glad to have her back, saying, 'Have you news from Arthur's court?' 'The best news, lady: I have succeeded in your errand. When shall I show you the chieftain who has come?' 'Towards midday tomorrow. Bring him to me, and I will clear the town for his arrival.' Luned went home, and the next day she dressed Owein in a tunic and surcoat and mantle of yellow brocade, with a wide border of gold thread in the mantle, and buskins of mottled cordovan buckled with the image of a gold lion. When they entered the countess's chamber she welcomed them and looked hard at Owein and said, 'Luned, this man does not have the look of a traveller.' 'What harm in that, lady?' 'Between me and God, none but he took my lord's life.' 'So much the better for you, lady – were this man not superior to your lord, he would not have overcome him. That is past, now, and there is nothing to be done about it.' 'Go home, then, while I seek advice,' said the countess.

On the following day she called the entire kingdom into one place and explained that the earldom had been subdued and could not be defended except by horse and arms and strength: 'Thus I give you this choice: either let one of you take me, or let me take a husband from elsewhere who can defend the fountain.' When her people had conferred they decided to let her take a husband from elsewhere; she brought bishops and archbishops from her court to marry her and Owein, and all the men of the earldom swore allegiance to him. Thereafter Owein held the fountain with spear and sword. Whatever horsemen came Owein overthrew them and held them for their full worth, and the ransom thus gained he shared with his barons and knights, so that in the entire world no man was more loved by his realm than he. Thus it was for three years.

One day Gwalchmei was out for a walk with Arthur. The emperor seemed grieved and afflicted, and Gwalchmei was saddened to find his companion in such a state, so he asked, 'Lord, what troubles you?' 'Between me and God, Gwalchmei,' said Arthur, 'I am longing for Owein, who has been gone for three years. I cannot live another year without seeing him, and I am certain that it is because of the tale of Kynon son of Clydno that he has been lost.' 'Lord, there is no need to marshal the realm on that account,' said Gwalchmei. 'If Owein has been killed we of your court can take revenge; if he lies imprisoned you can free him, and if he is alive you can bring him back.'

Gwalchmei's advice was accepted. Equipped with horses and arms Arthur and his men rode out in search of Owein, three thousand of them, not counting servants, with Kynon son of Clydno as guide. Arthur found the fortress where Kynon had stayed, and when he arrived the lads were shooting in the same place and the yellow-haired man was near at hand; when this man saw Arthur he asked him in, and Arthur accepted. They entered the fortress, and though they made up a great host their presence was not noticed. The girls rose to serve them, and whereas they had seen flaws in every other service there was none in that of these girls, nor was the work of the grooms that night any worse than the work of Arthur's own grooms.

The next day Arthur set out with Kynon as his guide;

they came to where the black man was, and Arthur thought this man far bigger than he had been told. After that they climbed to the top of the slope and journeyed through the vale until they came to the green tree, where they saw the fountain and the bowl and the stone. Kei went to Arthur and said, 'Lord, I know the meaning of all this, and I ask permission to throw the water on the stone and undertake the first adventure which follows.' Arthur consented and Kei threw the bowlful of water on the stone. Immediately there came thunder and a shower the like of which they had never heard nor seen, and the shower killed many of the servants who had accompanied Arthur. After that the sky brightened, and when they looked at the tree there was not a leaf on it. The birds alighted on the tree, and they were certain they had never heard songs like those the birds sang. Then they saw a knight on a pure black horse, dressed in pure black brocade and approaching boldly. Kei went against him and they jousted, and it was not long before Kei was thrown to the ground. Then the knight set up a pavilion, and Arthur and his host set up their pavilions for the night.

When they rose the next morning the jousting signal hung on the black knight's spear, whereupon Kei went to Arthur and said, 'Lord, I was unfairly thrown yesterday. If it please you, I will joust with the knight again today.' Arthur consented. Kei went to meet the knight and was unhorsed at once; the knight looked at him, then struck him in the forehead with his spear butt, so that it broke Kei's helmet and skull cap and skin and flesh to the bone, a wound as broad as the head of the spear. With that Kei returned to his companions, and thereafter each man in Arthur's retinue went to joust with the knight, and all were thrown until there remained only Arthur and Gwalchmei.

Then Arthur armed himself to joust, but Gwalchmei

said, 'Alas, lord, let me go out first.' Arthur consented, and Gwalchmei rode out to face the knight, he and his horse covered with brocade which the Earl of Anjou's daughter had sent, so that no one in the host recognized him. The two men charged and fought until evening, but neither came close to unhorsing the other. The following day they jousted with sharp spears, but neither overcame the other. The third day they came to joust with strong stout sharp spears; kindled with rage they set about each other on the stroke of noon. Each thrust at the other so that the saddle girths of both horses broke, and each man was thrown over his horse's hindquarters to the ground. They rose at once and drew their swords and fought, and the host were certain they had never seen two men as strong and splendid as these – had the night been dark, it would have been bright with the fire from their weapons.

Finally the knight gave Gwalchmei such a blow that his helmet turned on his face; the knight recognized him and said, 'Lord Gwalchmei, I did not recognize you because of your cloak. You are my first cousin – take my sword and armour.' 'Owein, you are master,' said Gwalchmei, 'you have won, now take my arms.' When Arthur perceived this he approached the warriors; Gwalchmei said, 'Lord, Owein has defeated me and will not take my arms,' but Owein said, 'Lord, it is Gwalchmei who has defeated me and will not accept my sword.' Arthur said, 'Give me your swords, and then neither of you will have overcome the other.' At that Owein threw his arms round the emperor's neck and embraced him, and the host came so quickly and in such numbers trying to see Owein and embrace him that they all but left corpses in their wake.

That night everyone went to his tent, and the next morning Arthur sought to leave. 'Lord, that would not be right,' Owein said. 'Three years ago I left you, and now this place is mine, and since I left I have been preparing a feast in anticipation of your arrival, for I knew you would come to look for me. You and your men must come with me to have a bath and rid yourselves of fatigue.' So they all went to the fortress of the Countess of the Fountain, where the feast that was three years in the making was consumed in three months, and they had never had a more comfortable or restful celebration. When Arthur finally made to leave he sent messengers to the countess asking her to allow Owein to accompany him, so that the nobles and ladies of the island of Britain might see him for just three months. The countess did not find this easy but she gave her consent, and Owein accompanied Arthur to the island of Britain. Once reunited with his kinsmen and banquet companions, however, he stayed for three years rather than three months.

One day, as he was dining at the Emperor Arthur's court in Caer Llion ar Wysg, a woman arrived on a bay horse with a curly mane that reached the ground; she was dressed in yellow brocade, and her bridle and what could be seen of her saddle were all of gold. This girl rode up to Owein and took the ring from his finger, saying, 'This is how one deals with a false treacherous deceiver – shame on your beard!' Then she turned her horse's head and left. The memory of his adventure returned to Owein and he became sad, and when he had finished his meal he went to his lodging, where he lay grief-stricken through the night. The next morning he rose and set out, not to Arthur's court, but to the four reaches and desolate mountains of the world. He wandered about until his clothes fell off and his body all but gave out and long hair grew all over him, and he kept company with wild animals and fed with them until they grew used to him. When he became so weak that he could not keep up with them he descended from the mountains into a vale and made for a park, the loveliest one in the world, and it was owned by a widowed countess.

One day this countess and her handmaidens were out

walking alongside a pond that was in the park, and half-
way along they saw the form and shape of a man and
were frightened; even so they approached and felt him
and looked him over carefully. They could see the blood
running through his veins and hear him moaning because
of the sun, so the countess returned to the castle and took
a cup full of precious ointment and gave it to one of her
handmaidens, saying, 'Take this ointment and these
clothes and that horse there and put them near the man;
rub him with the ointment until he revives, and then
watch to see what he does.' The girl went out and rubbed
all the ointment over Owein, and then she left the clothes
and the horse near by; she retreated a little way and hid
herself and watched, and after a short while she saw him
scratch his arms and rise and examine his skin, for he was
ashamed to see the ugly appearance he made. He noticed
the clothes and the horse; he crawled along until he could
draw the clothes from the saddle and put them on, and
then with difficulty he managed to mount the horse.

At that the girl showed herself and greeted him:
Owein was glad to see her, and asked what country and
place he was in. 'God knows, a widowed countess owns
this castle,' said the girl, 'and when the lord who was her
husband died he left her two earldoms, but now there is
only this one house which the young earl who is her
neighbour has not taken, because she would not be his
wife.' 'A pity,' said Owein, whereupon he and the girl
went to the castle. He dismounted and she led him to a
comfortable chamber and kindled a fire for him; then she
went to the countess and returned the ointment cup, and
the countess said, 'Girl, where is the ointment?' 'It is all
gone.' 'Girl, it is not easy for me to reproach you, but I
am distraught that you have used up one hundred and
forty pounds' worth for a man whose name you do not
know. Nevertheless, see that he is abundantly provided
for.' The girl did this, providing Owein with food and

drink and fires and baths and a bed until he was well
and his hair came out in scaly tufts. This went on for
three months, until his skin was whiter than before.

One day Owein heard a commotion in the castle and
great preparations being made and arms being brought in,
and he asked the girl, 'What commotion is this?' 'The
earl I told you of is coming to this castle with his hosts,
to try to destroy my lady.' 'Has the countess horses and
armour?' 'Indeed, the best in the world.' 'Then will you
ask her to lend me a horse and armour, that I might go
and look at this host?' 'Gladly,' said the girl, and she went
to the countess and told her of this conversation. The
countess laughed and said, 'Between me and God, I will
give him a horse and armour as a gift, and he has never
had a better horse nor better armour. I am pleased that
he is taking them before they can be seized by my enemies,
but I do not know what he wants with them.'

A handsome black Gascony horse was brought, with a
beechen saddle, and armour for both man and horse;
Owein dressed himself and mounted the horse and rode
out with two pages, both mounted and fully armed. They
could see no limit to the earl's hosts, so Owein asked the
pages which troop the earl was in. 'The one with the four
yellow standards, two before and two behind,' they
answered. 'Then go back and wait for me at the castle
gate,' said Owein. The pages returned, and Owein rode
through the first two troops until he met the earl, whom
he dragged from the saddle and put between himself and
the pommel of his own saddle, and then turned his horse's
head towards the castle. Through every difficulty he carried the earl along with him until he reached the castle
gate where the two pages were waiting; all went in, and he
gave the earl as a present to the countess, saying, 'Here is
your payment for the healing ointment which you gave
me.' The host pitched their tents round the castle. In
return for his life the earl gave back the two earldoms, and

in return for his freedom he gave back her gold and silver
and jewels and half his own realm; and moreover he gave
sureties for everything.

After that Owein left. The countess invited him with
his entire realm, but he wanted only to roam the far
reaches and deserts of the world. As he was journeying
thus he heard a great roar in the forest, then a second
and a third. Having entered the forest he found a large
cliff in the centre and a grey rock on the side of the cliff;
there was a cleft in the rock and a serpent in the cleft
and a pure white lion[6] beside the serpent, and whenever
the lion attempted to leave, the serpent leapt at it and it
let out a roar. Owein unsheathed his sword and approached the rock, and as the serpent came towards him
he slashed until it lay in two halves on the ground. After
that he took the road as before, and he saw the lion following and sporting about like a greyhound he had reared
himself. They journeyed until evening, and when Owein
thought it time to stop he dismounted and turned his
horse loose to graze in a level wooded meadow. He kindled
a fire, and by the time that was ready the lion had collected enough firewood for three nights. Then the lion
slipped away, and at once returned with a fine big roebuck; it dropped this before Owein and then lay down
between him and the fire. Owein took the buck and
skinned it and set chops on skewers round the fire, while
giving everything else to the lion. As he was thus occupied
he heard a loud moan, and then a second and a third;
he approached and asked whether it was an earthly
creature that made such a sound.

'Indeed it is,' came the answer. 'Who are you?' asked
Owein. 'God knows, I am Luned, handmaiden to the
Countess of the Fountain.' 'What are you doing there?'
'I was imprisoned for the sake of a young man who came
from the court of the emperor and stayed a short time

6. white lion: black lion in the Red Book text.

with my lady, and then visited Arthur's court and never
returned. He was the companion I believe I loved best
in the whole world. Two of the countess's chamberlains
reviled him in my presence and called him a false deceiver,
whereupon I said that the two of them together could not
stand against him. They then imprisoned me in this stone
vessel and said that I should not remain alive unless he
came to defend me by a certain day, no later than the day
after tomorrow, and I have no one to go and look for him.
His name is Owein son of Uryen.' 'Are you certain that
if this young man knew of your plight he would come to
defend you?' 'Between me and God, I am.'[7]

When the chops were cooked through Owein shared
them equally with the girl, and then they talked until the
next day, when he asked her where he might find food
and shelter for the night. 'Lord, go to the ford and take
the path along the river,' she told him, 'and after some
distance you will see a great fortress with many towers;
the earl who owns this fortress is the best man ever for
food, and you can spend the night there.' (No watchman
ever guarded his lord as faithfully as the lion had watched
over Owein the night before.)

So Owein saddled his horse and set out through the
ford until he saw the fortress. He approached and was
received honourably; his horse was well attended and
supplied with abundant food, and the lion lay down before its manger so that no one from the fortress would
dare approach it. Owein was certain he had never seen a
place where the service was as good, and yet each man
there was as sad as if he were dying. When they went to
eat the earl sat on one side of him and a girl on the other,
and Owein was certain he had never seen such a beautiful
girl; meanwhile the lion came and lay between his feet

7. Why does Owein not free Luned? The storyteller appears to
have borrowed an episode he did not understand.

under the table, and he fed it from every dish that was set
before him.

Owein had never seen such sad men. Half-way through
the meal the earl welcomed him, and he replied, 'High
time for you to cheer up.' 'God knows, it is not on your
account that we are sad, but rather because good reason
for sadness and grief has come.' 'What reason?' 'I have
two sons, and yesterday they went to hunt on the mountain, where there is a brute who kills men and eats them.
He seized my sons, and tomorrow is the day on which I
must give him this girl, or else he will kill my sons before
my eyes. While he has the look of a man he is no smaller
than a giant.' 'God knows, that is a pity,' said Owein.
'What will you do?' 'God knows, I think it more honourable that my sons, whom he seized against my will, be
killed than that I willingly give my daughter to him to be
violated and killed.'

After that the conversation turned to other matters.
Owein spent the night there, and the next morning they
heard an immeasurably loud noise, made by the large
man coming with the two sons. The earl wanted to close
up the fortress and abandon his sons, but Owein armed
himself and went out to try the man, and the lion followed. When the man saw Owein armed he advanced;
they fought, but the lion fought against the big man far
better than Owein did. 'Between me and God,' said the
man, 'I could handle you well enough if you did not have
that lion with you.' So Owein drove the lion back inside
the fortress and closed the gate, and then returned to fight
with the big man as before, but the lion roared when it
perceived that Owein was in difficulty. It climbed onto
the earl's hall and jumped onto the fortress wall and from
there bounded along until it found Owein, and then it
clapped the big man on the shoulder until its paw went
through to his knees, so that all his entrails could be seen
spilling out, and the big man fell dead.

Owein then gave the two lads back to their father; the earl asked him to stay, but he wanted to ride to the meadow where Luned was. There he saw the light of a great fire, and two fine lads with curly auburn hair taking the girl and throwing her into the fire. He asked what they had against her, and they told him the story, just as she had told it the night before, concluding, 'Since Owein has failed, we will burn her.' 'God knows, he is a good knight,' replied Owein, 'and I would be surprised if he knew about this girl and did not come to defend her. If you want me to stand up for him, I will fight you.' 'By Him who made us, we accept,' said the lads, and they set upon Owein until he was hard pressed by the two of them. When the lion came up, however, he had the better of it, and the lads said, 'Chieftain, we agreed to fight with you alone, and that animal is a fiercer opponent than you are.' Owein put the lion into the prison with the girl [8] and built a stone wall across the door. He went to fight with the two men as before, but his full strength had not yet returned, so that the lads were getting the better of it and the lion was continually roaring because he was in trouble. It tore at the wall until it found a way out, whereupon it quickly killed first one lad and then the other – thus they saved Luned from being burned. Owein and Luned went together to the realm of the Countess of the Fountain, and when he left he took the countess with him to Arthur's court, and she was his only wife as long as she lived.

After that Owein went to the court of the Black Oppressor and killed him, and the lion did not leave Owein until he had overcome that opponent. Having arrived at the man's court he made for the hall, and there he saw twenty-four girls, the most beautiful ever, only their clothing was not worth twenty-four pieces of silver, and they were as sad as if they were dying. He asked the

8. Has Luned been returned to prison?

meaning of their grief, and they said that they were the daughters of earls and that each had come with the man she loved best. 'When we came we were welcomed and accorded respect, and made drunk, whereupon the devil who owns this court came and killed our men and took our clothes and horses and gold and silver. Their bodies lie in this very house with the corpses of many others, and we are distressed at your arrival, chieftain, lest you too come to grief.' Owein thought this very sad. Going back outside he saw a knight approaching, welcoming him with love and joy as if he were a brother, but this was the Black Oppressor. 'God knows, I did not come here to seek your welcome,' said Owein. 'Then God knows, you will not get it,' answered the other. At once they made for each other and struggled fiercely, until with a great effort Owein bound his opponent's hands behind his back, and the latter asked for mercy: 'Lord Owein, there was a prophecy that you would come here and subdue me, and that you have done. I was a robber and this a plunder-house; spare my life, and for your sake I will become a host and turn this into a guest-house for the weak and the strong, for as long as I live.' Owein accepted that.

He stayed there that night, and the next morning he took the twenty-four girls, with their clothes and horses and what they had of goods and jewels, and set out for Arthur's court. Arthur had welcomed him before when he was lost, and he did so even more joyfully now. Those of the women who wished to stay in the court stayed and those who wished to leave left. As for Owein, he stayed in Arthur's court as chief of his lord's retinue from then on, and was dear to Arthur, until he went to his own land with the three hundred swords of Kynverchin[9] and his flight of ravens, and they were victorious wherever they went.

This is the story called the Tale of the Countess of the Fountain.

9. Kynverchin: Kynvarch is Owein's grandfather.

PEREDUR SON OF EVRAWG

FOR the most part, the events of 'Peredur' parallel those of its French counterpart, Crestiens' unfinished *li contes del graal* (or *Perceval*); however, the narratives do differ in two significant respects: 'Peredur' features an extended sequence of unintegrated and rather meretricious exploits just after the hero's reunion with Arthur, while following the Good Friday meeting with the hermit the tales part company, *li contes del graal* to continue with the adventures of Gauvain (Gwalchmei in Welsh), *Peredur* to move precipitously towards its conclusion. In the most important matter, though, these stories are sadly at one, for neither fully illuminates the mystery of the lance and Grail seen at the castle of the hero's (Fisher King?) uncle. Crestiens, of course, did not live to finish *Perceval*, and the ending of Peredur, while corroborating the revenge motif of Manessier (in his continuation of *Perceval*), seems horribly contrived, and leaves much unexplained too.

Inasmuch as Crestiens admits that Perceval is a Welshman, and inasmuch as the name Perceval (pierce-valley?) means little, it seems likely that Peredur is the more original form of the hero's name. Peredur, moreover, looks suspiciously like Pryderi (from the Four Branches). According to Welsh history Peredur and Gwrgi were companions in northern Britain of the fifth century, just as Pryderi and Gwrgi are companions in 'Math'. Then too, Pryderi and Peredur exhibit

striking similarities in personality: both are
naïve, free-wheeling types prone to serious errors
in judgement – though in *Perceval* the hero's
dégagé ingenuousness is seen as the natural
gaucherie of the Welsh rustic. Perhaps at an
earlier stage Pryderi–Peredur was both the focal
point of the Four Branches and the central figure
in the first Grail narratives.

Peredur Son of Evrawg

Earl Evrawg [1] possessed an earldom in the north, and he
had seven sons. Not by wealth did he maintain himself,
but by tournaments and combat and fighting, and as often
happens to those who follow the wars he was killed, and
so were six of his sons. The seventh son was named
Peredur, and he was the youngest; he was not old enough
to fight or go to war, or else he would have died like his
father and brothers. His mother was a refined and prudent woman who gave some thought to her son and his
realm, and on her own initiative she left civilization and
fled with him to a desert wilderness. She took no one in
her company save women and children and quiet con-
tented types who could not and would not fight or wage
war, and in the lad's hearing no one dared mention horses
or arms for fear of putting the thought into his head.

Every day Peredur would go to the forest of tall trees to
play and to throw holly darts, and one day he saw there
a herd of his mother's goats, along with two hinds who
were standing near by, and he marvelled to see these two
without horns when all the others had them, for he supposed that they were all goats and that these two had lost
their horns. By speed and strength he drove the hinds
along with the goats into the house for the goats at one

1. Evrawg = York, from the Latin Eburācum.

end of the forest, and then he returned home and said, 'Mother, what a strange thing I have seen near by: two of your goats have been running wild, and after roaming the forest for so long they have lost their horns. No man has ever had a more difficult task than I had in driving them inside.' Everyone rose to go and look, and when they saw the hinds they marvelled that anyone should have the speed and strength to overtake such animals.

One day three knights came down the bridle path along-side the forest: Gwalchmei son of Gwyar, Gweir son of Gwestyl and Owein son of Uryen, the latter bringing up the rear while pursuing the knight who had distributed the apples in Arthur's court. Peredur asked, 'Mother, what are these?' 'Angels, my son.' 'I will be an angel and go with them,' said he, and he went to the path to meet the knights. 'Friend, tell me,' said Owein, 'have you seen a knight go by yesterday or today?' 'I do not know what a knight is,' said the lad. 'It is what I am,' said Owein. 'If you tell me what I ask you, I will tell you what you ask me.' 'Gladly,' said Owein. 'What is that?' the lad asked, indicating the saddle. 'A saddle,' said Owein. Peredur asked what every-thing was and what was expected of it and what it was good for, and Owein told him in full what everything was and how it could be used. 'Proceed, now,' said Peredur, 'for I have seen the man you asked about, and I will follow you as a knight at once.'

Peredur returned to his mother and her company and said, 'Mother, those are not angels; they are knights.' At that she fainted dead away. Peredur, however, went over to the nags that carried firewood and brought food and drink to the desert from the outside world, and he chose a bony dapple-grey nag which seemed to him the strongest one; he strapped on a bundle as a saddle and went back to his mother, who was just then coming round. 'Do you wish to go then?' said she. 'I do.' 'Will you listen to some advice before you go?' 'I will if you speak quickly.'

'Then go to Arthur's court, where the best and bravest and most generous men are. When you see a church chant your paternoster. If you see food and drink and are in need, and they are not offered to you out of goodwill and understanding, then take them. If you hear an outcry make for it, especially if it is the cry of a woman. If you see a fine jewel take it and give it to someone, and you will earn a good name for yourself. If you see a beautiful woman, woo her, even if she does not wish it, for it will make you a better and nobler man.'

Peredur imitated with withes the trappings he had seen in every way; then he set out, carrying a handful of pointed darts. Two days and two nights he travelled through wilderness and desert without food or drink. He came to a great tangle of forest, far into which he could see a clearing with a pavilion in the guise of a church, so he chanted his paternoster. Upon reaching the pavilion he found the door open, and near that sitting in a golden chair a handsome chestnut-haired girl wearing a gold hairband with prominent stones, and a thick gold ring on her hand. He dismounted and entered, and the girl welcomed him. At the far end of the pavilion he saw a table with two bottles full of wine and two loaves of white bread and chops from suckling pigs, and he said, 'My mother told me that if I saw food and drink I should take it.' 'Go and eat, chieftain, and God's welcome to you.' Peredur went to the table and took half the food and drink for himself, leaving the rest for the girl, and when he had finished he returned to her and said, 'My mother told me to take a fine jewel if I saw one.' 'Take it, friend, I will not grudge you that.' He took the ring and knelt down and kissed the girl; then he took his horse and set out.

After that there rode up the knight who owned the pavilion, the Pride of the Clearing; he observed the hoof-prints and asked the girl, 'Who has been here since I left?' 'A strange-looking man, lord,' and she described

Peredur's appearance and manners. 'Tell me, has he been
with you?' 'By my faith, he has not.' 'By my faith, I do not
believe you, and until I meet him, to avenge my anger and
my shame upon him, you shall not spend two nights in
the same place.'

The knight set out to look for Peredur, but the latter
made for Arthur's court. Prior to his arrival there another knight had appeared and had given the gatekeeper
a thick gold ring to guard his horse, and then had entered
the hall. Arthur was there with his retinue and Gwenhwyvar and her ladies, and a chamberlain was serving
Gwenhwyvar from a cup; the knight took this cup from
her hand and poured its contents over her face and breast
and boxed her ears severely, and then said, 'Whoever
wishes to take this cup from me and avenge this insult
to Gwenhwyvar, let him follow me to the meadow, where
I will be waiting.' The knight took his horse and made
for the meadow, and everyone hung his head for fear of
being asked to avenge this insult, for they all felt that no
one would commit such an outrage unless he possessed
such strength and skill and magic and enchantment that
no vengeance could be taken.

At this moment Peredur arrived, entering the hall on his
bony dapple-grey nag with its decrepit trappings and fur-
nishings. Kei was standing in the middle of the hall, and
Peredur said, 'Tell me, tall man, where is Arthur?' 'What
do you want with Arthur?' 'My mother told me to come
and be ordained a knight by Arthur.' 'By my faith, you
have come badly equipped as to horse and armour.' At
that Arthur's host took notice of Peredur and began to
mock him and throw sticks at him, and they were glad
that such a spectacle had appeared and distracted atten-
tion from the other incident.

Thereupon the dwarf entered. A year earlier he had
brought his dwarf wife to the court to seek Arthur's hospitality, which they received, but they had in the course

of the year not spoken a word to anyone; when he saw
Peredur, however, the dwarf said, 'God's welcome to you,
Peredur, handsome son of Evrawg, chief of warriors and
flower of knights.' 'God knows,' said Kei, 'that was a silly
thing, to remain silent for a year in Arthur's court, with
your choice of talking and drinking companions, and then
in the presence of the emperor and his household to call
such a man chief of warriors and flower of knights.' Kei
boxed the dwarf on the ear so that he fell to the floor in
a dead faint. The dwarf's wife entered and said, 'God's
welcome to you, Peredur, handsome son of Evrawg, flower
of warriors and candle of knights,' whereupon Kei said,
'Girl, that was a silly thing, to remain silent for a year in
Arthur's court, without saying a word to anyone, and
then in the presence of Arthur and his warriors to call
such a man flower of warriors and candle of knights.' Kei
gave her such a kick that she fell in a dead faint. 'Tall
man, tell me,' said Peredur, 'where is Arthur?' 'Be quiet
and follow the knight who rode out to the meadow; take
the cup and overthrow him, and take his horse and
armour, and then you shall be made a knight.' 'Tall man,
I will do that.'

  Peredur turned his horse and made for the meadow,
and when he arrived the knight was riding about, arrogant in his power and might. 'Tell me,' said the knight,
'did you see anyone from the court following me?' 'The
tall man there told me to overthrow you and recover the
cup, and to take your horse and armour for myself.' 'Be
quiet. Return to the court and in my name call for Arthur
or another knight to come and fight with me; if someone
does not come quickly I will not wait.' 'By my faith,' said
Peredur, 'I will take your horse and armour and the cup,
whether you will or not.' At that the knight advanced
angrily and used his spear butt to strike him a powerful
blow between neck and shoulder. Peredur said, 'Lad, my
mother's servants would not play with me thus, but I will

play with you.' He aimed a pointed dart and hit the knight in the eye; the dart left through the nape of the neck and the man fell to the ground dead.

Meanwhile Owein son of Uryen was saying to Kei, 'God knows, you struck that man you sent after the knight a foul blow. He will be either overthrown or killed: if he is overthrown the knight will consider him a man of stature, and Arthur and his warriors will be eternally shamed; if he is killed they will still be shamed, and you will have sinned as well. May I lose face if I do not go and learn what has happened.' Owein rode to the meadow, where he found Peredur dragging the knight behind him, and so he said, 'Wait, chieftain, and I will remove the armour.' 'This iron tunic will not come off, it is part of him.' So Owein removed the armour and clothing and said, 'There you are, friend, now you have a horse and armour that are better than those you had – take them gladly, and come with me to Arthur, who will make you a knight.' Peredur replied, 'May I lose face if I go. Take this cup from me to Gwenhwyvar and tell Arthur that wherever I go I will be his man, and that I will serve him to his advantage as best I can, but tell him that I will not enter the court until I meet the tall man and avenge the insult to the dwarf and his wife.' Owein then returned to the court and related to Arthur and Gwenhwyvar and the entire household both the adventure and the threat to Kei.

Peredur set out, and as he journeyed he encountered a knight, who asked, 'Where are you coming from?' 'From Arthur's court.' 'Are you Arthur's man?' 'By my faith, I am.' 'This is a good place to declare that.' 'Why?' 'I will tell you. I have always been a waylayer and a robber of Arthur, and I kill any of his men I meet.' Without further delay they jousted, and it was not long before Peredur threw his opponent over his horse's hindquarters to the ground. The knight asked for mercy, and Peredur

said, 'You shall have that on your promise to go to
Arthur's court and tell him that I have overthrown you
in his honour and service. Tell him also that I will not set
foot in his court until I meet the tall man and avenge the
insult to the dwarf and his wife.' The knight gave his oath;
he travelled to Arthur's court and related the adventure
and the threat to Kei. Peredur continued, and in the next
week met sixteen knights; he overthrew them all, and sent
them to Arthur with the same story and threat. Kei was
thereupon reproved by Arthur and the household, and
was no little concerned.

Peredur rode on until he reached a great tangle of
forest, with a lake alongside, and on the other side a great
court surrounded by a handsome fortress. At the edge of
the lake a hoary-haired man sat on a brocade pillow; he
was dressed in a brocade garment, and there were lads
fishing from a boat in the middle of the lake. When the
hoary-haired man caught sight of Peredur he rose and
made for the court; Peredur too made for the court, where
he found the door open, and when he entered the hoary-
haired man was sitting on a brocade cushion, and a strong
crackling fire blazed. The household rose to meet Peredur,
helping him to dismount and disarm. Then the man
patted the end of the cushion with his hand and asked
Peredur to come and sit on it; they sat and talked, and
when it was time, the tables were set up and he was seated
at one side of the man, and they ate.

The meal being ended the man asked Peredur if he
was skilled at fighting with a sword, and the lad answered,
'I suppose that if I were to receive instruction I would be
skilled.' 'He who knows how to play with stick and shield
would know how to use a sword.' The hoary man had two
sons, one yellow-haired and one auburn-haired. 'Rise,
lads,' he told them, 'and play with sticks and shields.'
When the lads rose and did so the man said, 'Tell me,
friend, which of the two plays better?' 'I suspect the

yellow-haired lad could have drawn blood long ago had he
wished.' 'Then take the stick and shield from the auburn-
haired lad and draw blood from the yellow-haired one if
you can.' Peredur rose and took the stick and shield, and
he struck the yellow-haired lad until his eyebrow sagged
down to his eye and the blood ran in streams, whereupon
the man said to him, 'Well, friend, go sit down now. You
will be the best swordsman in this island. I am your uncle,
your mother's brother,[2] and you shall remain with me
for a while, learning manners and courtesy. Forget your
mother's words, for I will be your teacher, and I will make
you a knight. From now on follow this advice: though
you see what is strange, do not ask about it unless someone is courteous enough to tell you; any rebuke will fall
on me rather than on you, as I am your teacher.' Then
they were served and honoured in various ways, and
when the time came they went to sleep.

When day broke Peredur rose and took his horse, and
with his uncle's permission he left. He entered a great
forest and saw a level meadow at the far end, and beyond
that a great fortress and a handsome court; he made for
the court, and finding the door open approached the hall.
As he entered a handsome hoary-haired man was seated
to one side and surrounded with many squires, each of
whom rose to meet him, and their service was good. He
was seated at one side of the nobleman who owned the
court, and they talked, and when it was time to eat he
was seated on one side of the nobleman at the table. When
the meal was ended and they had eaten their fill, the
nobleman asked him if he knew how to use a sword, and
he answered, 'Were I to receive instruction I suppose I

2. The stress on sisters' sons in the northern Branches of the
Mabinogi – Beli, Penarddun and Brân; Brân, Branwen and Gwern;
Math, Dôn and Gwydyon; Gwydyon, Aranrhod and Lleu – suggests
a system of matrilinear descent. Thus, Peredur is certainly his
maternal uncles' heir.

would know.' Then take that sword and strike the
column.' There was in the middle of the hall a great iron
column, the circumference of a warrior's embrace; Peredur rose and struck this column so that both it and the
sword broke in two. 'Now put the pieces together and
join them.' Peredur put them together until they were as
before. A second time he struck so that both sword and
column broke in two, and then he joined them as before.
A third time he struck so that both sword and column
broke in two. 'Now join them once more,' said the nobleman, and Peredur put them together a third time, but he
could join neither sword nor column. 'Well, lad, go sit
down, and God's blessing upon you – you are the best
swordsman in the entire kingdom. You have come into
two parts of your strength, but the third is still wanting;
when you attain your full power you will yield to no
one. I am your uncle, your mother's brother, and the
brother of the man whose court you were in last night.'

Then Peredur sat to one side of his uncle and they
talked. He saw two lads entering the hall and then leaving for a chamber; they carried a spear of incalculable
size with three streams of blood running from the socket
to the floor. When everyone saw the lads coming in this
way they set up a crying and a lamentation that was not
easy for anyone to bear, but the man did not interrupt
his conversation with Peredur – he did not explain what
this meant, nor did Peredur ask him. After a short silence
two girls entered bearing a large platter with a man's head
covered with blood on it, and everyone set up a crying
and lamentation such that it was not easy to stay in the
same house. Then a chamber was prepared for Peredur
and he went to bed.

The next morning he rose, and with his uncle's permission set out. He came to a forest, at the far edge of
which he heard a cry, and making in that direction he
arrived to find a handsome auburn-haired woman and a

saddled horse standing near by. She was holding the corpse
of a man and trying to lay it across the saddle, but it
would fall to the ground and she would cry. 'Tell me,
sister, why are you crying?' 'Alas, accursed Peredur, little
consolation from my grief have you brought.' 'Why am I
accursed?' 'You are the cause of your mother's death.
When you set out against her will a pang of pain leapt up
within her and she died, and as you are the cause of her
death you are accursed. The dwarf and his wife whom you
saw in Arthur's court – that was the dwarf of your father
and mother. I am your foster-sister, and this is my husband, killed by the knight in the wood; do not approach
him yourself, or you too will be killed.' 'Sister, you do
wrong to rebuke me. Having tarried here so long I will
scarcely overcome him, and were I to stay longer I would
not overcome him at all. Leave off your crying, for help is
nearer now than it was before; I will bury the man, and
then I will accompany you to where the knight is, and if
I can avenge you I will.'

The body having been buried they rode to where the
knight was riding his horse in a clearing, and at once the
latter asked Peredur where he came from. 'I come from
Arthur's court.' 'Are you Arthur's man?' 'By my faith, I
am.' 'A good place for you to claim a relationship with
Arthur.' They attacked and at once Peredur overthrew the
knight, and the latter begged for mercy. 'You shall have
that on your promise to marry this woman, and to do for
her whatever good you are accustomed to do for women,
in return for having killed her innocent husband. You
shall go to Arthur's court and tell him that it was I who
overthrew you in his service and honour, and that I will
not set foot in his court until I meet the tall man and
avenge the insult to the dwarf and his wife.' Peredur
then took sureties. The knight set the woman on a horse
in his train and rode to Arthur's court, where he related
both the adventure and the threat to Kei; and Kei was

rebuked by Arthur and the household for having driven
away from the court so good a lad as Peredur. 'That
knight will never come to court,' said Owein, 'nor will
Kei venture out.' 'By my faith,' said Arthur, 'I will search
the wildernesses of the island of Britain until I find him,
and then he and Kei may do their worst to each other.'

Peredur, however, rode on until he came to a great
tangled forest where he saw the tracks of neither man nor
herds, only thickets and vegetation. At the far end of the
forest he saw a great ivy-covered fortress with many strong
towers; near the gate the vegetation was lusher than elsewhere, and from the embrasure a thin lad with reddish-
yellow hair said, 'Chieftain, shall I open the gate for you,
or shall I tell the head man that you have arrived?' 'Tell
him that I am here, and if he wishes me to enter I will.'
The page returned quickly and opened the gate, and
Peredur entered the hall; there he saw eighteen lads, lean
and red-haired and all of the growth and appearance and
age and clothing as the one who had opened the gate.
Their courtesy and their service were good: they helped
him to dismount, they drew off his armour, and then they
all sat and talked. Five girls came from a chamber into
the hall, and as for the chief girl Peredur was certain he
had never seen a sight as beautiful as she; she wore a tattered old brocade garment, once good, and where her skin
could be seen through this it was whiter than the flower
of the whitest crystal, while her hair and eyebrows were
blacker than jet and in her cheeks were two little red
spots redder than the reddest thing. She greeted Peredur
and embraced him and sat next to him, and not long after
that he saw two nuns coming in, one carrying a bottle full
of wine and the other with six loaves of white bread, and
they said, 'God knows, lady, this is as much food and drink
as our convent had.'

They went to eat then, and Peredur perceived that the
girl wanted to give more to him than to anyone else, so he

said, 'You are my sister, and I will share out the food and
drink.' 'No, friend,' she protested, but he said, 'Shame on
my beard if I do not.' He took the bread and divided it
equally, and the same with the wine to the measure of a
vial. When the meal was ended Peredur said, 'I would be
happy to have a comfortable place to sleep.' A chamber
was prepared for him and he went to bed, while the lads
said to the girl, 'Sister, we have some advice for you.' 'What
is that?' 'You shall go to the squire in the chamber near by
and offer yourself to him as he pleases, either as his wife
or as his mistress.' 'That is not a proper proposal. I have
never been with a man, and to offer myself to him before
he wooed me – that I could not do.' 'By our confession to
God, unless you do this we will leave you here to your
enemies.'

At that the girl rose, still weeping, and went to the chamber, and with the noise of the door opening Peredur woke
and saw her with tears streaming down her cheeks. 'Tell
me, sister, why are you weeping?' 'I will tell you, lord. My
father owned this court, along with the best earldom in the
world. The son of another earl was asking my father for
me, but I would not go to him of my own will, and my
father would not give me against my will, to him or to
anyone else. My father had no other children but me, and
when he died the realm fell into my hands; I was even less
eager to have the young earl than before, so he waged war
against me and seized all my possessions save for this one
house. The men you saw are my foster-brothers; they are
very brave and have fortified the house so that I could not
be taken as long as food and drink lasted. These would
have run out if the nuns you saw had not provided for us,
since they are free to travel through the land and the
realm, but now they themselves have neither food nor
drink. The earl and his hosts will attack this house no later
than tomorrow, and if he takes me my fate will be no better
than if I were given to the stableboys. Therefore I have

come to offer myself to you, in whatever way you please, if you will help us to escape or else defend us here.' 'Sister, go and sleep – I will not leave without doing one or the other.'

The girl left and went to sleep; next morning she rose and went to Peredur and greeted him. 'God reward you, friend,' he said. 'Is there any news?' 'None but good news, lord, so long as you are well. But the earl and all his forces have laid siege to the house, and no one has ever seen such a crush of tents, and knights calling on each other to joust.' 'Then saddle my horse, and I will rise.' The horse was saddled; Peredur rose and set out for the meadow, and when he arrived a knight was there riding his horse after having raised the signal to joust. He threw this knight over the hindquarters of his horse, and many others as well that day, and in the afternoon, towards sunset, a particular knight came to joust with him; this knight too was thrown and begged for mercy. 'Who are you?' Peredur asked. 'God knows, I am leader of the earl's retinue.' 'How much of the countess's realm is in your power?' 'God knows, a third.' 'Then return that third to her in full, with the good you have had from it, and supply food and drink for one hundred men, and horses and armour for them, and have all this in her court tonight. Moreover you shall be her prisoner, but you shall not be sentenced to death.' That was done at once.

The girl was joyful and happy that night – a third of her realm had been restored to her, and there was an abundance of horses and armour and food and drink in her court. They enjoyed themselves for as long as they wished, and then they went to bed. The next morning Peredur rose and set out for the meadow; that day he overthrew a great number until at the end of the day an arrogant knight appeared to fight him, and this knight too was overthrown and asked for mercy. 'Who are you?' Peredur asked. 'The earl's steward.' 'How much of the girl's realm is in your

power?' 'A third.' 'Return that third and the good you
have had from it in full; supply food and drink and horses
and armour for two hundred men, and surrender as her
prisoner.' That was done at once.

The third day Peredur set out for the meadow, over-
throwing more that day than he had the second, until
finally the earl came to joust with him; he too was overthrown and asked for mercy. 'Who are you?' Peredur
asked. 'I will not conceal it – I am the earl.' 'Well, then,
surrender the whole of the girl's earldom, and your own
as well; supply food and drink and horses and armour for
three hundred men, and put yourself in her hands.' Peredur spent three weeks overseeing their submission and the
girl's tribute, and after she was settled and the realm was in
order he said, 'With your permission, I will leave now.'
'My brother, is that your wish?' 'By my faith, it is – but for
love of you I would not have stayed so long.' 'Friend, who
are you?' 'Peredur son of Evrawg, from the north. If you
are ever threatened with danger or distress, tell me, and I
will rescue you if I can.'

Peredur set out, and far away he met a horsewoman on
a rangy sweated horse, and she greeted him. 'Sister, where
are you coming from?' She described her situation and her
journey, for she was the woman of the Pride of the Clearing. Peredur said, 'Well, I am the knight on whose account
you have suffered this disgrace, and he who brought it
upon you shall apologize.' At that a knight appeared and
asked him if he had seen such a knight as was being sought.
'Be quiet, for I am the one whom you seek. By my faith,
the girl is innocent of any wrong in connection with me.'
They jousted nonetheless; Peredur threw the knight, who
asked for mercy. 'You shall have that when you retrace
your path and proclaim the girl's innocence, and how in
compensation I overthrew you.' The knight gave his promise to that.

Peredur rode on, and seeing a castle on the mountain

ahead he made for it and pounded on the gate with his spear until there appeared to open it a fine auburn-haired lad, the size and weight of a warrior, but the age of a boy. Peredur entered the hall, where a tall handsome woman was sitting in a chair surrounded by handmaidens, and she was glad to see him; at dinner-time they went to eat, and after the meal she said, 'Chieftain, you would do well to find another place to spend the night.' 'Can I not sleep here?' 'Friend, there are nine hags here, and their father and mother as well. They are the hags of Gloucester, and by daybreak we will be as near to death as to making our escape, for they have overrun and laid waste the entire realm except for this one house.' 'Well, I would like to stay here tonight; if trouble comes, I will do what good I can, and I will do no harm.' Then they went to bed.

Towards dawn Peredur heard screaming; he rose quickly and went out in his shirt and trousers, with a sword round his neck, and when he arrived he saw a hag overcoming a screaming watchman, so he took his sword and struck her on the head until her helmet and skullcap spread out like a platter. 'Your mercy, Peredur, handsome son of Evrawg, and the mercy of God!' 'Hag, how do you know that I am Peredur?' 'It was prophesied and foretold that I would suffer harm from you, and that you would take horse and arms from me, and so you shall remain with me a while learning to ride your horse and handle your arms.' 'You shall have mercy upon your promise never to harm the realm of this countess.' Peredur took sureties to that effect, and with the countess's permission he accompanied the hag to the hags' court, staying there for three weeks and then choosing horse and arms and setting out.

In the evening of the first day he came to a valley, at the end of which was a hermit's cell; the hermit received him gladly, and he spent the night there. The next morning he rose and went out to find that snow had fallen during the night. A wild hawk had killed a duck in front of the cell, and with the noise of the horses the hawk rose and a raven alighted on the duck. Peredur stood there, comparing the blackness of the raven and whiteness of the snow and redness of the blood to the appearance of the woman he loved best: her hair was black as jet, her skin white as the snow, and the two red spots in her cheeks like the blood in the snow.[3]

Meanwhile Arthur and his retinue were searching for Peredur. 'Does anyone know the knight with the spear standing there in the valley?' asked Arthur. 'Lord, I will go and find out who he is,' said one of the men. The squire approached Peredur and asked him what he was doing and who he was, but Peredur was thinking so hard about the woman he loved best that he gave no answer; the man then struck at him with a spear, but Peredur threw him over his horse's hindquarters to the ground. One after another twenty-four knights came, but Peredur gave to none any answer other than the trick of jousting with each one and knocking him from his horse to the ground. Kei himself came and spoke rudely and harshly, but Peredur struck him under the jaw with his spear and threw him down hard, so that he broke his arm and his collar-bone. While he was in a dead faint from the hurt he had received his horse returned galloping wildly, and when the household saw the horse returning without its rider they hurried to the scene of the encounter. At first they thought Kei had been killed, but they saw that if a doctor set the bone and bound up the joints the patient would be none the worse. Peredur did not stir from his meditation at seeing the crush about Kei. The latter was brought to Arthur's tent, and Arthur had skilful doctors brought; he was upset over the hurt Kei had suffered, for he loved him very much.

Then Gwalchmei said, 'No one ought to be so dis-

3. In a similar episode in the Irish 'Exile of the Sons of Uisnech', Derdriu anticipates the arrival of Noísi.

courteous as to disturb a true knight from whatever meditation he is about – perhaps he is thinking of a loss which
he has sustained, or else of the woman he loves best. It
may be that discourtesy was shown by the man who saw
him last. Lord, if you wish, I will go and see whether this
knight has stirred from his meditation, and if he has I will
ask him politely to come and see you.' Kei was displeased,
and he spoke bitter envious words. 'Gwalchmei, I am certain that you will lead him back by the reins, though little
honour or glory will accrue from your overcoming a tired
knight worn out with fighting. Even so, you have overcome
many other knights, and while you have your tongue and
your fair words a thin linen tunic will be armour enough –
nor will you need to break sword or spear with the knight
you find in that condition.' 'You could speak more kindly
if you wished,' Gwalchmei replied. 'It is not right to vent
your anger and frustration on me, though I expect to bring
the knight along without breaking arm or shoulder.' Then
Arthur said, 'You speak like a wise and sensible man – go,
choose your horse and take whatever arms you need.'

Gwalchmei armed himself and made for Peredur at his
horse's easy gait, and he found the knight leaning on his
spear shaft and meditating still. He approached with no
sign of hostility and said, 'If I thought it would please you
as much as me, I would talk to you. I am a messenger from
Arthur, who asks you to come and see him. Two men have
come before me on this same errand.' 'That is true,' said
Peredur, 'they came discourteously and fought with me,
and I was displeased inasmuch as I disliked being aroused
from my meditation. I was thinking of the woman I love
best, and this is how I happened to remember her; I was
looking at the snow and the raven and the drops of blood
from the duck which the hawk killed, and thinking how
the whiteness of her skin is like the whiteness of the snow,
and the blackness of her hair and eyebrows like the raven,
and the two red spots in her cheeks like the two drops of

blood.' 'That was no ignoble meditation, nor was it strange that you disliked being distracted from it,' said Gwalchmei. 'Tell me, is Kei in Arthur's court?' 'He is. He is the last knight you encountered, and he came to grief: he broke his right arm and collar-bone with the fall he took from your spear thrust.' 'Well, I am not dismayed at having begun to take revenge for the insult to the dwarf and his wife.' Gwalchmei was surprised to hear the knight speak of the dwarf and his wife; he drew near Peredur and embraced him and asked what his name was. 'I am called Peredur son of Evrawg – who are you?' 'I am called Gwalchmei.' 'I am happy to see you – in every land I have encountered your reputation for strength and loyalty, and I entreat your companionship.' 'By my faith you shall have that, and give me yours.' 'Gladly,' said Peredur.

The two men set out in joyful friendship towards Arthur. When Kei heard them coming he said, 'I knew Gwalchmei would not need to fight with the knight, nor is it strange that he has won renown – he has done more with kind words than we by force of arms.' Peredur and Gwalchmei went to the latter's tent to take off their armour. Peredur put on the same kind of garment as his friend wore, and hand in hand they went to Arthur and greeted him. 'Lord, here is the man you have sought for so long,' said Gwalchmei. 'Welcome to you, chieftain – you must stay with me. Had I known you would progress so quickly you should not have left when you did – yet this was foretold by the dwarf and his wife, whom Kei injured and whom you have now avenged.' The queen and her handmaidens approached and greeted Peredur; they were happy to see him and made him welcome, and Arthur showed him great honour and respect.

They returned to Caer Llion. That first night in Arthur's court Peredur was walking in the fortress after dinner when he met Angharad Golden Hand. 'Sister,' he said, 'you are a kind, lovable girl, and I could love you best of all women, if you liked.' 'I give you my word,' said she, 'I do not love you, nor will I ever have you.' 'I give you my word, I will speak no word to any Christian until you confess that you love me best of men.'

The following day Peredur set out along the highway and the ridge of a great mountain, past which he saw a circular valley, wooded and rocky at the edges, with a floor of level meadows, and ploughed fields between the meadows and the forest, and in the centre of the forest great black houses of irregular construction. Having dismounted he led his horse towards the forest, and a little way in he saw the side of a sharp rock and a path leading to it; a lion fastened to a chain slept by the side of the rock, and beneath that yawned an immense deep pit filled with the bones of men and beasts. Peredur drew his sword and struck the lion so that it fell into the pit and hung by the chain; then with a second blow he struck the chain so that it broke and the lion dropped.

After that he led his horse across the side of the rock and into the valley, making for the fine castle he saw in the centre. In the meadow nearby was seated a great hoary-haired man, bigger than any man he had seen, while two young lads – one with yellow hair and one with auburn – were throwing knives with hilts of walrus ivory. Peredur made his way to the hoary man and greeted him. 'Shame on my gatekeeper's beard,' said the man, and Peredur realized the lion had been the gatekeeper.

The hoary-haired man and the lads then made for the castle, and Peredur joined them. It was a fine noble place: in the hall tables with great amounts of food and drink had been set out, and there entered from a chamber an old woman and a young one, the biggest women he had ever seen. Everyone washed and sat down: the hoary-haired man sat at the head of the highest table with the old woman next to him, while Peredur was seated next to the girl, and they were served by the two lads. The girl looked at Peredur and became sad, and when he asked her why she said, 'Friend, from the moment I saw you I have loved you best of men, and I am heartsick at the fate that will befall such a noble youth as you tomorrow. Did you see the black houses in the heart of the forest? Therein live the men of my father, the hoary-haired man yonder; they are all giants, and tomorrow they will fall upon you and kill you. This valley is called the Circular Valley.' 'Alas! Lady, will you arrange to have my horse and arms in the same lodging as myself?' 'Between me and God, I will gladly, if I can.'

When they thought it more timely to sleep than to carouse they went to bed, and the girl arranged for Peredur to have his horse and arms with him in his lodgings. When he heard the thronging of men and horses round the castle the next morning he rose, armed himself and his horse and rode out to the meadow. The old woman and the girl went to the hoary-haired man and said, 'Lord, secure the knight's promise to say nothing of what he has seen here, and we will see that he keeps his word.' 'By my faith, I will not,' said the hoary-haired man, so Peredur fought against the hosts, and by evening he had killed a third of them without being harmed by anyone. The old woman said to her husband, 'The squire has killed many already – grant him mercy.' 'By my faith, I will not.' The old woman and the beautiful girl went to an embrasure in the fortress to watch; Peredur met the yellow-haired lad and killed him, whereupon the girl said to her father, 'Lord, grant this knight mercy.' 'Between me and God, I will not.' Peredur encountered the auburn-haired lad and killed him too, and the girl said, 'You would have done better to grant the squire mercy before he killed your two sons. Now you will scarcely manage to escape yourself.' 'Go in person, girl, and beg him to show us mercy, though we have shown none to him.'

The girl went to Peredur and begged mercy for her father and those of his men who had escaped alive. 'He shall have that on his promise to go with his men and do homage to the Emperor Arthur, and to tell Arthur that Peredur is the man who did him this service.' 'Between me and God, we will do that gladly.' 'You are to be baptized, and then I will ask Arthur to give this valley to you and your heirs forever.' They went in, where the hoary-haired man and the big woman greeted Peredur. 'Since I gained control of this valley no Christian but you has left with his life,' said the man, 'yet I will do homage to Arthur, and will accept baptism and the faith.' Then Peredur said, 'I thank God I have not broken my vow to the woman I love best: that I would speak no word to any Christian.' They spent the night there, and the next morning the hoary-haired man and his retinue left for Arthur's court; there they did homage, and Arthur arranged for their baptism. The man told Arthur it was Peredur who had overcome him, and Arthur gave the valley to the man and his retinue as Peredur had requested, and with Arthur's permission they returned to the Circular Valley.

Peredur himself set out the next morning, crossing a long stretch of desert without finding a single dwelling until at last he came to a poor small house, and there he heard how there was lying on a gold ring a serpent which had not left standing a dwelling for seven miles round. He went to where he had been told the serpent lay and fought with it fiercely and ardently and bravely, until he killed it and took the ring for himself.

After that Peredur wandered for a long time without speaking a word to any Christian, until he began to lose his colour and looks from longing for Arthur's court and his companions and the woman he loved best; he set out for the court, and on the way he met Arthur's retinue, with Kei riding ahead on an errand. Peredur recognized each of them, but none recognized him. 'Where are you coming

from, chieftain?' asked Kei, and a second time and a third,
but no answer did he get, so he struck Peredur in the thigh
with his spear, and lest he should have to speak and break
his vow, Peredur rode on without retaliating. 'Between
me and God, Kei,' said Gwalchmei, 'that was an evil blow
to strike a knight for not being able to speak,' and when
they returned to court he said to Gwenhwyvar, 'Lady, see
what a wicked blow Kei struck a knight for not being able
to speak. For God's sake and mine, have the lad treated
and made well by the time I return, and I will repay you.'

By the time the men returned from their errand a knight
had come to the meadow near Arthur's court, and was en-
treating opponents to joust with him; those who went were
overthrown, and for the next week this man overthrew a
knight every day. Arthur and his men were coming from
church when Arthur saw that the knight had hoisted the
signal to joust. 'Men,' he said, 'by the valour of men, I will
not go from here until I have my horse and arms, in order
to overthrow that strange knight.' Servants went to fetch
these for Arthur, but in returning they met Peredur, who
took both horse and arms and rode to the meadow. Everyone who saw him go to joust with the knight made for the
rooftops and the hilltops and the high places to watch
the encounter. When Peredur signalled with his hand that
they should begin the knight charged, but Peredur stood
fast and did not move. Then Peredur gave the spurs to his
horse and made a ferocious attack, sharp and terrible,
proud and eager, and struck a poisonous-sharp, bitter-
severe, warrior-like blow under the helmet, lifting his opponent out of the saddle and throwing him a great distance away. Afterwards he returned horse and arms to the
servants, and made for the court on foot, where he was
called the Mute Knight.

When Angharad Golden Hand met him, she said, 'Between me and God, chieftain, if you could speak I would
love you best of men – by my faith, though you cannot

speak I will love you best all the same.' 'God reward you, sister. By my faith, I will love you.' Then it was perceived that this was Peredur; he became the companion of Gwalchmei, and Owein son of Uryen, and all of Arthur's retinue, and he stayed at the court.

Arthur was at Caer Llion ar Wysg, and one day he went hunting, taking Peredur with him. Peredur unleashed his dogs, and they killed a stag in the desert. Some way off he could see signs of habitation, and when he approached he found a hall, three swarthy, bald-headed lads playing gwyddbwyll by the door and three girls seated on a couch, all dressed in gold garments suitable for noble folk. He went to sit on the couch, whereupon one of the girls looked at him closely and began to cry, and he asked her why. 'For sorrow over the death of such a handsome youth as you.' 'Who will kill me?' 'Were it not dangerous for you to remain here I would tell you.' 'I will hear you, however much danger there be in remaining.' 'The man who owns this court is our father, and he kills all who come here without his permission.' 'What sort of man is your father to kill everyone thus?' 'A man who commits forceful and violent acts against his neighbours without compensating them.'

At that Peredur saw the lads rising to clear the pieces from the board. He heard a great noise, and following that a great black one-eyed man entered. The girls rose to meet him; they took his clothes from him and he sat down, and when he had collected himself and rested, he looked at Peredur and asked who this knight was. 'Lord, this is the handsomest and gentlest lad you ever saw,' said the girl, 'for God's sake and that of your own courtesy, be reasonable with him.' 'For your sake I will be reasonable and spare his life for tonight.' Peredur went over to the fire and ate and drank and talked with the girls, and when he had become intoxicated he said to the man, 'I marvel at the strength which you claim to possess. Who put out your eye?' 'It is my custom to spare no one who asks me what you have asked, neither as a gift nor for ransom.' 'Lord,' said the girl, 'though he spoke frivolously, it was due to drunkenness and intoxication. Keep the promise you made just now.' 'For your sake I will do that gladly, and I will spare his life for tonight.'

Peredur spent the night there, and the next day the black man rose and armed himself and sought him out, saying, 'Rise up, man, and meet your death!' 'If you wish to fight me, black man, either put aside your armour or else give me arms of my own.' 'Could you fight if you had arms? Take whatever you wish.' So the girl brought Peredur such arms as he liked, and he fought with the black man until the latter had to ask for mercy. 'You shall have that while you are telling me who you are and who put out your eye.' 'Lord, I will tell you – I lost the eye fighting against the Black Serpent of the Barrow. There is a hillock called the Mournful Mound, and in that mound a barrow; a serpent lies in the barrow, and in the serpent's tail is a stone with this property: whoever holds it in one hand will have as much gold as he wishes in the other. I lost my eye fighting against that serpent. My name is the Black Oppressor, and I am called that because I never left anyone round me without doing him violence, nor did I ever grant compensation.'

Then Peredur said, 'How far is this mound you speak of?' 'I will recount the stages and tell you how far it is. The day you leave here you come to the court of the sons of the King of Suffering.' 'Why are they called that?' 'Because a monster from the lake kills one of them every day. From there you come to the court of the Countess of the Feats.' 'What feats has she?' 'She has a retinue of three hundred men, and every stranger who comes to her court is told the feats of her retinue. The three hundred men sit next to the lady, not out of discourtesy to the guests, but to enable them to describe their feats. The day you leave that court

you will come to the Mournful Mound, around which the
owners of three hundred tents have gathered to watch the
serpent.'

'Since you have been a tyrant for so long, I will see that
your oppression does not continue,' and with that Peredur
killed the Black Oppressor. The girl who had begun to
talk to him said, 'Were you a poor man when you arrived
you will be rich now with the treasure of the black man
you have killed; moreover, you can see that there are many
pleasing girls in this court, and you might woo any one
you like.' 'Lady, I did not leave my country for a wife. I see
handsome lads here – let each of you make a match with
the one she likes best. As for your goods, I want none of
them, for I do not need them.'

From there Peredur rode to the court of the sons of the
King of Suffering; when he arrived he saw only women,
who nonetheless rose to give him a joyful welcome. As they
began to talk he saw a horse approaching with a body laid
across its saddle. One of the women rose and took the body
from the saddle and bathed it in a tub of warm water that
was near the door, and then she rubbed it with precious
ointment, whereupon the man rose alive and went to Peredur, greeting him and making him welcome. Two other
men came in on their saddles, and the girl revived them
as she had the first. Peredur asked why this was, and they
told him that in a cave there was a monster which killed
them every day.

They spent the night there. The next day the lads set
out; Peredur asked to go along, for the sake of their ladies,
but they refused, saying, 'If you are killed there, you will
have no one to revive you.' They left; Peredur followed,
but they slipped away and he lost them, and then he met
the most beautiful woman he had ever seen, and she was
seated on top of a mound. 'I know where you are going –
to fight with the monster – and it will kill you, not bravely,
but with cunning. A stone pillar stands at the door to its

cave, so that it sees everyone who enters but no one sees it, and from the safety of this pillar it kills everyone with poisoned stone spears. If you will promise to love me best of all women, I will give you a stone, so that when you enter, you will see it but it will not see you.' 'I give you my word that I loved you when I first saw you. Where will I find you?' 'When you seek me, look towards India.' She put the stone in his hand, and then she disappeared.

Peredur rode on towards a river valley whose edges were forested, with level meadows on both sides of the river; on one bank there was a flock of white sheep, and on the other a flock of black sheep. When a white sheep bleated a black sheep would cross the river and turn white, and when a black sheep bleated a white sheep would cross the river and turn black. On the bank of the river he saw a tall tree: from roots to crown one half was aflame and the other green with leaves. Beyond that a young lord sat on a mound with two white-breasted brindled greyhounds on leashes lying alongside, and Peredur was certain he had never seen such a royal-looking lad. In the forest opposite he could hear the staghounds flushing a herd of deer. Then he greeted the lord and the lord greeted him. He saw three paths leading from the mound, two highways and a third smaller road, and he asked where these led. 'One leads to my court, and I suggest that you either go on to my wife, or else stay here and see the staghounds chasing the exhausted deer out of the forest and into the open – you shall see the best greyhounds ever, and the strongest for stags, killing the deer close by the water. When it is time to eat my groom will bring my horse to meet me, and you shall be welcomed by us tonight.' 'God reward you. I will not stay, but will journey on.' 'The second road leads to a fortress where food and drink can be bought, while the narrower road leads to the monster's cave.' 'With your permission, lord, I will go there.'

When Peredur approached the cave he put the stone in

his left hand and his spear in his right hand; having entered and perceived the monster, he cast his spear through it and cut off its head. Then his three companions greeted him at the mouth of the cave and said it was foretold that he would kill the tyrant. He gave the head to the lords, and they in turn offered him his choice of their three sisters, and half their possessions as well. 'I did not come here for a wife, but if I wanted one, perhaps I would want your sister most.'

After that Peredur went on his way. When he heard a noise behind him he looked back, and saw a man in red armour coming along on a red horse; this man overtook him and greeted him in the name of God and man, so Peredur greeted him as a friend. 'Lord, I came to ask a favour of you,' said the man. 'What is that?' 'Accept me as your man.' 'If I were to take you, whom would I be getting?' 'I will not conceal my identity from you – I am called Edlym Red Sword, an earl from an eastern land.' 'I marvel that you offer yourself as man to one whose lands are no greater than your own, for I have nothing but an earldom myself, but if it suits you to come along as my man I will have you gladly.'

They rode on to the countess's court and were given a joyful welcome, and they were told that their seating below the retinue was a custom of the court and entailed no discourtesy, for anyone who overthrew her three hundred men could sit next to the countess, and she would love him best of men. Peredur overthrew the three hundred men and sat next to her, and she said, 'I thank God to have as brave and handsome a lad as you, as I do not have the man I love best.' 'Who was the man you loved best?' 'By my faith, Edlym Red Sword was the man, though I have never seen him.' 'God knows, Edlym Red Sword is my companion, and here he is. It was for his sake that I played with your retinue, and he could have done it better had he wished. I will give you to him.' 'God thank you, kind knight, I will have the man I love best,' and that night the countess and Edlym slept together .

The next day Peredur set out for the Mournful Mound, and Edlym said, 'By your hand, lord, I will go with you.' They rode forth to where they could see the mound and the tents. 'Go to those men,' said Peredur, 'and ask them to come and do homage to me.' Edlym went to them and said, 'Come and do homage to my lord.' 'Who is your lord?' 'Peredur Long Spear.' 'Were it permitted to execute a messenger you would not return to your lord alive for making such an arrogant request as that kings and earls and barons should go and do homage to him.' Edlym returned to Peredur, and Peredur told him to go back and give them their choice of doing homage or fighting with him; they chose to fight, and that day he overthrew the owners of a hundred tents. The next day he overthrew the owners of a hundred more, whereupon the third hundred decided to do him homage. Peredur asked them what they were doing. 'We are watching over the serpent until it dies, and then we will fight each other for the stone, and the strongest of us will win it.' 'Stay here while I go to look at this serpent,' said Peredur. 'No, lord, we will all go to kill the serpent together.' 'I do not wish that, for if it is killed I will win no more fame than the rest of you.' He went against the serpent and killed it, and then returned and said, 'Tell me what you have spent here, and I will pay it in gold.' He paid them all what they said they were owed, and asked nothing of them save the acknowledgement that they were his men. Then he said to Edlym, 'Go to the woman you love best, and I will go my way. I will repay you for having come along as my man,' and he gave Edlym the stone. 'God reward you, and make your way easy,' said Edlym.

Peredur then came to the loveliest river valley he had

ever seen, with many pavilions of different colours, and
even more marvellous than that was the multitude of
watermills and windmills. He met a big auburn-haired
man with the look of a miller and asked who he was.
'Head miller over all these mills.' 'Will I find lodging with
you?' 'You will, gladly,' whereupon Peredur went to the
miller's house and found it a pleasant, attractive dwelling. He asked the miller to lend him money to buy food
and drink for himself and for the people of the house,
promising to repay before he left, and he asked why there
was such an assembly. 'You must be either a stranger or
a fool,' said the miller. 'The Empress of great Constantin-
ople is there, and she wants none but the bravest men, as
she has no need of wealth. Food enough for all her troops
cannot be brought, and that is why there are so many
mills.'

That night they rested, and the next morning Peredur
rose and dressed and saddled his horse and went out to the
tournament. He saw among all the pavilions one which
was lovelier than any he had seen, and a beautiful lady
looking out through the window. He had never seen a
lovelier woman. She wore a brocade garment, and as he
gazed at her a great love overcame him; he looked at her
from morning to noon, and from noon to night, and then
the tournament ended. He put aside his arms and asked
the miller to lend him money, thus angering the miller's
wife – nevertheless the miller granted the request. The
second day he did what he had done the first, and at night
he returned to his lodging and borrowed money from the
miller; the third day he was in the same place, looking at
the girl, when he felt a great axe-handle blow between
the neck and shoulder, and when he looked round, there
was the miller, who said, 'Either turn your head away or
else go to the tournament.'

Peredur smiled at the miller, and went to the tournament. He overthrew everyone he encountered that day;

the men he overthrew were sent as a gift to the empress, while the horses and armour were sent to the miller's wife in consideration of the money lent. He took part in the tournament until he had overthrown everyone, sending all the men as prisoners to the empress, and the horses and armour to the miller's wife in return for the loans. The empress sent for the Knight of the Mill, asking him to come and see her, but he refused the first messenger and the second, and the third time she sent a hundred knights to ask him to come, saying that if he did not come of his own will they were to use force. They went and said they were the empress's messengers, but he played a good trick on them, trussing them up like roebuck and throwing them into the mill ditch. Then the empress sought advice of a wise man in her council. 'I will go as your messenger,' he said, and he went and greeted Peredur and asked him for the sake of his love to come and see the empress. Peredur and the miller went; he sat down in the first place he came to in the pavilion, and the empress sat next to him, and they conversed a little before Peredur said good-bye and returned to his lodging.

When he came to see her the next day he found not one spot in the pavilion less well-furnished than any other, for they did not know where he would sit. He sat next to the empress and they talked affectionately, and as they were thus they saw enter a black man holding a gold cup full of wine; he dropped to one knee before the empress and asked her not to give the cup save to one who would fight him for her. She glanced at Peredur, and he said, 'Lady, give me the cup.' He drank the wine and gave the cup to the miller's wife. Another black man came, bigger than the first, holding a monster's claw shaped like a cup and full of wine; he gave it to the empress and asked her not to give it to anyone who would not fight him for her. Peredur said, 'Lady, give it to me.' She gave it to him, and he drank the wine and gave the cup to the miller's

wife. Finally came a man with curly red hair, bigger than
the other two, holding a crystal cup full of wine; he bowed
on one knee and gave the cup to the empress, asking her
not to give it to anyone who would not fight him for her.
She gave it to Peredur, who sent it on to the miller's wife.

That night Peredur went to his lodging; the next day
he rose and armed himself and his horse, and rode to the
meadow, where he killed the three men. After that he
went to the pavilion, and the empress said to him, 'Kind
Peredur, remember the promise you made me when I
gave you the stone that enabled you to kill the monster.'
'What you say is true, lady, and I will remember.' According to the story Peredur ruled with the empress for
fourteen years.

Arthur was in his chief court at Caer Llion ar Wysg.
Seated on a brocade mantle in the middle of the floor
were four men: Owein son of Uryen, Gwalchmei son of
Gwyar, Howel son of Emhyr of Brittany, and Peredur
Long Spear. These four men saw enter a black, curly-
haired woman, riding a yellow mule. She held rough
thongs for beating the mule, and she had a rough, un-
lovable appearance: her face and hands were blacker
than pitch, and yet it was her shape rather than her
colour that was ugliest – high cheeks and a sagging face,
a snub, wide-nostrilled nose, one eye speckled grey and
protruding, the other jet black and sunken, long teeth
yellow as broom, a stomach that swelled up over her
breasts and above her chin. Her backbone was shaped like
a crutch; her hips were wide in the bone, but her legs
were narrow, except for her knobby knees and feet. This
woman greeted Arthur and the retinue, except for Peredur, for whom she had only harsh uncivil words. 'Peredur,
you deserve no greeting, and I give you none. Fate was
blind to give you fame and talent. When you went to the
court of the lame king and saw the squire carrying a
sharpened spear, with a drop of blood running from the

point to the lad's fist like a waterfall,[4] and other marvels as well, you asked neither their cause nor their meaning. Had you asked, the king would have been made well and the kingdom made peaceful, but now there will be battles and killing, knights lost and women widowed and children orphaned, all because of you.'

Then she said to Arthur, 'Lord, with your permission, my lodging is far from here – it is nowhere but in Castell Syberw,[5] and I do not know whether you have heard of that. Five hundred and sixty-six true knights are there, each with the woman he loves best, and whoever desires to win renown at arms and jousting and fighting will win it there if he deserves it. Moreover, I know where he who wishes the greatest honour and glory can win it: there is a castle on a high mountain, and a girl inside, and the castle is besieged. Whoever lifts that siege will win the greatest fame there has ever been.' Then she left.

'By my faith,' said Gwalchmei, 'I will not sleep in peace until I discover whether I can rescue the girl.' Many in Arthur's retinue had the same thought, but Peredur said, 'By my faith, I will not sleep in peace until I know the story and the meaning of the spear that the black woman spoke of.' As they were all making preparations, there rode to the gate a knight the size and strength of a warrior, and equipped with horse and armour; he approached and greeted Arthur and the entire retinue except for Gwalchmei. He carried on his shoulders a gold-chased shield with a bar of azure enamel, and the same colour was on all his armour. To Gwalchmei he said, 'You killed my lord through treachery and deceit, and I will prove it against you.' Gwalchmei rose and said, 'My pledge against you,

4. Actually, Peredur saw three drops of blood running from a spear carried by two lads, and in the court of his second uncle and not the lame one. Here the relationship between asking about the marvels and the well-being of the ailing king is finally established.

5. Castell Syberw: proud castle.

here or where you wish, that I am neither deceiver nor traitor.' 'I desire our combat to take place in the presence of my king.' 'Gladly. Lead on, and I will follow.' The knight rode forth, while Gwalchmei made ready; many arms were offered him, but he wished none but his own. He and Peredur dressed themselves and set out together because of the great friendship between them, but they did not ride together, for each one went his own way.

Early in the day Gwalchmei reached a valley, where he could see a fortress and a great court inside, with proud tall towers all round. He saw a horseman coming out through the gate, riding a glossy black palfrey, wide-nostrilled, smooth-stepping, proud and even-gaited, alert, quick and free-striding; this man owned the court, and Gwalchmei greeted him. 'God be good to you, chieftain. Where do you come from?' 'I come from Arthur's court.' 'Are you Arthur's man?' 'By my faith, I am.' 'Then I have good advice for you, for I see you are weary and worn out – go to my court and spend the night there, if you like.' 'I will, lord, and God repay you.' 'Take this ring as a token to the gatekeeper and make for the tower; my sister is there.'

Gwalchmei rode to the gate and showed his ring and made for the tower; when he arrived a great fire was blazing with a high smokeless flame, and a noble beautiful girl was sitting in a chair close to it. She rose and greeted him, and made him welcome, and he went to sit next to her; they ate their dinner and then turned to conversation, and as they did so a handsome hoary-haired man appeared, and said, 'Alas, you shameless whore, if you knew how improper it is to sit and play with that man, you would not do so.' The man withdrew his head and disappeared, and the girl said, 'Chieftain, if you would take my advice, you would secure the door for fear of danger from that man.' Gwalchmei rose, but before he could reach the door the man appeared as one of sixty fully-armed men ascending the tower, so he took the gwyddbwyll board and prevented their coming up until the earl returned from hunting.

At that the earl returned and asked, 'What is this?' 'A bad business,' said the hoary-haired man. 'This shameless creature is sitting and drinking with the man who killed your father – he is Gwalchmei son of Gwyar.' 'Stop all this, and I will go in,' said the earl; then he welcomed Gwalchmei and said, 'Chieftain, if you knew you had killed our father, it was wrong of you to come to our court. Though we cannot take vengeance, God will do so.' 'Friend, I came here neither to admit killing your father, nor to deny it. I am on an errand for Arthur and for myself, and I ask for a year's respite until I return from that errand. By my faith, when I return to this court I will either admit the deed or else deny it.' They gave him the respite willingly, but that is all the story has to say about Gwalchmei and this adventure.

Peredur set out and roamed the island seeking news of the black woman, but he found none. He came to a land he did not know in a river valley, and as he was travelling through that valley he met a rider in the garb of a priest, and asked for his blessing. 'Alas, poor wretch, you deserve no blessing, nor would it absolve you of having taken up arms on such a holy day.' 'What day is this?' asked Peredur. 'Good Friday.' 'Do not reproach me, for I did not know that. It is a year today since I set out from my own country.' Peredur dismounted, and taking his horse by the bridle led it some distance along the highway until he came to a side road; he took this through the forest and on the other side found a towerless fortress and signs of dwellings. He made for the fortress, and meeting the same priest at the gate again asked for a blessing. 'God's blessing upon you,' said the priest, 'and the better for you to travel with it. You shall spend the night here.' Peredur stayed there that night, but when he sought to leave the next day, the priest said, 'This is no day to travel. You shall stay with me today and tomorrow and the day after, and as to that which you seek I will guide you as best I can.' On the fourth day Peredur sought to leave, and he begged the priest to tell him of the Fortress of Marvels. 'I will tell you what I know. Cross the mountain yonder; on the far side there is a river, and in the valley the court of a king. The king was there at Easter, and if you are ever to learn of the Fortress of Marvels, you will learn of it there.'

Peredur set out, and when he reached the river valley he met a number of men going out to hunt, among them a man of noble bearing, whom he greeted. 'Chieftain, you may either go to the court or else come hunting with me,' said the man. 'I will send a retainer to commend you to a daughter of mine in the fortress, and she will give you food and drink until I return. If your errands are the sort that I can help with, moreover, I will do so gladly.' The king sent a short yellow-haired lad to accompany Peredur, and as they arrived at the court the daughter had just risen and was going to wash, so Peredur went to her and she welcomed him joyfully and made room for him at her side. They ate their dinner together, and she laughed aloud at whatever he said, so that everyone in the court heard. The short yellow-haired lad said to the girl, 'By my faith, if you ever had a man it is this knight, and if you have no man, your heart and soul are set on this one.' Then he went to the king, saying that the knight he had met was probably his daughter's man, 'And if he is not I expect he will be shortly, unless you prevent it.' 'Lad, what is your advice?' 'I advise you to send bold men against him and hold him until you are certain of his intentions.'

Thus the king sent men against Peredur, and they took him and put him in gaol. The girl went to her father and

asked why he had imprisoned the knight from Arthur's
court, but the king said, 'God knows, he shall not be free
tonight, nor tomorrow nor the day after; he shall not come
from where he is.' She did not oppose her father, but she
went to Peredur and said, 'Is it unpleasant being here?'
'I would not mind being free.' 'Your quarters and the
conditions here will be no worse than the king's, and you
will have the best entertainers in the court at your command. If it is more pleasing than before to have my bed
here, so that we can talk, you shall have that gladly.' 'I
will not refuse that.' So Peredur remained in prison that
night, and the girl kept the promise she had made.

The next morning there was an uproar in the city.
'Alas, kind lady, what uproar is this?' asked Peredur. 'My
father's hosts and all his men are coming to this city today.' 'For what purpose?' 'There is an earl near by with
two earldoms, and he is as powerful as a king. Today he
and my father will meet.' 'I beg you to obtain horse and
armour for me, so that I can go and look at the battle – I
give my word that I will return to prison.' 'I will do that
gladly.' She got these for him, with a pure red covering
over the armour and a yellow shield on the shoulder; he
went to battle and overthrew those of the earl's men he
met, and then returned to prison. The girl asked him how
he had fared, but he said not a word, so she went to her
father and asked which of his retainers had fought best,
and he answered that the man, whom he did not know,
had worn a red surcoat over his armour and a yellow shield
on his shoulder. She smiled and went to Peredur, and he
was well respected that night.

Peredur killed the earl's men for three days on end,
but before anyone could recognize him he always returned
to prison. On the fourth day he killed the earl himself,
and when the girl asked her father for news the king said,
'Good news: the earl has been killed and the two earldoms are mine.' 'Do you know who killed him, lord?' 'I

do – the knight with the red surcoat and the yellow shield.'
'Lord, I know who that is.' 'For God's sake, who?' 'The
knight who lies in your prison.' The king went to Peredur
and welcomed him and said he might name his reward
for the service he had performed. When they sat down to
eat Peredur was seated with the king on one side and his
daughter on the other, and after the meal the king said, 'I
will give you my daughter as a wife, and half my kingdom
with her, and the two earldoms as a present.' 'May the
lord God reward you, but I did not come here seeking
a wife.' 'Chieftain, what do you seek?' 'I seek news of the
Fortress of Marvels.' 'The chieftain aims higher than we
expected,' said the girl. 'You shall have news of the fortress, and a hundred guides through my father's realm and
abundant provisions – and chieftain, you are the man I
love best.' Then she told him, 'Cross the mountain yonder, and you will see a lake with a fortress in it, and that is
called the Fortress of Marvels. We know nothing of the
marvels, but that is the name of the fortress.'

Peredur made for the fortress and found the gate open,
and when he reached the hall that door was open; inside
he saw a gwyddbwyll set, and the pieces playing by themselves. The side he helped lost the game, and the other
side's pieces shouted as if they were real men; this angered
Peredur, so he gathered the pieces into his lap and threw
the board into the lake, whereupon the black woman
appeared. 'May you not receive God's welcome – you do
evil more often than good.' 'What do you have against
me?' 'You have lost the empress's board, and she would
not wish that for her empire.' 'Can it be recovered?' 'It
can if you go to the fortress of Ysbidinongyl. A black man
there ravages many of the empress's lands; kill him and
you will get the board. If you go there, however, you will
not return alive.' 'Will you guide me there?' 'I will show
you the way.'

Peredur went to the fortress of Ysbidinongyl and fought

with the black man until the latter asked for mercy. 'I will grant that if you return the empress's board to where it was when I entered the hall.' The black woman came and said, 'God curse you for your perverse sparing of the tyrant who is ravaging the empress's lands.' 'I gave him his life in order to obtain the board.' 'The board is not where you first found it; go back and kill him.' Peredur did that, and when he returned to the court the black woman was there. 'Woman, where is the empress?' 'Between me and God, you shall not see her until you destroy an oppressor that is in yonder forest.' 'What sort of oppressor?' 'A stag as fleet as the swiftest bird, with a single horn on its forehead as long as a spear shaft and as sharp as the sharpest thing. It grazes on foliage and whatever grass there is in the forest and kills every animal it finds, and those it does not kill die of hunger. Worse than that, it comes every night and drinks up the water in the fishpond so that the fish are left exposed, and the greater part of them die before the water returns.' 'Woman, will you show me this animal?' 'I will not. No one has dared go to the forest for a year; however the empress's little dog will flush the stag and drive it towards you, and the stag will attack you.'

The dog went as guide; it flushed the stag and drove it towards Peredur, and as the stag charged he let it go by and cut off its head with his sword. As he was looking at the stag's head there approached a horsewoman; she took the dog up into the sleeve of her cape, and set the stag's head, a red-gold collar round its neck, between herself and the pommel. 'Chieftain, you have acted discourteously by killing the finest jewel in my realm,' said she. 'I was requested to do it. Can I win your friendship?' 'You can. Go to the crest of the mountain and you will see a bush, and at the foot of the bush a stone. Seek a man to fight with you three times there, and you shall win my friendship.'

Peredur set out, and finding the bush called for a man to fight with him, whereupon there arose from under the stone a black man on a bony horse, both of them wearing great rusty armour. They fought, and as often as Peredur overthrew the black man the latter would climb back into the saddle. Finally Peredur dismounted and drew his sword, whereupon the black man disappeared with both horses, so that not even a second glimpse of him was to be had. Peredur walked along the ridge of the mountain, and on the other side he saw a fortress in a river valley; he made for that, and as he reached it he saw a hall with the door open. As he entered a lame hoary-haired man was sitting at one end of the hall, with Gwalchmei next to him, and he could see his horse in the same stable as Gwalchmei's steed. They welcomed him, and he went to sit on the other side of the hoary-haired man, and at that a yellow-haired lad came and knelt before him and sought his friendship, saying, 'Lord, I came to Arthur's court in the form of the black woman – when you threw away the gwyddbwyll board, when you killed the black man from Ysbidinongyl, when you killed the stag and fought with the black man from the stone. I carried the bleeding head on the platter, and the spear with the stream of blood running from the point. The head belonged to your first cousin, whom the hags of Gloucester killed, and they lamed your uncle as well. I am your first cousin also. It was prophesied that you would take revenge.'

Peredur and Gwalchmei decided to send to Arthur and his retinue and ask them to come. They began to fight with the hags, and one of them killed one of Arthur's men right in front of Peredur, and he ordered her to desist. She killed another man in front of him and again he ordered her to desist, but she killed a third man, whereupon he drew his sword and struck her on the helmet so that helmet and armour and her head split in two. She screeched and told the other hags to flee, saying that this was Peredur, the man who had been with them learning horsemanship and who was fated to destroy them. Arthur and his men struck the hags of Gloucester and killed them all. Thus it is told of the Fortress of Marvels.

GEREINT AND ENID

OF the Three Romances 'Gereint' is by far the least obtrusively marked by mythological motifs; it is also the most thoroughly refined and rationalized, and, perhaps in consequence, the best narrated. As in 'Owein' the hero wins his lady, then loses her and must win her back, not by force of arms, but by asking forgiveness. Only whereas Owein loses interest in his wife, Gereint fears that Enid has lost interest in him.

Gereint's name brings to mind that of Constantine's general Gerontios, as well as the frequent appearances of the name Gerontios in Cornish history – though Gereint is not a historical figure. On the contrary, he sports a fully realized fictional personality: cautious in approaching a better-armed opponent; generous in his terms to the same defeated opponent; reluctant to leave the tournament circuit for the responsibilities of home; doting upon his wife; immediately suspicious of her; inordinately stubborn in his conviction of her infidelity; childish in his dejection over not being allowed to enter the hedge of mist. Through all this Enid is merely steadfast and enduring.

Arthur is somewhat more visible here than in 'Owein' or 'Peredur': he organizes the hunt for the white hart, and with the help of his dog Cavall (who in 'Culhwch' corners Chief Boar Ysgithyrwyn) he kills the animal himself. Later, he compels Gereint to accept treatment for his injuries.

The meaning of the hedge of mist episode re-

mains a mystery. In the corresponding section of
Crestiens' *Erec* the hero's opponent is named
Mabonagrain, but the connection, if any, with
Mabon son of Modron is not clear.

Gereint and Enid

Arthur was accustomed to hold court at Caer Llion ar
Wysg, and at one time he did so through seven Easters
and five Christmases. Once he held it there at Whitsuntide, for it was the most accessible spot in his kingdom,
whether by land or sea. Arthur had assembled nine
crowned kings, all his men, together with earls and barons,
for these were his guests at every important feast, unless
they were kept away by some difficult matter. When court
was held at Caer Llion thirteen churches were set aside
for Masses: one for Arthur and his rulers and guests, one
for Gwenhwyvar and her ladies, one for the steward and
the suppliants, one for Odyar the Frank and other officers,
and nine other churches for the nine captains, especially
Gwalchmei, since he was the most distinguished by the
degree of his fame and his fighting ability and his noble
bearing. No one church might hold more than we have
mentioned above. Glewlwyd Strong Grip was Chief Gatekeeper, but he did not trouble himself over this service
except on one of the three important festivals; during the
rest of the year the duties were shared by his seven
assistants: Gryn, Penpingyon, Llaesgymyn, Gogyvwlch,
Gwrddnei Cat Eye, who could see by night as well as by
day, Drem son of Dremidydd and Clust son of Clustveinydd, all of them Arthur's warriors.

On Whit Tuesday the Emperor Arthur was sitting and
carousing when there entered a tall auburn-haired lad in
a tunic and surcoat of ribbed brocade, with a gold-hilted
sword round his neck and low-cut cordovan shoes on his

feet. 'Hail, lord,' said the man, coming before Arthur.
'God be good to you, and His welcome to you,' said
Arthur. 'Have you any news?' 'Lord, I have.' 'I do not
recognize you,' said Arthur. 'I wonder at that, for I am
your forester from the Forest of Dean – Madawg son of
Twrgadarn [1] is my name.' 'Tell us your news.' 'Lord, I
will. I saw in the forest a hart the like of which I have
never seen before.' 'What is there about it for you never
to have seen its like?' 'Lord, it is pure white, and out of
arrogance and pride in its lordliness it will travel with
no other animal. I have come to you for advice on the
matter.' 'I will do what is best,' said Arthur. 'Early tomorrow morning I will go and hunt it; tonight I will inform those in the guest houses, and Rhyverys (Arthur's
Master of Hounds) and Elivri (Arthur's Head Groom) and
everyone else.'

They decided on that, and Arthur sent the page on
ahead. Gwenhwyvar said, 'Lord, will you allow me to go
out tomorrow and watch the hunting of the hart which
the page spoke of?' 'I will gladly.' 'I will go then.'
Gwalchmei said, 'Lord, would it not be right to allow the
hunter who succeeds in cutting off the head – whether he
be mounted or on foot – to present it to his lover, or to a
companion's lover?' 'I will gladly allow that,' said Arthur.
'The steward will be held responsible if everyone is not
ready to go hunting in the morning.'

They spent a quiet evening with songs and entertainment and conversation and enough service, and when they
all thought it time for bed they went. They woke at dawn,
and Arthur called upon the chamberlains who guarded
his bed, no less than four squires: Cadyryeith son of
Gatekeeper Gandwy, Amren son of Bedwyr, Amhar son of
Arthur and Goreu son of Custenhin; these men came
and greeted Arthur and dressed him, and he was surprised

1. Twrgadarn: strong tower.

that Gwenhwyvar had not woken or even turned over in
bed. The men wanted to wake her, but he said, 'Do not
wake her, as she would rather sleep than watch the hunt.'
Then Arthur set out, and he could hear two horns being
blown, one near the lodging of the Master of Hounds and
one near the lodging of the Head Groom; the full complement of all his hosts came and they set out, crossing
Wysg and leaving the highway and travelling through excellent fine land until they reached the forest.

After Arthur had left the court Gwenhwyvar woke and
called on her women to dress her, saying, 'Women, I received permission last night to go and watch the hunt, so
let one of you go to the stables and have brought such
horses as are fit for women to ride.' The woman who went
found only two horses, so Gwenhwyvar and one hand-
maiden rode out across Wysg and followed the trail of
men and horses. As they were travelling thus they heard
a loud thundering noise, and when they looked back they
saw a knight on a huge willow-grey colt, the rider an
auburn-haired young man, bare-legged but royal-looking.
He wore a gold-hilted sword on his thigh, a tunic and
surcoat of brocade, low-cut cordovan shoes on his feet, and
a mantle of green purple with a gold apple in each corner, while his horse's gait was proud and high-stepping,
swift and lively, short and even.

This man overtook Gwenhwyvar and greeted her. 'God
be good to you, Gereint,' she answered. 'I recognized you
as soon as I saw you. God's welcome to you. Why did you
not go hunting with your lord?' 'I did not know when he
went.' 'I wondered how he could go without me, either.'
'Well, lady, I was asleep, so I did not know when he left.'
'Of all the young lads in the kingdom, I think you are
the best for companionship. We can enjoy the hunt as
much as the hunters, for we will hear the horns being
sounded, and the dogs being unleashed and their starting
to bay.' They went to the edge of the forest, and Gwen-

hwyvar said, 'Now we will hear the dogs being unleashed.'

At that they heard a great commotion, and they saw a
dwarf riding towards them, a whip in his hand, his horse
tall and robust, wide-nostrilled, ground-covering, strong
and proud. Next to him they saw a woman on a proud,
handsome, even-gaited, pure-white horse, and she wore a
garment of gold brocade; next to her rode a knight on a
huge mud-spattered war-horse, both man and beast wearing heavy gleaming armour. Gereint and Gwenhwyvar
were certain they had never seen man or horse or armour
of such impressive size, and all three rode close together.

'Gereint, do you know that great knight yonder?' asked
Gwenhwyvar. 'I do not, and that strange heavy armour
permits neither face nor countenance to be seen.' Then
Gwenhwyvar said, 'Woman, go ask the dwarf who the
knight is.' The girl went to meet the dwarf; he drew near
when he saw her coming, and she said, 'Who is the knight?'
'I will not say.' 'As you are so discourteous, I will ask him
myself.' 'By my faith, you shall not.' 'Why not?' 'Your rank
does not entitle you to talk to my lord.' The girl nonetheless turned her horse's head towards the knight, whereupon the dwarf struck her across the face and eyes with
his whip, so that the blood welled forth. The girl rode
back to Gwenhwyvar, moaning with pain. 'That was a
cruel thing the dwarf did,' said Gereint. 'I will go find out
who the knight is.' 'Do,' said Gwenhwyvar.

Gereint rode over to the dwarf and asked, 'Who is the
knight?' 'I will not say.' 'Then I will ask him myself.' 'By
my faith, you shall not. You are not so honourable as to
deserve to speak with my lord.' 'I have spoken with a man
who ranks with your lord.' Gereint turned his horse's head
towards the knight, but the dwarf overtook him and struck
him as he had struck the girl, so that the blood coloured
his mantle. He put his hand on the hilt of his sword, but
on reflection he considered that it was no revenge to kill

the dwarf only to have an armed knight take him cheaply, for Gereint was without armour. He rode back to Gwenhwyvar, and she said, 'You acted wisely and sensibly.' 'Lady, with your permission, I will go after him yet. The knight must eventually make for dwellings, and there I will find armour, either on loan or in exchange for surety, with which to try myself against him.' 'Go, then, but do not close with him until you have good armour. I will be anxious until news comes.' 'Lady, if I escape alive, you shall have news by late tomorrow afternoon.'

With that Gereint set out. The trio took the road below the court of Caer Llion, crossing the ford at Wysg and travelling through excellent and lovely flat plains until they came to a walled town with a fortress and castle at one end. They entered at the other end, and as the knight rode through, every family rose to greet and welcome him, but when Gereint arrived he looked at every house to see whether he recognized anyone, and he did not, nor did anyone recognize him, so that he might obtain the favour of armour on loan, or for surety. Every house he saw was full of men and horses and arms, and shields being polished and swords burnished, and armour washed and horses shod.

The knight and the lady and the dwarf made for the castle; everyone there was glad to see them, and from gates and battlements and everywhere people all but broke their necks thronging to greet them and make them welcome. Gereint stood looking to see whether the knight would stay in the castle, and being certain that he would, he looked round and saw some distance from the town an old tumbledown court and a battered hall. As he recognized no one in the town he made for the old court, but when he arrived he saw scarcely anything but an upstairs chamber and a marble staircase leading from it, and on the stair a hoary-haired man was sitting in old torn clothes. Gereint stared hard for a long time, until the man said,

'Lad, what are you thinking?' 'I am thinking that I do not know where to go tonight.' 'Then stay here, chieftain, and you shall have the best I can offer.' 'I will do that, and God reward you.'

Gereint then approached and dismounted in the hall, and leaving his horse there he accompanied the man upstairs. In the chamber a very old woman was seated on a cushion; she was dressed in a ragged old brocade garment, and he supposed that in her prime she would have been the most beautiful women he had ever seen. There was also a girl near by, wearing a shift and mantle that were very old and beginning to tear, and he was certain he had never seen a girl as full of abundant grace and beauty as she. The man said to the girl, 'Tonight this gentleman has for his horse no groom but yourself.' 'I will wait upon him and his horse as best I can.' She pulled off Gereint's boots and provided his horse with straw and grain, and then she made for the hall and returned to the chamber, where the man said, 'Go to town, now, and have brought here the best supply of food and drink that you can get.' 'I will do that gladly, lord.'

She went to town, then, and while she was gone they talked, but she returned almost at once, bringing with her a lad who carried a bottle of bought mead on his back and a quarter of a young ox; in her hands the girl brought a portion of white bread and a loaf of the finest wheat. 'I could not get better supplies than these, nor would I be credited with better.' 'Good enough,' said Gereint. They had the meat boiled, and when it was ready they sat down, Gereint with the man on one side and the woman on the other, and the girl serving them. They ate and drank, and when they had finished Gereint began to talk with the hoary-haired man, asking him if he was the first owner of the court. 'I certainly am, for I built it, and I also owned the fortress and castle you saw.' 'Alas, man, how did you lose it?' asked Gereint. 'I lost a great earldom as well, and this is how: I had a nephew, my brother's son, whose lands I took with my own. When he came to power he claimed his realm, but I refused him, so he made war on me and took everything I had.'

Then Gereint asked, 'Gentle sir, will you tell me of the arrival of the knight who came to the fortress with a lady and a dwarf? Why is there the preparation of arms that I saw?' 'I will tell you. The preparation is for tomorrow, for a game the young earl plays. They place in the meadow two forked sticks, and across the forks a silver rod and on the rod a kestrel, and there is a tournament for the kestrel. The host of men and arms and horses that you saw in the town have come for the tournament, and each man has brought the woman he loves best, for he who has not brought his lady may not joust for the kestrel. The knight you saw has won the hawk for two years, and if he wins it a third time it will be sent to him without his having to come for it, and he shall be known as the Knight of the Kestrel.'

'Good sir, what advice have you concerning that knight and an insult which I and an attendant of Arthur's wife Gwenhwyvar both received from the dwarf?' And Gereint told the hoary-haired man the episode of the insult. 'It is not easy to advise you, since you profess to love no girl or lady so that you might joust with the knight. You could take this armour that was mine, and my horse, should you prefer it to your own.' 'God reward you, good sir. My own horse is good enough for me, since I am accustomed to it, but I will take the armour. Will you allow me to profess to love that girl there, your daughter, at the appointed time tomorrow? If I survive the tournament my love and loyalty will be hers as long as I live, and if I do not survive she will be as chaste as before.' 'I will do that gladly. Since you have settled on this idea you will have to have your horse and arms ready tomorrow at daybreak, for at that time the Knight of the Kestrel will make his proclamation – that is, he will ask the woman he loves best to take the kestrel, as she deserves it best. He will say, "You have had it the last two years, and if anyone disputes your claim I will defend it by strength." For that reason you must be there at daybreak, and the three of us will be there with you.'

They settled on that and went to bed at once. Before dawn they rose and dressed, and at dawn the four of them were standing on the bank of the meadow. The Knight of the Kestrel made his proclamation and asked his love to take the hawk, but Gereint said, 'Do not take it, for here is a girl who is lovelier and finer and nobler than you and who deserves it better.' 'If you mean to maintain that the kestrel is hers, then come and joust with me,' said the knight, so Gereint went to the end of the meadow, furnished as he was with a horse and some strange heavy rusted worthless armour. They charged at each other and broke their spears, and likewise the second and third time and thereafter, breaking the weapons as fast as they were brought. When the earl and his host saw the Knight of the Kestrel getting the upper hand a shout of gladness and rejoicing would go up from him and his number, while the hoary-haired man and his wife and daughter would be saddened. The hoary-haired man provided Gereint with spears as he broke them, and the dwarf did the same for the Knight of the Kestrel.

Finally the hoary-haired man went to Gereint and said, 'Chieftain, you see in my hand the spear that was mine the day I was made a knight; I have never broken it, and it has a very good blade. None of your spears has availed.' Gereint took the spear and thanked the man. At that the dwarf also brought a spear to his lord, saying, 'You see here a spear that is no worse. Remember that no knight has ever withstood you as long as this one.' 'Between me and God,' said Gereint to the dwarf, 'unless sudden death carries me off he will be none the better for your help.' From a great distance Gereint urged on his horse and closed in, warning his opponent and then striking him a blow on the strongest part of the shield so that it split, and his armour broke in the direction of the blow; his girths broke and he and the saddle were thrown over the horse's hind-quarters to the ground. Gereint at once dismounted and angrily drew his sword, advancing in a ferocious rage; the knight rose and drew his sword, and they went at each other on foot until the armour of each had been shattered by the other and the sweat and blood were running into their eyes. When Gereint had the better of it the hoary-haired man and his wife and daughter were glad, and when the knight was uppermost the earl and his party rejoiced.

When the hoary-haired man saw that Gereint had received a heavy painful blow he quickly drew near and said, 'Chieftain, remember the insult you suffered at the dwarf's hand – was it not to avenge that, and the insult to Arthur's wife Gwenhwyvar, that you came?' At that Gereint recalled the dwarf's words; he collected his forces and raised his sword and struck the knight on the top of the head, breaking through head-armour and skin and sinking into flesh until it struck bone, whereupon the knight fell to his knees and threw his sword away and begged Gereint for mercy, saying, 'My wrongful arrogance has prevented my asking mercy until too late. Unless I am granted time to see a priest and confess my sins to God, I shall be none the better for mercy.' 'I will show mercy on condition that you go to Arthur's wife Gwenhwyvar and make good the insult her attendant suffered at the hand of your dwarf. I am satisfied with what I have done to you in return for the injury I suffered, but you are not to dismount from the time of your departure until you are before Gwenhwyvar, to make such amends as Arthur's court decrees.' 'I will do that gladly. Who are you?' 'Gereint son of Erbin. Now tell me who you are.' 'Edern son of Nudd.' Edern was thrown onto his horse and so went off to Arthur's court, with the woman he loved best before him, and his dwarf too, and there was loud weeping. (The story so far.)

•

The young earl and his host approached Gereint and greeted him, and invited him to come to the castle, but he said, 'I will not. I will stay in the place where I stayed last night.' 'As you will not accept the invitation now, accept such provision as I can have brought to the place where you were last night, and I will have drawn a bath to relieve you of your fatigue and weariness.' 'God reward you. Now I will go to my lodging,' said Gereint, and he did that. Earl Niwl and his wife and daughter went with him, and when they reached the upstairs chamber they found that the chamberlains of the young earl had brought their service to the court and were preparing all the houses and supplying them with straw and fire; shortly the bath was drawn, and Gereint stepped in and his head was washed. The young earl himself came as one of forty knights, what with his own men and the guests from the tournament; Gereint came from the bath and the earl asked him to go into the hall and eat. 'Where are Earl Niwl and his wife and daughter?' 'They are in the upstairs chamber,' said a chamberlain, 'putting on the clothes which the earl brought for them.' But Gereint said, 'Let the girl wear nothing but her shift and mantle until she goes to Arthur's court, for Gwenhwyvar to dress her as she sees fit,' and the girl did that.

Everyone then entered the hall and washed and went to eat. This is how they sat: Gereint with the young earl and Earl Niwl on one side, and the girl and her mother on the other, and after that according to the degree of honour. They ate and were served generously with an abundance of different dishes, and after that they began to talk, and the young earl invited Gereint for the following day. 'Between me and God, I will not,' said Gereint, 'for this girl and I are going to Arthur's court. I feel that Earl Niwl has suffered enough of grief and tribulation, and it is largely to try to obtain a better provision for him that I am going.' 'Chieftain, it is not my fault that Niwl is without a realm.' 'By my faith, he will not remain so unless death carries me off.' 'Chieftain, with regard to the disagreement between myself and Niwl, I will gladly accept your advice, as you will judge impartially between us.' 'I ask nothing but that he be given what belongs to him, and the good he has been deprived of from the time of his loss until today.' 'For your sake, I will do that gladly.'

Then Gereint said, 'All those here who ought to be Niwl's men should do him homage now,' and those men all did, and everything was settled; the castle and the town and the realm were returned to Niwl, and all that he had lost, down to the smallest jewel. Niwl said to Gereint, 'Chieftain, the girl you avowed on the day of the tournament is ready to do your will, and she is at your command,' but Gereint answered, 'I wish only that she remain as she is until she arrives at Arthur's court, for I want Arthur and Gwenhwyvar to give her to me.' The next day they set out for Arthur's court, and that is Gereint's adventure so far.

•

Meanwhile, this is how Arthur was hunting the hart. He assigned the men and dogs hunting posts and unleashed the dogs against the hart, and the last dog unleashed was Arthur's favourite, a dog named Cavall. This one left the other dogs behind and caused the hart to turn and pass Arthur's position, whereupon Arthur overtook it and cut off its head before anyone else could attack it. The horn announcing the kill was sounded and everyone gathered,

and Cadyryeith came to Arthur and said, 'Lord, Gwenhwyvar is over there, alone save for one attendant.' 'Then
ask Gildas son of Caw and the scholars of the court to
accompany her home,' and that was done. During their
return they debated to whom they should give the hart's
head: one man wanted to give it to the lady he loved
best, another to the lady that he loved best, so that all
the retainers and knights were quarrelling sharply over
the head. As they reached the court Arthur and Gwenhwyvar heard their quarrelling, and the queen said, 'Lord,
my advice is that the hart's head should not be given until
Gereint son of Erbin returns from his errand,' and she told
her husband the story of that errand. 'Gladly, let that be
done,' said Arthur, and so it was agreed.

The next day Gwenhwyvar alerted the fortress to be
on the look-out for Gereint's arrival, and after midday
there was seen a hunchbacked little man on a horse,
and behind him a woman, or a girl, as it seemed, and
behind her a great bowed-over knight, head down and
very sad, and wearing poor smashed armour. Before they
reached the gate a watchman went to Gwenhwyvar and
told her what people they had seen and the sort of appearance these people made, and he said, 'I do not know
who they are.' Gwenhwyvar said, 'I know – that is the
knight whom Gereint pursued, and I suspect that he is
not now coming of his own will. If Gereint overtook
him, then he has avenged the smallest insult to my hand-
maiden.' The gatekeeper came to Gwenhwyvar and said,
'Lady, there is a knight at the gate, and no one has ever
seen a more terrible sight: his armour is battered and
broken, and the colour of his blood is getting the better
of his own colour.' 'Do you know who he is?' 'I do – he is
Edern son of Nudd. But I do not know him.'

Gwenhwyvar went to the gate and saw the knight enter,
and she would have grieved over such a sight had he not
permitted so ill-mannered a thing as the dwarf to accom-

pany him. Edern greeted her, and she answered, 'God be good to you.' 'Lady, greetings to you from Gereint son of Erbin, the bravest and best of men.' 'Did he encounter you?' 'He did, and not to my advantage, but that is my fault and not his. Lady, Gereint sends you his greetings, and along with them me, whom he has compelled to come here, in order to make amends for the hurt your hand-maiden suffered from my dwarf. He has forgiven me his own insult, since he supposed my life to be in danger, but he placed a firm, bold, manly, warrior-like charge on me to come here and do your will.' 'Alas, sir, where did he overtake you?' 'In the place of the games and competition for the kestrel (the town now called Caerdyv).[2] He had no retinue save three very poor shabby-looking creatures: a very old hoary-haired man and an old woman and a good-looking young girl, all wearing shabby old clothes. Gereint avowed his love for the girl and parti-cipated in the tournament for the kestrel, for he said that his lady deserved the falcon better than mine; we jousted, and he left me as you see me now, lady.' 'Sir, when do you expect Gereint to arrive?' 'Lady, I presume that he and the girl will arrive tomorrow.'

Then Arthur approached, and Edern greeted the king. 'God be good to you,' said Arthur, and he looked at the knight for a long time and was surprised to see him in such a state, for he thought he recognized him. 'Are you Edern son of Nudd?' 'Lord, I am, after suffering very serious injuries and almost unbearable wounds.' He re-lated the entire adventure, whereupon Arthur said, 'Well, Gwenhwyvar ought to show mercy, from what I hear.' 'Lord, I will show such mercy as you wish, for my dis-grace is as much an insult to you as is your own.' 'Then this is the fairest thing,' said Arthur. 'Let physicians be called for this man until it is known whether he will live. If he lives, let him give such compensation as is ordered

2. Caerdyv = Cardiff.

by the best men in the court, and let him give sureties; if he dies, the death of so good a lad as Edern is too much for the insult to the attendant.'

'I think that fair,' said Gwenhwyvar, so Arthur himself stood surety for Edern, along with Caradawg son of Llŷr, Gwallawg [3] son of Llenawg, Owein son of Nudd, Gwalchmei and many other men. Arthur had his chief physician Morgan Tud called, and said to him, 'Take Edern son of Nudd and have a chamber prepared for him, and treat him as well as you would me if I were wounded. Let no one disturb him in his chamber other than yourself and those assistants who minister to him.' 'Lord, I will do that gladly,' said Morgan Tud. Then the steward said, 'Lord, where should the girl be sent?' 'Let her go to Gwenhwyvar and her handmaidens,' and that was done. (Their story so far.)

The next day Gereint approached the fortress. Gwenhwyvar had men out watching lest he arrive unnoticed, and a watchman came to her and said, 'Lady, I believe I have seen Gereint and the girl. He is mounted and dressed in walking clothes, while the girl is very white, and I suspect she is wearing a linen garment.' 'Every woman make ready to meet Gereint and greet him and give him a joyful welcome,' said Gwenhwyvar, and she herself went out to meet Gereint and the girl. Gereint went to Gwenhwyvar and greeted her. 'God be good to you,' she said, 'and welcome. You have carried out a fruitful and prosperous errand, well-judged and praiseworthy, and God reward you for sending me such a handsome compensation.' 'Lady, I wished you to have the compensation you chose. Here is the girl for whose sake you were avenged.' 'God's welcome to her, and no wrong for us to welcome her either.'

They went inside and dismounted, and Gereint went

3. Gwallawg: one of the kings who fought against Hussa at the end of the sixth century.

to Arthur and greeted him. 'God be good to you,' said
Arthur, 'and His welcome to you. Though Edern son of
Nudd has been hurt and wounded, still, you have performed a worthy errand.' 'That was not my fault, rather
it came of Edern's arrogance in refusing to identify himself. I would not leave him until I knew his name, or
until one of us overcame the other.' 'Sir, where is the girl
I hear you have avowed?' asked Arthur. 'She has accompanied Gwenhwyvar to the latter's chamber.' Arthur went
to see the girl, and he and his companions and everyone
in the court welcomed her, and all were certain that if her
dress and appearance were to match her beauty, they
would never have seen a lovelier girl. Arthur gave her to
Gereint, and the bond that was made between two people
at that time was made between Gereint and the girl. She
had her choice of Gwenhwyvar's clothing, and whoever
saw her so dressed saw a radiant and beautiful sight. That
day and evening they spent with plenty of songs and
various dishes and liquors and numerous games, and when
it was time to sleep they went to bed; in the chamber of
Arthur and Gwenhwyvar a bed was made up for Gereint
and Enid, and that night they slept together for the first
time.

The next day Arthur satisfied the suppliants on
Gereint's behalf, providing an abundance of gifts, while
Enid became acquainted with the court, and won such
companions that no lady in the island of Britain was
better spoken of. 'I was right to propose that the hart's
head be given to no one until Gereint's return,' said
Gwenhwyvar, 'for we ought to give it to Enid daughter
of Niwl, the girl of greatest renown. I do not expect anyone will deny her this, as between her and everyone there
is nothing but tenderness and affection.' They all approved, Arthur included, and so the head was given to
Enid; thereafter her fame increased, and she had even
more companions than before. Gereint loved tournaments

and the heat of combat, and he returned victorious every time; thus it was for one year, and two, and three, until his fame had spread over the face of the kingdom.

*

One day Arthur was holding court at Caer Llion ar Wysg, during Whitsuntide, when there came to him wise and sensible, scholarly and eloquent messengers, and they greeted him. 'God be good to you, and His greeting to you. Where do you come from?' 'Lord, we come from Cornwall, and we are messengers from your uncle Erbin son of Custenhin. Our message is for you: such greetings as an uncle ought to send his nephew and a man his lord, and to tell you that he is growing weak and feeble and approaching his end. His neighbours, perceiving this, trespass on his territory and covet both land and realm. He entreats you, lord, to permit his son Gereint to come to save the land and defend the boundaries, for he says that Gereint would do better to employ the flower of his youth and vigour in defending his own boundaries, rather than in worthless tournaments that bring him only fame.' 'Well, go change your clothes and eat, and rest from your journey,' said Arthur, 'and you shall have an answer before you leave.'

The messengers went to eat, and Arthur considered how it was not easy for him to let Gereint go from the court, nor was it fair or handsome of him to prevent his cousin from guarding his kingdom and its boundaries, inasmuch as his father was unable to defend them. Gwenhwyvar was no less troubled and distracted, nor were the women and girls, for they all feared Enid would leave them. They spent that day and evening well supplied with everything, and Arthur told Gereint the content of the message which the men of Cornwall had brought. 'Well, lord, I will do your will in this matter, regardless of the advantage or disadvantage to me,' said Gereint.

'Then here is my advice. Though I regret your departure, go to your own realm and defend its boundaries, and take with you as large a company as you wish. Take those of my loyal followers you love best to be your guides, and those of your relatives and fellow knights whom you love.' 'God reward you, I will do that,' said Gereint. 'What murmuring is this I hear between you?' asked Gwenhwyvar. 'Does it concern companions for Gereint on his journey?' 'It does,' said Arthur. 'Then I must consider companions and provisions for Enid,' she said. 'Those are wise words,' said Arthur. They went to bed, and the next day the messengers were permitted to depart, having been told that Gereint would follow.

Three days later Gereint set out, and these are the men who accompanied him: Gwalchmei son of Gwyar, Rhioganedd son of the King of Ireland, Ondyaw son of the Duke of Burgundy, Gwilym son of the ruler of France, Howel son of Emhyr of Brittany, Elivri Rich in Arts, Gwynn son of Tringad, Goreu son of Custenhin, Gweir Great Valour, Garanhon son of Glythvyr, Peredur son of Evrawg, Gwyn Llogell Gwyr, a magistrate of Arthur's court, Dyvyr son of Alun of Dyved, Gwrhyr Interpreter of Languages, Bedwyr son of Pedrawd, Cadwr son of Gwryon, Kei son of Kynyr, Odyar the Frank, Arthur's court steward, 'and Edern son of Nudd,' said Gereint, 'as I hear he is able to ride and I want him to come.' Arthur said, 'Though he is well, it is not right for him to go until there is peace between him and Gwenhwyvar.' 'Gwenhwyvar could let him go with me in exchange for sureties.' 'No, if she gives her permission, let her do so freely and with no sureties, for the man has suffered enough hurt and distress for the harm his dwarf did to the girl.' So Gwenhwyvar said, 'Well, lord, whatever seems right to you and Gereint in this matter, that I will do.' She allowed Edern to go freely, and there were many others who accompanied Gereint.

They set out then, the best-looking host ever seen, and made for the Havren, and on the far bank of the river Gereint's foster-father was at the head of the best men of Erbin son of Custenhin. They gave him a glad welcome, and many women from the court accompanied Gereint's mother in coming to see Enid daughter of Niwl. All the court were overjoyed to meet Gereint, because of their love for him, because of the renown he had won since his departure, and because he meant to defend the dominion and maintain its boundaries. They went to the court, where they were generously supplied with a variety of dishes and different liquors and ample service and numerous songs and games. And in honour of Gereint all the nobles of the realm were invited in that night to see him.

They spent that day and night enjoying themselves sensibly, and early the next day Erbin rose and summoned Gereint, along with the best of his companions, and said to him, 'I am a weak, aged man. While I was able to defend the realm for you and myself I did so, but now that you are a young man in the flower of your youth and vigour you must do so.' Gereint said, 'Well, I did not ask you to place control of your realm in my hands, or call me away from Arthur's court.' 'I am giving it into your hands now, and you must take the homage of your men today.' But Gwalchmei said, 'Better to fulfil the requests of the suppliants today, and to take the homage of your realm tomorrow.' The suppliants were called into one place, and Cadyryeith went to gather their intent and ask each one what he wanted; Arthur's retinue began to distribute gifts, and at once the Cornishmen came and began to do likewise, and so eager were all to give that the distribution did not last long, neither did anyone who came with a request leave unsatisfied.

They spent that day and night enjoying themselves sensibly and early the next day Erbin called on Gereint to

send messengers to ask his men whether it was convenient for him to come and receive their homage, and
whether they were troubled or offended or had anything
against him; Gereint sent to the Cornishmen to ask them
that, and they replied that they were exultant and joyful
at the prospect of his coming to receive their homage. He
took the homage of those who were there, and they were
all together for the third night. The next day Arthur's
retinue asked to leave. 'Your departure now would be too
painful,' said Gereint. 'Stay with me until I have received
the homage of those of my best men who mean to come
to me.' They stayed until this was done; Gereint and Enid
guided them back as far as Dyngannan, and there they
parted. Then Ondyaw son of the Duke of Burgundy said
to Gereint, 'First journey along the borders of your dominion and mark their extent closely and carefully; then if
trouble afflicts you, tell your companions.' 'God reward
you, I will do that.' Gereint and a knowledgeable guide
from among the best men of his realm set out for the borders of the country, and he took careful note of the farthest
limit shown him. As had been his custom in Arthur's
court he went to tournaments and encountered the boldest
and strongest men, until he was as famous in that region
as he had been before with Arthur, and had enriched his
court and companions and noblemen with the best horses
and arms and the best and rarest jewels. He did not leave
off until his reputation had spread over the face of the
land.

When Gereint perceived how his fame had grown, he
began to prefer comfort and leisure, for no one was worthy
of combat with him. He loved his wife, and the routine
of the court and songs and entertainment, so he dwelt in
the court for a time; then he began to love being alone
in his chamber with his wife, until that was pleasanter to
him than anything else. He began to lose the hearts of his
noblemen, and his hunting and sport, and the hearts of

all the people at court, until there was a murmuring against him and reviling of him in secret by these people, because he had forsaken their company for the company of a woman. When these mutterings reached Erbin he spoke to Enid and asked her whether it was she who was causing this in Gereint and encouraging him to forsake his people and his retinue. 'By my confession to God, it is not I,' she said, 'for nothing could displease me more than that.' Nevertheless she did not know what to do – it was not easy to tell Gereint what was being said, and it was no easier to listen to it and not tell him, so she became very anxious.

One summer morning they were in bed. He was on the outer, protective side, while she was awake in the glass chamber; the sun was shining down on the bed and the coverlet had slipped from over his chest and arms, and he was asleep. She gazed at the magnificence of his good looks and said, 'Woe is me, if on my account these arms and chest are losing the fame and fighting ability they once possessed,' and at that the tears streamed down until they fell on his chest. That and the words she had spoken woke Gereint, and he was disturbed by the thought that she spoke not out of concern for him, but out of love for another man with whom she wished to be alone. At that thought he lost all peace of mind. He summoned a squire and said, 'Have my horse saddled and my arms made ready, and be quick about it. And you,' he said to Enid, 'rise and dress and have your horse fitted out, and bring along the worst riding dress you have. Shame on me if you return until you learn if I have lost my strength as completely as you suppose, or if being alone with the man you were thinking of will be as you expected.' Enid rose and put on a simple dress and said, 'Lord, I know nothing of your thoughts.' 'Nor shall you yet,' he replied.

He went to Erbin and said, 'Sir, I have an errand to do, and I am not certain when I will return – look after your

realm until I do.' 'That I will,' said Erbin, 'only I wonder at this sudden departure. Who will go with you? For
you are not a man to travel through England alone.'
'Only one person will accompany me.' 'Then God protect
you, son, for there is many a man in England with a
grievance against you.' Gereint went to his horse,
equipped as it was with strange heavy glittering armour,
and he told Enid to mount her horse and ride out in
front and stay well ahead. 'Whatever you see or hear about
me, do not turn back, and say nothing to me unless I speak
to you first.'

They rode out, then, and their road was neither the
pleasantest nor the most travelled, but the wildest and
surest for thieves and robbers and wild beasts. When they
reached the highway they followed that until they saw a
great forest, and as they made for the forest there appeared
four armed knights, one of whom was saying, 'This is a
good chance for us to take the two horses and the armour,
and the woman as well, for we will have no trouble as
far as that single sad-looking droopy-drowsy knight is concerned.' Enid overheard this talk, but for fear of Gereint
she did not know whether to speak or be silent. 'God's
vengeance on me,' she said, 'if I do not prefer death at
Gereint's hand to death at another's. Though he may kill
me, I will speak, lest he be killed without warning.' She
waited for Gereint to draw near, and when he did so she
said, 'Lord, did you hear what those men said about you?'
He raised his head and looked at her angrily. 'You are to
do as you were told and be silent. Your concern means
nothing to me and is no warning, and though you wish my
death and destruction at the hands of those men yonder,
I am not afraid.'

At that the foremost knight couched his spear and
charged; Gereint met him, and not feebly, either, for he
side-stepped the rush and struck the knight boldly on the
shield so that it split and his armour broke and the spear

went half a yard into him, throwing him over his horse's hindquarters to the ground. Angered by the death of his companion the second knight advanced, but he was thrown with one blow and killed like the first, while the third and fourth subsequently advanced and were killed in the same way. Enid was sad and unhappy to see this. Gereint dismounted and stripped the armour from the slain men and put it on their saddles; he knotted the reins together and then mounted his horse and said, 'Take the four horses and drive them before you, and stay in front of me as before. Say nothing to me unless I speak to you first, for by my confession to God, if you disobey me you shall suffer for it.' 'My lord, I will do my best to obey you.'

They travelled on into the forest until they reached a great level plain with a dense tangled copse in the middle, and from that copse approached three knights, both horses and riders being fully equipped and armed. The girl scrutinized them closely, and as they drew near she overheard their talk: 'Here is a fortunate arrival, four horses and four suits of armour for no trouble. We will get them easily for all that dejected-looking knight can do, and we will have the girl in our power as well.' 'That is true,' thought Enid, 'for he is weary after fighting with those other knights. God's vengeance on me if I do not warn him,' and she waited until Gereint drew near. 'Lord, do you not hear the talk of those men concerning you?' 'What is that?' 'They are saying they will get this booty cheap.' 'Between me and God, I am less displeased by what these men say than I am by your talk and disobedience.' 'Lord, I spoke only lest you be taken by surprise.' 'Then be quiet, for your concern is worthless to me.'

At that one of the knights couched his spear and charged, striking effectively, he thought, but Gereint met the thrust easily and deflected it. Then he advanced and struck the other squarely, and with the advance of man

and horse all his opponent's armour did not avail; the
head of the spear and a length of the spear shaft went into
the knight, and he was thrown over his horse's hindquarters to the ground. The other two knights approached
in their turn, but they fared no better than had the first.
Enid stood and watched, on the one hand afraid that
Gereint might be wounded in combat with the men, and
on the other joyful to see him triumph. Gereint dismounted and bound the three suits of armour to the three
saddles; he knotted the reins so that there were now seven
horses tied together, and then he mounted his own horse
and ordered Enid to drive the horses on ahead. 'As you
will not obey me, I am none the better for telling you to
be silent.' 'Lord, I will do my best, but I cannot conceal
from you the violent hateful talk which I hear from the
strangers who journey through this wilderness.' 'Between
me and God, your concern is worthless to me.' 'From now
on, lord, I will be silent as long as I can.'

Enid rode on, keeping the horses before her and staying
well ahead of Gereint. From the copse they travelled
through good open country, lovely and beautiful, level
and distinguished, and far away they saw a forest, and
apart from the near edge they could see no end or limit
to it. As they approached that forest there emerged from
it five bold, fierce, powerful knights, mounted on strong,
wide-boned, ground-devouring, wide-nostrilled war-
horses, with plenty of armour covering both man and
beast. When these knights had drawn near, Enid heard
this conversation from them: 'This is a good chance for
us – we will get all these horses and the armour cheaply
and with no trouble, and the girl as well, for all that
feeble, worn-out, sad-looking knight can do.' She was
greatly distressed to hear the men talk so, for she did not
know what to do; finally deciding to warn Gereint, she
turned her horse's head, rode back and said, 'Lord, had
you heard the talk of those men as I did, you would be

more anxious than you are.' Gereint gave her a cool,
bitter, mocking smile and said, 'I hear you doing what I
forbade you to, but perhaps you will live to regret it.'

At that the men encountered him, and Gereint, exuber-
ant and victorious, overcame all five. He bound the five
suits of armour to the five saddles and knotted the reins
so that there were twelve horses tied together, and these
he delivered to Enid, saying, 'I do not know what is the
good of giving you orders, but this once, as a warning to
you, I will do so.' So Enid rode on to the forest, keeping
well ahead as Gereint had commanded, and had it not
been for his anger he would have been sorry to see the
trouble so excellent a girl had with so many horses.

They journeyed into the forest; it was deep and broad,
and soon night fell and Gereint said, 'Woman, there is no
point in trying to go farther.' 'Lord, we shall do as you
wish.' 'Best to turn off into the forest to rest, and to wait
until day to go on.' 'Gladly, let us do that.' Gereint dismounted and lifted her to the ground, saying, 'I am so
tired I can do nothing but sleep – you stay up and watch
the horses.' 'Lord, I will do that.' Gereint slept in his
armour, and so they passed the night, which in that sea-
son was not long. When Enid saw the light of day she
looked round to see whether he was awake, and at that
moment he woke. 'Lord, I have wanted to wake you for
some time,' she said, but he was silent, annoyed that she
had spoken without permission. At length he rose and
said, 'Take the horses and set out, and ride ahead as you
did yesterday.'

After a short time they left the forest and came to flat
open country, with meadows on one side and men cutting
hay with scythes. When they came to a river their horses
bent and drank, and then they climbed up a lofty hill,
where they met a slender young lad with a towel round his
neck and a bundle in the towel, but they did not know
what was in the bundle. The lad had a small green pitcher

in his hand, with a cup over the mouth of the pitcher, and he greeted Gereint. 'God be good to you,' said Gereint, 'where do you come from?' 'I come from the city you see before you. Lord, would you mind if I ask you where you come from?' 'I would not. I came through the forest back there.' 'You did not come through it today?' 'No, I spent the night in the forest.' 'I do not suppose that you were comfortable there, or that you had food or drink.' 'Between me and God, I did not.' 'Then take my advice and have your meal with me.' 'What have you?' 'A breakfast I was taking to the mowers, nothing but bread and meat and wine. If you wish it, sir, they shall have nothing.' 'I do, and God repay you.' Gereint dismounted, and the lad lifted the girl to the ground. They washed and went to eat; the lad sliced the bread and poured the wine and served them with everything, and when they had finished he rose and said to Gereint, 'Lord, with your permission, I will go after food for the mowers.' 'First go into town and find me lodging in the best place you know, and the roomiest for the horses; take whichever of the horses you like, and the armour with it, to pay for your service and your gift.' 'God repay you – that would be repayment enough for a service greater than I have rendered.'

The lad went to the town and paid for the best and most comfortable lodging he knew of, and after that he took his horse and armour to the court, and went to the earl and related to him the entire adventure. 'Now, lord, I will go to meet the knight and show him his lodging.' 'Go, gladly, and if he wishes to come here he will receive a joyful welcome.' The lad went to meet Gereint, and told him that the earl would welcome him to his court, but Gereint wanted only to go to his own lodging; he found an ample comfortable chamber, with plenty of straw and coverings, and a roomy comfortable place for the horses, and the lad obtained ample provision for them. After they had undressed, Gereint said to Enid, 'Go to the far end of the chamber and do not disturb me – you may call the woman of the house if you wish.' 'Lord, I will do as you say.' The man of the house came and greeted Gereint and said, 'Chieftain, have you had your dinner?' 'I have.' The lad said, 'Do you wish drink or anything else before I go to see the earl?' 'In fact, I do.' So the youth went out into the town and brought back drink, and shortly Gereint said, 'I cannot help but sleep.' The lad said, 'Well, while you sleep, I will go and see the earl.' 'Do that, gladly, and return when I asked you to.'

Gereint slept, then, and Enid did too. When the lad went to the earl, the latter asked him where the knight's lodging was, and the lad told him, saying, 'Now I must go and serve him.' 'Then go and greet him for me, and say I will come to see him presently.' 'I will do that.' When it was time for Gereint and Enid to wake the lad returned; they rose and walked out, and when it was time for their meal they took it, with the lad serving them. Gereint asked the man of the house if he had companions he would like to invite, and the man said he did. 'Then bring them here, and give them their fill of the best that can be bought in the town, at my expense,' and so the best men of the host's acquaintance were brought to eat their fill at Gereint's expense.

After that the earl came in a party of twelve true knights to see Gereint, and Gereint rose to greet him. 'God be good to you,' said the earl, and then they all went to sit down, each according to his rank, and the earl asked Gereint what sort of journey he was on. 'I intend simply to look for adventure and do the errands I like.' The earl looked at Enid carefully, until he was certain he had never seen a lovelier girl, nor a finer one, and he set his heart and soul on her. 'Have I your permission to go over to that girl and talk with her?' he asked Gereint, 'for I see that she is somewhat estranged from you.' 'You have my permission, gladly.'

The earl went to Enid and said, 'Woman, you cannot enjoy journeying with that man.' 'It is not unpleasant for me to travel the road he travels.' 'You have neither servants nor handmaidens to wait on you.' 'I would rather follow him than have servants and handmaidens.' 'I have a good idea: I will give you power over my earldom if you will stay with me.' 'Between me and God, I do not wish that. I promised myself to that man first, and I will not betray him.' 'You do wrong. If I kill him, then I will have you as long as I wish, and when I do not want you I will turn you away. If you do this of your own will, however, then we will be inseparable and happy together for as long as we live.' She thought over what he was telling her, and at length she decided to encourage him in his presumption. 'This is the best plan, chieftain: lest I be accused of unfaithfulness beyond measure, come here tomorrow, and carry me off as if I knew nothing about it.' 'I will do that,' he said, and he rose and took his leave and departed with his men.

Enid said nothing to Gereint of the man's conversation with her, lest she should make him angry or anxious or distressed. When it was time they went to bed, and at first she slept a little, but at midnight she woke and arranged Gereint's armour so that it would be ready for him. Fearful and trembling she went to the edge of Gereint's bed, and slowly and softly she said to him, 'Lord, rouse yourself and dress, for this is what the earl said to me and what he intends to do,' and she told him of the entire conversation. Though he was angry with her he heeded the warning, and dressed himself, and when she had lit a candle for him to dress by he said, 'Leave the candle and ask the man of the house to come here.' She did that; the man of the house came, and Gereint asked him, 'Do you know how much I owe you?' 'Good sir, I do not believe it is much.' 'Whatever I may owe, take the eleven horses and the eleven suits of armour.' 'God re-

ward you, but I have not spent on you the worth of even
one suit of armour.' 'Well, then, you will be so much the
richer. Sir, will you guide me out of town?' 'Gladly. In
what direction do you wish to travel?' 'In the one opposite
to that of my arrival.'

The innkeeper guided him until he had all the directions he needed, and then Gereint told Enid to ride
ahead, which she did, while the innkeeper returned home.
He had scarcely arrived when the greatest commotion that
anyone had heard arose, and when he looked out he saw
eighty fully-armed knights surrounding the house, led by
the Brown Earl, who asked, 'Where is the knight who was
here?' 'By my hand, he is a good distance away, for he left
quite a while ago.' 'What sort of ruffian are you to let him
go without telling me?' 'Lord, you did not command me
to keep him – if you had, I would not have let him go.'
'What direction do you suppose he took?' 'I know only
that he took the highway.' The earl and his men turned
for the highway, and observing hoofprints they followed
these. When Enid saw the light of day she looked behind
her and saw mist and a great fog, and she thought, 'By my
faith, I will warn him – better to die by his hand than to
see him killed without warning.' 'Lord,' she said, 'do you
not see the man advancing towards you, and the other
men with him?' 'I see, and I see that despite my orders
you will not be silent. Your warning means nothing to
me – now be quiet.'

Gereint turned to the knight, and at the first charge
threw him to the ground under his horse's hooves. As long
as there remained a knight out of the eighty, Gereint
would throw the man at the first rush; from better to best
they came at him, except for the earl, but at last the earl
himself came and broke one spear shaft, and then another.
Then Gereint turned on him and thrust his spear against
the strongest part of the shield, so that it split and all the
earl's armour broke, and he himself was thrown over his

horse's hindquarters to the ground, where he lay in peril
of his life. At the noise of Gereint's horse approaching he
recovered his senses, and said, 'Lord, your mercy,' and
Gereint showed mercy. Between the hardness of the
ground where the men were thrown, and the ferocity of
the blows they had received, there was not one man without a bitter-deadly, sadly-wounding, powerful-bruising
fall.

Then Gereint set out again on the highway, with Enid
well ahead. Before them they saw the loveliest valley anyone had seen, with a great river running through it, and
a bridge over the river; the highway led to the bridge and
over it, and on the other side there was the handsomest
walled town anyone had seen. As they made for the bridge,
they saw approaching through a dense little copse a man
on a great tall even-gaited horse, spirited but responsive.
'Knight, where are you coming from?' asked Gereint. 'I
am coming from the valley below.' 'Sir, will you tell me
who owns this lovely valley and walled town?' 'I will,
gladly. The French call him Gwiffred Petit, and the
Welsh call him the Little King.' Then Gereint said, 'I am
going to cross the bridge and take the lower road below
the town.' 'Do not cross the bridge and enter his land
unless you wish to encounter him, for it is his custom to
let no knight enter his territory without combat.' 'Between
me and God, I will take the road for all that,' said
Gereint. 'Then I think it likely that you will be shamed
and humiliated.' Angered and fierce-hearted, Gereint set
out along the road, as he had intended; he did not take
the road from the bridge to the town, but the one that
led along the ridge of rough country, high and elevated,
with a distant view.

As he was riding along he saw a rider coming after him
on a war-horse, strong and robust, bold-stepping, wide-
hoofed and barrel-chested. Gereint had never seen a
smaller man than he saw on this horse, and both horse and

rider wore plenty of armour. Having overtaken Gereint
the little man said, 'Tell me, chieftain, is it out of discourtesy and arrogance that you would cost me my
honour and have me abandon my custom?' 'It is not — I
did not know this road was forbidden.' 'As you did not
know, come with me to my court to make amends.' 'By my
faith, I will not. I will not go to the court of your lord
unless he is Arthur.' 'Now by Arthur's hand, I must have
compensation from you, or I will have suffered a great
injury.' They charged each other at once. A squire came
to supply them with spears as they broke, and each dealt
the other harsh painful blows until the shields lost their
colour. Gereint found this fighting unpleasant, because
his opponent was small and hard to hit and dealt severe
blows. They did not tire until their horses fell to their
knees, and then at last Gereint threw the other headfirst
to the ground; they leapt to their feet and fought, and
each dealt the other strong, severe, heavy, painful, ferocious, sharp blows, piercing helmets and breaking mail-
caps and battering armour, until they could scarcely see
for the sweat and blood.

Finally Gereint grew furious; he pulled himself together, and fierce-angry, courageous-swift, cruel-ferocious,
he raised his sword and struck his opponent on the top of
the head, a mortally painful, venomous-bold, bitter-cruel
blow, so that the head-armour broke, and skin and flesh
parted and the wound went to the bone. The Little King's
sword was thrown a field's distance away from him, and
in God's name he begged Gereint's protection and mercy.
'Though your manners were bad and you were unreason-
able, you shall be shown mercy as long as you travel with
me and do not attack me again, and if I meet with trouble
you are to rescue me.' 'Lord, you shall have that gladly,'
and Gereint took his word. Then the Little King said,
'Lord, you must come to my court and relieve your weariness and fatigue.' 'Between me and God, I will not go.'

Gwiffred Petit looked at Enid, and he was saddened to see the multitude of woes that afflicted so noble a lady. He said to Gereint, 'Lord, you do wrong not to rest and take comfort, for in your condition you are not likely to overcome any adversity you might encounter.'

Gereint wished only to proceed, however; he mounted his horse, bloody and uncomfortable, while Enid rode on ahead, and they made for a forest which they saw in the distance. It was very hot, and between the sweat and blood Gereint's armour stuck to his skin, so when they reached the forest he paused under a tree to avoid the heat, and he felt more pain than when he had been wounded. Enid halted under another tree, and they heard horns and an assembly, for Arthur and a host had dismounted in the forest. Gereint was considering how he might avoid them when a man on foot spotted him. This man was a servant of the steward; he went to his master and told him of the knight he had seen in the forest, whereupon the steward had his horse saddled and took his spear and shield and rode to where Gereint was. 'Knight, what are you doing there?' he asked. 'I am halting under a shady tree, in order to avoid the heat and the sun.' 'Where are you going and who are you?' 'I am looking for adventures, and going whatever way I please.' Then Kei said, 'Well, come with me to see Arthur, who is near by.' 'Between me and God, I will not.' 'Then you shall be compelled.' Now Gereint recognized Kei, but Kei did not recognize Gereint, and so he charged with the best that was in him, but Gereint grew angry and struck Kei with the butt of his spear, so that the latter fell headfirst to the ground. He had no wish to do the steward further harm, however.

Kei was terrified and ran off wildly. He mounted his horse and rode to his lodging, from where he went to Gwalchmei's pavilion and said, 'Sir, I have heard that in the forest yonder one of the lads saw a wounded knight in shabby armour. You would do well to go and look at him.' 'I do not mind going,' said Gwalchmei. 'Then take your horse and some of your arms, for I hear he is rather short with those who come his way.' Gwalchmei took his spear and mounted his horse and rode to where Gereint was. 'Knight,' he said, 'what sort of journey are you on?' 'Doing my errands and looking for adventures.' 'Will you tell me who you are, or will you come to see Arthur, who is near by?' 'I will not identify myself, nor will I go to see Arthur.' He recognized Gwalchmei, but Gwalchmei did not recognize him. 'It will never be said of me that I let you go without knowing who you are,' said Gwalchmei, and he thrust his spear into Gereint's shield until the shaft splintered and the horses were head to head. At that he recognized his opponent. 'Alas, Gereint, is it you?' 'I am not Gereint.' 'Between me and God, Gereint, this is a wretched, ill-advised journey,' and Gwalchmei looked round until he discovered Enid, whom he greeted and welcomed, and then he continued, 'Gereint, come and see Arthur, your lord and first cousin.' 'I will not go – I am not in a condition to see anyone.'

At that a squire appeared, coming to speak with Gwalchmei, and Gwalchmei sent him back to tell Arthur that Gereint was there wounded and in a sorry state, and would not come to see him; he whispered to the squire, out of Gereint's hearing, 'Ask Arthur to move his pavilion nearer to the road, since Gereint will not come of his own will, nor would it be easy to compel him in his present condition.' The squire went and said this, and Arthur moved his pavilion to the edge of the road, whereupon Enid took heart. Then Gwalchmei coaxed Gereint along the road to where Arthur was encamped, and the squires were setting up a tent at the edge of the road. 'Hail, lord,' said Gereint. 'God be good to you. Who are you?' said Arthur. 'This is Gereint,' said Gwalchmei, 'and of his own will he would not have met you today.' 'Well, he lacks advice,' said Arthur. At that Enid went to Arthur and greeted him, and he said, 'God be good to you. Let someone help her dismount.' One of the squires having done so, Arthur asked, 'Alas, Enid, what journey is this?' 'Lord, I do not know, save that I must travel the road he travels.' 'Lord, with your permission, we will leave now,' said Gereint. 'Where will you go? You cannot leave now unless you wish to assure your death.' 'He would not let me invite him here,' said Gwalchmei. 'Well, he will let me,' said Arthur, 'and he shall not leave until he is well.' 'Lord, it would please me best if you permitted me to leave.' 'Between me and God, I will not permit it.'

First Arthur had a girl summoned to take Enid to Gwenhwyvar's pavilion, and Gwenhwyvar and her women were overjoyed; they helped Enid out of her riding-dress and gave her another garment. Then Arthur summoned Cadryeith and told him to set up a pavilion for Gereint and the doctors, and ordered him to provide a good supply of everything that was needed; Cadryeith did all this, and he brought in Morgan Tud and his assistants. After Arthur and his company had spent nearly a month treating him Gereint went to the king and asked permission to leave. 'I do not know if you have fully recovered,' said Arthur. 'In truth, I have, lord.' 'It is not you I will believe, but your doctors,' and he called them in and asked if this were true, and Morgan Tud said it was.

The next day Arthur permitted Gereint to depart, and he prepared to complete his journey, while Arthur himself left that same day. Gereint told Enid to ride well ahead as she had done before; she took the road and followed the highway, and as they were riding they heard close by the loudest scream in the world. Gereint said, 'Halt here, and wait while I seek the explanation of that scream.' 'I will do that,' said she. Gereint came to a clearing near the road, and in that clearing he found two horses, one with a man's saddle on it and the other with a woman's; a knight in armour lay dead, while a young

woman in riding-dress was standing over him and screaming. 'Lady, what has happened to you?' 'I was travelling
with the man I love best, when there came three giants,
who with no reason or cause killed him.' 'What road did
they take?' 'The highway.' Gereint returned to Enid and
said, 'Go to the lady in the clearing and wait for me there
– if I return.' She was saddened by this command, but she
nevertheless went to the lady, who was painful to hear,
and she was certain that Gereint would never return.

Gereint pursued the giants until he overtook them.
Each one was bigger than three men, and each had a huge
cudgel on his shoulder. He advanced and caught one giant
in the middle with his spear, and then he pulled the spear
out and struck a second giant. The third, however, turned
and struck him so that his shield split and his shoulder
stopped the blow; all his wounds opened and the blood
ran out. Gereint drew his sword and advanced, and struck
such a bold, ferocious, painful, powerful blow that it split
the head and neck down to the shoulder, and the giant
dropped dead. He left the three giants there and returned
to where Enid waited, and when he saw her he fell from
his horse to the ground dead. Enid gave a terrible, loud
heart-rending scream and ran to where he had fallen.

The Earl Limwris [4] was travelling along the road with
his company, and when they heard the cry they crossed
the road, and the earl said to Enid, 'Lady, what has
happened?' 'Good sir, the man I loved best and always
will love – he has been killed.' 'And what has happened
to you?' the earl asked of the other lady. 'The man I loved
best has been killed also.' 'What killed them?' 'The giants
killed the man I loved best, and this other knight went
after them, and as you see he has lost blood beyond
measure. I do not suppose he has returned without killing
some of them, if not all.' The earl had them bury the
knight who had been left dead; however, he believed there

4. Limwris: in Crestiens' *Erec*, li mors, 'death'.

was life left in Gereint, so he had him brought back in the hollow of his shield, to see whether he would live.

The two women went to the earl's court, and when they arrived Gereint and the bier were placed on a table in the hall. Everyone changed out of his riding-clothes, and the earl asked Enid to change and put on another dress. 'Between me and God, I do not wish to.' 'Lady, do not be so sad.' 'It will be difficult to convince me why I should not be.' 'I am telling you there is no need to be sad, regardless of whether that knight lives or dies, for I have a good earldom here, and you shall have control over it, and myself as well. So take heart and cheer up.' 'By my confession to God, I will not be merry as long as I live.' 'Come and eat.' 'Between me and God, I will not.' 'Between me and God, you shall.' He dragged her to the table against her will and repeatedly asked her to eat. 'By my confession to God, I will not eat until the man on the bier does.' 'You cannot fulfil that, the man is all but dead.' 'I will do my best.' Then he offered her drink from a bowl, saying, 'Drink this bowlful and you will change your mind.' 'Shame on me if I drink before he does.'

'Well,' said the earl, 'it is no better being kind to you than being unkind,' and he boxed her ears. She gave a loud piercing scream, and cried far more than she had before, and it occurred to her that were Gereint alive she would not have her ears boxed so. With the reverberation of that scream Gereint came to his senses. He sat up and found his sword in the hollow of his shield, whereupon he rushed at the earl and struck him a ferocious-bold, venomous-painful, fierce-powerful blow so that the man was split, and only the table stopped the sword. Everyone left the tables and fled – it was not the living man they feared most, but the one who had risen from the dead to kill them. Then Gereint looked at Enid, and he felt two sorrows, one over her losing her colour and looks, and the other in knowing that she had been in the right. 'Lady, do you know where our horses are?' 'I know where yours went, but not mine. Yours went to that house yonder.' He went to the house and brought his horse out, and mounted it, and he lifted Enid up and set her in front of him, and so they rode out.

They were travelling as if between two hedges, and day was giving way to night, when they saw between them and the horizon spear shafts following, and they heard the noise of horses and the clamour of a company. 'I hear something following us,' Gereint said, 'so I will put you on the other side of the hedge.' At that a knight advanced and couched his spear, but when Enid saw that she said, 'Chieftain, whoever you are, what fame can you win by killing a dead man?' 'Alas, is this Gereint?' said the man. 'Between me and God, it is. Who are you?' 'I am the Little King, coming to help after I heard that you were in trouble. Had you taken my advice, you would not have met with this misfortune.' 'Nothing is done against God's will, though advice brings much good with it.' 'Well, I have advice for you. Come to the court of my brother-in-law, which is close by, and you shall have the best treatment in the realm.' 'We will go gladly,' said Gereint. The Little King gave Enid one of the squires' horses, and they rode to the baron's court, where they were greeted joyfully and cared for and waited on. The next morning doctors were sought and found, and soon they came and Gereint was treated until he was entirely well. While he was being treated the Little King had his armour repaired so that it was as good as new. When they had spent a month and a fortnight there the Little King went to Gereint and said, 'Let us go to my own court, now, to rest and be comfortable there.' 'If you please,' said Gereint, 'we would travel one day more, and then return.' 'Gladly,' said the Little King.

Early the next morning they set out, and Enid travelled with them, happier and more joyful that day than she had

ever been. They came to a highway and saw it fork; on
one road a man was walking towards them, and Gwiffred
asked where he was coming from. 'I come from doing
errands in the country.' 'Tell me,' said Gereint, 'which of
these roads is better for me to travel?' 'This one is better,
for if you go by the other you will not return alive. Below
there is a hedge of mist, and enchanted games within, and
no man who has gone there has ever come back. The court
of Earl Owein is there, and he permits none to lodge in
the town save those who go to his court.' 'Between me and
God, that is the road I will take,' said Gereint.

They did that and reached the town, taking lodging in
what seemed to them the nicest and pleasantest spot, and
a young man came and greeted them. 'God be good to
you, sirs. What business have you here?' 'We have taken
lodging and will stay the night.' 'It is the custom of the
man who owns the court not to permit gentle folk to lodge
here, but to have them come to the court. Will you come?'
'We will, gladly,' said Gereint. They accompanied the
squire and were welcomed at the court; the earl came into
the hall to meet them, and he asked that tables be set
up. They washed and went to eat, and this is how they
sat: Gereint on one side of the earl and Enid on the
other, with the Little King nearest Enid and the countess
nearest Gereint, and everyone else according to his rank.
Gereint began to think about the game, and supposing
that he would not be allowed to go, he stopped eating.
The earl noticed him lost in thought and supposed that
Gereint had stopped for fear of having to go to the game;
and he was sorry he had ever instituted these games, if
only so as not to lose a man as excellent as this. If Gereint
had asked him to call off the game he would have done so
gladly. 'Chieftain,' he said, 'what are you thinking of that
you do not eat? If you are fearful of going to the game
you will not have to go, and for your sake no one will
ever have to go again.' 'God reward you,' said Gereint,

'but it is rather that I do wish to go to the game, and to be directed to it.' 'If that is what you want most, you shall have it gladly.' 'In truth, it is.'

They ate and were served generously with various dishes and numerous drinks, and when the meal was finished they rose; Gereint called for his horse and arms and dressed himself and his horse, and the entire company went to the hedge. The top was no lower than the highest point they could see in the sky, while on every stake but two there was a man's head, and there were a good many stakes, both in the hedge and through it. The Little King said, 'May anyone accompany the chieftain?' 'No,' said Earl Owein. 'In what direction does one go?' asked Gereint. 'I do not know,' said the earl, 'but take the direction that is easiest.'

Boldly and without hesitation Gereint entered the mist, and when he emerged he found a great orchard and a clearing within; there stood a brocade pavilion with a red canopy and the entrance open, and next to that an apple tree with a great hunting-horn hanging from a branch. He dismounted and entered the pavilion, and inside there was nothing but a girl sitting in a gold chair, with another chair opposite her vacant, so he sat in the vacant chair. 'Chieftain, I advise you not to sit in that chair,' said the girl. 'Why?' 'The man who owns it has never permitted anyone else to sit in it.' 'I do not care if he takes it badly that I sit here.'

At that they heard a great commotion outside the pavilion, and when Gereint looked out after the cause he saw a knight on a proud, high-spirited, wide-nostrilled, broad-boned war-horse, with a covering for both sides of horse and rider, and plenty of armour under that. 'Tell me, chieftain,' this knight said to Gereint, 'who gave you permission to sit there?' 'I did.' 'You were wrong to shame and disgrace me so. Rise now, and afford me compensation for your discourtesy.' Gereint rose, and they began to fight at once; they broke one set of spears, then a second and a third, and each rained proud-swift, bitter-harsh blows on the other. At last Gereint grew angry. He spurred his horse forward and struck the strongest part of the shield so that it split and the spear point penetrated the armour. The knight's girths broke and he was thrown an arm and a spear's length over his horse's hindquarters to the ground, whereupon Gereint drew his sword to cut off his head. 'Alas, lord, mercy, and you shall have whatever you wish.' 'I wish only that these games cease, and that the hedge of mist and the magic and enchantment disappear.' 'Lord, you shall have that gladly.' 'Then disperse the mist.' 'Blow on that horn, for as soon as you sound it the mist will vanish. Until a knight who had overthrown me sounded the horn, the mist could not vanish.' Enid, from where she was, worried and fretted, fearing for Gereint, but he came and blew the horn, and as soon as he did so the mist disappeared.

Then the company gathered and peace was made among them all. That night the earl invited Gereint and the Little King in and the next morning they parted and Gereint went to his own realm. From that time forth he ruled prosperously, with prowess and splendour, and won praise and fame for himself and for Enid ever after.

INDEX

NOTE: In this index *c* and *k*, which represent the same sound, are listed together under *c*; and *ch*, *dd*, *ll* and *th*, all distinct sounds, appear after *c*, *d*, *l* and *t* respectively. Also, *F* and *R*, with which only foreign words begin, precede the native *Ff* and *Rh* respectively.

FOR THE BEST IN PAPERBACKS, LOOK FOR THE 🐧

In every corner of the world, on every subject under the sun, Penguin represents quality and variety – the very best in publishing today.

For complete information about books available from Penguin – including Puffins, Penguin Classics and Arkana – and how to order them, write to us at the appropriate address below. Please note that for copyright reasons the selection of books varies from country to country.

In the United Kingdom: Please write to *Dept E.P., Penguin Books Ltd, Harmondsworth, Middlesex, UB7 0DA.*

If you have any difficulty in obtaining a title, please send your order with the correct money, plus ten per cent for postage and packaging, to *PO Box No 11, West Drayton, Middlesex*

In the United States: Please write to *Dept BA, Penguin, 299 Murray Hill Parkway, East Rutherford, New Jersey 07073*

In Canada: Please write to *Penguin Books Canada Ltd, 2801 John Street, Markham, Ontario L3R 1B4*

In Australia: Please write to the *Marketing Department, Penguin Books Australia Ltd, P.O. Box 257, Ringwood, Victoria 3134*

In New Zealand: Please write to the *Marketing Department, Penguin Books (NZ) Ltd, Private Bag, Takapuna, Auckland 9*

In India: Please write to *Penguin Overseas Ltd, 706 Eros Apartments, 56 Nehru Place, New Delhi, 110019*

In the Netherlands: Please write to *Penguin Books Netherlands B.V., Postbus 195, NL–1380AD Weesp*

In West Germany: Please write to *Penguin Books Ltd, Friedrichstrasse 10–12, D–6000 Frankfurt/Main 1*

In Spain: Please write to *Longman Penguin España, Calle San Nicolas 15, E–28013 Madrid*

In Italy: Please write to *Penguin Italia s.r.l., Via Como 4, I-20096 Pioltello (Milano)*

In France: Please write to *Penguin Books Ltd, 39 Rue de Montmorency, F-75003 Paris*

In Japan: Please write to *Longman Penguin Japan Co Ltd, Yamaguchi Building, 2-12-9 Kanda Jimbocho, Chiyoda-Ku, Tokyo 101*

FOR THE BEST IN PAPERBACKS, LOOK FOR THE 🐧

PENGUIN CLASSICS

A Passage to India E. M. Forster

Centred on the unresolved mystery in the Marabar Caves, Forster's great work provides the definitive evocation of the British Raj.

The Republic Plato

The best-known of Plato's dialogues, *The Republic* is also one of the supreme masterpieces of Western philosophy whose influence cannot be overestimated.

The Life of Johnson James Boswell

Perhaps the finest 'life' ever written, Boswell's *Johnson* captures for all time one of the most colourful and talented figures in English literary history.

Metamorphoses Ovid

A golden treasury of myths and legends which has proved a major influence on Western literature.

A Nietzsche Reader Friedrich Nietzsche

A superb selection from all the major works of one of the greatest thinkers and writers in world literature, translated into clear, modern English.

Madame Bovary Gustave Flaubert

With *Madame Bovary* Flaubert established the realistic novel in France; while his central character of Emma Bovary, the bored wife of a provincial doctor, remains one of the great creations of modern literature.

Aeschylus	**The Oresteian Trilogy**
	(Agamemnon/The Choephori/The Eumenides)
	Prometheus Bound/The Suppliants/Seven
	Against Thebes/The Persians
Aesop	**Fables**
Ammianus Marcellinus	**The Later Roman Empire (AD 353–378)**
Apollonius of Rhodes	**The Voyage of Argo**
Apuleius	**The Golden Ass**
Aristophanes	**The Knights/Peace/The Birds/The Assembly**
	Women/Wealth
	Lysistrata/The Acharnians/The Clouds/
	The Wasps/The Poet and the Women/The Frogs
Aristotle	**The Athenian Constitution**
	The Ethics
	The Politics
	De Anima
Arrian	**The Campaigns of Alexander**
Saint Augustine	**City of God**
	Confessions
Boethius	**The Consolation of Philosophy**
Caesar	**The Civil War**
	The Conquest of Gaul
Catullus	**Poems**
Cicero	**The Murder Trials**
	The Nature of the Gods
	On the Good Life
	Selected Letters
	Selected Political Speeches
	Selected Works
Euripides	**Alcestis/Iphigenia in Tauris/Hippolytus**
	The Bacchae/Ion/The Women of Troy/Helen
	Medea/Hecabe/Electra/Heracles
	Orestes/The Children of Heracles/
	Andromache/The Suppliant Women/
	The Phoenician Women/Iphigenia in Aulis

FOR THE BEST IN PAPERBACKS, LOOK FOR THE 🐧

PENGUIN CLASSICS

Hesiod/Theognis	**Theogony** and **Works and Days/Elegies**
Hippocrates	**Hippocratic Writings**
Homer	**The Iliad**
	The Odyssey
Horace	**Complete Odes and Epodes**
Horace/Persius	**Satires and Epistles**
Juvenal	**Sixteen Satires**
Livy	**The Early History of Rome**
	Rome and Italy
	Rome and the Mediterranean
	The War with Hannibal
Lucretius	**On the Nature of the Universe**
Marcus Aurelius	**Meditations**
Martial	**Epigrams**
Ovid	**The Erotic Poems**
	The Metamorphoses
Pausanias	**Guide to Greece** (in two volumes)
Petronius/Seneca	**The Satyricon/The Apocolocyntosis**
Pindar	**The Odes**
Plato	**Early Socratic Dialogues**
	Gorgias
	The Last Days of Socrates (Euthyphro/ The Apology/Crito/Phaedo)
	The Laws
	Phaedrus and **Letters VII and VIII**
	Philebus
	Protagoras and Meno
	The Republic
	The Symposium
	Theaetetus
Plautus	**The Pot of Gold/The Prisoners/ The Brothers Menaechmus/ The Swaggering Soldier/Pseudolus**
	The Rope/Amphitryo/The Ghost/ A Three-Dollar Day

FOR THE BEST IN PAPERBACKS, LOOK FOR THE 🐧

PENGUIN CLASSICS

Saint Anselm	**The Prayers and Meditations**
Saint Augustine	**The Confessions**
Bede	**A History of the English Church and People**
Chaucer	**The Canterbury Tales**
	Love Visions
	Troilus and Criseyde
Froissart	**The Chronicles**
Geoffrey of Monmouth	**The History of the Kings of Britain**
Gerald of Wales	**History and Topography of Ireland**
	The Journey through Wales and **The Description of Wales**
Gregory of Tours	**The History of the Franks**
Henryson	**The Testament of Cresseid and Other Poems**
Walter Hilton	**The Ladder of Perfection**
Julian of Norwich	**Revelations of Divine Love**
Thomas à Kempis	**The Imitation of Christ**
William Langland	**Piers the Ploughman**
Sir John Mandeville	**The Travels of Sir John Mandeville**
Marguerite de Navarre	**The Heptameron**
Christine de Pisan	**The Treasure of the City of Ladies**
Marco Polo	**The Travels**
Richard Rolle	**The Fire of Love**
François Villon	**Selected Poems**

PENGUIN CLASSICS

ANTHOLOGIES AND ANONYMOUS WORKS

The Age of Bede
Alfred the Great
Beowulf
A Celtic Miscellany
The Cloud of Unknowing and Other Works
The Death of King Arthur
The Earliest English Poems
Early Christian Writings
Early Irish Myths and Sagas
Egil's Saga
King Arthur's Death
The Letters of Abelard and Heloise
Medieval English Verse
Njal's Saga
Seven Viking Romances
Sir Gawain and the Green Knight
The Song of Roland